The Quayside Poet

A Fenland Mystery

Diane Calton Smith

Published by New Generation Publishing in 2018

Copyright © Diane Calton Smith 2018

First Edition

The author asserts the moral right under the Copyright, Designs and Patents Act 1988 to be identified as the author of this work.

All Rights reserved. No part of this publication may be reproduced, stored in a retrieval system or transmitted, in any form or by any means without the prior consent of the author, nor be otherwise circulated in any form of binding or cover other than that which it is published and without a similar condition being imposed on the subsequent purchaser.

This book is a work of fiction. People, places, events and situations are the product of the author's imagination. Any resemblance to actual living persons is purely coincidental.

www.newgeneration-publishing.com

New Generation Publishing

For Christine

In memory of Nan and the Smutties

Also by Diane Calton Smith:

Fenland Histories:

A Georgian House on the Brink (2015)
(Winner of a Cambridgeshire Association for Local History [CALH] award)

Webbed Feet and Wildfowlers (2017)

Fenland Mystery:

Quiet While Dollie Sings (2016)

Thomas Clarkson's 'slave chest' at Wisbech and Fenland Museum.
Photo by kind permission of the museum.

FOREWORD

So much that ought to be thrown away....

She set the rusting old tin on her knee and eyed its contents wearily. So much clutter, so many relics of times and deeds long past, too many memories of people she had never loved and who had never loved her.

The pile of documents, letters and photographs, all of them tattered and faded, slipped through her stiff, arthritic fingers. Only an old postcard, inherited long ago, attracted a second glance. A First World War cartoon of a confused looking German, dressed only in his underwear and spiked helmet, grinned foolishly back at her and brought a glimmer of a smile to her jaded, unhappy features.

The rest of the pile was not worth keeping. No one ever came now, to ask how she was or to stake a claim to some unlikely inheritance.

A cursory knock at the door was followed by the immediate entry of one of the carers. She gave the old lady a brief, professional smile as she collected her empty tea cup.

'Looking at your old photos again, Edith?'

'What's it look like?' she snapped, her retort sounding peevish and unreasonable even to her own ears. It was hardly the carers' fault if there was nothing original left to say. They were her only visitors and companions these days.

Alone again, Edith considered tossing the contents of the tin into the waste paper basket, but it was too far away from her chair and she couldn't summon the energy to move. She closed her eyes, her fingers finding the lid of the tin and closing it with a squeak of hinges.

When she awoke, the tin had gone.

ONE

Diary of Joshua Ambrose, Wednesday, 1st May 1799

The cuckoo was abroad this morning even before I made my early way down to the river. I could hear him in the willows behind the old warehouses, loudly repeating his two-tone song. I never caught sight of the elusive little bird; I envy his ability to avoid mankind.

I come here often now. Whatever the weather, I steal time to wander down to the riverside before the day with its numerous dreary duties claims me. In darkness or in light, I come to this place on the grassy bank, a sheltered corner hidden by scrub from the road and beyond the reach of tidal mud. Only during the greatest, rarest of storms and highest surges has the dark water risen far enough to blight the grass and the wild flowers that come in spring.

Here, I can be free for a short while, lazily watching as the brown water presses on below, hell-bent toward the quayside.

It gives me time to think, to muse, just to be. For now I am more certain than ever, that whatever else we may be, we are merely here to do another's bidding.

TWO; Early December 2017

The Odd One Out

Monica had missed the old place.

Her key was turning, slipping in the ancient lock the way it always did, the door eventually creaking open. The old walls of the museum seemed to shudder as the alarm screeched out, shaking dust motes into dark corners and shocking the tired rooms with its noise. Monica felt for the keypad by the door, thumbing in the pass code and cutting off the alarm mid-screech.

It was dark in the Poet's House Museum, the deep bank of December cloud permitting hardly a glimmer to shine through, yet still she was reluctant to switch on the overhead lights. Their harsh illumination was just too much for her pounding head and sleepless eyes, the results of long flight delays following a fortnight's family holiday.

The lighting was wrong for the museum, anyway, she decided, too jarring for the otherwise peaceful atmosphere of the Poet's House. When funds allowed, she would have to talk to the trustees and get it sorted out. That and the drains. Her nose told her that the steadily worsening drain problem had not gone away.

She went from room to room, opening window shutters and letting in the pale, half-hearted light. Reaching her office, she listened with mounting impatience to the long tape of voice mail, jotting down a few numbers before turning to the computer and facing a seemingly endless list of emails. Mostly junk, she concluded, or trivial business that could wait.

With a cup of strong coffee to bolster her ebbing enthusiasm, she replied to the most urgent messages and deleted a lot of the rubbish before turning to her schedule of winter conservation jobs. She underlined a couple of the most pressing tasks and started to plan her week.

Between the end of the summer season and the pre-Christmas special event, the Poet's House Museum opened only for a few weekends. The rest of the time was dedicated to conservation and research, though the list of work to be done never seemed to get any shorter. January and February would be easier, though. During those two months each year the museum closed altogether, allowing Monica and her small team to catch up.

The phone on her desk seemed to jump in surprise as it began to ring, as if rudely awoken from a doze. She picked it up reluctantly. As the voice on the other end unravelled its woes, she smiled in a long suffering sort of way.

'No, Dad. It was great, it really was,' she replied, trying to sound reassuring, '....no, just tired. No, kids will be kids; it was fine. Of course not, Dad. Don't worry. Love to Mum and Adela....'

Monica put her head in her hands as the call ended. She was a constant disappointment and worry to her family. Never smiley enough, never patient enough with her sister's two small children. It had been a long fortnight in Malta. She'd ended up making a lot of use of the local buses and going on solitary trips around the small island, just to regain some peace and put a temporary distance between her and her loving but energy-sapping family. She felt something like affection for them, but could never be with them for long without needing a break.

She'd always been the odd one out. Her parents and older sister Adela were tall, striking, fair-haired, bouncy and sociable individuals, while she was short and dark haired, painfully anti-social and brittle with people.

Now at the age of thirty three, the need for solitude, even after short doses of company, was more desperate than ever. That was why this job at the museum suited her, with its long hours spent alone in the old place. It was also why she'd never married or had any other long term relationship worth mentioning. She'd never been able to bear any man's company for long, always relieved when a relationship, no matter how trivial, ended, and she could return to her solitary ways.

As children, she and Adela had once sat together and looked into the mirror of the bedroom they shared, comparing Adela's long, straight, blond hair and angelic mid-blue eyes with Monica's curly brown hair and chestnut coloured eyes. Adela, always fond of fairy tales, had suggested that Monica might be a changeling. She'd thought it a romantic idea that her dark haired, younger sister might be a gift from the fairies. Adela hadn't meant to be cruel. It just wasn't in her, but her theories hadn't been helpful to Monica.

Mulling over her sister's words and worrying over other suspicions, Monica had once asked their mother whether she had been adopted. Her mother had smiled kindly; her eyes that were as blue as Adela's had been full of compassion as she'd given her younger child a hug and told her that she was theirs, all right. Monica just had her genes from her dad's family, whoever they were. It didn't help that Monica had never met them. She might have enjoyed sharing her odd looks and ways with them, but an old quarrel had resulted in the two sides of the family never meeting again and she was not destined to see these fabled dark haired, strange people.

As the years passed, she had learned to hide her feelings more. She was better now with colleagues, even with strangers, more polite, thankfully. She'd even made the odd friend, but then that had been the trouble. Most of them had been odd.

A squall of rain hit the office window, as if someone had thrown a handful of pea gravel at it. Water gushed down the thin pane and distorted her view of the dustbins in the yard outside. She went over to the corner work table and depressed the switch on the lamp, flooding the work surface with light. Fetching a heavy plastic crate full of tarnished brass from the store room, she lifted it on to the table, spreading out layers of clean paper on which to work. She pulled out the high backed work chair and settled comfortably on it, picking up her cloth. She selected a particularly grimy candlestick, beginning to polish it as the grit-hard rain continued to pelt the window.

And then the whispering started.

She froze, her hands paused in mid-polish, every part of her listening. The whispering, against the background of falling rain, seemed to be coming from everywhere at once. At first, it seemed mostly to be coming from the reception hall at the front of the house, but she'd only just been in there and knew the room to be empty. There was no one else in the building and anyway, the place had been closed up for the past two weeks.

She was not imagining it. The whispering was there, clear and insistent, the hissing sound of secrets shared. Slowly,

Monica pushed back her chair and stepped out of the office, into reception. She could still hear it, but it was quieter now, as if coming from the back of the building. She frowned and made exasperated noises, but despite protests from her common sense, she made her way towards the back stairs. She was greeted only by silence. The whispering had moved again, apparently coming now from her own office. That, of course, was impossible. There had to be a rational explanation. To Monica, there was a rational explanation for everything.

The shrill, abrupt blast of the door bell startled her. Even the whisperers seemed to clam up in surprise. Who on earth would be calling on a Monday morning in December? Everyone knew the place was shut. She strode through the shadowed building towards the front door and pulled it open.

The woman who stood on the door step was soaked to the skin. With her pale hair plastered to her forehead, she glared at Monica as if the weather were somehow her fault. Her eyes were the colour of flint, and about as friendly.

Monica winced as she uttered an automatic, fairly polite greeting.

Oh, hell. This was all she needed.

THREE

Diary of Joshua Ambrose, Tuesday, 4th June 1799

A joyous morning; one for writing, for thinking, not for the usual walk to our wretched warehouse. I went anyway, of course, after my usual sojourn by the riverside. More peace for us all if the old man thinks I'm trying.

He was in Rudderham's Coffee House last night. Nearly bumped into him, but heard his self-satisfied laugh just in time and was able to back out of the door. Through the grimy panes I could see him boring poor Mr Peckover and Mr Clarkson half to death. Why a good man like Mr Clarkson puts up with his arrogance I cannot tell. He is tired enough from all his campaigning without having to endure fools like my father. It is perhaps more in Mr Peckover's interests to be polite. It would make poor business sense for him to ignore a good client, and father is certainly that. The Wisbech and Lincolnshire Bank benefits greatly from merchants such as my father.

I ended up in Joseph Moules' Coffee House on South Brink instead, sipping my lukewarm coffee with little joy, dear old Sam's sweaty armpits being too close to my nose for comfort.

For now, I must do as the old man wishes. I must continue to work in the family business, becoming ever more cunning under his watchful eye. As he does, I shall continue to let others brave the seas while I sit in the mouldering safety of our warehouse office, trading in the goods which arrive so conveniently on the tall sailing ships in the Port of Wisbech.

Few townspeople like my father, but they seem to admire his talent for turning goods into gold. Such a pity, they mutter behind their hands, that his son's heart is not in it, that he is puny and sickly and that old Ambrose has no other sons to rely on. He can hardly expect his two daughters to continue in the trade.

The quayside was an orchestra of sound this morning, off-key but vibrant with grating, hollering noise. A few people waved as I strolled by, their voices joining the discordant sound as the bright June sun dazzled the water and cracked the mud on the river banks.

Our silk was being unloaded as I passed; I recognised the packages with their London marks. Silk is a fairly safe commodity, better by far than sugar.

When all the trouble first blew up a few years back, when the principled, good people of England started to refuse to buy slave-grown sugar from the West Indies, father was as sour as hell. He'd made a fortune already from the produce of slave labour, but that fact has never disturbed his conscience.

As Mr Clarkson's anti-slavery campaign went on, and the Member of Parliament for Hull, Mr Wilberforce, made increasing impact with his powerful speeches to parliament, people began to listen. The more conscience-driven customers started to turn their backs on slave-grown West Indian sugar. With impeccable timing, father had just taken delivery of a huge shipment of the stuff. Our warehouse groaned under the weight of sugar, all beautifully refined in London and shaped into glistening loaves. And no one wanted it.

And despite the fact that I shared his shame and the warehouse full of unwanted sugar, I was secretly pleased that people were at last listening to Mr Clarkson.

Still there is no buyer for the wretched stuff. We have had to resort to silk, wine, coffee, tea and other such luxuries. In fact, we trade in anything which the hearts of our good townsfolk desire, anything which can be shipped into the Port of Wisbech.

As I watched our silk being unloaded and carried into the warehouse, I hoped this delivery would keep father sweet for most of the day. We certainly have enough orders to keep him happy.

Perhaps my wishes were granted, because the old man gave me that funny look of his, the one where he raises one eyebrow, as I entered our depressing old office. That funny look is what passes as a smile for him, and I made the most of it, keeping my head down for the rest of the day. After all, the view through the window from my tall desk, of the ugly warehouse entrance and all its mess, is never a great distraction. I carried out my duties like a true Ambrose, writing invoices and penning letters.

For the time being, it is best that he believes I am proud to be the son of Elijah Ambrose, merchant of this town and the dullest, most arrogant man to walk its streets.

FOUR; Mid December 2017

Foul Water

'Ole lot needs rippin' out, mate. Rippin' out an' new stuff puttin' in, know whatta mean?'

'Can't do that, Bertle, no budget for it. Can't you just clear the blockage?'

Monica felt a bit embarrassed, addressing Bertle's backside like this. As he disappeared under the sink, rattling at the pipes to release the trap, he presented her with nothing more inspiring to talk to than the cleavage above his worryingly low-slung jeans. There was a lot of grunting and he reversed awkwardly out, a torrent of black, lumpy water following him, most of it missing the bucket.

Albert Collins, of "Bert'll Crack It (Call Us Anytime for all your Plumbing, Handy-Man and Electrical Needs)" was better known locally as Bertle Bodgit. Whenever something needed repairing in the museum, it was Bertle who was called in. This was mainly out of habit and not because he was good. As Monica left the kitchen, he was kneeling on the floor tiles and peering thoughtfully into the bucket.

'Opening the museum in ten minutes,' she called over her shoulder, 'any chance you'll be done by then?'

'Dart it, mate, dart it very much,' he muttered, eyeing the white pipe that disappeared behind the next cabinet, 'Might be 'ere for a bit.'

The pong of foul water, which had been steadily worsening since Bertle had started work, followed Monica like a malevolent cloud into reception, where her dark haired assistant, Bernadette, was busily tipping bags of change into the old till.

'We've run out of rose air freshener,' Bernadette stated philosophically, 'but I could always use the sample perfume spray from the shop stock.'

'No, don't do that. I'll go to Aldi as soon as we've opened, and pick up a new aerosol.'

'Why did you have to wait until this morning to have the plumbing seen to? Of all days, the Saturday we open for Christmas?' Bernadette had never been slow to speak her mind.

'Because,' sighed Monica, 'today was the earliest Bertle could fit us in and he assured me it would be a quick job that would be finished an hour ago.'

'And you believed him?'

Winter sun was slanting in through the small Georgian panes of the front windows, showing up every old finger print and ghost of sticky tape used in seasons gone by. This close to Christmas, with the Poet's House Museum decked out in seasonal greenery and with mince pies and mulled wine on offer, Monica was hoping for decent visitor figures. They certainly needed the income. The trustees who ran the museum were forever reminding her of the need to increase visitor numbers and maximise shop takings. Smelly drains were not helpful.

By five to twelve a few people had gathered in the tiny front garden, hanging around in the cold and staring expectantly at the closed door. She couldn't afford to have them wandering off again.

'Ready if I open now?' she asked Bernadette, who was still counting her fifty pence coins. The assistant dropped the lot in and shrugged.

'OK, let's go for it.'

Welcoming the visitors with her brightest smile, Monica waited until Bernadette had sold the small group their tickets and told them about the seasonal offers, before she went back to check on Bertle.

It didn't look good. The cupboard next to the sink unit had been removed now and a grubby length of white pipe lay on the floor, a pool of dark water seeping out of one end.

'Soon be there now, mate,' Bertle greeted her cheerfully, 'Just cleared a load of muck artta this pipe. That'll be your blockage. Just have to put it all back together and bob'll be your uncle, sortta thing.'

She strode out through the front door into the fresh winter air, the bright, low sun disappearing behind buildings and glaring out again as she walked along. The traffic approaching the town bridge along Nene Quay was tailed back from the lights, extra pre-Christmas volume adding to the congestion. The faces of the drivers she glanced at wore an almost uniform look of finger-tapping frustration as over-excited kids, seated in the back of most of the cars, headed for local seasonal fun. On busy days like these, the old quayside seemed an unlikely setting for a museum, especially one which celebrated the life of the town's famous poet and which was at its best when quiet and peaceful.

To be fair, though, in Joshua Ambrose's day, this quayside where he spent his short life would not have been much quieter than it was today. The noise then would have been a different kind, of course. Though there would have been no cars or lorries, the quayside would have been a scene of almost constant activity, with ships arriving on the tide and being unloaded and reloaded throughout the day. Joshua would have walked along this road, which in those days had been little more than a muddy track, each day to work in the family warehouse and office near the bridge.

His had been a very different world, Monica considered. The times he lived in, with all their problems and difficulties, seemed far removed from modern troubles, but the poetry he wrote still meant something to today's readers. It could still communicate with people living now, could even reach people in traffic jams or with plumbing to fix or who went to Aldi for their shopping.

The Blunt family trust, which in 1985 had opened the house as a museum to honour the life and work of one of its earliest residents, had, in Monica's opinion, done a fine job. Although the last of the family had died soon after setting up the trust, the trustees had continued the work. They had stripped back what they could of the modern additions to the three storey merchant's house, leaving the panelled walls and elegant fireplaces intact.

As its curator, Monica did her best to present the house as sympathetically as possible, so that lovers of Joshua's poems could visit and understand more about the man.

She had made a Reading Room on the top floor, where visitors could sit in peaceful surroundings and browse through the selection of books available there. On the first floor she had furnished the two large main rooms to recreate the family's drawing and dining rooms. There had been plenty of furniture stored in the attic and cellars which she'd been able to use, items which were believed to have belonged to the Ambrose family.

Joshua, with his sisters Rebecca and Rachel and his parents Elijah and Elizabeth, would once have used the silk upholstered chairs, sat at the walnut table, even sipped from the tiny tea bowls which Monica had discovered stacked and covered in a crate.

The ground floor had been remodelled years ago, the once elegant and lofty entrance hall and side rooms divided to create a reception hall and gift shop at the front, Monica's office, a store room, loos and the kitchen. The limited refreshments on offer were served in the small Victorian Garden Room at the back of the building. This extension had been added long after the poet's death, so wasn't ideal, but it was far too useful to pull down.

In the basement were the cellar, a murky, damp chamber once used to store wine, and the original, long abandoned kitchen used in Joshua's time.

Monica's long term plans for the museum included opening the old kitchen to visitors, but she was realistic about it, knowing that funds were short. A far more achievable ambition was to open Joshua's bedroom on the top floor, and she already had the go-ahead from the trustees to do that. The rather spartan room next to the Reading Room had long been believed to have been the poet's. As a boy, he'd been fond of carving his name on things and the wooden mantelpiece in that room was still scarred with his initials. It was as if he were continuing to stake his claim to the place.

Although little spare furniture remained to furnish Joshua's room, the trustees had agreed to her purchasing a few items for it. The plan was to have the room ready for opening at the start of the new visitor season in March. She couldn't wait to get started. As soon as Christmas was over and the place closed its doors to visitors for two months, she could get stuck in.

Aldi was heaving with pre-Christmas shoppers and it was gone half past twelve by the time Monica returned to the museum via the side entrance, clutching the air freshener and a bag of sugar. The stench of drains hit her like a blanket of fog.

It was still busy in reception, despite their problems. Bernadette was in full flow, bright and cheerful, welcoming and apologetic about the smell.

Monica, perhaps over keen to make amends, uttered a swift warning before spraying the area liberally, choking the atmosphere with lily of the valley. A few people started coughing violently, but, thought Monica with irritation, they'd have to put up with it. It was either that or the drains.

'Oh, Miss Kerridge! So good of you to try, but you've made things worse now, haven't you?'

The sugary sweet voice rang out loud and clear as Monica left reception, but she ignored it. Right now, she really couldn't stand another dose of Victoria Sharpston, the museum's keenest and most irksome visitor. She opted for the kitchen and Bertle instead.

A third cupboard had now been removed and reposed crookedly in one corner, next to another pipe which was longer and filthier than the first. The window was wide open, which was a minor blessing, and Bertle was leaning out of it, watching the lack of activity in the drain below.

'Nah,' he muttered, turning back into the room. 'Still nuffin coming art of it. I've cleared art the pipes from the sink to the wall. Blockage must be in the last bit, sortta thing, the bit under the end cupboard what goes art through the wall.'

'Bertle, Angie will be here in a few minutes and she'll need to start getting food ready,' Monica sighed heavily, 'not that anyone's going to want refreshments. This stink is going to put them all off.'

'Don't you worry mate. I'll get the last bitta pipe cleared and then bob'll be your uncle, sortta thing.'

'That's what you said last time.'

Angie's usually pale face blanched a few more shades when she entered the room, bang on time at a quarter to twelve. She nodded wordlessly as she listened to Monica's explanation, nervously pushing strands of her flame red hair beneath her catering hair net. Monica recognised the warning signs, that Angie was far from happy at work. She couldn't afford to have anyone leave so close to Christmas and she knew she ought to find the time to speak to her, to find out what was wrong.

Opening the fridge door, she showed Angie the provisions she'd bought.

'These mince pies are from the place up the road. Thought they looked almost homemade....' Monica gave up her explanation as Bertle's grunting and wrestling with the pipes drowned out her voice.

Angie gave her a faint, sympathetic smile as she carried the boxes of mince pies into Monica's office, where she began setting them out on baking trays. Exposing food, even for a few seconds, to the foul air of the kitchen felt like a major health and safety issue. Covering the trays with cloths, she carried them back into the kitchen and placed them inside the heated oven. Monica began to prepare the mulled wine in the big catering pan on the hob, avoiding Bertle's backside as she poured in readily prepared chopped apples and oranges. The coffee machine was gurgling away in the corner, competing with Bertle's clattering and swearing under the worktop, when Bernadette's dark head appeared around the door.

'Monica....' she whispered, 'it's our favourite visitor again....she needs a word.'

Monica, who had hoped the woman would have gone by now, heaved another heavy sigh and walked into reception.

Victoria Sharpston had a way of filling a room all by herself. It wasn't so much her physical size, though there was no particular shortage of that, but her very demanding presence. Her arms were folded over her ample bosom and her greasy pale hair was scraped behind her ears, the ends disappearing into the generous folds of her purple woollen scarf. The smile she bestowed on Monica had all the glow of a burned out tea light.

'Good afternoon, Miss Kerridge, I hope you can spare the time to speak now. Been having trouble receiving emails lately, have you?'

She was using that whiney, treacly voice again, the one she probably thought was appealing. It was as insincere as her smile and as unconvincing as lily of the valley covering the smell of bad drains.

'No, all received perfectly, as were your texts,' Monica retorted, straight faced. 'I didn't reply straight away as I decided to double-check with the trustees. But their decision is still no, I'm afraid. I apologise for not yet getting back to you, but I only received their reply this morning.'

And quite honestly, replying to another of Victoria's missives was way down her list of priorities.

'But how can that be reasonable? I....'

'Mrs Sharpston,' Monica interrupted, continuing the use of surnames which her visitor seemed to prefer, 'Joshua Ambrose's scrapbook is a very fragile document. It is kept in the display cabinet so that visitors can see it, but its pages are so delicate that the trustees cannot allow anyone to handle it.'

'But I need to look at it. You know very well that I need it for my research.'

'There is a perfectly legible printed copy of the book upstairs. You're welcome to look at it as often as you need. I'll even make another copy for you to take away, if you like. Surely that will help?'

'But....' the sugary tone was developing a few crusty edges now, 'there's nothing like handling the original, is there? And surely, for one of the family....'

'The family?' Monica eyed her curiously. There was a glint in the woman's slate-hard eyes which suggested that she'd scored a point.

'Oh, yes. As you know, I've been researching my family tree for a while now, and it's pretty clear that I'm Joshua's descendant. Joshua is my ancestor! Isn't that wonderful?'

Great alarm bells were clanging in Monica's head, though she was not yet sure why. She managed to crack a smile that ended up more like a wince.

'Lovely. But the situation remains that, although you are welcome to a copy, I cannot allow you to handle the original scrapbook. It's just....' something angry inside her made her add, 'it's just too precious.'

Victoria's mouth twitched, but she made no reply. Above the purple scarf, her face was flushing with indignation. Monica left her by the guide book stand, returning to Angie and Bertle and the remains of the kitchen.

Bertle was standing by the sink, having turned both taps fully on, and was watching the results of his struggles with glee. The water, instead of just sitting there, looking dirty and mournful, now gushed and gurgled its way down the plug hole.

Even Angie was smiling. She had removed her hair net and was preparing to serve refreshments in the Garden Room.

'There you are, mate. Bob's your uncle!' declared Bertle with undisguised pride.

'You did it!' She sounded pathetically grateful, but after the morning's problems and a dose of Victoria, this was a very welcome development.

It was only a case now of Bertle putting all the kitchen cupboards back and screwing on the doors again. Already, the air smelled better, more mulled wine than drain. Any newly arriving visitors would never know there'd been anything wrong.

They might even want mince pies.

FIVE

Diary of Joshua Ambrose, Friday 21st June 1799

The cellar is well stocked with barrels again and it is a cheerful sight. We have port wine and Madeira from Portugal, all up from London yesterday, on the morning tide.

I must confess that when trading in wine a merchant's life is not a miserable one. I find myself eager enough to satisfy even father's wishes, to seek out buyers in the town. Indeed, there is no shortage of them. Yesterday, father sold a barrel of the Madeira to Mr Peckover on North Brink. Though he is a Quaker, I am glad to say Mr Peckover has not given up the pleasure of wine and his cellars are amongst the best stocked in Wisbech.

As for my own endeavours, I spent an agreeable hour or two this morning at the Castle with Mr Medworth.

I do wonder why he persists in calling his admittedly fine mansion a castle. For all its admirable architecture, there is not a turret or a keep in sight and owes the grandeur of its title to the building which once stood there, William the Conqueror's castle. Mr Medworth, I suspect, is guilty of more than a little pomposity in holding on to this name for his residence.

He sampled plenty, in trying to decide whether to take the port or Madeira. I sampled both too, to keep him company. The sacrifice was well worth it. In the end he became a little confused over his choice and decided to order a barrel of each for his cellars.

By the time I was out of the Castle and making my way through the building site he has created in his grounds, the world was swimming before my eyes in a shocking way. I had to lean against the Butter Cross while I regained my composure.

Perhaps I was making a spectacle of myself, for I'm sure some of the fellows engaged in building Mr Medworth's new houses were peering at me from behind the scaffolding. I suppose it was an amusing sight, a wine merchant who can't take his drink. But I confess I am particularly fond of the Madeira.

Quite apart from this, a situation has developed which I must address. We have a vermin problem in the house cellars. It is not a concern for the wine, for that will be gone soon enough, but the kitchen maid finds our unwanted lodgers troublesome. Tilly finds their presence behind the kitchen dresser too much to bear and the house fairly shakes with the sound of her squealing. Mrs Jarvis, the new cook, hates her noise even more than she does the rats, so we must find another house cat. Our old tom cat died in the spring and the rat population is taking advantage, I think.

SIX; Early January 2018

First Thoughts

Monica had always known they had only part of the story. It just didn't make sense on its own, this sad collection of scraps from Joshua Ambrose's life.

Working under the light from the bright desk lamp on the first day back after New Year, she placed the large but delicate leather bound scrapbook on its foam support.

Everywhere was so quiet. She wondered whether she had come back to work too soon, whether the nation had been given an extra bank holiday she'd forgotten about, for there was no one about. There were no sounds even from the street outside, and very little traffic. The heavy rain that had been falling since first light enhanced her feeling of isolation, made the town feel like it was still recovering from a bad hangover.

She had just spent a painstakingly long time in giving Joshua Ambrose's scrapbook its annual, very careful clean. This was the book which Victoria Sharpston wanted so badly to handle, this book of paper cuttings, drawings and random thoughts.

Their keenest visitor had spent hours in the Reading Room, poring over the facsimile document which was available for everyone to read. For some reason, though, this wasn't enough for her. She wanted to get her broken, dirty nails into the original. Why? Did she believe there was something within its fragile pages which would give her further clues about the Sharpston family history? And could she truly be descended from the poet himself, or was she just deluded?

Even if Victoria had the original book in her hands, it was unlikely to tell her any more than it had Monica. There were just too many gaps and too many tantalising, agonisingly vague little clues.

The scrapbook was quite a bulky item, its thirty, roughly A4 sized pages stitched together inside a tooled leather cover. Because its owner had pasted in so many paper cuttings and other items, the pages had fanned out and become stiff and brittle. The scrapbook had evidently been given to Joshua at an early age by his prosperous parents. Pictures of bubble headed people with banana smiles, playing with something that looked like a kite, framed the oversized letters which spelled out "J E Ambrose age 6". More pictures followed, of houses, trees and horses.

The next few pages showed the slow progression to more sophisticated drawing. There was a sketch of his two sisters, Rebecca and Rachel, with their mother. They looked as if they were reading something and the picture was neatly dated as March 1785, making Joshua fifteen at the time. This was one of the easy things about researching his life. He wrote dates on everything, almost as if he knew how preciously short his life would be.

As the pages progressed, the sketches grew more elaborate. There was a well known one of North Brink, which took up the whole of one page. Surprisingly, the Brink had changed little since then. Bank House, which had later became Peckover House, was clearly shown, but without its two later side extensions. The little thatched Quaker Meeting House, which had preceded the later Victorian building, was also shown, with the river bank in the foreground.

This was where the scrapbook became interesting. Joshua had begun to add little notes, random thoughts, comments about his day, all of them dated. In themselves they were not significant, but they were tiny clues which, added together formed a sketchy picture of his life. On later pages he had pasted newspaper clippings with penned comments of his own underneath. There was a piece from The Morning Chronicle dated Tuesday, May 12th 1789, reporting on William Wilberforce's first anti-slavery speech in the House of Commons. Below that was a cutting about one of Thomas Clarkson's speeches in London. Underneath the Clarkson piece Joshua had written, 'Excellent speech. A truly inspiring man,' indicating that at the age of nineteen he had travelled to London to listen to this great Wisbech born man speaking. Joshua's support of the anti-slavery movement was well documented.

The following pages were filled with assorted lines of his own poetry, some of which had later been developed into finished work and the odd remnant that had never been seen again. There were abbreviated sentences referring to everyday events in his adolescent years, such as running errands for his merchant father and escaping to down a flagon or two of ale with his good friend Sam Mayberry. He was obviously fond of his mother and sisters, judging by his portraits of them. Other references to the people in his life told of less devotion. His stony comment, written in 1799, "Seeing Ada again this evening. No avoiding it," showed just how little enthusiasm he had about the girl his father expected him to marry.

The whole scrapbook, all thirty pages of it, was a treasury of thoughts, poetry ideas, drawings and tantalising clues that led practically nowhere. Among its most frustrating notes was almost its last. On a dog-eared corner of a page towards the back of the book was a smeared, almost illegible note which simply stated, "See diary."

See diary? There *was* no diary. But why had it not survived when the scrapbook had? The lack of written information about this Georgian poet was what made Monica's job so difficult. You had to be the keenest detective to find out anything at all and Monica knew she had exhausted every clue in the book. Why on earth, then, did Victoria think she could find out more from its pages?

There was still the great clanging of alarm bells in her head whenever Monica thought of the woman. There was no way Victoria was going to get her hands on the scrapbook.

A movement from outside drew Monica's attention and she peered through the office window into the rain soaked yard. One of next door's grey cats streaked towards the dustbins, making for the cat flap in Mrs Paynter's back door. It was hard to tell which of her three cats it was.

The elderly lady had named them Smokey, Smudge and Sooty but, all of them being grey without obvious markings, they were practically indistinguishable from each other to the casual eye. As Mrs Paynter's eyesight had worsened, she'd given up telling which cat was which and had merged their three names into "Smutty".

Collectively, the cats had become fondly known as the "Smutties" and they frequently found their way into the museum during open hours. They had become popular with regular visitors, who saw them as part of the attraction of the place. The staff and volunteers liked to have them around too and regularly fed them when their owner was out.

As lunch time approached, the world outside the museum seemed gradually to awaken. Though she had no view of the street from her office, Monica could hear more activity. There was the sound of a kid yelling something and a clang as someone kicked a can into the gutter.

She sighed, feeling restless. It was all very well doing research that led nowhere and polishing bits of brass, but she really needed to be getting on with her new project in Joshua's bedroom. The trouble was, that until Bertle Bodgit managed to come and help her, she couldn't get started, and he was busy fitting in urgent plumbing jobs that had accumulated over Christmas. He'd promised to come as soon as possible, but the wait was frustrating.

The only members of staff at the museum, apart from Monica, were Bernadette and Angie, both employed on part time, seasonal contracts and who came in only when the museum was open. Everyone else worked on a voluntary basis. What the museum really needed was a volunteer handy-man. In fact, it needed several more volunteers. Monica was feeling very short handed and knew she needed to get some kind of advertisement into the newspapers before the new season started. As things stood, there was only Bertle who could help her with this job and his time cost money. And he wasn't there!

Something in the house slammed. She lifted her head and frowned, not at all sure where the noise could have come from.

Not a door, for all the doors in the museum were closed to preserve what warmth there was on this cold, damp January day. Perhaps it was the kids outside again.

She picked up the next book to be cleaned and placed it on the folded white cloth inside the three-sided frame on her work table. Beneath the table was a vacuum cleaner, switched to its lowest setting, its hose secured so that it appeared through the back of the frame, its end covered with a piece of gauze. As she brushed the book with a soft badger hair brush the low powered suction removed the dust she had loosened. Holding the book close to the hose, she brushed along the top, bottom and side of its closed pages. Then, opening it carefully, she brushed the end pages, back and front. This book, she was happy to see, was in good condition and needed no further attention. It could be replaced on the newly dusted bookshelf for another year.

As well as the precious scrapbook, the museum owned many of Joshua's books, a number of which were sitting on Monica's work table, ready for cleaning. She picked up one of the museum's first editions of Joshua's work, his earliest published anthology, "First Thoughts". This, and the first edition of his following work, "Common Poems", only left the security of their glazed and locked bookcase once a year for cleaning.

She turned "First Thoughts" carefully over in her hands. The spine of its faded leather cover was only a centimetre wide, its once boldly gilded lettering worn away and almost indecipherable now. She placed it on the folded sheet, ready for the very lightest of dusting.

Some of the books in the museum's collection were of less interest and, because they had been so infrequently read, needed little maintenance. Apart from the precious first editions, there were volumes from the poet's own collection, some of them given to him by friends. Though their content provided little in the way of helpful information, a few offered interesting clues. "The Spirit Guiding Us", for example, promised nothing at first glance. Its blue cloth spine was badly faded, while its pages looked pristine, as if they had rarely been turned. This sad little book had clearly spent most of its life on a book shelf, had hardly ever been glanced at. To Monica, however, it was one of the most fascinating books in the collection. It was also one of the most annoying.

Having cleaned the edges of its pages, she opened the book and looked once more at the faded ink lettering on the front end paper.

Something in the house slammed again and she made an irritated noise with her tongue. She really ought to go and investigate. Perhaps she had left a window ajar. She'd go and look in a minute. She tried to concentrate.

"To my dear friend Ambrose, as you travel south once more. May God go with you." There was a signature underneath, something which looked like "Jon". The tiny letters filled only the very top right hand corner of the page and immediately beneath them was a faded date, 1801.

It was the date which puzzled her. So little was known of Joshua Ambrose's life, apart from what could be pieced together from letters, the scrapbook and prefaces to early publications of his work, written by people who remembered him.

Born in 1770, he was the son of a fairly wealthy Wisbech merchant. Having two sisters, Joshua was expected to join his father in the family business and one day take over from him. He was also expected to marry Ada Imbridge, the daughter of a far wealthier merchant living on North Brink. However, he never married, most likely due to the bad health he suffered for most of his adult life.

Most of Joshua's free time was devoted to writing his now famous verses. In 1799, at the age of twenty nine, he spent some time in Dorset in the hope that its warmer climate might ease his chest problems. It was there that he wrote some of his most loved poetry. These "Common Poems" were thought to have been inspired by his walks on Corfe Castle Common. In 1800 he published his first anthology, appropriately called "First Thoughts", followed by the second, "Common Poems," in 1801. Later that same year he died of consumption and because of this, it was believed that he'd never had the chance to revisit Dorset.

This book, however, signed by a friend, suggested otherwise. If the date was correct and Joshua really had returned to Dorset, it had to have been just before his death. There was so much Monica didn't know.

Something slammed for a third time, hard and heavy, on to floor boards. This time she had to go and look.

All seemed to be in order in the kitchen. The store room, the staff and visitors' loos and the Garden Room at the back also appeared undisturbed. In reception, however, the problem was immediately obvious.

Spread in a thick layer on the floor was practically the entire stock of guide books, which had fallen from the display stand on the shelf above.

Perhaps steady vibration from traffic had gradually nudged the books towards the edge of the shelf. That was quite possible but didn't explain how the neatly stacked spare stock behind the display had also fallen. It had been sitting safely at the back of the shelf for months.

She bent down and began to pick up the slim, glossy books. Those on top of the pile were splayed spine up and wide open, like a flock of shiny, multi-coloured seagulls.

The first one she handled didn't seem to be damaged by its fall, but had opened at a most unlikely place. Rather than at the middle pages, where you would expect a book to fall open, it was spread wide to display page four. This was the page on which the opening lines of Joshua's most beloved poem, "The Walk", were set out in bold font;

"We walk
And nineteen thousand stars awake
To dance upon thy brow."

Monica began to stack the books. The second one was also opened at page four. So was the third. She frowned, continuing to collect the books together. The whole pile of more than forty guide books had fallen open at the same page.

A less logical and sensible person, Monica thought, might imagine that someone was trying to tell her something.

But what? And anyway, Monica was far too busy to look for clues in a pile of fallen books.

SEVEN

Diary of Joshua Ambrose, Saturday 6th July 1799

Quite took the shine off things, seeing the old man was there, but I took my place with Sam in the second row regardless. Sam was doing plenty of fidgeting and scratching, but he'd had no time to change out of his work clothes and his stockings seemed to be giving him trouble. Knowing Sam Mayberry as I do, I would wager it had been far too long since he'd surrendered his clothing to the laundry.

And of course they were all there, occupying the front row of seats in Rudderham's Coffee House, all the great and the good of Wisbech. There to listen or just to be seen. The portly Mr George Imbridge, the town's wealthiest merchant, had enthroned himself in the centre of the row and of course father had made sure he was seated right next to him. No doubt he spent the whole evening dropping compliments into Mr Imbridge's ear.

To father's right, sat the Reverend Dr Caesar Morgan, vicar of this parish and a kindly old fellow. He was deep in conversation with Dr Oglethorpe Wainman, the surgeon living on North Brink. On Mr Imbridge's other side was Sam's employer and Dr Wainman's neighbour, Mr Jonathan Peckover, partner of the Wisbech and Lincolnshire Bank and a well known supporter of the anti-slavery movement. Next to him, and taking up more space than he ought to, was Mr Medworth of the Castle. Even from where I sat, I could hear him droning on to his banker about his plans to develop the town. I noticed that Mr Peckover was nodding but saying little, perhaps hoping he would take the hint and be quiet.

At least, on this occasion I could be confident about not bumping into Mr Imbridge's daughter, ladies not being permitted entry to coffee houses. It was a relief; a bit of Ada goes a long way.

At last, a hush fell over the assembly and the tall figure of Mr Clarkson made his entrance. I'd heard him speak in London, of course, but that was a good ten years ago now, and if anything, despite the exhaustion that is clearly etched on his face, he is more convincing, more magnificent than ever.

As he speaks of the horrors on board the slave ships, the appallingly cramped conditions, the brutality, the evil and inhumanity of it all, he seems to be able to summon the images before your eyes. He brings alive the vile reality of it and, hearing all of this, there could not have remained one decent soul in that room who condoned slavery.

Perhaps, I thought, even my father's hard heart may have softened. If such a miracle has occurred, however, it won't last long. I watched the back of his head as he nodded and tut-tutted in all the right places, but I wager that by tomorrow he'll have forgotten all about it. He will only remember his slave-grown West Indian sugar gradually deteriorating in the warehouse. The poor wretches, who have no choice but to produce it, will cease to be of any account to him.

Mr Clarkson had brought his slave chest with him. The items inside it have become a regular feature of his speeches, bringing his audience face to face with the very instruments of cruelty he describes. Tonight, he brought out heavy hand cuffs, leg shackles and branding irons, explaining how they are used in the brutal treatment of African slaves. He told us too of other cruelties, punishments inflicted on these poor souls once they reach the West Indies.

Only when Mr Clarkson had filled the coffee house with shocked silence, only when he was satisfied that the full impact of his message had been absorbed, did he turn to the gentler items in the chest.

He displayed skilfully carved wooden artefacts, beaded and colourful woven cloth, carved ivory and even handfuls of spices. These were all things of beauty and of culinary use which could become highly valued throughout the British Empire, he said. We could trade in goods, not in people. At this point, I noticed Mr Imbridge's large head nodding vigorously, but father's remained quite still.

As Mr Clarkson's speech came to an end, there was an enormous round of applause. We were all standing and cheering, and for a moment he seemed to glow. For a second or two his tired, greying face and thinning, untidy red hair were forgotten and he looked strong and full of vigour again, younger than his thirty nine years.

At moments like this, he must believe that one day his exhausting campaigning, the frustration and endurance of so much opposition to what he, his brother and fellow abolitionists are trying to achieve, will be worth it.

He is currently supposed to be taking a break from his campaigning. His health has suffered from overwork and too much travelling on horseback, and he has been advised to rest from his endeavours. He is living on his Lake District farm with his new wife, Catherine, but I imagine that while visiting his home town of Wisbech, he couldn't resist giving a speech or two. I believe that tonight he is glad he did.

Sam and I said little as we walked out, collars raised against the chill air of the windy quayside. We were both too deep in thought to say very much. The tide was in and we could hear the brown water smacking against the wooden hulls of the moored ships, the thump of heavy ropes against the furled sails.

Mr Clarkson's words were still running around in my head and at first I was unaware of the girl who tugged at my arm. Ada.

'How dreadfully moving, Joshua! I was quite determined to hear what Mr Clarkson had to say, and Mr Rudderham was so obliging, allowing me to listen at the coffee house window! Mama would never have approved! But, even so, she and I do our little bit for the cause. We are not without influence, you see, and can make sure that Wisbech households continue to boycott the sugar. Look, Joshua!'

She waved her wrist in front of my eyes, showing a pretty little ceramic medallion framed in gold and set into a chain bracelet. On the medallion was the tiny image of a kneeling slave in chains and around the edge was engraved "Am I not a man and a brother?"

'Is it one of Mr Wedgewood's ceramic pieces?' I queried, 'The ones he's making to spread support for the abolition of slavery?'

'It is indeed, Joshua! And is it not a handsome thing? Papa had it fashioned into a bracelet for me. Mr Clarkson approves of these medallions greatly. He says it's good to see the potters, who usually make such trivial things, doing something useful. Papa is doing his bit too. He is bringing in sugar from the East Indies now. They don't use slaves to make the sugar there, you see, so it commands a higher price. Even so, he is assured of buyers. But Joshua, I quite forgot to ask, how do you do?'

Dear Ada, always so keen to talk, so determined and spirited and, on this occasion, so very sad for the fate of others. Her lively mind and kindly nature can distract a man for seconds at a time from her plain features and slightly protruding teeth.

Tonight, despite my reluctance to see her, there was something in her sincerity, her warmth and her need to help others, which touched my heart. As she turned to go, I reached out to offer her my arm, but her spiky elbow was in the way and I simply bowed instead.

Yes, tonight, in the dim light of Rudderham's candlelit windows, she was almost pretty in her vehemence. In some ways, perhaps Ada isn't so bad after all.

Since I am obliged to marry her, that's just as well, I suppose.

EIGHT; Mid January 2018

Of All the Cheek

There was someone at the door, but that shouldn't have been possible.

No one had phoned from the entrance to the flats, so no one should have been able to reach Monica's door. Whoever it was must have sneaked in behind a delivery or some other careless visitor who hadn't closed the gate properly behind them. The thought made her cautious.

Monica was still getting used to the security system, with its keypad and telephone at the entrance to the flats, having moved there only a few months previously. Her old house had been quite a way out of town and when her neighbour and friend, Rosie had left town, the appeal of living there had gone with her. Monica had sold up and moved to this flat in a Victorian house close to the museum. Not only was it convenient for work, it was also small, just big enough for one person and easy to maintain.

There were just three flats in the gothic styled house, one on each floor. Hers on the first floor contained the house's original drawing room, now her sitting room and kitchen combined. Together with the single bedroom and bathroom, her flat had enough original features, including a decorative fireplace, handsome door surrounds and coving, to keep her happy. Monica was only content living in old houses.

'Who's there?' she demanded, her voice sounding grouchy enough to put most people off. No answer. She moved closer to the old panelled door and shouted again.

'What do you want?' Again, no answer, but she thought she could hear pacing along the bare boards of the landing. She shrugged and went to make coffee. She didn't intend to waste any more of her Saturday morning on idiots.

'It's only me, Miss Kerridge. I only wanted a quick word.' The voice was weedy and thin, but still recognisable.

Of all the cheek....Monica wrenched open the door.

'This is my home. How dare you push your way in here?' she demanded, as Victoria Sharpston came into focus in the badly lit hallway. The woman looked a sorrowful mess, her mascara running and her hair looking greasier than usual. Monica's indignation stuttered and faltered as Mrs Sharpston's pitiful voice continued.

'I'm sorry, Miss Kerridge. I know I shouldn't have come here, but a man was calling at the upstairs flat and I managed to get in behind him. This need for information is really getting to me. I just need one more clue....'

'What on earth about?' Though, of course she knew.

'I've traced our family right back to Edmund Ambrose and there's always been a rumour that we were descended from Joshua himself. The trouble is that I can't find a connection between Edmund and Joshua.'

'Who the hell is Edmund?' It was a name which hadn't even featured in Monica's research and she couldn't deny she was curious. 'Come in, Victoria. You look frozen,' she relented, deciding to drop the use of surnames, which was almost as annoying as the woman herself.

'He's my great, great, great, err, however many greats, grandfather,' answered Victoria, still using the wounded, weedy voice. She walked into the flat and sat obediently in the armchair Monica indicated.

'But there *is* no Edmund in Joshua's family tree.'

'Not in the one you have at the museum, no. But you see, I believe there was another branch to that tree, that Joshua had a son. And that son was Edmund, my ancestor.'

'That's ridiculous! We know he never married Ada because he was too ill. He doesn't even seem to have liked her much. If he'd had a child, surely....'

'I know all that,' cut in Victoria dismissively in a voice that was steadily losing its weediness, 'The family house, now your museum, was subject to old entailment laws, as we all know. It always had to pass to the nearest legitimate male relative on the death of the old owner. Joshua would normally have inherited the house from his father, but when he died early, the only male relative the family knew about was Richard Blunt, the baby son of Joshua's sister, Rachel. I believe, however, that Joshua had a son. One that his family didn't know about.

'Hasn't it ever occurred to you, Monica, how romantic the Common Poems are? Why would Joshua go on about love like that if there was no one special in his life? Do the comments he makes in the scrapbook about poor old Ada strike you as inspiration for such poetry?'

'No, but....' Monica bit off the objection she was going to make, reluctantly having to admit that Victoria had a point.

'And why were those romantic poems written in Dorset? Think about it. All the Fenland lines he wrote were about nature, plants, flowers, the Fens themselves. He was not in love here. But, then he went to Dorset, a place full of glorious landscapes and every plant he could ever wish to describe, yet he hardly mentions them. Suddenly, his poems are all about love.'

'I agree your point, but there's no mention of any woman's name. Nothing to suggest he met anyone at all.'

'Perhaps not, but I believe he met a girl in Dorset and that they had a child who took his name. I believe that through that child, Edmund, I am descended from our poet. That is why, Monica, I need to look at the original scrapbook. I can't help feeling there's some tiny clue that's been missed before....'

'Victoria', Monica sighed, fed up with this subject now, 'you know you can't handle the book. Even if I agreed to let you touch it, the trustees would never allow it. It is their decision. Please do not keep asking the same question. It's getting extremely annoying.'

'All right,' said Victoria, pulling herself out of the big old armchair, 'then my only option is to go to Dorset and find out for myself. I cannot leave this thing now.'

Her voice had miraculously returned to full strength, having gradually lost its pitiful whining. Her frail and needy act hadn't achieved much.

Monica opened the door and watched Victoria make her shadowy way down the stairs. Though she hadn't given ground, Monica felt disturbed. Many of the woman's observations rang far too true for comfort.

It was also true that the family tree which had been constructed by the museum was fairly thin and lacking in detail, but it contained all they knew of the Ambrose family's successors. It could be summed up like this:

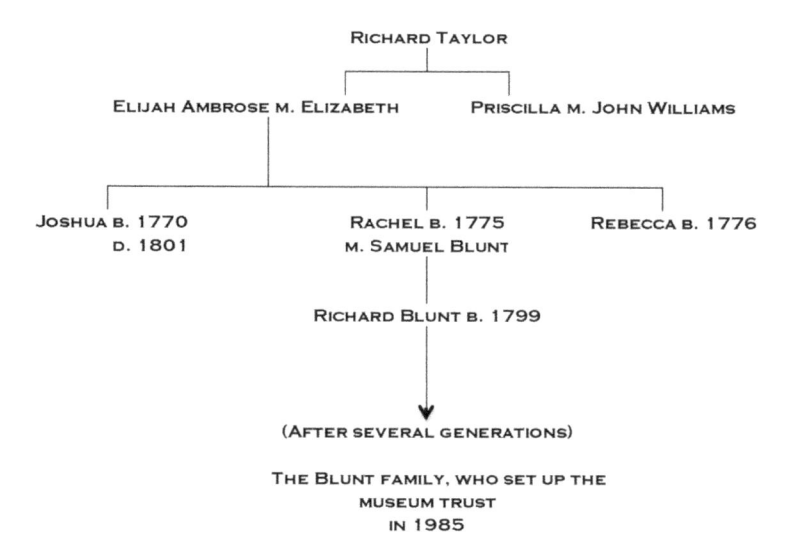

```
                        RICHARD TAYLOR
                              |
         ┌────────────────────┴────────────────────┐
ELIJAH AMBROSE M. ELIZABETH              PRISCILLA M. JOHN WILLIAMS
         |
   ┌─────┼─────────────────────┐
JOSHUA B. 1770      RACHEL B. 1775       REBECCA B. 1776
D. 1801             M. SAMUEL BLUNT
                          |
                  RICHARD BLUNT B. 1799
                          ▼
                 (AFTER SEVERAL GENERATIONS)

             THE BLUNT FAMILY, WHO SET UP THE
                      MUSEUM TRUST
                         IN 1985
```

What more could Victoria hope to dig up in Dorset? She seemed to Monica to be relying on fantasies, assumptions rather than facts.

And while she was away, Monica would at least have a few weeks' peace.

NINE

Diary of Joshua Ambrose, Monday 8th July 1799

I had seen her before, the tiny mewing thing, but she is a rare sight, keeping well out of everyone's way. She is very thin, the very runt of the litter. She is doubtless the last to feed from any kill, her stronger siblings keeping the best of the food for themselves.

This morning, while making my way across the yard to the warehouse, I caught her watching me. To be more truthful, I saw two eyes peering out from behind the old hand cart in the corner. She darted away before I could get close, but this afternoon I put out some fish tails, kindly provisioned by Tilly from the kitchen. It is in Tilly's interest, of course, this search of mine for a new house cat.

I kept watch from the window and after an hour or so I was rewarded for my patience. I watched as the kitten found the courage to come out from her corner and sniff hungrily at the fish. She seemed quite alone. Her brothers must have been away on the quayside, gorging themselves on vermin.

I mean to win her trust and take her home. I'm sure that with a bit more feeding she will be strong enough to become as good a mouser as any other cat on the quayside.

She already has a name. This poor, weak little thing, with her amber and white colouring, is to be called Tabitha.

TEN; Early February 2018

Bertle's Battle

'Blummin' thing don't wanna shift.'

At long last they were making some sort of progress. Bertle was doing a lot of grunting in the corner, heaving away at a stubborn old cupboard that had been attached to the wall for nearly two hundred years and was refusing to let go without a fight.

'Suppose that's why nobody bothered to take it out before,' replied Monica.

Joshua's bedroom had now been cleared of the junk that had been filling it for decades. Only this cupboard remained, clinging to the filthy wall and overlooking dull floorboards which were rough and splintered from years of neglect.

It was already the first week of February and Monica had to accept that her new project would not be ready for the start of the new season on March the first. She was still determined to open the room as soon as possible, though, and already the Wisbech Standard had published a small feature on her plans. They'd included a photo of the room before work had begun and she'd hoped to send them an updated picture of the completed project before March. That would have to wait a bit longer now.

She was managing to get other things done, however. She had spoken to Angie that morning, something she'd been meaning to do since before Christmas, ever since she'd noticed how unhappy the catering assistant looked. It seemed that Monica had caught her just in time, because Angie had been planning to give in her notice. She objected to working in a haunted building, she'd explained. It wasn't so bad when she was able to stay in the kitchen and Garden Room, because the strange goings-on didn't seem to happen there, but she hated volunteering upstairs and in reception.

'But surely you don't believe in any of that rubbish!' Monica had retorted. It had been the wrong thing to say, because obviously Angie did believe in it. Unlike Bernadette, Angie found nothing intriguing about the unexplained sounds and happenings. To her, they were just downright disturbing.

In the end, Monica had had to apply a little tact and Angie had agreed to keep her part-time catering job on the condition that she did no more voluntary work as a room steward. This compromise had left Monica even shorter of stewards, but she'd held on to her kitchen assistant. At least she hoped so. If Angie didn't have second thoughts.

Monica had to admit she was struggling. Things weren't exactly going badly, but she didn't feel fully in control either. Being so short of voluntary help, nothing was being done on time. The old wine cellar was still piled high with furniture for Joshua's room and other bulky items, meaning that she couldn't reach her conservation records. These were documents which she still hadn't had time to transfer on to computer files and which she needed now for work. She simply hadn't expected the furniture to be stuck there, leaning against the filing cabinet, for so long.

And until this monstrosity of a cupboard in Joshua's room was removed, the trustees couldn't send in the decorators. And until the painting was done, the furniture couldn't be moved up from the cellar.

'Nah, it really don't wanna budge,' Bertle confirmed as he squatted for a while on the dusty floor, 'Been nailed to the wall with six inchers. Look at that!' He waved a long, ancient looking iron nail in the air before tossing it on to the pile in the corner.

'Sorry it's a difficult job, Bertle. I'll go and make you a cup of tea.'

'Make it a mug, mate. Three sugars. Some of them oatcakes wouldn't go amiss, neither.'

Monica smiled to herself as she went downstairs to put the kettle on, reaching for the Hobnobs from the biscuit tin. Bertle would get there in the end; he always did. The kettle wheezed and sighed as it heated up, reaching its usual crescendo as it came to the boil. It clicked off abruptly, allowing other sounds to make themselves heard. From upstairs came the noise of Bertle's battle with the cupboard; noise she expected to hear, no trouble at all. It was the murmuring which she found disturbing.

It sounded as if two or more people were standing in reception, having a private discussion.

No wonder Angie found it so creepy in this house. Monica had to admit that, however logical and dismissive you were, the place had a strangeness about it. She frowned, pouring the boiling water into the mugs and swishing the tea bag around in Bertle's while trying to find rational explanations for the noises.

First it had been the whispering, now this. She stood still and listened. The voices sounded male, but were so quiet that she couldn't be sure. Leaving the tea bags in the mugs, she went through to reception, just to satisfy her curiosity, but of course the room was empty. She could still hear the murmuring. She could make out the rise and fall of the voices without being able to hear any words. Checking the storeroom and the loo, Monica concluded that the voices were coming from the stairs. She shrugged and left them to it, going back to making the tea.

Removing the teabags from the mugs, she heaped in Bertle's sugar and added milk, carrying them and the biscuits towards the back hallway. She certainly wasn't afraid of the old house's strange noises, but they were really getting on her nerves now. Monica hated situations that couldn't easily be explained.

At the foot of the stairs she paused, listening hard. Nothing but silence.

The murmuring had stopped. There was nothing to worry about. Perhaps she just needed a hearing check.

When she reached Joshua's room, Bertle's head had disappeared inside the great, unwieldy cupboard.

'Are you there, mate?' came his muffled voice from inside the cupboard, 'Only, if they've gone I could do with an 'and 'ere.'

'Of course,' she said, putting the tea on the floor and striding over to where he was pulling hard on one side of the cupboard. 'What do you mean, if they've gone?'

'Yeah, that's it, if you could put your 'ands there and just pull when I say. Them people what you were talking to. It's just that I could do with an 'and for a minute. One tug and bob'll be your uncle, like.'

They gripped the side of the cupboard and pulled. There was a gratifying scraping sound as the released woodwork tore away from old paint and plaster. One more tug and the huge cupboard was out of the corner at last.

'Bob's your uncle! Musta been fastened by at least thirty of them nails! Never meant nobody to take the thing art. Iggerant lot didn't know nuffin abart woodwork in them days.'

Despite his grumbling, Bertle looked triumphant. He was sweating a lot and wiping one grimy hand across his forehead, leaving a streak of dirt there.

'Well done, Bertle. Have a cup of tea.' She dragged two chairs from the Reading Room next door and they sat companionably, drinking tea and admiring the dark patch of cobwebbed and filthy grey wall left behind by the cupboard. It hadn't seen the light of day for two centuries.

'Lovely,' slurped Bertle with satisfaction, dunking his Hobnob, 'nicely stewed, just the way I like it. Just look at that ol' paint. Told you there was no need for them fancy paint scraping jobs you 'ad done. All you needed to do was wait and see. That's your original colour. Mucky grey. Bound to have it in some la-de-da posh paint collection. Should've listened to ol' Bertle and saved yourselves a bitta money.'

He was right. The original colour of the paintwork was right before her eyes and confirmed what the paint scrapes from other rooms had shown. The colour they needed to paint Joshua's room in was dove grey.

'Bertle....I need to ask you about what you said earlier, when you said I was talking to people. There was no one here. I just went down to make tea. Why did you think there were other people here?'

'Oh, I dunno. Just a load of mutterin' an' stuff. Sounded like it was art on the landing, know whatta mean? Thought it was you talking to people.'

'No,' said Monica quietly, 'No, it wasn't me.'

She went back downstairs while Bertle cleared up. The heavy cupboard, which had survived its removal from the corner in fairly good shape, would now have to be hauled downstairs. Like everything else, its final resting place would probably be in the cellars.

She left a quick message on Justin Loveridge's voice mail, letting him know that she was at last ready for the decorators to paint Joshua's room. Justin was one of the Poet's House trustees, the one who oversaw most of the house's day to day running and the one Monica saw most of. Putting down the phone, she noticed how quiet the house was. Even Bertle's noisy clearing up and thumping about had paused. The silence didn't last for long.

'Monica mate!' he yelled down the stairs, 'You might wanna come and look at this!'

She tore upstairs, imagining all sorts of horrors, but Bertle was just kneeling in the corner, rubbing at a filthy but otherwise harmless looking skirting board.

'Look at that!' he exclaimed. She approached the dark corner, her eyes scanning the discoloured grey wall with its black, dust laden cobwebs, and the dun coloured skirting. Apart from all the dirt, she could see nothing.

'Nah, you can't see nuffin from there. You have to get down 'ere, sortta thing.' She crouched down on the dusty floor and peered at where his finger was rubbing the skirting board. 'From over there you can't see it, but when the light from the window....there, that's it, look at that, mate!'

She moved her head, trying to see what he was showing her, and there, sure enough, something was marked on the skirting. The dim light did not help, but as she ran her fingers across the board she could feel, rather than see, that something had been carved there. She tried switching on the overhead light, but the shadows it cast made the carving even harder to make out. She went downstairs for a torch and shone it directly on to the inscription.

Crude lettering, its style already familiar to her from Joshua's inscription on the mantelpiece, had been carved into the wood with a knife. Just a name, a date and something lozenge shaped, like an elongated 'o'. A ring, perhaps?

ELEVEN

Diary of Joshua Ambrose, Tuesday 9th July 1799

Father took the carriage to visit a farmer in Leverington this morning. He had high hopes of a good order for our tea and I imagine he was not disappointed, for the business took him most of the day. With him out of the way, I was free to get on with more important matters.

Tilly had found me a basket, which I left just inside the warehouse all morning. I put out more fish scraps, but it took the cat a tediously long time to raise the courage to come out from behind the old cart. After an hour or so, I saw her approach the food and begin cautiously to eat. She looked, if possible, even weaker than she had yesterday, despite the small meal she had eaten, and I decided to waste no more time.

When I picked her up I realised how shockingly frail and thin she is. I could feel her ribs clearly and was careful not to cause her further harm by my inexpert handling. She hardly resisted at all, going compliantly into the basket, and I carried her along the quayside towards home.

Coming towards me were Mrs and Miss Imbridge, who presumably were taking the air. If so, they would have done better to find somewhere more salubrious for their walk. This part of the quayside, where the sewer empties its filth into the river, could not be described as the most fragrant district of town.

I bowed as we met, of course, as well as one can when carrying a basketful of cat. We made the usual polite enquiries about each others' health and that of our families, and all the time I was desperate to get the poor creature in the basket home.

'Oh how sweet!' exclaimed Ada when I explained the situation, 'May I look?'

'Sadly, I must refuse,' I replied with a smile, 'Tabitha may escape and that would do her no good at all.'

Ada giggled but Mrs Imbridge just looked haughtier than usual. Despite her obvious dislike of me, however, she joined with her daughter in reminding me that I must soon call for tea.

At last they let me go and I managed to get the cat home. Rebecca, eager to see our future little mouser, came down to the kitchen to look, while Tilly lifted the poor thing out of the basket.

'She will recover,' pronounced our maid as she examined the small creature, 'A few days of feeding and she'll get her strength back.'

She lifted the cat gently into the corner where she had prepared a small box lined with rags, to serve as a bed. There was a dish there too, for her food. Tilly, I can see, is going to enjoy caring for our patient.

'She is such a pretty thing,' announced my sister as she followed Tilly and the cat into the corner, 'Tabitha, did you say, Joshua? I would have called her Marmalade. Her colouring reminds me of orange preserve, but Tabitha will do very well!'

Mother will not disapprove, for we are all aware of how much we need a house cat. Father will not care one way or another, so long as our little weakling learns to hunt.

TWELVE; Early February 2018

Splinters

Justin Loveridge, trustee of the Poet's House Museum, had arrived within half an hour of Monica's second call, attracted like a bespectacled bee to an ancient honey pot. He was kneeling on the dusty planks of Joshua's room, ignoring the splintered wood and debris left behind by Bertle's hasty sweeping up.

'Can we be sure this was written by Joshua?' he queried as he peered through his gold rimmed circular lenses at the carved letters. His face was only centimetres from the inscription; Monica hadn't realised before how short sighted he was.

'Not a hundred percent, of course,' she replied, 'but the lettering is practically identical to his carving on the mantelpiece. The cupboard that was hiding the writing, going by the style of the thing, must have been attached to the wall in the early eighteen hundreds. As far as we know, the poet himself was using this room until his death in 1801. That only leaves time for one, maybe two possible later occupants before the cupboard was installed. All that makes it highly likely to have been written by Joshua.'

'Makes sense,' agreed Justin with a grunt as he eased himself painfully from the boards to a standing position. He brushed down the knees of his trousers with his hands and winced. 'Think I picked up a few splinters. So, that leads to the obvious question. Who was Susanna?'

'I don't know,' confessed Monica, 'her name never appears in letters, poems, or any notes written by other people about him. There's certainly nothing about her in the scrapbook, but....' Her words tailed off indecisively.

'Bit of a puzzle, then,' acknowledged Justin.

He joined Monica at the window and they watched the traffic passing below on Nene Quay for a few seconds. The view from Joshua's old room on the second floor was not the most attractive of the town. Although the path beside the river bank opposite had been neatly paved and made more decorative by a number of large planters, in February they were hardly at their seasonal best. There was no view of the river itself from here, its banks being hidden behind a substantial brick wall, the need for which became obvious at times of high rainfall and flood alerts.

In Joshua's day, the only flood defences along this busy quayside had been the high river banks. Wisbech and the surrounding Fenland, even by then, had endured centuries of damage through regular flooding. At one time, the sea had reached as far inland as Wisbech itself and the Saxons had constructed sea banks and drainage ditches to protect the developing town and the Fenland from the ever present threat of high water. The modern brick walls which bordered the river all the way through town were the latest defences against the old enemy.

'What makes me think there's something else going on?' continued Justin, interrupting her thoughts, 'What were you going to add when you thought better of it?' She looked at him with uncertainty and shrugged.

'It's all a bit insubstantial, but....'

'Go on.'

'We have a regular visitor who is beginning to make a bit of a nuisance of herself. She's convinced that she's descended from our poet through some fanciful link. She is adamant that Joshua had someone in his life beside Ada Imbridge and that they had a son. She thinks the Common Poems, being mostly romantic, are signs that he met this other person while in Dorset. But because there was absolutely no evidence to support any of it, I just ignored her....'

'And now we have the mysterious Susanna and what looks like a ring.'

'Quite, and what's more, our helpful poet who liked to date everything has even told us that Susanna was part of his life in 1801....'

'....two years after he visited Dorset for his health.'

'Exactly. If he met someone down there, it could mean this visitor, Victoria Sharpston....'

'The one who wanted to borrow the scrapbook? Yes, I remember.'

'Mmm, it could mean she has a point. If Victoria saw this inscription now she'd be beside herself with joy, convinced that....'

'Then, for now, when we open this room to visitors, we don't draw attention to it. We'll have the room decorated as planned, but we'll protect the carving and keep it out of sight somehow. I'll give it some thought. We'll tell no one who doesn't have to know about it, until we know more. Do you have any ideas about how you could find out more about this?'

'Victoria obviously thinks she can. She's poking around in Dorset even as we speak.'

'In that case, why don't you go down there yourself? When this other woman is no longer hanging about, I mean, and when the weather is better? The trust doesn't have a lot of money in the coffers, but I think under the circumstances we could justify the expense of a short stay in Dorset for you. Perhaps you could sort out some dates with Bernadette, see when she could cover for you?'

'Sounds good!' enthused Monica, 'Perhaps I could go in April or May, before our busy season starts.'

He smiled and they began to descend the stairs.

'I'll get home then,' he concluded as he shook her hand vigorously at the front door, 'and find some tweezers for the splinters in my knees. Keep me up to date with anything else you discover in the meantime!'

She smiled as she watched him turn from the small herb garden in front of the museum on to the pavement outside. Talking to him had made her feel more positive and the thought of doing some delving around in Dorset felt quite appealing.

She was still smiling as she turned the key in the lock, but her good mood soon ebbed away when the murmuring started again. It began behind her, in reception, gradually building in volume as it spread throughout the building, rising like a swarm of bees to fill every room.

This time, she didn't even try looking around.

'Oh, shut up,' she muttered irritably, and went back upstairs to continue clearing up.

THIRTEEN

Diary of Joshua Ambrose, Saturday 13th July 1799

So there I was, turning my hat in my hands like a fool, until their man servant took it discretely from me.

The house on North Brink has a very handsome hall to be left waiting in. You could almost call it stately. Not so grand of course, as Mr Peckover's Bank House a few doors along, (a fact of which father regularly reminds us,) but certainly superior to the Ambrose residence on the quayside. The chequered floor tiles of the hall were streaked with late morning sunshine as I waited. Partially open doors allowed me glimpses of half hidden rooms from where muffled voices reached my ears. Indistinct murmurs, laughter. The morning sounds of a contented household.

And then she was there, flying down the stairs in a manner of which her mama would never have approved. Quite indecently keen to greet me! Why the devil she should be, I don't know. I've never given the poor girl the slightest encouragement.

'Joshua! And about time! Come on up and take tea with us.'

And despite my reservations, I found myself responding to Ada's enthusiasm, bounding up the stairs behind her to the drawing room, where sat Mrs Imbridge very properly. She placed the embroidery she had been employed with on a side table as we entered.

'Ah, Mr Ambrose, how very nice!' she said, trying hard to be welcoming, 'We have just ordered tea.'

Ada smiled broadly and settled herself on the green silk sofa, folding her hands demurely in her lap. I took my seat by the fireplace, remembering to admire Mrs Imbridge's Bow porcelain figures, which she likes to have noticed. I found myself wondering how I would manage to live in such a sedate manner for the rest of my life, for it is something I must consider. One can only delay these things for so long and soon I must "speak". Everyone expects me to propose marriage; father, mother, Ada and the Imbridges.

'The weather stays very fine,' announced Ada when the silence had run on for too long.

'Not at all what one expects in summer,' I replied drily, but Mrs Imbridge failed to notice the irony. Ada squirmed a bit, indicating that she noticed only too well.

The tea arrived and was served in fashionable new tea bowls made by the Caughley factory. They had been modelled with tiny handles attached to them, quite the latest thing, and I sipped from the dainty items, dutifully admiring their blue and white design. The charade went on as I endeavoured to answer Mrs Imbridge's polite observations as if they were examples of the most sparkling wit and originality.

I knew that Ada was bursting to talk of more interesting things, such as Mr Clarkson's talk last week. I could see her fingering her new bracelet with its anti-slavery medallion, as if that were all that occupied her thoughts. Her mother, however, would not have approved of political talk, however much she may have agreed with our views, and so we continued to talk of our families' health and the weather.

Ada may not be pretty, but more and more I find that I admire her wit and spirit. She is a little too energetic for my taste, always ordering a fellow around, but the time has come, at the great age of twenty nine, when I must take a wife. Ada is as good a girl as any.

Tea duly sipped and a suitable half hour elapsed, Mrs Imbridge was just rising from her seat to bring my visit to an end, when the most dreadful fit of coughing seized me. Struggling to retain as much dignity as possible, I thanked them for their hospitality and left in a hurry, quite forgetting my hat. I made it just as far as my favourite part of the river bank, where I sprawled on the rough grass, coughing violently.

I had thought this illness had run its course, that at last I might be free to enjoy a little good health. But I know the signs and they are worrying. I hate to imagine what Ada and her mother might think of me and my conduct.

FOURTEEN; Mid February 2018

A Pile of Old Books

There was nothing Monica could do about the mysterious Susanna and the inscription on the skirting until she went to Dorset in April, but in the meantime there was plenty to get on with. She still had Joshua's room to finish, amongst other things.

The decorators were busy upstairs, covering the dirty, cobwebbed walls with fresh dove grey paint. With its single small window, the room would still be gloomy, but at least it would smell fresher and look fairly authentic. Justin had come up with the idea of protecting the carving on the skirting board with a small patch of cellophane, leaving the area free of new paint and hiding it from view by standing a chair in front of it. With any luck, not even the vulture-eyed Victoria would notice.

On a Friday in mid February, Monica left the house in the care of the decorators and walked along Nene Quay towards the town bridge. In the canvas bag she carried was the book from Joshua's collection, the one with the message signed by "Jon".

When she and Justin had discussed the signature, they'd agreed that the most obvious man of that or a similar name living in Wisbech at the time the book was signed in 1801, was Jonathan Peckover. A partner of the Wisbech and Lincolnshire Bank, in 1794 he had moved into Bank House on North Brink, the property now known as Peckover House and which was in the care of the National Trust. However, it couldn't be taken for granted that

Jonathan Peckover and Joshua had been acquainted, let alone friends who exchanged gifts.

In 1801 Jonathan Peckover would have been forty seven years of age, while Joshua would have been thirty one. While it might be assumed that in a small town everyone of a certain class knew everyone else, the difference in their ages and professions meant it was likely that they'd never become more than acquaintances.

Monica was hopeful that a little more digging around might tell her more, and Peckover House was a sensible place to start.

As she crossed the road to the bridge, she glanced up at the Clarkson Memorial, its lofty spire reaching to the bright winter sky. Sheltered within the structure was a very formal looking Thomas Clarkson, the Wisbech born anti-slavery campaigner. Countrywide, it was William Wilberforce, the Member of Parliament for Hull, who was the better known, but it was Clarkson's tireless campaigning which had provided the MP with the evidence he needed to succeed eventually in the abolition of slavery in the British Empire.

The statue didn't in the least resemble Rufus Sewell's portrayal of Clarkson in the film "Amazing Grace", but who today knew what the man had really been like? Joshua would have known, though. Like Jonathan Peckover, Thomas Clarkson had been part of the Wisbech Joshua knew. Thomas had been born in 1760, in the house which stood close behind his memorial. Ten years older than Joshua, he'd been the son of the headmaster of the local grammar school.

All in all, quite an interesting group of characters to be living in a small Fenland town at the end of the eighteenth century.

As Monica turned on to North Brink, a gust of cold wind caught her, blasting away the fragile warmth of the winter sun as it blew its way down the passage by the old Nat West Bank. Monica pulled her coat around her and buttoned it up hastily, hurrying past the old merchants' houses on the Brink. Their handsome frontages lining both banks of the river, they too had been part of Joshua's world, and the house she was approaching had been the most prestigious of them all.

She opened the black iron front gate of Peckover House and walked up the path to the side entrance. Being a Friday, the house was closed to visitors, so she pressed the brass bell and waited.

It was a very long wait. Whenever someone rang the doorbell, whoever was on duty might have to walk from the far reaches of the house's several floors to reach the door. Monica knew from previous experience not to be impatient. She folded her arms against the cold and took a few steps around the small porch, admiring the neat front garden with its first snowdrops and pruned back shrubs. Now and again, she thought she heard rustling from inside the house, but the sounds died away to nothing, offering no promise of the door being opened. In the end, her patience ran out and she gave the bell a series of sharp rings, pulling up her collar against the wind which was aimed with perfect precision into the porch. The sun appeared to have given up for the day.

This time she was sure she could hear distant feet on far away stairs. Then there was a voice in the hall, speaking in a resigned, long-suffering sort of way, then a key fumbling in the lock. A long, pale, tired face, with dark rings around the eyes, appeared in the narrow opening of the door. The face stared at her in puzzlement, as if totally clueless as to her identity.

She had known Mark Appledore, the House Manager, for years and was used to his vagueness, but this morning was too cold for mucking about.

'Mark, it's me, Monica. We have an appointment.'

'Oh, Monica Kerridge. Absolutely. Yes, of course we do, yes. In you come, then, Monica Kerridge.'

He opened the door fully, his tired features breaking into a faint smile which looked like it hurt.

'Apologies for the attire,' he pronounced in his cultured voice as he led her through the dark reception hall and along the narrow back corridor towards the main hall of the house, 'only we've been clearing out the cellars and it's as cold as hell down there.'

Monica smiled, glancing at his clothing as he led her through the well lit, elegant hallway. He was wearing a long tweed coat that reached to the floor and almost managed to hide his trousers. The trousers, which were baggy and far too short, displayed a bit too much of his socks, which were liberally decorated with tiny Christmas puddings. Wound several times around his neck was a bright red woollen scarf, protection against the cold and possible damp of a Georgian cellar.

'It's nice of you to help,' Monica acknowledged as she caught up at last with Mark's long legged stride. They were passing through the shuttered Morning Room, the part of the house which in Joshua's day had been used as the library. The books had later been moved to an even grander location.

'Ah', he replied ruefully, 'as to that, I have to confess that the old brain cells have completely forgotten what you asked me about on the phone.'

Mark had produced a huge bundle of keys from his coat pocket and was opening the door before them with one of the longest.

'I have a book to show you,' Monica reminded him, 'and I'm interested in the collection of books you have here....the ones you think belonged to the Peckovers. You mentioned on the phone that a few of them might even date back to the first Jonathan Peckover and I wondered if I could have a look at them.'

The door was thrown open to reveal the "new" library, a large Victorian extension added in 1878 by Alexander, Lord Peckover, to house his huge book collection. The light in the library was muted, its windows half covered by blinds to protect the books and furniture from bright daylight. Mark flicked on the electric switches by the door with a flourish and Monica's eyes adapted to the dappled illumination from three crystal chandeliers.

'Ah, yes, that's right,' said Mark, recalling at last some of their phone conversation. He peered at her with bleary eyes and brushed back his long, dark fringe from his face as they seated themselves at the oval library table, 'Let's have a look at it then.'

Monica lifted the small book with its faded blue cloth cover out of her bag and handed it to Mark. He was silent for a while, turning the little volume over in his long, elegant fingers.

'Good heavens,' he said at last, '"The Spirit Guiding Us" by Jabez Crow. Bet this was a real page-turner in its day! It's certainly the kind of book that Jonathan might have had in his collection, being a series of Quaker essays.'

'That's helpful to know,' nodded Monica, 'but it's this which really intrigues me.' She opened the front cover to show the tiny writing in the top right hand corner of the end paper. 'I need your advice about how this might relate to Jonathan Peckover. It could be an important clue in the research I'm doing about Joshua Ambrose's life.'

Mark held the open page at a distance from his face, having forgotten to bring his reading glasses, and read, '"To my dear friend Ambrose, as you travel south once more. May God go with you." Then a squiggle and the date 1801. Intriguing. So, you're thinking this was written by Jonathan Peckover?'

'I don't know. I was hoping you'd recognise the signature or the writing. The signature starts with what looks like "Jon" and, as you say, it's a collection of Quaker essays, Jonathan's kind of reading material.'

'Indeed. I'm afraid we have little to compare the handwriting with but we do have a record of his signature somewhere. I would have to check, but I must say it looks familiar. Also, judging by the subject matter and the fact that the two men must have been acquainted, I'd say this was very likely to have been written by our Jonathan. Unfortunately, and this is a damned shame,' he gestured towards the long row of tall bookcases, 'most of the books in this collection didn't belong to the Peckovers at all. Many of them are on loan from other collections. Although Alexander, Lord Peckover, was a great collector, and added his valuable collection to those of his predecessors, his books were sold, along with practically everything else from the house, at an auction in 1948.'

'When the house came to the National Trust?'

'Indeed. But, as I probably waffled on about on the phone, we do have a small number of books which we believe did belong to the family. Over the years, various kind people have found a few and donated them and....'

He rose from his chair and crouched down in front of one of the book cases, pulling open the door of a small cupboard set into the bottom shelf.

'....you could start by having a look down here.' He peered at the row of faded books, closing one eye as if he had a headache. 'On this shelf are a few of the books which have made their way back to us and which we think belonged to the Peckovers. Others in this cupboard here....' he gave a stack of books a poke and the pile collapsed with a great thud.

He stuck his head into the cupboard, uttering a muffled series of heavy duty expletives as he attempted to reassemble the pile. '....As I was saying, others in this cupboard have not been sorted and most of them are in pretty poor condition, but they look like they may have belonged to the family. You're welcome to have a browse through. I'm off to get some lunch now, so I'll leave you to it. When I come back I'll look out a facsimile of Jonathan's signature I have in the office. At least, I think that's where I last saw it. We can compare that with the signature in your book. In the meantime, make yourself at home. Just put everything back in the right place, or I'll have the house steward yelling at me.'

Monica bestowed upon him her broadest smile and most gracious thanks and lost no time in placing herself before the shelf and the contents of the small cupboard. Things were looking promising, she told herself.

And she didn't care who called her sad, but there was little she liked more than an hour to herself and a pile of old books.

FIFTEEN

Diary of Joshua Ambrose, Sunday 28th July 1799

What can I write, other than that I have been confined to this wretched bed, with endless coughing and fever, for a fortnight now? Tabitha is my most faithful companion, staying for hours at a time, curled up to sleep on my bed. In the three short weeks she has been with us her condition has improved considerably. She is gaining weight and confidence, already strolling about our home as if she has always been a part of it. Everyone has become fond of her. Even father has no complaint, which is a wonder in itself.

Apart from Tabitha, of course, Mother and Rebecca check on me constantly. Their kind attention and concern never falter. Father peers at me occasionally from the doorway, as if I were some curious specimen in a laboratory. I am a mystery to him. How can so fine a figure of a man be cursed by such a weakling son?

Our house was a happy one on Sunday. Rachel arrived in her carriage from Outwell, bringing her baby son, Richard, to show to us. My state of health meant I was obliged to remain at a distance from them, but it was good to see my mother's face light up at the sight of her elder daughter and new grandson. My sister seems happy with her farmer husband; his estate is considerable and their home is newly built and handsome. She talks of pleasing society in the village and her particular friendship with the vicar's wife. I am glad for her.

I have produced very few lines of merit lately. This sick bed brings little inspiration. I long to be out on the Fen again and as soon as I am fit enough to ride, I shall spend some hours in solitude there. Lately, I have felt some improvement in my condition. In the last few days I have awoken feeling more like my old self. Sometimes, there are even a few lines in my head and I hurry to write them down.

Not a soul to be seen in the landscape,
Only wheeling birds dropping down to rest
And feed.
Crisp winter fields and washes;
God
Is here
At home
With me.

Mother suggests that I spend some time in the south when I am well enough to travel. She thinks the warmer climate of Dorsetshire will be of benefit to my health, and God knows I need it. Even father agrees to do without me in the warehouse for a while. I'm hardly of any use to him as I am.

It appears it has been decided. Before the summer ends I will go to visit my mother's sister, Aunt Williams, in Ponders Mullen, Dorsetshire.

SIXTEEN; Mid February, 2018

A Bit of Luck

Most of the books on the shelf were of the heavily religious sort. Dry, hard to digest tomes, written in language surely never meant to be read, their message lost in impenetrable waffle.

Amongst the books which Mark had pointed out were several on Quaker philosophy, various versions of the Bible and the kind of Victorian travelogues that did nothing to persuade you to leave home. There was also a hefty volume written about the sterling work of the Friends' Ambulance Service during the First World War and other conflicts. The Peckovers had been strong in their Quaker beliefs and most of their reading matter reflected that. Monica turned her attention from the shelf to the books inside the small cupboard.

She had been kneeling on the polished floorboards of the library for around half an hour and one foot was beginning to go to sleep. She eased herself into a more comfortable position and reached for the first books from the pile which had collapsed beneath Mark's fumbling fingers. There was an edition of Tennyson, its spine held on with tape, and a dog-eared volume of Wordsworth. Beneath them were a book on chess with its back cover missing, a well read one on tennis, and a very non descript, thin leather volume with a battered and scuffed front cover.

Its once gilded title had long since faded from the spine and Monica had to pick it up in order to tell what it was. Butterflies stirred in her stomach and began to flutter as she pulled herself to her feet, holding the small, fragile book as carefully as she would a baby bird.

"Common Poems" by J E Ambrose. It was a rare first edition of Joshua's second published collection of poetry.

The fact that this book existed among the few remaining items belonging to the Peckover family was interesting, but in itself meant nothing. One of the family could easily have bought the book without even knowing Joshua, and yet its presence gave her hope that she was on the right track.

In anticipation, she opened the book, but both the front and back end papers were blank. Disappointment mounting, she turned page after page, but still found nothing.

Despite this, she couldn't bring herself to let go of the small volume. She continued to hold on to it as her eyes ran over the titles of the remaining books in the pile. There was no more poetry there, nothing else of any help to her. She carried "Common Poems" over to the window to take a closer look at it. Even though the blinds were almost fully closed, she could still see more clearly by the natural light seeping through them than by the artificial illumination from the chandeliers. She rechecked the blank end papers for any impression that might have been left from erased pencil marks, but no matter from which angle she viewed the pages, there was nothing there and never had been.

It was only when she closed the book that she knew her persistence had not been in vain. There was something protruding from the bottom of the book about half way through, a piece of paper that had dropped down.

Opening the book, she fished out the tiny scrap of paper. It had been folded in half, as if used long ago as a bookmark. Very carefully, she placed the book on the table and eased open the paper.

There it was; Joshua's handwriting. Faded ink on a torn and creased piece of paper.

"In grateful thanks for your counsel as I travel once more in hope. JEA."

No date this time and no clue as to whom he had addressed the note. Unusual for Joshua. And why not just write in the front of the book? Why hide this message on a scrap of paper that could have been thrown away at any time?

But "Common Poems" had not been published until 1801, the year of his death, so the absence of a date under the initials for once didn't matter. Joshua was referring to travelling again, and in hope. In hope of what? If it had been Jonathan he was writing to, it made sense that this gift had been made around the same time as Joshua had received the Jabez Crow book from Jonathan.

The two notes in the two books, one from Jonathan wishing Joshua luck with his travels, the other from Joshua thanking Jonathan for his advice, suggested that Joshua was going south for a specific reason.

This supported Victoria Sharpston's theory that something significant had happened to Joshua while staying in the south. It didn't mean that she was right, of course, just that a few clues were beginning to point that way. This thought clouded Monica's excitement a little. The thought of Victoria was enough to spoil anything. She was still smiling, though, when Mark returned. He was keeping one of his eyes closed, as if his headache had worsened.

'Had a bit of luck,' he announced through his pain. 'Found Jonathan Peckover's signature facsimile in a folder full of useful bits. Take a look.'

He placed the folder in front of her and she studied the photo-copied signature. It looked as if it had been copied from some sort of legal document.

Jonathan had written the first three letters of his Christian name clearly, but the last five letters had disappeared into a curving scroll which merged into the "P" of Peckover. It read more like Jon than Jonathan, and so when she compared it with the message inside the front cover of "The Spirit Guiding Us" by Jabez Crow, the similarity was obvious.

'It's him,' she said quietly. 'This is the same signature.'

'I would agree. So Jonathan gave a book to Joshua Ambrose.'

'And received one in return, it appears,' she added, showing him her new discovery. He rubbed his eyes and, managing to keep them both open, peered painfully at the scrap of paper from inside "Common Poems".

'Remarkable. Quite remarkable,' he muttered, 'So the two must have struck up a friendship. The Quaker banker and the merchant poet. We ought to put together a joint exhibition based on this, you know.'

'You're right!' she smiled, noticing that he'd lost some of his listlessness. He looked inspired suddenly, as if his tiredness, aches and pains had been forgotten. He clearly had a real love of his job and a genuine interest in new discoveries.

'You can have a copy of that piece of paper if you like, Monica Kerridge,' he offered with a grin.

'Thanks, Mark, for all your help. This has been so useful.'

'And likewise for your persistence. I am glad to have been of service,' he said formally, as if about to bow.

Back in the cold winter street, the sun was once more attempting to make an appearance. Little flecks of golden light flitted across the fronts of buildings before being snuffed out like candles by the sharp east wind.

With Mark's photocopy folded carefully inside "The Spirit Guiding Us", Monica headed back to the museum. She would have to phone Justin Loveridge now and bring him up to date.

For better or for worse.

SEVENTEEN

Diary of Joshua Ambrose, Monday 5th August 1799

It was so pleasing to return to something resembling good health, that even our old warehouse was a welcome sight to me today. I spent the morning overseeing the packaging of orders for our Indian muslin.

This fabric, newly arrived from London, is in great demand. The most fashionable ladies want it for their gowns and we are fortunate to have some of the town's worthiest citizens among our customers. Mrs Peckover of Bank House, as well as her neighbour Mrs Wainman and her two daughters, will soon be attired in the latest pale muslin. Ladies of other notable families will quickly follow their example, to be sure.

Father, naturally, is swelling with pride. Our silk, muslin, wine, tea and coffee are selling almost as quickly as we can import them, and bringing in satisfactory profits. The damp and mouldering sugar loaves in the warehouse are almost forgotten.

It will be good to be away for a while.

Our physician, my old friend George Western, assures me that in another seven days I shall be fit enough to travel, and so I am busy with my plans.

I have written to Aunt Williams in Ponders Mullen, Dorsetshire today, to warn her of my imminent arrival.

EIGHTEEN; March 2018

Pink Smile

During the first days of March, gales had torn their way across the country, leaving fallen trees, dislodged roof tiles, damaged cars and queues outside fence suppliers in their wake.

St Peter's Garden was still strewn with branches and other debris from trees and dustbins as Monica made her way along the path. The wind had dropped now, leaving pale sunshine that seeped through light clouds like a mild apology. Out of the shade, the midday temperature was encouraging enough for the good folk of Wisbech to venture outside again.

Monica found a free bench to sit on near the fountain. She opened her packet of cheese sandwiches, ignoring the curious glances of two men seated on the opposite bench. They weren't really interested in her, engrossed in eating their chips while discussing something dramatic in a foreign language. The public garden had a community feel about it on most days, but on this Friday following the storm it was more popular than ever. For some it was a place to sit and chat, for others somewhere to stroll or exercise dogs. By the church porch, two women were chatting while one pushed a buggy back and forth. Tucked under a pink blanket in the buggy, her baby slept, oblivious of the laughter and the occasional shout which rang out across the garden.

There was very little left of the old church graveyard these days, most of it having been transformed decades ago into St Peter's Garden. In the shady flower beds wind-battered daffodils were emerging from loosened buds, their golden trumpets competing with the last of the snowdrops.

Monica had looked before at the few remaining headstones and large table tombs and had found nothing. She had also looked more than once through the old parish records held at the Wisbech and Fenland Museum, which showed that Joshua had been both baptised and buried in this church. She knew that there was no mention of a marriage in the records, but even so, with the new name of Susanna cropping up, she couldn't resist another quick look at the stones.

She'd had a mixed morning. Thanks to the help of a couple of volunteers, Joshua's bedroom was almost ready. Today they had moved the final pieces of furniture into the newly decorated room and it was almost beginning to look lived in. It was now scheduled to open to visitors on the following Saturday, only two weeks later than planned. Considering how delayed the start of the project had been, that wasn't bad at all.

The first hour of the day had been a lot less rewarding, however. Monica had spent a tedious hour on the internet, searching through old marriage records. It had been the logical thing to do, to check whether anything new had been uploaded to show a marriage between the mysterious Susanna and Joshua. She had not been surprised to find nothing.

As far as she was concerned, this was a good thing. She wanted more than anything to prove Victoria wrong, but a quick internet search was far from conclusive. Not all parish records had been uploaded; some had been lost, become illegible or destroyed over the centuries.

Joshua, of course, may not even have married Susanna. Perhaps he had promised to and nothing had come of it. The child who Victoria believed to be her ancestor could still have been born to Joshua and Susanna, married or not. Yet Monica found it hard to believe that Joshua, being so correctly brought up in his middle class family, would have treated someone he loved so poorly. In those days, such behaviour would have meant ruin for Susanna and her child.

If there was any truth in Victoria's theory about being descended from Joshua, the family tree which Monica was so familiar with would be completely changed. Adding a new branch would transform it to something like this:

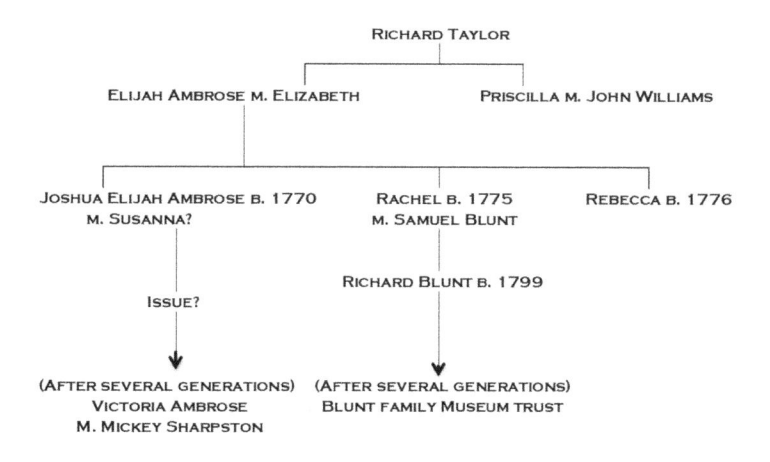

```
                        RICHARD TAYLOR
                   ┌──────────┴──────────┐
   ELIJAH AMBROSE M. ELIZABETH        PRISCILLA M. JOHN WILLIAMS
   ┌───────────────┼───────────────┐
JOSHUA ELIJAH AMBROSE B. 1770   RACHEL B. 1775      REBECCA B. 1776
   M. SUSANNA?                  M. SAMUEL BLUNT
                                    │
                              RICHARD BLUNT B. 1799
         │                          │
       ISSUE?                       │
         ▼                          ▼
(AFTER SEVERAL GENERATIONS)   (AFTER SEVERAL GENERATIONS)
     VICTORIA AMBROSE          BLUNT FAMILY MUSEUM TRUST
   M. MICKEY SHARPSTON
```

There had to be something to prove Victoria wrong. Surely she was wrong? Monica had to find something.

As she made her way round to the west side of the church, the temperature dropped suddenly, the sun disappearing behind thicker cloud. She stopped to zip up her jacket. Even on warm days, the sun rarely seemed to touch the dark patches of earth between the yews and the gravestones, allowing algae to creep in and take over. It carpeted the crevices between the paving stones and spread like old green velvet across graves to colour the faces of angels, who puffed out their cheeks regardless.

Monica made her slow way between the grave stones on the west and south sides of the church. As before, she saw that any inscription old enough to be of interest to her was severely worn away, leaving only a few faint letters or numbers behind. Her search told her nothing new. There was no mention of Susanna, even of Joshua himself. Though presumably he'd once had a headstone, nothing remained of it now.

Inside the church, she practically knew the inscriptions on the memorials by heart. She was aware that the likelihood of discovering anything new was miniscule, but still she looked. Standing alone in the airy and peaceful church, she looked at the very same memorials that Joshua would have glanced at almost every Sunday of his life. Perfectly preserved in wood and plaster, ruffed and gowned Puritans still knelt and prayed, keeping their watch over the chancel. Perhaps Joshua had wondered, as she did, what their seventeenth century Puritan lives had been like and what sort of people they had been.

Leaving the church, she began to walk back towards Nene Quay but paused outside the Wisbech and Fenland Museum. A sign had been tied to the front railings, advertising their new exhibition and, in no hurry to return to work, she went in.

She had always been drawn to this beautiful old museum. One of the earliest purpose-built museums in the country, it still displayed its collections in the original Victorian wooden and glass cabinets. Staffordshire figures, in all their naivety, shared a room with Napoleon Bonaparte's breakfast set of fine porcelain. Fossils and Egyptian exhibits sat in curious proximity to Roman pots.

There were no electronic teaching aids, no touch screens, no inter-active gizmos. And that was its charm. You could browse or research on so many subjects, while enjoying the peace of this treasure house within its charming, ever-so-slightly crooked, old building.

She headed first for the new exhibition of historical maps in the modern extension at the back of the building, immersing herself in the detail of seventeenth century cartography. Now extinct water courses, tiny towns marked with huge windmill symbols and the oddly spelled landmarks of ancient Fenland, kept her interested for a while as she lost herself in thought. Returning to the main body of the museum, her footsteps echoed with unseemly loudness and she stopped to look, as she always did, at the Thomas Clarkson display.

Overseen by a handsome mannequin of an African slave, was an informative exhibit on Thomas Clarkson, his brother John, and their hard fought campaign against slavery.

During the course of his long and exhausting campaign, Thomas had delivered many powerful speeches throughout the country and had become well known for his use of a particular visual aid. His famous wooden chest, together with many of its original contents, was well displayed in the cabinet.

Monica was still reading information printed on the large boards in the cabinet when she became aware of someone standing behind her. She ignored whoever it was, continuing to read about the campaigners' long uphill struggle and the final passing of the Slavery Abolition Act in 1833.

The person was still there, behind her. In an otherwise empty room it was both unnecessary and annoying.

'Hello Monica,' sounded the over-sweet voice in her ear as she turned round, 'So sorry to hear about all your trouble.'

A woman with too much wiry blond hair surrounding a pale face and glossy pink lips, was standing there. The pink lips were set in a phoney smile.

'I beg your pardon?'

The woman stuck out a hand.

'You probably don't remember me. Philippa Renshaw. I've visited the Poet's House quite a few times.' The hand was still there and Monica shook it, just to get rid of it.

'What do you mean, all my trouble?'

'Oh, didn't mean to give offence,' the woman's smile remained in place, moving around her words. Some of the pink gloss had smudged on to her teeth. 'Perhaps it's nothing, but I heard your museum was at risk, that it's in some kind of trouble....'

'Where did you hear this?' Monica snapped. Her tone made no impression on the pink smile.

'Oh....couldn't really say. Perhaps it was someone I was talking to last week. I move in so many circles, you see. I meet so many people. As I said, it may be nothing.'

Philippa Renshaw moved on, taking her ghastly pink smile with her. Monica was left alone with the mannequin of the slave, who looked as clueless as she did. She wandered out of the museum to the small square, trying in vain to shrug off the discomfort Ms Renshaw had given her. Monica had the feeling that her uneasiness was exactly what the woman had intended. For whatever reason, her words had sounded deliberate, practised.

And they had hit their mark. Despite her efforts to forget the stupid woman, the day was ruined. Its only real progress, in getting Joshua's room ready, was forgotten.

What the hell was going on?

NINETEEN

Diary of Joshua Ambrose, Sunday 11th August 1799

My God is in the green wood,
In the sacraments,
The tall spire, the singing choir,
In every new unfurling leaf.
Lord and Goddess too,
The spark, the light
Of life itself.

They were all at church this morning, the town's most worthy and swaggering, hogging all the best seats at the front and in the gallery. Father, of course, made sure that the Ambrose family and servants took up more than their fair share of the front pews, while the poorer members of the congregation made do with benches somewhere behind us.

The sermon wasn't one of the Reverend Dr Morgan's most stimulating. Too much sin and hellfire and not enough hope. I found my eyes wandering to the lofty heights of the great place, looking at the carved stone faces decorating the arches. As I sat there, I thought too of the memorials to long-dead worthies that adorn the walls of the chancel. Their ancient, pious faces above stiff ruffs and collars have always fascinated me. Were they once flesh and bone like me? Did they once sit where I sit now, staring at even older carvings?

Then I found myself wondering whether Ada were there, whether she'd slipped in while we were seated and I'd missed her. It is curious how lately I've thought of her more. Being confined to a sick bed for weeks was no pleasure at all, yet not once did she or any other member of her family call to enquire after my health. Perhaps her mother was put off by my distasteful coughing that day. It must have been most unsightly.

Outside, we all shook hands with the vicar, who twinkled his kindly eyes at us in a way that defied belief that he could run on like that about hellfire and damnation. Dr and Mrs Wainman, the surgeon and his wife who live next door to Bank House on North Brink, came to speak to Dr Morgan then. I think I caught something about their daughter Marian's forthcoming marriage. Miss Marian Wainman is a true beauty with a lively mind to match and I hope the fellow is worthy of her.

While engaged in my eavesdropping, I saw father strolling casually over to where Mr Medworth was beating the ears of a group of Capital Burgesses about his plans for the town's improvement. The houses he is building on the land surrounding his mansion in the centre of town are almost completed and doubtless he will sell them at great profit. The houses are, I must confess, elegant and handsome. Joined together in a terrace, they form a crescent shape. It is rumoured that he plans to build another such terrace and thereby extend his crescents into a full circus of houses around his mansion.

Circus, grumbles father in some of his more humorous moments, is the right word for it. Mr Medworth's houses with their good looks will benefit the town, but his plans for the rest of Wisbech are too far-reaching and ambitious for most worthy citizens to contemplate. And his building site, with its noise and commotion, promises to spread through our midst and dominate the town forever.

It is said that when the building of the crescents is completed, he means to change the use of his mansion, the Castle itself. According to coffee house gossip, he proposes to sell the place to the grammar school, so that it can be used as the master's house, or some such other nonsense. Further, he wishes to cut a road through some old buildings he has purchased to lead from the crescent to the market place. From there, he plans to cut another road through, connecting with Ship Lane and giving easier access to the Lynn road. As well as creating a new approach to the town, the road would also connect the new master's house with the rest of the school.

It seems that not all of his plans are falling on sympathetic ears. Our Capital Burgesses, the very gentlemen who run the town and make all the decisions that matter, are not easy to win over. I could not help observing their looks as they listened to Mr Medworth by the south porch. If he had hoped for nods and smiles, he must have been severely disappointed by their sneering, superior faces.

While father was listening to Mr Medworth's monologue, mother, Rebecca and I were left alone for a few minutes. It was then that mother spied Mrs Imbridge.

'Heavens,' she remarked quietly to Rebecca, 'What on earth is she wearing on her head?'

It wasn't hard to spot the new headgear bobbing about between the yew trees. The headdress enveloped Mrs Imbridge's hair completely, making her head look like a hideous boiled egg. As if that were not enough, two enormous blue feathers stitched to the egg danced and waggled in time with Mrs Imbridge's every movement.

I am sure that Mrs Imbridge's hat was not the only thing on my mother's mind. Though she would not admit it to me, she cannot be unaware of the absence of calls lately from that family.

Rebecca and I watched as mother stepped carefully between the grave stones, trying to avoid the worst of the mud. We saw her pause as she approached Mrs Imbridge, who was enjoying some highly amusing exchange with Mrs Morgan, the vicar's wife. The three ladies curtseyed briefly before speaking, politeness no doubt saving them from the danger of saying anything that mattered.

We were so busy keeping an eye on everyone else, that neither of us saw Ada approaching. She was wearing a small lilac straw bonnet that made her rather sharp features look softer somehow.

'Ada!' I must have sounded foolishly keen and I moderated the tone of my greeting to add, 'What a fine morning!'

'It is indeed. Good to see you in improved health, Joshua.'

'Thank you. I had hoped to call on you and Mrs Imbridge yesterday, but events overtook me,' I confessed. I could feel my sister watching my clumsy attempts at courtship with some amusement. She knows I am trying hard, that I am playing the game, trying to do my duty.

Ada gave another curtsey and smiled.

'I wanted to tell you that I am going away tomorrow,' I continued, 'My physician....'

'So soon? To Dorsetshire so soon?' Her forlorn look surprised me. I had assumed that her staying away during my illness meant a cooling off on her part.

'It will not be for long,' I tried to reassure her, 'and as soon as I am home I look forward very much to calling on you again....'

She answered me with a sad smile.

'I confess,' I heard my sister addressing Ada, perhaps to lighten the mood, 'that I am curious about Mrs Imbridge's new bonnet.' Rebecca was clearly trying not to laugh.

'Ah, yes! It's a turban!' replied Ada with an admirable attempt at cheerfulness, 'Quite the new thing! Aren't the feathers amusing? Papa ordered it for mama from a London milliner. He promises to order one for me next time.'

'No!' I cried before I could stop myself, 'The bonnet you are wearing is most becoming. It must not be changed for a thing!'

Ada blushed and smiled shyly. Rebecca's smile was broad and there was a lot of suppressed humour in it.

Committing myself to marriage is one thing, but committing myself to marriage with a woman wearing a feathered boiled egg, is quite another thing altogether.

TWENTY; Mid March 2018

One of Us

It was looking pretty good now, Monica had to admit. Mid March and only a couple of weeks late in opening.

With the simple pale linen bedcover and pillows, the small bedside chest and candle stick, and the small collection of books that stood on the mantel shelf, Joshua's room was ready to receive visitors. There was one further item in the room. In the corner by the window, as if someone had been sitting there to read, was a low backed Windsor chair, its back legs conveniently hiding a certain area of skirting board.

Monica was fairly satisfied that the newly discovered carving was hidden from view. A small oblong of transparent plastic had been tacked to the wood over the lettering, protecting it from damage and the new paint which had transformed the rest of the room. To the casual eye, the patch was invisible. Even to a suspicious eye, the writing could hardly be seen beneath the plastic.

The lighting in the room was deliberately subdued; there was just one low-energy ceiling light over the fireplace. The west facing window benefitted from the sun only in the late afternoon, which gave the room a cosy, bedtime feel. Monica had added to this ambiance with a fake fire in the grate, where piled up pine cones and red cellophane were lit from below by hidden LED lights to give the fire a realistic look.

It was one o'clock now. From downstairs came the sounds of the heavy front door being opened. She could hear

Bernadette's voice, already welcoming people. Angie's was there too, meaning that they were busy enough for Bernadette to need help in reception. Angie would not be enjoying having to work there, Monica thought. She ought to go down and help.

She took one last look around Joshua's bedroom, her winter project. In a moment the first visitors would be walking up the stairs to see it. She could hear a hum of voices in the stair well already and was gratified that people were responding to that week's articles in the Wisbech Standard and the Fenland Citizen.

Something caught her eye as she turned to leave the room. A grey shape slinked past her, a flicker of movement that merged with the shadows. Her heart missed a beat. The shape crouched in the dark corner behind the chair, springing deftly on to the crisp, white linen of the bedcover. Sniffing the bed suspiciously, it began to pad round in a circle, preparing for a snooze.

'Oi, Smokey, not on there!' No response. Monica thought she was beginning to recognise which one of next door's cats was which, but the three sleek, grey visitors were so alike that this could equally be one of its siblings, Smudge or Sooty. She gave up guessing, as clueless as the cats' owner, and resorted to their collective name.

'Smutty, geddoff!'

This time there was a twitch of the almost entirely tucked in tail, which probably meant the cat had heard but had no intention of obeying the command. Despite herself, Monica grinned. She liked the cats being around and they were popular with most of the visitors, but the pristine new bed cover in Joshua's room was not the place for them. She bent down and picked up the cat, who protested mildly, wriggling in her arms as she carried him out of the bedroom. She laid him gently in one of the specially designated Smutty baskets in the small box room next door.

Rapid footsteps sounded on the wooden stairs as Monica emerged from the box room and Angie appeared, puffing heavily from the exertion of running up two flights of steps.

'Monica! A woman's here to see you. Can you come?'

Monica muttered something uncomplimentary under her breath as she followed Angie down the stairs. She had hoped that Victoria would stay away a bit longer, that their opening day for the new room would not be blighted by another of her visits. It seemed her hopes had been in vain.

The woman stood apart from the other visitors, her back to the room as she gazed out of the window. A black woollen beanie hat covered most of her dark bobbed hair and she'd either lost weight while away in Dorset, or she was not Victoria.

She was not Victoria. Monica was so relieved that she found herself smiling and accepting the woman's business card more enthusiastically than was strictly necessary.

'Marcia Hunter....' began the stranger without returning the smile. She wore instead an other-worldly, strange expression as she gazed around the room without appearing to see it.

'....yes?' prompted the curator.

'I do apologise. It's just that I find myself overwhelmed by the energy in this building....Marcia Hunter, of Phenland Phantom Phinders.'

She couldn't be serious. Monica glanced at the card in her hand to make sure she'd heard correctly. She had.

'I'm afraid we're extremely busy at the moment,' she said, indicating the queue at the reception desk. There was so much noise in the room that she could hardly hear herself speak, let alone her eccentric visitor.

'Yes, I do see that I've chosen a bad time to visit,' acknowledged Marcia with her ethereal look, 'I'll call again some other time, when you are quieter....you see, I feel there is work to be done here. This house is so.... so full of feeling, such an obvious presence of....'

Don't tempt me, muttered Monica under her breath as Marcia's sentence faded away to nothing.

'However,' she replied crisply instead, seeing another family enter and join the queue, 'Now is simply not the time to discuss anything, I'm afraid. I really must go.'

'Well, keep the card and one of us will call at another time. Good day to you, Miss Kerridge.'

One of us? It sounded eerily threatening and who on earth said good day anymore? Monica tossed the card into the bin and went to greet the next people in the queue, apologising for the wait and doing her best to keep everyone happy.

By two o'clock more than fifty visitors had arrived, a number which the small museum had never before had to cope with in such a short period of time. When the flow of visitors eventually began to slow down, Monica went to help Angie in the tea room, brewing extra coffee and preparing cream teas.

The newspaper articles had worked wonders. The town had always been fond of its poet and Monica was constantly encouraged, as well as surprised, by the number of their regular visitors and how far people were prepared to travel to this tiny museum. She'd known visitors to come from as far away as Canada before, obviously not solely to visit the poet's birthplace, but with the museum on their list of places to see.

Now, with an extra room open, especially one as important as the poet's own bedroom, the future looked very promising. Monica, Bernadette and Angie worked without a break all afternoon, but it was in the knowledge that the hard work was worth it.

So, of course, Victoria had to turn up and spoil it.

She chose her moment well, entering the house at the very end of the afternoon when there were no other visitors. She'd washed her hair for a change, as if celebrating a special occasion. She'd even gone to the trouble of curling her blond locks and her hair tumbled over the shoulders of her red coat.

'Good afternoon, Monica, do you have a moment?' Judging by the emptiness of the place, it was clear that Monica did. Unfortunately.

'Afternoon, Victoria, good holiday?'

'A wonderful holiday, thank you,' she chirped, 'I spent three happy weeks of exploring, walking and enjoying all the sights, you know. And I made some interesting discoveries....'

Monica knew she was expected to jump in at this point, demand to know what discoveries these were, but she took her time. She walked slowly to join Bernadette, who was pretending not to listen, behind the counter.

'Discoveries?' prompted Monica at last, 'What have you been discovering?' She asked the question as if to a child who'd been fishing in rock pools all day.

'That I,' Victoria enunciated, 'am most definitely descended from Joshua Ambrose, our poet.'

'I see, but you thought that already.'

'But now I know for sure, Monica. Before I went to Dorset, I didn't know for certain that my ancestor, Edmund Ambrose, was connected to Joshua. Now I do. I have filled in the missing gap!'

'Well that's....'

'Marvellous, isn't it? I'm so happy! So thrilled! It means that my family once lived in this house, that my ancestor once wrote his poetry here, ate here, slept here. It gives me such a feeling of belonging, Monica! Just imagine!'

Monica allowed a smile in response, but her hackles were up, prepared for whatever was coming next. Because with Victoria you always had to expect something else.

'So, I'll be off, then! I'll leave you to your cashing up and sorting out and I'll be in touch. Byee!'

'Hell,' uttered Bernadette as the red coated woman sailed out of the door, 'She'll be in touch, she says. What is she up to?'

'I do not know,' replied Monica in a voice that had lost all its pleasure from the day's success, 'but I have a very bad feeling about this. The sooner I can get to Dorset, the better. If she found something there, I can find it too. We have to know what we're up against.'

'Sounds serious.'

Monica nodded. She had the feeling that things were going to get a lot more serious.

TWENTY ONE

Diary of Joshua Ambrose, Thursday, 15th August 1799

It is good to be out of London again. As a merchant I cannot ignore its value as a trading place, nor its mighty port, which draws in bounty from all over the globe, but one night spent in its dirt, noise and smoky air is more than enough for a Fenland born fellow such as I.

Last night was my third on the road and in truth I cannot complain about the journey so far. At last the chaise has brought me into the pleasant lanes of Surrey and by tomorrow we shall be in Hampshire.

Already, I feel the benefit of fresher, more wholesome air. This glorious, rolling landscape opens out a new vista with every turn in the road and from the crest of every hill. I am sure that my health will improve a hundredfold by being in these southern climes.

This slow travel suits me. Perhaps it could be achieved more quickly with fewer nights spent on the road, but I see no benefit in such uncomfortable haste. By the end of tomorrow I should have arrived at my destination and that will be soon enough.

In time, all the delights of Ponders Mullen and the hills of Dorsetshire will become familiar to me.

TWENTY TWO; Early April 2018. Day One of Holiday

Watching Eyes

It had rained on and off for most of the journey, making progress slow and tedious. Monica's one break for coffee and a quick meal had been the usual mooch around an enormous motorway complex, dodging crowds, vending machines and enough cuddly toys to fill the nation's nurseries. Her only true relaxation would come at the end of the journey, and at long last that was near.

As soon as she had passed Wareham, the distant, towering dominance of Corfe Castle beckoned her along the road, drawing her ever closer to the village. Right on cue, the rain decided it had fallen enough for one day and dissolved into drizzle, leaving no more than a fine mist on the Renault Clio's windscreen. The windscreen wipers began to screech, having too little to do, as she entered the village of Corfe Castle. Soon she was driving at minimum speed along West Street, craning her neck in vain to make out the numbers on cottage doors. In the end, she had to park the car and walk along the narrow road, finally locating the cottage she had rented for the week.

Daffodil Cottage was as sweet as its name, but even on first sight it was in obvious need of care and attention. Charmingly ancient, its grey stones were held together by desiccated wooden beams and its front steps, which led up a sharp incline to the door, were carpeted with weeds.

Monica's eyes swept over its faults and saw only the cottage's charm. She found herself smiling with pleasure as she lugged her suitcase up the wet, slippery steps and fitted her key into the surprisingly modern lock. Despite her tiredness, she continued to smile as she closed the door behind her, putting down the case on the stone flagged floor and breathing in the atmosphere of the cottage. One step inside the door and it felt like home.

The landlord had thoughtfully left the heating on for her and the house felt immediately cosy and welcoming. There were just three rooms downstairs; a sitting room dominated by a huge fireplace, a small kitchen and a tiny bathroom. From the kitchen window stretched the view of the long garden with its twisted orchard trees, which looked almost as old as the house. In the distance she could see the green expanse of Corfe Common.

The upper storey was accessed through a latched plank door and a winding stairway which ended in a tiny bedroom. Its heavily beamed ceiling was so low that even Monica with her short stature had to take care not to knock herself silly when walking around the bed. Beyond this room was a further bedroom with twin beds and a floor that dipped alarmingly in the centre. She retreated to the first room and left her case there.

She went back down the stairway, with its impossibly tiny treads and sharp bend, to make herself a drink. Filling the kettle, she looked out of the window, watching a pair of chaffinches as they flitted between the branches of a gnarled apple tree. She wallowed in the silence of the cottage, standing motionless by the window while she waited for the kettle, before remembering that she'd left her box of provisions, including the jar of coffee, in the car.

Once her small supply of groceries had been packed away, she took her mug of coffee into the long back garden. The drizzle had stopped at last, leaving the late afternoon sky a watery white, patterned with tiny far off streaks of brightness. They were hints, perhaps, of better weather to come.

The lawn needed cutting, the recent weeks of rain having made a tussocky meadow of it, and the flower beds by the back door were overgrown with weeds. By the time she had reached the end of the garden, her shoes were soaked, but it seemed unimportant. She gazed over the tired old planks of the back fence towards a small gathering of horses that grazed on the common, enjoying the rain drenched pasture and the fresh air of their perfect landscape.

Her tiredness having caught up with her, she decided not to go out that evening and to make do with the pasty she'd bought at the motorway stop. Tomorrow she would go shopping and start to explore, but tonight she was too comfortable in her new home, however temporary, to move.

She was awoken by the dust cart at eight o'clock the next morning. The crew must have known where the holiday cottage bins were kept, because already they were being up-ended at the back of the cart, wheels spinning aimlessly in the air. She watched from the small bedroom window as the bins were wheeled back home then, pulling on her dressing gown, she made her careful way down the perilous stairway. Outside she could hear the dust cart grumbling and wheezing its way down the road, leaving silence behind.

Just being in the cottage for a few short hours had already triggered a change in Monica. True, she had not yet stepped out into the street or even begun to see what she could discover, but there seemed no hurry. Her week seemed to stretch endlessly before her and very unusually she felt no worry or panic. Drinking her coffee, eating cornflakes from her supplies and using the milk left thoughtfully in the fridge by the landlord, she felt a rare sense of calm.

The first thing she needed to do was to shop for food. She'd decided to do all her shopping locally on this brief working holiday, to make the most of village life for a few days. She started as she meant to go on, leaving her small red Renault parked next to the cottage and walking into the village centre.

On a Friday morning in early April, the village of Corfe Castle had to be one of the most pleasant settings imaginable for a walk to the shop.

Although there were, of course, a number of newly built homes, the vast majority of houses had lined the village's streets for centuries. Constructed from the same distinctive grey Purbeck stone as the castle itself, many of the most picturesque houses were huddled together in terraces. They showed signs of great age, but they wore them with pride and dignity, each uneven roof line, drooping window ledge and slanting door frame displayed like badges of virtue. Window boxes, colourful with spring flowers, jutted out to make the narrow pavements even narrower. Here and there, little passageways led intriguingly from gaps between the terraces, their ancient flagstones worn in the centre by the feet of many generations.

The picture postcard village centre, with the ruins of the great castle towering above it, was utterly charming, and Monica couldn't stop a great smile from lighting up her face as she turned from West Street on to the small square. There was an excellent bakery, where she bought bread, cakes and sausage rolls, the entrance to the Model Village, several very pretty gift shops, the large National Trust shop, a newsagent, two good looking pubs and the village stores.

The Corfe Castle Village Stores sold everything she needed and was a pleasure to visit. Shopping in the traditional way, with a basket on her arm, choosing from fresh and frozen goods, many of them produced locally, was a delight which suited her new peaceful mood. Even the beer was locally produced, made by a brewery named after the River Piddle in Dorset. Though not much of a beer drinker, she couldn't resist buying a couple of bottles of Silent Slasher produced by the Piddle Brewery. By the time a bottle of wine had been added to her bags, they were bulging dangerously and far too heavy, but she hefted them out of the shop and lugged them back through the square.

The castle entrance was busy already; a party of school children was climbing down from a bus and the hum of their excited chatter was mounting with each moment. Even had Monica not been weighed down by her shopping, she knew she could not yet justify a visit to the castle. Much as she longed to climb up there and explore the ruins, there was too much to do first. She only had a week and knew she ought to make a start with her research. She headed straight home to the cottage.

After unpacking her purchases, she changed into walking boots and ventured out again. She had decided to begin by retracing Joshua's footsteps with a walk on the common. Obviously, there would be no new discoveries made like this, but she wanted to get a feel for the place where Joshua was believed to have written many of his poems. It just felt like the right place to start.

The watery white sky was beginning to brighten as she set out, the faintest glimmer of sunshine touching the road ahead for a few brief seconds before shivering away again. It was chilly in the shade of the trees lining the end of West Street, where the gated road entered the common, and she zipped up her jacket, pushing her hands into her pockets as she crossed the cattle grid.

At first she took the wrong path. Turning right at the gate, the track plunged suddenly down a steep slope which the recent heavy rain had turned into a mud slide. The pale clay mud stuck to her boots before she had gone very far and she had to give up, her feet sucking out of the thick, wet mud as if covered in cement. The effort of pulling herself back up the slope almost sent her sprawling into a broad puddle liberally splattered with fresh cowpats, to the great interest of a herd of cows which had gathered to watch. She could almost feel them sniggering, the buggers, chewing on mouthfuls of grass and snorting.

She returned to the gate and this time headed off in the opposite direction, following the faintly worn track through the grass and down into a shallow dip where alders and willow saplings grew in profusion.

The path continued downwards, crossing a slim bridge of wooden planks over a narrow stream and the boggy ground that bordered it. There was just a single hand rail to the bridge and she leaned against it for a while, peering into the clear water. The stream was far too shallow to support larger fish like the brown trout found in the Corfe River, but a complete microcosm, a universe of life in miniature, was there before her eyes. Mayfly nymphs, tiny wriggling worms and the smallest fish imaginable propelled themselves through the water, apparently unconscious of the larger world around them.

Before the path began to lead uphill, it passed through a dip where the ground had been churned up by the hooves of too many cows and the boots of too many human walkers. It had become a mire of sticky clay and mud. The only way around it was by finding foot holds by the elder bushes bordering the path. Holding on to branches to steady herself, she leapt between the slightly firmer patches and was soon following the path upward again. There the ground was firm underfoot and her boots soon shed their clumps of wet mud.

Monica's feeling of isolation was complete and perfect. This green expanse, which was now safe in the care of the National Trust, was a rare survival of the common land which had once surrounded most English villages and towns.

For centuries, people living close to Corfe Common had depended on the right to graze their animals on its pasture and to collect firewood from its woodland. Even now, there were local people who enjoyed this ancient right and paid a fee to the Trust so that their horses and cattle could graze there. As the path led Monica towards the top of the ridge, the wide, green and wooded landscape gradually opened around and below her. Here and there, contentedly grazing on the fresh, spring grass, were small herds of horses, masters of this rare and splendid place.

There had been a period in the eighteenth and nineteenth centuries when industry had been allowed to disturb the peace of the common. Wide scale clay extraction had taken place and the clay sent up to Staffordshire for use in the production of pottery. Josiah Wedgewood, apparently, had been a very good customer and must have brought a level of prosperity to the area. By the late nineteenth century, however, the extraction had finally come to an end.

Apart from that period, when large areas of the common must have been scarred and much of its peace destroyed, these acres of grassy hills, vales and copses would have seen little change over the centuries. There was evidence that life had gone on there for millennia.

Close to the top of the ridge, almost hidden by scrub and tall grass, was a burial mound thought to date from the Bronze Age. Apparently, there were also traces on the common of Celtic field systems, signs that the Iron Age tribe of Durotriges had once prospered there. Monica found it staggering just how long this area had been occupied by mankind.

She could well understand its attractions. Even as a walker, an hour or so spent there was good for the soul. It was a balm to fill her lungs with the clear, clean air and to fill her heart with peace and solitude. It had been a long time since she had last felt so contented and free.

And of course it was there that Joshua was believed to have written much of his romantic poetry. It was there that he had walked and contemplated, perhaps composing lines in his head as he made his way along the many winding paths.

From the top of the ridge she could see the village of Kingston in the distance and, turning round, the broken keep of Corfe Castle in the opposite direction. Far away, traffic moved along the road, but its noise hardly reached her. Apart from the animals, she was alone. There was not another human soul in sight.

Which was why it made no sense at all that suddenly, out of nowhere, she knew she was being watched.

There were eyes on her. She could feel them distinctly, and though she could not explain how, she knew it to be a man who watched. And yet she was quite alone. Even further down the hill, where the burial mound lay close to the path and provided a degree of cover, there was no movement, no sense that anyone was there at all.

The peace and contentment which only a few seconds ago had felt complete, had vanished, leaving her with only the strong desire to escape. Rapidly she began to walk back down the hill, navigating once more around the muddy bit and trotting over the narrow bridge. Still there were eyes on her back, following her retreat.

She would come back, she fiercely promised herself. When this hidden threat was no longer there, she would explore the common again, but today her walk was well and truly over.

She crossed the cattle grid and unlatched the gate at the edge of the common, entering West Street and heading for home. It was only then that she turned round.

Standing by the gate she had just passed through was a man. He was leaning against the metal bars of the sturdy gate and appeared to be engrossed in a large, fold-out map. He looked ordinary enough, a dark haired, clean shaven man of medium height, dressed in a dark waterproof and jeans. He was the only human being she had seen since arriving at the common and he seemed to have appeared from nowhere.

Monica was only half aware that she had begun to retrace her steps, that she was pacing purposefully back up the road towards the gate. As she grew close to the man, she saw him raise his eyes, glancing casually at her at first, then his face registering surprise as he noticed her furious expression.

'Just what did you think you were doing?' she demanded, 'Scaring me witless like that? You may have found it entertaining, but actually it was bloody frightening.'

'I'm sorry, I don't....' the man uttered, looking perplexed and baffled. Certainly not as creepy as she might have expected.

'You were following me!' she accused, 'Why? I was just having a walk. What's your problem?'

The man still looked confused, but was beginning to collect himself. He was folding the large map in his hands, as if giving himself time to think.

'Look,' he said, his voice quite stern, like a headmaster's she remembered from primary school, 'I can see you've been frightened, but I assure you I was not following you. In fact, this is the first time I've clapped eyes on you. If you think you were being followed, it might be a good idea to report it to the police.'

She found herself on the back foot suddenly, her anger dissolving, embarrassment creeping in to fill the gap. She backed away from him, shaking her head.

'I'm sorry. It's not fair to accuse you, but you were the first person I've seen since arriving on the common. It was a shock. It was very creepy.'

'That's OK. Don't let it put you off walking here. It's a grand place.' He smiled then, olive-green eyes crinkling in a comfortable, pleasant face. She didn't dare trust him, though. She was far from recovered from the fear she had felt.

After another awkward apology she left him in peace with his map. She was glad to return to the silence of Daffodil Cottage and its absence of watching eyes.

TWENTY THREE

Diary of Joshua Ambrose, Friday 23rd August 1799

This is a good place to be.

My Aunt Williams is a kindly woman, though I fear not one who enjoys good health. Any small amount of exercise seems to tire her and she is often very pale in the face. She says it is nothing, that she is quite well and happy to have my company.

She asks constantly after her sister and I do my best to oblige. In the evenings after dinner we sit and enjoy the peace and warmth of the summer evenings and I tell her all the interesting snippets I can think of, of family life and memories which show my mother at her happiest. She likes to hear about Rachel's visits with her baby son, as well as family dinners when father is in a good humour and harmony reigns in our home. I choose not to tell her about the dark days, when father's ill temper spreads through the house like an evil fog and everyone, including mother, knows it best to stay away from him.

My aunt lives well as a widow, enjoying her high standing in the village of Ponders Mullen and a pleasant degree of society. Her home is the graceful old manor house opposite the church, a house which has been in her late husband's family for generations. To me, it seems a home where the sun always shines, even when the clouds show that to be impossible. My aunt has been kindness itself to me and is quite determined to restore me to perfect health. She feeds me until I am fit to burst, on home cured bacon and delicious pies, baked by her ever smiling cook, Mrs Mollifer.

We find ourselves involved in more social engagements than I would like. It seems that the principal families of Ponders Mullen are determined to become acquainted with Mrs Williams' nephew. We have received many friendly morning calls and are obliged to make many in return. We also have a number of invitations to dine and poor Mrs Mollifer's smile has dulled to something less radiant. She can even be heard grumbling away in the kitchen as she readies herself and the other servants for the dinners which my aunt must offer in return.

When we are not entertaining or being entertained, I spend most of my time out of doors. It is fortunate that my aunt is unperturbed by this habit of mine. Sometimes she takes a little turn about the village with me, but she tires quickly and needs to be taken home again and settled with her painting. She loves to sketch and to paint and there is always some village scene or grouping of people which engages her interest and keeps her absorbed for hours at a time.

When I wander further afield, she is happy to lend me her bay, a sweet tempered horse who seems to know his way from Ponders Mullen to nearby Corfe Castle without much guidance from me. I suspect my aunt is glad of the respite from my chatter and enjoys being alone sometimes. My own peace comes while walking on the common around Corfe Castle and I find I am drawn there as easily as is the bay.

The Greyhound Inn occupies a prominent position in the village square of Corfe Castle, opposite the crumbling old Parish Church of St Edward. The whole village is overlooked by the castle ruins on the hill, a constant reminder of its once powerful presence. The landlord of the Greyhound has agreed that I leave my horse in his care while I wander on the common. It is a good arrangement and there's certainly no penance in sampling a flagon or two of ale at the end of the day when my weary legs carry me back to the inn.

I find the company of the local people refreshing. No talk of shipping or trade here. Many of the villagers are employed as clay cutters on the common and discussion in the Greyhound ranges from their daily toils to the concerns of local sheep farming. The villagers' voices, with their pleasant West Country burr, are pleasing to the ear.

And so on most days, when social engagements allow, I walk on the common. I am easily lost in day dreams as I wander and words come into my head, but they are lazy lines that fit nothing and go nowhere. Perhaps the latest bout of sickness has left me weaker than I thought. My head is fuzzy, my thoughts unformed, trailing off into fantasy without conclusion, sensible or otherwise.

Even the common itself has problems. Despite the need for employment in this and neighbouring villages, the spoiling of this wild and ancient place is terrible to see. I know the potters of Staffordshire must take their clay from somewhere, but the extraction of the stuff is turning parts of this heaven into hell. The clamour of industry, the shouting of men as they rip up the turf and load up their carts, leaving churned up tracks across once tranquil pasture, is dreadful indeed. Yet without this evil, where would Mr Wedgewood find his clay? I am as guilty as any man in eating my supper from his plates.

This morning I made my way up to the ridge, an exposed, windy spot from where, looking in opposite directions, both the village of Kingston and the castle at Corfe can be seen. Despite the wind, which funnels its way up through the Purbeck Hills, this is a peaceful spot, the noise and mess of industry being sufficiently distant to be forgotten for a while.

Not far away are a number of ancient burial mounds, hillocks which crown the natural hills. Scrubby elder trees, gorse and long grass littered with tiny wild flowers gather around these mounds, as if to guard them, making them private places to sit and think. There is one in particular, just off the beaten track, which lends a perfect view of the castle ruins on the neighbouring hill. Even from here, the castle is a commanding presence. No matter its ruinous state, it draws the eye and the imagination. Its ivy covered walls are still majestic, whatever ill has come to it in the past.

I mean to explore the castle soon. The landlord of the Greyhound tells me that I would be free to do so. Occasionally, he says, the odd curious minded fellow is seen having a poke around up there, and I am as odd and curious minded as the next man.

I had expected the view of the castle to inspire better lines, but my brain remains as dull as the clay-clouded puddles in the valleys of the common. Only a few awkward words come to me, joined together with tortured phrases that have no business being there. Most of my note book remains reprovingly blank, the only filled pages a mess of deletions and ugliness.

My efforts have so far yielded only this:

Ivy now the sole embrace
Of walls which very long ago
Did grace the glance of lords and kings
And suffer deeds of many fools.

Battered, bruised, besieged by birds,
Your broken walls memorial
To what was once both feared and proud,
Your erstwhile lofty self.

Dah-dee-dah-dee. Oh dear, perhaps father is right. I fear the life of a merchant will always be my lot.

The birds, I suppose, are jackdaws. It is hard to tell from this distance. Long ago, there were ravens at the castle, but it is said they fled at the first whiff of trouble. The landlord tells me that the faithless creatures abandoned the castle to its fate just before the place was blown to bits by Cromwell's thugs.

Jackdaws are certainly in evidence on the common, plodding around in that self important way of theirs, scattering all the small birds into cover and emptying the place like Sam's armpits in Rudderham's on a Friday night.

I must give the poetry time. No good will come from forcing the mind when it is so reluctant to work. For now, I will endeavour to enjoy the unpolluted parts of this common and try not to hurry things.

Though I must confess I am eager for something to happen.

TWENTY FOUR; Early April 2018. Day Two of Holiday

The Man from the Common

Noise boomed out through the door as she opened it, blasting like a physical force on to the pavement and nearly taking her back out with it.

Monica hadn't realised that the Greyhound would be hosting live music that night, but clearly everyone else knew. In the bar there was standing room only. She hesitated for a moment, considering going to the Bankes Arms next door instead, but then the crowd immediately in front of her dispersed to a pre-booked table and left the barmaid looking straight at her.

The girl with long, straight, dark hair and a heart shaped nose stud was all smiles as she filled Monica's glass with Thatcher's Gold.

'Band must be popular,' shouted Monica above the din.

'Very. Lizzy and Co. They play a lot of old Thin Lizzy, but they write their own songs as well. Seen them plenty of times before and they're pretty cool.'

Monica nodded and shouted her thanks as she took her cider. Having no seat, she braced her feet on the wooden floor to avoid being knocked over by the jostling groups on each side of her, and sipped her drink. From where she stood at the end of the long bar she couldn't see much of the band. Occasionally she caught sight of an elbow or a twirling drumstick poking out from behind a group of people, but other than that it was just their music which reached her, very loud and clear.

Between numbers, normal pub sounds resurged; raised voices, laughter and the clinking of glasses. Despite the crush, everyone seemed more than happy. At tables tucked into every corner and crevice, people were eating, elbows tucked in tightly to avoid losing their beer-battered cod to the cable knitted front of a passing drinker.

After a while, a few of the tables began to empty and some of the waiting groups sat down, leaving space around the bar. Eventually, Monica managed to sneak her bottom on to one of the bar stools close to where she had been standing. In one of the short pauses between songs she ordered another cider and scampi and chips from the menu.

After her experience on the common that afternoon, it was reassuring to have plenty of people around her. It was an unusual feeling for her, normally preferring solitude, but the discomfort she'd felt on the common persisted.

Having had time now to think things through, she knew she shouldn't have accused the stranger. He had most likely been totally innocent. Perhaps her fear had been an overreaction, but at the time it had been intense, a natural reaction to feeling observed and followed. All the stories she'd read in the papers, about attacks on women in isolated places, had done nothing to ease her peace of mind.

After a short pause, the front man of Lizzy and Co said a few words about how glad they were to be back in Corfe Castle, his amplified voice booming and bouncing off the old walls. He announced the next number, and as the opening bars of "The Boys Are Back in Town" pounded out, Monica's food arrived.

Like the rest of the food served in the pub, the scampi and chips were artistically presented. The chips had been up-ended into a miniature steel chip pan basket, surrounded by substantial piles of mushy peas and scampi, on a plate designed to look like newspaper. It tasted as good as it looked. The band wasn't making a bad hash of things either, Monica contemplated as she downed her cider and munched her way through the scampi. Unfamiliar chords began to fill the room as the band announced one of their own compositions. Not bad at all, she considered, growing decidedly mellower.

By the time "Parisienne Walkways" was lulling everyone in a fair imitation of the original version, Monica was feeling well disposed towards everyone. From her seat at the end of the bar she could see a bit more of the guitarist, who managed to look a bit like Gary Moore from late seventies posters. That was, if you ignored the double chin and beer gut. The vocalist, however, wasn't in the least like Phil Lynott, his long blond hair making any attempt in that direction a bit of a non-starter.

Of the rest of the band she could see nothing. There were still too many heads in the way, as well as constant movement behind the bar. Her seating position meant that in order to see the band she had to look across the full length of the bar, but she didn't really mind. The atmosphere was good and she was lucky to have a seat at all.

As she finished her cider, her eyes wandered from the band, across the backs of the heads at the bar. One of them, she noticed, was turned towards her, the owner of the head looking straight at her. Her heart gave a deep, slow thud of warning and she looked away.

Her plate was removed from the bar top and she was glad of the distraction, murmuring unheard thanks to the immediately disappearing barmaid. She picked up her glass again, but realised it was empty. The bar staff were all busy serving. No hope of an instant refill.

Her panic resurged as still she felt the eyes on her. After more seconds than were comfortable, she felt, rather than saw, the staring head withdraw from the bar, and she breathed a long, cautious sigh of relief.

'Hello....'

She jumped. Foolishly, she actually jumped. She felt ridiculous. The man from the common was standing right next to her, squeezed in between the tightly packed bar stools.

'Look, I really didn't mean to alarm you. Obviously I did, so I'm sorry. You had a bit of a fright today. I just wanted to ask if you were all right, that's all....'

His voice was solid, reassuring, the sound of common sense. It had a nice depth to it. No particular accent that she could decipher, and unlike earlier, there was a touch of friendliness about it. There was nothing creepy about it, but then....

She half turned to face him. He didn't *look* creepy either. Ordinary. Just an ordinary dark haired man in something like his forties, dressed in dark coloured walking clothes, which suited him.

'I'm sorry,' she said at last. 'You must think I'm an idiot.'

'Of course not. I saw you were scared, that's all. I *would* ask if I could get you a drink, but that would just convince you of my identity as the pervert of Corfe Common....'

She smiled, saying nothing.

'....Yet, if I *didn't* buy you one after making that excuse, you'd just think I was mean.'

She laughed, her caution billowing away like a wafted swarm of flies. Already, he'd caught a barmaid's eye and was ordering her another cider, pulling money from his pocket.

'Thank you,' she smiled. The last notes of "Parisienne Walkways" filled the pub, then dissolved into loud applause.

When she turned back to him, he had gone.

TWENTY FIVE

Diary of Joshua Ambrose, Monday 26th August 1799

Who is she?

I saw her by the stone bridge on the common this morning. Head down, purposeful, as if walking were a task to be done.

She did not see me; I am sure of that. I was sitting in my usual place, on a fallen branch amongst a clump of willows to the side of the path. I was struggling with my writing, as usual, my pencil employed more in deleting than in composing.

And yet there she was, treading prettily from the cobbles of the bridge to the torn up, muddy grass, her fair hair escaping from her straw bonnet.

And then she had gone, hurrying away and out of my sight, a solitary inspiration on a cloudy, indifferent day.

TWENTY SIX; Early April 2018. Day Three of Holiday

Tyrant Grown Old

It was still dark in the room; not enough light even to make out the heavy shapes of beams in the low ceiling above her head.

The cottage was in total silence; no obvious reason for her having awoken so abruptly. Yet something had alerted her and now she was fully awake, heart booming, eyes staring up towards the invisible beams.

It had only been a dream, she realised. Nothing to worry about, just a rapidly fading dream. She had to concentrate hard to remember any of it at all.

She'd dreamed she was walking on the common and someone had been following her along the path. A man. She'd glanced back, but hadn't been able to see much of his face at first. His hand had been raised to hold on his hat, to stop it being blown away by the wind, and his sleeve had been obscuring his face.

She'd felt no fear of him to begin with, however closely he followed her along the path. He was wearing a jacket with a high turned over collar, displaying a loosely tied cream cravat at his throat. He was very thin and fair haired, and when he'd allowed his hand to drop and show his face, she'd noticed the intense blue of his eyes.

That had been when her heart had started to pound, when she'd seen his eyes. They'd shone from his pale, lean face and had looked right into her own. They had startled her into waking, escaping the fear of once more being watched.

This man was definitely not the one from the pub and the common. This was another stranger altogether, one whose intensity she was not likely to forget in a hurry.

She turned over and tried to sleep again, but did more fidgeting than dozing. Eventually, morning light began to creep into the room, outlining the dark beams and showing them against the white painted ceiling. She gave up with sleep and went downstairs to shower and get ready for the day.

Saturday brought its usual bustle to the village square. A minibus was dropping off a group of German tourists, who gathered before the Bankes Arms and gazed as one towards the ruin on the hill. The castle, even in its present dilapidated state, probably attracted as many visitors as it had in its medieval heyday. It certainly still drew every eye upwards, towards its commanding presence, and Monica, with her great love of all things ancient, couldn't wait to get up there and explore it for herself.

But first she had a job to do. Already she'd been there a whole day without making any kind of progress and she had to get started. The logical place to begin was the village church, the Parish Church of St Edward, and she turned on to its path from the village square. Although the internet had shown no trace of any marriage Joshua might have had, it still had to be worth looking at the local churches, at any headstones or records that may have survived.

The church was unlocked but silent, the door creaking open to reveal its Victorian grandeur. The small guide book Monica purchased told her that there had been a church there since the twelfth century, but that the damage it had suffered over time meant that it had had to be rebuilt in the 1850s. Soldiers from Cromwell's army had used the place as a free hotel and stabling for their horses, while engaged in the destruction of the castle in the 1600s. They had been the sort of house guests you couldn't wait to get rid of, their abuse of the ancient church going even so far as to use parts of it for target practice.

And so, the church she was visiting today was not the structure which Joshua would have known in his time. The building he would have been familiar with would still have born the scars of Cromwell's men's vandalism. Monica left the quietness of the church, her disappointment mounting as she saw what was left of the graveyard.

Most of the headstones had been removed long ago to leave a grassy, open space, a haven of peace away from the busy square. For the last hundred and fifty years or so, burials had taken place in nearby cemeteries, initially across the road in East Street and later in an even newer one off West Street. No clues remained, therefore, from the time she was interested in. She would have to look at the parish registers, if they still existed, in order to find anything at all. Even there, she was unsure of how to start. And there was no one to ask, just the persistent stillness of the church.

She tried to rein in her impatience. Sunday would be the day for finding out more from churches. From the notice board she noted the time of the morning service and planned to be there. With any luck, tomorrow she would be able to speak to the rector or church warden and obtain permission to see the old records.

The rest of Saturday stretched ahead without a plan or the smallest idea of where she could start her investigation.

She was, she realised with sinking spirits, a pretty clueless detective. Miss Marple she was not. She tried to shrug off her frustration, pointing out to herself that even driving around local parishes to look at headstones would be better done on a Sunday. Today, she decided, there was little option. Today she would be a tourist.

From the square, she walked over the bridge which crossed the deep, dry moat and passed through the dark castle entrance. As she stepped into the bailey, a man in a National Trust polo shirt emerged with a cheerful greeting from a wooden hut by the path and checked her membership card. She continued along the neatly gravelled path, crossing the bailey and climbing the slope to the south-west gatehouse.

As she crossed the small bridge over one of the old defensive ditches and entered the broken gatehouse, the sun eased its way through the weakening cloud cover. The warmth it brought didn't last long, cheering the ancient grey stone for just a few precious seconds. It was enough, though, to lighten Monica's mood and allow her to put aside her worries and make the most of her free day.

The explosions which had undermined and destroyed the gatehouse had probably been a disappointment to Cromwell's men. Instead of reducing the structure to rubble, the assault had only managed to split the building in two. The left side seemed to have dropped a few feet, but had remained upright, settling into its new, sunken position where it had remained ever since. Just the top of its doorway peered out now on to the side of the path. The other half of the gatehouse had stayed where it was. It was missing only its roof, its back walls and practically everything else, when she thought about it.

Pretty much buggered really, as the tourist behind her put it. Monica silently agreed with him. But at least this half of the gatehouse still had the feel of a room about it, a place which had once sheltered guards on duty. It had been the workplace of generation after generation of soldiers who had witnessed just about everything that life could throw at them.

Monica continued along the path as it curved upwards to enter what remained of the towering keep. Wind blew pitilessly through its floorless, ceiling-less storeys, its massive walls carpeted with thick green moss, a parody of the rich tapestries which had once hung there. Only the view through the slit-like window was left to remind visitors of the extent of the surrounding landscape the castle had once commanded.

For centuries, the whole of the Isle of Purbeck would have existed in the shadow and protection of this mighty castle on its high mound. It had eventually been brought low by the ravages of civil war, but that it lived on at all was testament to its solid build quality and the care of the National Trust. The Trust had cleared away centuries of neglect, rubble and brambles, but what remained of the castle was a sad reminder of its former glory. It was like a fearsome tyrant grown old and mellowed, one who put up with his great grandchildren climbing all over him, even smiling a bit.

Monica stayed among the castle ruins for over an hour, wandering between the towers on the outer walls and the remains of the Gloriette, the residence added by King John in the early 1200s. Monica had never been all that sensitive in picking up the atmosphere of a place, but there was certainly something about this castle which attracted her and made her reluctant to leave.

In the grassy bailey, a man in medieval costume was beginning a demonstration of falconry. She watched for a while as the bird circled the ancient stones and returned to the gloved hand of his master. She was happy to delay her departure from the castle, but in the end she obeyed the growling of her stomach and went to seek lunch.

She was just leaving the bakery on the square with her bag of bread and pasties when she stopped short, the two German tourists immediately behind her almost colliding with her back.

A man of medium height with dark hair and wearing dark walking gear was strolling across the road towards her, one arm outstretched as if about to wave. Not him again, she muttered under her breath. But then the arm had continued upward to scratch his head and he'd veered away, into the entrance of the Greyhound. Not him at all.

Her shoulders slumped and she wandered over to the market cross to sit on its base and eat her pasty. Her mood, despite the hazy sunshine and her walk around the castle, could have been better. Lurking amongst her thoughts was something she vaguely recognised as disappointment.

She sipped from her water bottle, contemplating her next move, and could think of nothing more useful than further sight-seeing. As pleasant as it was, it was doing nothing to ease her sense of responsibility. The museum trustees had paid generously from their limited funds for this trip and she felt duty bound to unearth something of value before she left on Thursday morning.

The coaching entrance doors to the model village stood open and the sign drew her in without further hesitation. She bought her ticket and entered another Corfe, a village in miniature based on a time before Cromwell had given the castle its new look.

The model village was, like the original, made of Purbeck stone, its grey houses remarkable copies of the real things. Even from her limited knowledge of the village, she was able to identify several houses and pubs as she stepped along the small streets on her way to the castle.

High on its grassy hill, the perfectly intact castle was protected by high, solid stone walls. Its towers and gatehouses, no longer broken and tumbled down the banks, protected the fore building, keep and Gloriette. A long flight of steps led from the upright and mighty south-west gatehouse, providing a convenient yet steep approach to the great hall for the people of substance who visited.

The model of the castle as it once had been was fascinating. It was particularly interesting since Monica had just walked through its ruins. The model was skilfully made, the attention to detail staggering, and must have taken years of dedicated work to perfect.

She wandered home after an hour, walking back down West Street to her cottage, and pulled bags of calamari rings and chips out of the newly stocked freezer for dinner.

She would have liked a quick walk on the common before eating, but after the previous day's panic, late afternoon in spring didn't seem the best time to go there. Although she was already talking herself into believing that the whole incident had been no more than her imagination, a morning walk, when there would be other walkers about, would be more sensible.

In the morning she would feel better, be able to think more clearly. She would go for an early walk and attend the church service at 10.30am.

Then she would get to work on her sleuthing. It was about time.

TWENTY SEVEN

Diary of Joshua Ambrose, Tuesday 27th August 1799

I saw her again today.

I had been up by the old ruins and my mind was still busy with what I'd found there. Mostly, it was disappointment. The castle ruin is a sad place; that which still stands is smothered in ivy. The rest lies tumbled in heaps of stone, covered by nettles, docks and brambles. It is difficult to approach most parts of it, so high and impenetrable have become the weeds that guard it. With a strong dose of imagination, it is still possible to imagine how impressive the keep might once have been, but I have to conclude that the ruins are far more interesting from a distance than they are from close up.

From the castle, I had walked up through the village and on to the common. Heading for the top of the ridge, I was taking more notice of a pair of goldfinches flitting around in a thorn bush than I was of the path before me.

And then, there she was, the girl from yesterday, stepping down the hill towards me. There was that same purposeful look on her face, as if she had an obligation to fulfil. She glanced at me, as was natural when passing someone on a narrow hill path, but she quickly averted her eyes. I raised my hat as we passed, aware in that one brief glance of her bright eyes. I saw the troubled look in them, and something like sadness.

Yet, having passed her, there was no more I could do. I stood aimlessly on the ridge, gazing down at her as she walked away, my captivated eyes following her, perhaps felt by her, perhaps urging her even faster from my sight. I could not run after her, could not speak to her as I longed to do. We are not acquainted and cannot hope to be.

But at the very least, I have regained one thing through this encounter. Inspiration has returned and has grasped my stumbling attempts to write, making my efforts whole again.

Words flow from my pencil now, flying on to paper with rapid, uncontained fervour, coloured with melancholy. But it is good, this melancholy; it has awoken my soul. Never before in all my days have I longed so much for another glimpse of a girl.

After two brief encounters, I am hers!

TWENTY EIGHT; Early April 2018. Day Four of Holiday

The Fustiness of Biscuits

The morning service at St Edward's was fairly well attended, with around sixty adults and children, probably a mixture of parishioners and visitors. Monica had plenty of opportunity during the hour long family service to admire the Victorian stained glass and architecture. As pleasant as it was, however, she knew that if Joshua had come to church here at all, it would have been to a much older building.

If he had been here at all. She didn't even know that much. All she knew was that he'd visited Dorset, but it was a big county. His Common Poems had always been associated with Corfe Common, but that didn't mean he had stayed in Corfe itself.

The rector was a pleasant, smiling man who looked after several parishes. It must be frustrating for him, Monica thought, constantly to be greeting holidaying visitors to his churches, people he knew he would never see again. Despite any such feelings, though, he listened with apparent interest to Monica's request to see the old parish records before beckoning over one of the church wardens.

The warden bustled over at his summons, an efficient, busy looking woman in a grey suit with a large blue brooch on the lapel. She removed her glasses to speak, allowing them to dangle from a chain around her neck.

'Goodness, those records are popular lately! If you'd asked me a few months ago I'd have wondered where to find them, but I've only just put them away, as it happens.'

'Someone asked for them recently?'

'Indeed. A pleasant woman, though rather insistent, if I remember correctly. Keen to study her ancestry. What are you researching, dear?'

'Kettle's on the boil,' breezed another woman, teetering past on high heels. The warden called some sort of reply after the retreating figure, something about the biscuits being fusty, while Monica was still forming a reply in her head. It was no longer needed, however. The warden was obviously more concerned about the fustiness of the biscuits than with the demands of yet another nosey visitor.

'I'm afraid I won't be able to dig the records out until tonight,' she concluded, 'and I'm afraid the registers from that time are extremely fragile, so great care has to be taken when looking at them. They include records of baptism, banns, marriage and burial from around the time you're researching. I know, because the other lady was very keen to look through all of it. Could you come back tomorrow morning? I can have the books set out on that table over there,' she pointed towards the south side of the church, where a few leaflets and maps of the village had been set out, 'say about ten o'clock?'

'I'll be here,' smiled Monica, 'and thank you.'

Outside, the sun was shining, lighting up the walls of the castle and catching the outstretched wings of distant jackdaws, turning them golden as they moved above the great structure. She'd heard it said that ravens too could once more be seen at the castle, circling above the ruins at twilight. Having departed in the 1600s, they had only recently returned to roost in the keep. She hoped she might catch sight of them before she left.

Since it was Sunday, some of the shops were closed but there were still plenty of people in the square. The newsagent and gift shop on the corner was busy already. Two little boys were charging from its door in knightly armour, breastplates fastened over their T-shirts and wearing plastic helmets that sprouted red feathers. Waving their wooden swords in the air and yelling a battle cry, they belted towards the entrance to the castle. Following close behind, their parents walked at a sedate pace, chatting comfortably and looking like they'd seen it all before.

Monica grinned, wondering how daft she'd look in a Maid Marion outfit. The prospect of looking at the old registers the next day had cheered her up, though it could well lead to nothing. That afternoon, it might be useful to....

'Don't jump!'

She jumped. He was sitting on the base of the market cross, the man from the common. No mistake that it really was him this time. He must have just finished eating a sandwich because he was screwing up a triangular cardboard packet, twisting it between his fingers.

'Whatever I do makes you nervous,' he complained, 'Even warning you not to jump out of your skin makes you jump out of your skin! How can I be so alarming?'

She felt her shoulders relax a bit. He was smiling now, not a big, wide smile, but a tentative one, as if afraid a show of teeth might scare her.

'I'm sorry,' she muttered, 'it wasn't you, it was just....'

'....the fact that we keep bumping into each other?'

'And because of what happened up on the ridge, on the common. I'm not normally a nervous person, but I felt someone watching me and so when I saw you....' She found herself sitting down beside him.

'Yes, I understand that, but I'd just walked round from the cemetery direction. I hadn't been anywhere near the ridge.'

'I really am sorry. You were in the wrong place at the wrong time and I suppose I'm a bit distracted at the moment. I'm trying to get started with some research, you see, and I'm getting nowhere and time is slipping by.'

She stopped herself. What was she doing, gabbling away like this to a total stranger? What was wrong with her? She didn't even know his....

'My name's Archie, by the way,' he stuck out a slim hand, 'Well actually it's Archibald Newcombe-Walker, but that's a hell of a mouthful.'

She laughed, glancing sideways at him, and he was grinning too, a bit toothily. He wasn't handsome, that was for sure, but he had nice eyes. Large and an unusual olive green colour. And very shiny when he smiled.

'Monica Kerridge. Not much I can shorten that to, I'm afraid.' She'd taken the proffered hand and was shaking it, still smiling.

'So, what's the research all about?'

She wasn't sure how to reply, but she'd invited this by talking too much. She decided just to outline the bare facts, that she was trying to trace a marriage that may have taken place in the local area, between 1799 and 1801, and that it was connected to her work at a small museum in Cambridgeshire. She added that she had an appointment to look at the church registers in St Edward's the next day.

She thought he looked surprised for moment, but the expression quickly faded. He nodded and made no comment.

'Yes, I realise it sounds trivial,' she said hurriedly, as if having to defend her own work and actions, 'a lot of fuss over nothing. It's a long way to come just to look something up, but there's a lot hanging on this. Jobs could well be at risk and more besides.'

She was still ridiculously nervous, talking to him. She could hear it in her own voice.

'I was just thinking about your options,' he replied, as if he too had to explain himself. 'Have you looked round other parishes? At that time there would have been a lot more small churches around here. Not all of them remain, but most of them do. Some might even have parish records that haven't been uploaded to the internet.'

'Yes,' she agreed, 'I was thinking of doing that this afternoon. At least it'll feel like I'm doing something, because I'm running out of ideas already and I've hardly started.'

'Once you make a start, the rest will follow. It's the beginning which is the hardest bit.' He stood up, stretching slightly. 'I'm going to walk over to Kingston this afternoon. It's not exactly a long walk, but I thought I'd have a look round when I get there. So, good luck! I hope you find something. Perhaps see you later!'

From the newsagent's she bought a map which showed all the small villages and hamlets which were dotted around Corfe Castle. Walking back to the cottage, she picked up her car and drove out of the village in the sunshine, skirting the great castle-topped hill. The road took her through the gap in the Purbeck hills, and with the map spread over the passenger seat, she planned a rough route in her head.

Driving along the main road towards Wareham, she passed through Norden and Furzebrook, before turning back and branching off towards Church Knowle, then on towards Kimmeridge. Wherever she spied a church spire in the distance, she turned off the road to find it. Whenever that church had old gravestones, she walked between them, peering at their faded inscriptions. In several cases, she was obliged to wade through banks of nettles and briars to reach the longest forgotten of them.

Sometimes there was nothing much wider than a bridle path leading to a hamlet. In a couple of places, though a village was mentioned on the map, nothing remained of it but a cluster of ancient, tumble-down buildings. In yet more hopeless cases, the parish church had been closed long ago, its boarded up windows staring sadly and mutely over the nettled remains of its graveyard.

Monica was aware of how inadequate her amateur sleuthing was, but she kept on trying. Even where the headstones were too eroded by centuries of weather to tell her anything, if the church was old enough to have been there in Joshua's day she searched for a notice board and jotted down any phone number she could see. She intended to contact the parish priest or church warden later and then try to see their records.

After more than an hour of searching the parishes on one side of Corfe Castle, Monica turned back and headed in the other direction, towards Langton Matravers. Her findings were no more helpful there. It was all very scenic and pleasant, but she made few additions to her list of telephone numbers. As she turned into Kingston, she felt so frustrated with her lack of progress that she found herself hoping she'd bump into the man from the common, that he might have lingered there before turning back to Corfe. He had seemed interested in her research, but he was probably just being polite.

But he wasn't in Kingston, not that she could see.

He had a name now, she reminded herself as the car bumped over pot holes and clumps of earth left behind by tractor tyres. The thought of him no longer made her nervous. Archibald Newcombe-Walker was harmless, she was sure. He was even rather nice, but it would be better not to involve anyone else in her inadequate attempt to solve the museum's mysteries.

By the time she'd parked the car beside her cottage, there were just eight phone numbers written on her notepad. At least half of them had been copied from notices which were so faded that some of the digits had been almost indecipherable. She'd had to make more than a few guesses. Not very encouraging for a day's work.

She decided to walk on the common before going back inside. There were a few weekend walkers about and she was able to explore the paths and grassy hills without fear. Once more, she came to the narrow footbridge over the chalk stream and looked down into the brown tinted water.

As before, she found the stream very peaceful, a balm for her worries, and the more she watched, the more she saw. The miniscule fish still followed their invisible current, while tiny shrimps basked in the faintly sunlit water. When she raised her eyes, they were soothed by the sight of distant grazing horses on the hillside. Untroubled by the world's problems, they gave the occasional flick of their tails or raised their heads to breath in the peace of the Sunday afternoon.

Monica felt considerably less anxious by the time she returned to the cottage to change her clothes. Never the less, her meal in the Greyhound that night was dominated by her worries and was rather lonely.

TWENTY NINE

Diary of Joshua Ambrose, Wednesday 28th August 1799

My aunt has tried to help but is unable to do much.

After having her ears battered by my incessant talk last evening over supper, my aunt believes that my mystery girl is the niece of Mrs Blackstock. Despite my pitiful infatuation, my knowledge of the lovely creature is next to nothing, and my aunt had very little information to guide her. Even so, she thinks she knows who she is.

Mrs Blackstock is a widow of meagre means who has a cottage on the Wareham Road. She is, I am informed, a good and respectable woman, the widow of a clay cutter. Until her recent illness, she worked in the village as a seamstress, producing garments of good quality for local families. Her failing health has caused a considerable decrease in income and, to add to her misfortune, she is now in need of considerable care and nursing. Her younger sister, having married a tenant farmer from Dorchester and having three grown daughters to help on the farm, has been able to spare one of them to help Mrs Blackstock. My girl, therefore, is likely to be this niece.

No wonder her look is so troubled! Concern for her aunt's health and welfare must worry any kindly soul.

Aunt Williams looks troubled too. I know I have burdened her with my foolish yearnings and that she is only too aware of the understanding which exists between Miss Ada Imbridge and me. We both know that on my return to Wisbech I must honour that understanding. Even were I free to love where I wished, this beautiful girl is of quite the wrong social standing for my family to tolerate. Worse, I know nothing about her, not even her name. My aunt's knowledge does not reach so far.

There is one course of action which my aunt deems proper, and that is our paying a visit to Mrs Blackstock. My aunt's position in the village makes such a visit, to an ailing widow, appropriate.

With strict warnings ringing in my ears, Aunt Williams is planning for us to call on this widow and her niece within a day or two. She cannot approve of what is in my heart, but she is my mother's sister and shares her gentleness. I cannot help but feel that she understands.

And so I am to meet my girl. However hopeless my feelings, I can at least learn her name.

THIRTY; Early April 2018. Day Five of Holiday

Icy Water

They had seemed so full of promise at the start, those brittle church register pages. Monica had gone through line after line of faded, partly erased ink, her hope renewed with the beginning of each new page. The flowing script, which had diligently recorded baptisms on one page, banns and marriages on the next, followed by burials on the third, had gradually written the story of the parish.

Children baptised by the parish priest would be mentioned again a couple of decades later, on the banns and marriage pages. The priest, who recorded all this detail throughout the long years of his incumbency, must have known that one day the same names would make a final return to his pages, under burials, when a successor of his would write them down. They were all known to him, these people. They were living souls with problems, joys and sorrows, and yet their only remaining memorial was this faded ink on crumbling pages.

Some names were shown as having banns of marriage read out in church, without mention of the marriage itself. This had been where the wedding had taken place in another parish, usually where a man went to be married in his bride's church. Monica paid these names particular attention, thinking that even if Joshua had married elsewhere, if he'd been staying in the parish of Corfe Castle, his banns might have been read there.

Yet nowhere in any section was there a single Ambrose. Monica even checked for similar looking names, allowing for changes in spelling, which was common at the time. There was nothing. If a marriage had taken place at all, it had to have been elsewhere, perhaps in one of the parishes she had stumbled around yesterday.

It was beginning to look unlikely that Corfe Castle had been the village Joshua had stayed in. He could have ridden to the common from any of its surrounding villages. If anything was to be found at all, she would have to spread her net wider, and that was likely to take longer than the two and a half days she had left.

As she left St Edward's it was raining and the square had emptied. The rain had brought a chill with it and the jacket she had pulled on in a hurry that morning had become inadequate.

On its hill, the castle stood alone, its rain-darkened stones devoid of visitors.

Monica zipped up her jacket as she left the square, walking back along West Street. The cottages which pressed against the shining pavement managed to look almost as appealing in the rain, their window boxes bright with dwarf tulips, mauve and white aubrietia.

Across the road, a group of sightseers was sheltering from the rain beneath the arches of the small town hall. Seeing them there, a thought struck Monica and she slowed her steps.

When she had first explored the village she'd made a mental note of the small museum which housed its collection on the ground floor of the town hall. At the time, she'd been more focussed on looking at parish records, but she had meant to return on the off-chance that the museum's collection held any clues.

The Corfe Castle Town Trust Museum was one of the smallest she had seen, though only part of its collection was on view. Displayed behind glass and sheltered by the arches of the equally small town hall building, it was open to anyone who cared to look and was free of charge. It was a small, pleasant museum in a small, pleasant village.

The group of tourists continued like a large multi-coloured armadillo along the road, under the cover of their umbrellas. Left alone with her thoughts, Monica shook her wavy, dark hair free of some of the rain that had soaked it. Her hair was probably turned to frizz by now, she thought, but it didn't really bother her.

Despite the limited display space, the museum's exhibits were varied and interesting. They told the story of the village, from its ancient past to the present day. There was a series of old photos showing a way of life long gone, but many of the buildings were still recognisable. There was information about the extraction of clay in the eighteenth and nineteenth centuries, as well as the ancient local practice of quarrying Purbeck stone. Though she never came close to forgetting what she had come to find out, she quickly became engrossed, and it was some time before she saw the little notice in one corner of a window. Only part of the collection was on display, it reminded its visitors, due to limited space. If any researcher needed to look at the full collection of letters, books and poetry, they could email for an appointment.

She had her phone out in seconds, her cold fingers fumbling over the website address. She waited long, frustrating seconds for the site to appear, then even longer for the contact page to be found. She wrote a quick message explaining her limited time in the village and requesting an early appointment, then clicked "send" and hoped for the best.

Perhaps it was her imagination, but the weather seemed to be brightening up. The rain was certainly less insistent now, and with a change of heart she headed back into town instead of going straight home.

The newsagent had a display of postcards just inside its door and she paused to look. Most of the cards showed modern and atmospheric images of the castle, but a few sepia toned photographs showed views of the village from times past. Some of them were similar to the pictures she had just been looking at in the museum and she was especially drawn to these cards. Standing next to her, a little girl was picking up a grey plastic sword and pulling it from its rubbery scabbard. She was being told that, no, she couldn't have one. Her little brother was waving a lime green fishing net in her face and chuckling. Perhaps the family was planning to go to Lulworth Cove when the rain stopped.

She was suddenly immersed in memories of her sister Adela and their parents, of days out when they were young. She remembered long, happy hours with Adela and their fishing nets, playing in the rock pools of any beach the family happened upon. At those times she had felt close to her sister and not so very different from the rest of the family.

In this nostalgic mood, with her rose tinted glasses firmly in place, she bought two postcards and decided to send them. It wasn't her family's fault, she knew. She was the prickly one, always had been.

Though the rain had slowed to a faint drizzle, it was still too wet to be writing postcards out of doors. It was a good excuse to seek the shelter of a pub. Helped along by a midday snack, she could compose something suitable to go on the cards, before she went off the idea of sending them.

The Bankes Arms was doing a healthy trade, drawing in early season visitors out of the rain, as well as the locals who sat by the bar, exchanging gossip.

Monica ordered coffee and a sandwich and sat by the window with her postcards. She began with her parents, telling them about her working holiday, trying to sound light and chatty, but not going quite so far as to wish they were here. Her sister's was more difficult, but with only a small space on the card to fill, she did her best. No doubt they'd all think she was having a funny turn when they received them.

She was just sticking on the stamps when she heard his voice.

After such a short time, she wouldn't have expected to be familiar with it, but she knew it instantly. And it was coming from the stairs end of the pub, the stairs from the bedrooms upstairs. When he came into view he was with a tall, elegant, if a little old fashioned, woman. Red haired, perhaps in her thirties, she wore a sober, dark, vintage tweed suit which was lightened only by a green silk scarf at her throat. Monica felt suddenly very plain, acutely conscious of her wet, bedraggled hair, lack of make-up and shapeless clothing. She also wished she were invisible.

So this was where he was staying, she thought, and no one said he had to be single.

Even so, it felt as if icy water were hitting her stomach. She tried not to look, but still she saw them. He and the woman were talking, laughing as they stood at the entrance to the bar. Her court-shoed heels tapped loudly as she took her leave of him and strode across the floorboards, the sound seeming to drown out all other noise in the bar. As Monica's sandwich and coffee were brought to her table, she glanced up to thank the barman and realised that Archie had not moved, that he was still standing there.

'May I join you?' He looked hesitant, as if asking a big favour. She just felt confused.

'Of course...are you having lunch?'

'Might just have a pint, actually.' He went to the bar, allowing her time to collect her thoughts and recover from her unexpected reaction.

'I just wondered how you got on with your search through the church registers,' he said, returning with his beer and taking a long swig.

'Didn't get anywhere, I'm afraid, but I've asked the village museum for an appointment to look at their collection. Apparently they have local books, letters and poems....'

In the end she told him everything; all about Victoria and her claim to have found proof of the marriage which made her a direct descendant of the poet. Then she described in a very few words her own lack of progress.

He listened attentively and thoughtfully as he sipped his beer.

'I don't want to push in,' he ventured at last, 'but if you'd like any help with your search while you're down here, I'd be happy to oblige. I like a bit of detective work and sometimes two heads are better than one.'

'That would be good,' she responded to her own surprise. 'I really could do with some help, but wouldn't your, err...'

He looked totally blank and she felt herself blushing like a teenager.

'Your, err...wife? Girlfriend?' This was getting ridiculous. 'Wouldn't she mind if you helped me?'

'Doubt it. I had one once, but she's back in Leamington. We don't talk a lot now.' He was smiling as he said this, obviously not too distressed by his past domestic problems. He finished his beer in one long swallow.

'I thought the lady....' she pointed lamely towards the entrance to the stairs where she'd seen them together.

'Oh, that lady! I don't know who she is. We just started chatting as we came downstairs. Suppose she's staying here too.'

Monica smiled, swallowing the pathetic relief she felt.

'How long are you staying here?' she asked, as casually as she could manage.

'Just a few more days. I've spent longer than I meant to in Dorset already, because it's such a beautiful county. I'm in the middle of a long motoring holiday and the plan is to go to Devon next, then Cornwall, Wales, and finally back home to Leamington Spa. I've just sold my share in the business, you see, and I wanted to take some time out before making any decisions about the future. So,' he concluded, 'If you need my help I'm all yours.'

She thanked him with a smile, getting out her phone to check for any reply from the Corfe Castle Town Trust Museum. She was quite surprised to see one already.

'Tomorrow morning!' she enthused, 'Do you want to go with me? They suggest ten o'clock.'

'Tuesday. Yes, I'll be there. And in the meantime, I'll have a think about other ways we might find information.'

'And I'll get back to the cottage and try phoning some of the numbers I picked up from the parish notice boards yesterday. If we can manage to see some more church registers, that might help.'

He gave her a big, toothy smile, one that made her feel she was part of a small but enthusiastic team. The way ahead was no more certain, but it was beginning to feel more structured, and with Archie's help she had a lot more chance of success.

She was half way down West Street before she remembered the two postcards in her pocket. She had to retrace her steps to the square, but she was still smiling when eventually she found the post box and dropped them in.

THIRTY ONE

Diary of Joshua Ambrose, Thursday 29th August 1799

Miss Susanna Harrington. My girl has a name. She also has a voice and as charming a voice as I ever heard. She is well informed too. Whatever my father might think of people of a lower social standing, her family has made sure that her education does not shame her.

The visit was perhaps not the easiest for either Mrs Blackstock or my aunt, the first being too frail to be able to receive visitors with any alacrity and my aunt clearly distressed by the plight of this respectable, good woman.

Miss Harrington knows that soon she must return to the family farm near Dorchester, as she is needed there. There is, however, no improvement in Mrs Blackstock's health and it is clear that she will be unable to manage alone. She faces, therefore, the loss of her village home. She will have no choice but to go to live with her sister and the other Harringtons on the farm.

Miss Harrington assures her that she will be well cared for in her new home, that all her needs will be met, but it is clear that the loss of her cottage is a distressing prospect for the lady.

Tea was charmingly served by Miss Harrington, who met my eye with a smile and a blush. That one look made the visit perfect for me. We stayed no longer than twenty minutes, Miss Harrington curtseying prettily in the doorway as we left. My aunt said little as we walked home, but what she did say conveyed more concern about

Mrs Blackstock's plight than my attraction to an unsuitable young lady.

Her long silences must also have had much to do with the effort of walking. Though the distance was short, it was obviously too much for my aunt, who I think must begin to make more use of her carriage. She leaned heavily on my arm and needed to pause several times. I confess to being concerned about her.

Yet, Miss Susanna Harrington and I have now been introduced. We need never more pass without speaking when we meet while taking the air. I shall make sure that from now on I take the air as much as possible.

Corfe Castle Common beckons with greater promise than ever.

THIRTY TWO; Early April 2018. Day Six of Holiday

The Perils of Flood and Fire

It had been raining all night and still showed no sign of letting up. With its solid stone walls and small windows, the cottage was dark and gloomy and the view of the garden through the rain smeared kitchen windows was forlorn. A crestfallen looking blackbird was perched in one of the wet apple trees, its small body hunched under the shelter of young leaves.

Monica searched through her bags for her folding umbrella and tried to summon some optimism for the day ahead. Her efforts the previous afternoon had been far from inspiring. Working her way through the short list of telephone numbers from Sunday's drive around the local parishes, she had hoped for some progress, but the results had been disappointing.

Of the eight numbers she had written down, three had been copied from such faded and damaged notices that she'd obviously jotted them down wrongly, because they were unobtainable. Another rang out unanswered, without switching to voice mail, but two others had at least given her the option of leaving a message. In both cases she'd done so without much hope. The final two had been answered.

One of them had been picked up by an elderly and very talkative church warden, who happened to know from another recent enquiry, (no prizes for guessing from whom), that the registers from the end of the eighteenth century were missing. They had, he'd informed her, been lost long ago. He'd then begun a long lament about the perils of flood and fire to old documents, and how modern digital records would last for even less time. Something needed to be done about it, he'd gone on to explain, before it was too late. Monica had listened as patiently as she could, agreed, thanked him, and had finally rung off.

The final number on the list had been answered by the sister of the vicar of a small parish. She'd informed Monica that the vicar and his wife were away until next week. On their return, she was sure that Monica would be welcome to look at the registers. Great. She'd be back in Wisbech by then.

Maybe something would eventually come from these enquiries, but she had the feeling she was still nowhere near to finding the information she needed.

At a quarter to ten, just as she was leaving the house and locking the front door behind her, her mobile rang. She lowered the open red umbrella on to the wet path at the top of the front steps while she fumbled with the flap of her pocket. Finding her phone at last, she answered it eagerly, hoping it was a reply to one of the messages she'd left yesterday.

But it was Bernadette, ringing from the Poet's House.

'Monica, I'm sorry to disturb you on holiday, but I thought you should know while you're down there....'

'You're in early! Are we so busy?'

'We are. Justin asked me to come in earlier every day this week, catch up a bit, you know. Reason I'm phoning, that woman....Victoria Sharpston, has just called in, ringing the bell like she owns the place and has the right to come in before we open....'

'This doesn't sound like good news.'

'It isn't. She informs us that she's decided to seek legal advice.'

'What?'

'Apparently, because she's proven that she's a direct descendant of Joshua Ambrose, she reckons the house should have passed to her, not to the Blunt family, who set up the museum trust. She says the property was passed down the wrong line because no one at the time knew that Joshua had married and had a son.'

Monica hardly knew what to say and the silence ran on.

'Thanks for letting me know, Bernadette,' she managed to say eventually, 'and don't worry. I'll find out what I can and will be back for Friday's meeting with the trustees. Would you let Justin know what you've told me, please? I'll talk to him at the meeting.'

As she replaced the phone in her pocket, she noticed that the umbrella was missing. Heaving a great sigh, she ran down the steps and caught sight of it making its way along the road. She followed its big, red shape, watching it scud and wheel from puddle to puddle, feeling too stunned by Bernadette's news to care about how silly she looked, chasing an umbrella down the road.

The situation at home sounded bleak and she had an impulse to cry. She curbed it of course. Monica didn't do things like that.

THIRTY THREE

Diary of Joshua Ambrose, Friday 30th August 1799

Whether it was by her design as well as by mine, I cannot know, but somehow we contrived to meet this morning on the same path as before, close by the top of the ridge on the common.

This time, however, we stopped to talk. I asked after her aunt, she after mine. At first our conversation was halting and awkward. We looked at our shoes a lot. Long, awkward silences were broken by both of us rushing in at the same time, so that neither of us could be heard. But after that our words slowed and became harmonious and we talked easily.

She could not stop for long. Having had a lift to the market in Corfe on a farmer's cart, she was on her way to Kingston to run a few errands for Mrs Blackstock. She had to hurry back to attend to her aunt's needs.

And so she went on her way, but not before I had promised to call on her and Mrs Blackstock again tomorrow.

THIRTY FOUR; Early April 2018. Day Six of Holiday

A Song for Summer Time

'So, what are we looking for?'

Archie had already reached for one of the books from the piles of maps, letters and other documents that filled the centre of the table. The museum curator had been very helpful, leaving everything ready for them and saying he'd be back later.

'Anything that mentions the name Ambrose or any reference to his poetry. Or anyone called Susanna. We don't even know her surname. Yes, I know it's vague, but....'

She'd told him about Bernadette's phone call as soon as they'd met by the museum door. He'd been waiting there in his usual jeans and dark coloured walking clothes when she'd arrived with her red umbrella and wet hair.

'In that case,' he'd replied, referring to Victoria's latest threat, 'we'd better get working. Until you find what she found, you won't be able to fight it.'

The first hour in the airy room at the back of the town hall was mostly passed in silence. They glanced through many books from local collections, mostly on the area's geography or history. The books would have been extremely interesting to anyone carrying out Dorset based research, but were of no real help to them. There was a very early collection of Thomas Hardy novels as well as dozens of letters, most of them dating from no earlier that the first World War.

'Someone here liked your poet, at least,' commented Archie after a while. He held up a small, leather bound volume. 'This is an edition of his "Common Poems". I don't suppose it's all that significant that it's here?'

'Not really,' she considered, 'there's no reason why his books wouldn't have been spread throughout the country, even in his own lifetime. He had "Common Poems" published in 1801, not long before his death. Is that a first edition?'

He turned the front pages carefully.

'Looks like it. No reprint dates or anything.'

Monica returned to the letter she was reading. It had been written by someone in the village to a relative in Dorchester in the early 1800s. The writing was tiny and looped, very hard to make out in several places. It mentioned people in the village, local gossip, and she was scanning it for any clues. Archie went back to his book.

'Not exactly Wordsworth, was he? I mean, these poems are pretty and all that, but a bit fluffy. Did he get any better?'

She bristled. It felt like a personal affront.

'Maybe his talents weren't quite equal to Wordsworth's, but he's loved for his work. People can still identify with the feeling in his poetry, even if he isn't counted among the greatest poets of all time. And, he's especially loved in the Fens. Like Thomas Clarkson, the anti-slavery campaigner, and Octavia Hill, the co-founder of the

National Trust, he was born in Wisbech. He is one of ours. One of our boys!'

'Just winding you up,' he grinned, 'Thought you'd say that. This poem here, "A Song for Summer Time," reads to me like he was running out of time. It's obviously a love thing, as if he feared there'd be nowhere for him and a girl to meet once the summer ended. Sounds illicit.'

'True....Victoria made a lot of that too. That and several other poems hint at secret meetings and running out of time. That was what led her to assume that Joshua had married someone from around here.' Monica had forgotten the letter, hadn't even realised that it had dropped from her hand.

'Well, she may have a point,' Archie said, 'There's no way this was about fond memories of a girl back home. This is a real relationship, something going on at the time he was writing. And it was happening here; you only have to look at the scenery. I mean, listen to this;

"And yet I sing
My song for summer time
And still we laugh and
Love and seek the sun.
Our sheltering hills
Must yet repel
Autumn's whining call.

They must stay deaf
To its lament, and we...."

The "sheltering hills" are a bit of a give away, both about secrecy and location. No hills in your Fens! However, there's nothing to suggest he married the girl. Maybe they just had a fling.'

'Except for the engraving of the ring on the skirting board in his bedroom,' pointed out Monica, 'but Victoria doesn't know about that. So, somehow she's found something else to prove that a marriage took place. She's so convinced that her ancestor was the *legitimate* son of Joshua that she's seeking legal advice.'

'Someone has written in the front of this book,' went on Archie, holding the pages close to his face, 'I don't suppose it'll help us much, but this says, "PD Williams, Ponders Mullen".'

'Joshua's mother's sister married a Williams. Joshua's aunt became Mrs Williams. Not exactly an uncommon name, though, so it's most likely nothing. Ponders Mullen is only up the road from here. I was there on Sunday, actually. It was one of the many tiny hamlets I drove to. I think it was one which shared a vicar with several other parishes. It was on my phone list and....' she groped around in her handbag to locate her notepad, 'yes, it was the number which just rang out and I couldn't leave a message.'

'I think we should go there. We need to check every lead. Have you gone through everything you need here?'

'Afraid so. Let's go and have another look at Ponders Mullen. It's not much to go on, though....'

'But it's better that nothing at all. I'll get my car from the pub while you find the curator and give him your thanks. I'll meet you in the square in five minutes.'

Archie's black Nissan X-Trail made much easier work of the narrow lanes of the Isle of Purbeck than Monica's little Renault had done. The sun came out as they drove along, cheering up the rain-washed countryside. The car's high seating position meant that they could see what was coming towards them around bends and, as luck would have it, Archie only had to squeeze the Nissan against the hedge once, while a tractor rumbled past.

The village of Ponders Mullen was as well kept as it was small. There were a few charming, beautifully maintained old cottages spaced out along the lane which led to two larger houses opposite the church. One of them looked Victorian and had probably once been the vicarage. Like all the other houses in the village, it was immaculate, its front garden a well ordered palette of spring colour set around a freshly mown lawn. The house next door was the larger of the two and was set back from the lane behind a tall yew hedge and a neat white gate. The limited view over the gate showed the house's classical Georgian frontage and a handsome iron portico around the front door.

Across the narrow lane from the two houses, the church slumbered peacefully in the April sunshine. It looked twelfth, maybe thirteenth century, and was obviously still well looked after. The grass around the ancient, leaning grave stones had recently been cut, leaving only the odd rebellious spiky clump in awkward angles between broken masonry. Monica, with Archie's help this time, explored the churchyard for a second time, examining any inscription that remained legible.

'May I help you?'

The voice rang out imperiously, more like a reprimand than an offer of assistance. An elderly, well groomed woman stood by the lych gate to the churchyard, a schnauzer puppy on a lead at her side. She was obviously expecting them to explain themselves. They straightened up from the stone they had been looking at and ambled over to her. The little dog had no reservations about the strangers and jumped up to be petted as soon as Archie and Monica drew near.

'Now, now Jessie. We know we don't do that, don't we?' Jessie took no notice and Archie bent down to stroke his newly trimmed, soft grey head.

'Perhaps,' said Monica, deciding to take the lady's offer literally, 'perhaps you could. I work for a museum in East Anglia and I'm researching a family who I believe lived here a long time ago. Two hundred years ago, actually, but I just wondered whether anyone remembers their descendants? Their name was Williams.'

'The Williams family? Well, of course. Everyone remembers them, even though they sold up and cleared off in the 1950s.' The woman seemed somewhat mollified by the mention of the museum. It suggested respectability and the likelihood that these strangers might be worthy of her time. 'They owned most of the land around here, most of the houses too at one point. The original lords of the manor. In the end it was the usual thing. Problems with farming, falling profits and no sons to keep things going. They sold up and went. Not sure where to, I'm afraid.'

'That's interesting, thank you,' said Monica chewing her lip, 'So I'm guessing from what you've just said that this house here,' she indicated the older of the two large residences across the road, 'would once have been their home?'

'You are quite right. It was home to the Williams family from the mid 1700s. Owned by Londoners now,' she added, shaking her head sadly and tossing her neatly permed curls, 'but we must accept change. If you need to know more, the vicar will be here for the morning service at eleven o'clock on Sunday. Perhaps he can help. And now, Jessie and I must go home for our luncheon. Come along, Jessie!'

'You don't happen to know,' Monica called after her retreating back, 'how I can get in touch with the vicar in the meantime, do you? Only I....'

'Telephone number's on the notice board,' Jessie's owner called behind her, 'Good bye!'

They watched the elderly lady and her excitable companion make their way to the front door of the Victorian house, the one which looked like the old vicarage.

'The number which rings out and no one answers,' mumbled Monica as Jessie and her owner entered the house. 'I shall just have to keep trying, because this parish register could be interesting. The PD Williams who owned Joshua's collection of poems may or may not have been his aunt, but he had to be staying *somewhere.* This village couldn't have been more than a short ride on horseback from Corfe Common and was probably larger in those days. And I know my imagination has no place in our investigation, but the Georgian house over there, the old manor owned by the Williams family, looks just the sort of place Joshua would have stayed in.'

'You're right, imagination is of no use to us, but as you say, we really should look at the records. If Joshua did stay here, even if he married in a different parish, there should be a record of the banns being called here.'

Monica nodded thoughtfully and made her way along the path to the untidy church notice board. It was completely out of keeping with the small, neat village, as if its upkeep were someone else's job, someone who rarely bothered with it. The woodwork was peeling and the pane of glass covering the notices was cracked. Water had seeped in and blurred most of the dog-eared pieces of paper pinned inside, but at least the vicar's phone number was still legible. Once more, Monica entered the number on the keypad of her phone and put it to her ear, listening as it rang out, on and on, without reply.

'Never mind,' said Archie, 'Let's go and have "luncheon".'

THIRTY FIVE

Diary of Joshua Ambrose, Saturday 31st August 1799

I arrived far too early this morning at Mrs Blackstock's cottage. The short walk down the lane from my aunt's house had taken but a quarter of the time I had allowed and, armed with a basket of cakes and bread, I was obliged to kick my heels in the dust for a bit. When at last the old church clock chimed ten o'clock I went to knock at the cottage door.

Susanna herself opened it, with a smile that was far too knowing. I suspect she'd seen me hanging about from an upstairs window. She must know how hopelessly infatuated I am.

Poor Mrs Blackstock looks ill indeed. She was sitting in her high backed chair by the hearth, where Susanna had lit the first fire of the season. Already, the morning air has a hint of autumn about it and Mrs Blackstock feels the cold keenly. It is indeed a worry that her niece must soon return to the family farm. If Mrs Blackstock's health does not improve, she will be obliged to leave with her.

We spoke about this situation for a few minutes, all of us shaking our heads without coming up with anything to remedy the situation. Apart from sympathy for their circumstances, I have to admit to feeling sorry for myself. Susanna's departure looms ever closer and we all made the effort to move on from this unpleasant subject.

'Do you walk often on the common, Mr Ambrose?' asked Susanna very charmingly.

'Almost every day,' I said, 'Of course, there is great pleasure to be had in the society of Ponders Mullen, but I am also at liberty to ride and walk. And you, Miss Harrington, do you find the time to walk there much?'

'My aunt needs me to run errands in Corfe and Kingston most days and Mr Elliott is very obliging, letting me ride in the farm cart. When my errands are done, if it is not too long after one o'clock, I like to take the air on the common'.

'Susanna benefits a great deal from the exercise,' nodded Mrs Blackstock, 'looking after a troublesome old invalid can be no pleasure at all.'

'Caring for you is no trouble, aunt. You know how I delay going home!'

Mrs Blackstock only smiled at this, her look directed more at the fire than at either of us.

'Perhaps we may chance to meet when next on the common,' I rushed in while Mrs Blackstock was still observing the fire, 'I find noon an agreeable hour for exercise....'

'Indeed it is, Mr Ambrose,' cut in Mrs Blackstock, turning her smile on me, 'and at this time of year the midday sun is less scorching than in June.'

I knew that Susanna's aunt was laughing at us, but I'm sure neither of us minded too much. The entertainment of watching two awkward lovers pretending not to make plans, was probably doing her good.

My half hour visit soon came to an end and reluctantly I pulled myself from my chair. I had not expected half so much from this visit and can hardly believe my good fortune. Susanna is clearly as keen to meet as I.

And now I am home again, ready to dine with my own dear aunt, who asks so kindly after Mrs Blackstock and her niece. I suspect she will be glad when Miss Harrington and I have gone our separate ways and life in Ponders Mullen reverts to more suitable normality, but she is good enough not to tell me so.

THIRTY SIX; Early April 2018. Day Seven of Holiday

Fishermen's Socks

They had not wasted their time the day before; it just felt like they had.

Rain rattled hard on the windscreen as they drove to Dorchester in Archie's Nissan on Wednesday morning. It had been his idea to widen their search to the Dorchester area, because after Tuesday's trip to Ponders Mullen and another useless trail around churchyards and small, rural museums, they really were getting nowhere.

Today was Monica's last full day in Dorset. She had to leave on Thursday morning, the cottage being let to someone else, and she had to be back at work on Friday. Yet another meeting with the trustees awaited her and, unless things changed significantly, she'd have nothing useful to report to them.

And the vicar of Ponders Mullen was still not answering his phone.

The Dorset County Museum in Dorchester, according to Archie, housed collections from all over the county. Though it was true that their searches through local collections had yielded little, he'd insisted that the museum in Dorchester might be more helpful.

They parked close to the museum and made their way along the street under separate umbrellas that kept bumping into each other. They soon arrived at the museum, a splendid, galleried place, a showpiece of

Victorian architectural detail which housed a variety of collections.

This being a rainy Wednesday in April, they practically had the place to themselves and, despite the pressure of time and lack of progress, Monica could not resist having a quick look round.

There was an interesting section on the Durotriges, a Celtic tribe which had settled in Dorset during the Iron Age. Monica had already discovered that some of their land had covered the area of Corfe Common, and from the museum's display she read about the great tribal hill fort at Maiden Castle. There was an account of the tribe's battles against the Roman invaders and even the skeleton of a Durotriges tribesman, an arrow head still implanted between his ribs. She was just becoming engrossed when Archie dragged her off.

The section dedicated to local writers and artists was beautifully set out. Thomas Hardy, of course, was well represented, as was the poet William Barnes. Even famous writers who had visited the county and written about parts of it, such as Jane Austen, had their own, dedicated space. There was nothing on Joshua Ambrose, but that was hardly surprising. He was a Fenman who had merely written a few of his poems in Dorset and his fame could hardly be said to match Miss Austen's.

Even so, they looked carefully at each display, their eyes scanning letters and documents through the cabinet glass, just in case there was some small mention, some tiny clue.

There were paintings in plenty; water colours by local talented artists from the past, as well as oils and sketches in pencil and charcoal. The scenes these pictures represented were of the most interest and Archie and Monica stopped to look.

There were many inspiring views of the ruined Corfe Castle through the ages, captured by generations of artists. In varying stages of dilapidation and thickness of ivy covering, the old stones had been sketched from all angles. There were also numerous paintings of Corfe's village streets in less picturesque times, when sagging roofs had meant leaks more often than quaintness.

Next to these, in a glass topped cabinet, was a series of other water colours, clearly all by the same artist. Their grey and peachy hues depicted scenes which neither Monica nor Archie recognised. None of the paintings had been framed, or even put on to backing paper, simply placed on folds of creamy coloured fabric. The colours were almost as fresh as when the artist had finished his work. And although the scenes were unfamiliar, the signature....

'Edmund Ambrose. I do not believe it.' It was Archie who first made the discovery.

They stared at the faintly penned signature at the bottom right hand corner of one of the paintings, then saw the name repeated on the large label at the back of the case. They were both smiling, as if they'd struck gold. At last this felt like progress.

'They all seem to be of the same village,' observed Archie, 'the same bridge here and again here, and then there's this house that crops up twice, and it's obviously the same church.'

'But was this the village Edmund lived in, or just somewhere he liked to paint?' Monica queried, 'And of course, we don't even know whether he's *our* Edmund Ambrose....'

'True. Perhaps there's something written on the back of them which might help,' suggested Archie.

'That's a thought. I wonder if we could....excuse me!' Monica had seen a museum guide pass by the door to the room, hands behind her back and walking slowly.

The guide retraced her steps and entered the room, her soft soled shoes hardly making a sound on the wooden floor. She was smiling, perhaps pleased to be asked something on such a quiet day.

'Do you happen to know whether there's anything written on the back of any of these paintings?' asked Monica. The guide frowned, removing her glasses and putting them back on.

'Have to say I've never been asked that one before. I would have to open up the cabinet and have a look and I don't know....'

Monica hurriedly explained her situation, that she was the curator of a museum in Cambridgeshire and was researching the Ambrose family. The lady nodded, muttered something and wandered soundlessly away, returning after a couple of minutes with a huge bunch of keys on an oversized ring. She searched through them for several long seconds, eventually locating a tiny cabinet key and placing it in the lock.

The heavy bunch of keys left hanging from the delicate brass keyhole was further weighed down by an enormous celluloid disc which practically shouted, "Visit Dorset!" in big red letters. The disc offered no picture, nor any other incentive for anyone to obey its command, just those two big red words. As a marketing tool, Monica thought irrelevantly as she waited for the cabinet to be opened, it was pretty useless.

The guide looked grim as the key turned in the lock, perhaps unsure of whether she should be doing this. She and Archie perhaps looked a bit dodgy, considered Monica. Carefully, one by one, the guide turned the paintings over, replacing each one meticulously before moving on to the next. There was nothing written on any of them. But for a few paint smears, they were all completely blank. Monica sighed.

'What were you hoping to find, dear?' Now that the cabinet was locked again and the "Visit Dorset" disc with all its keys was safely back in her hand, the guide had visibly relaxed.

'I'm not sure really....any clue as to whether the artist was the son of Joshua Ambrose, the poet I'm researching, or....'

'Oh dear, I'm sorry but I haven't the faintest idea about that.'

'....or even the name of this village in the paintings....'

'Oh, I can tell you that, dear. It's Lower Beckton. Close to where I live, actually. Not far out of Dorchester, on the Cerne Abbas road. The village is quite changed now, of course, with housing estates added around the outside, but the village centre is unspoiled. It's only a few minutes away from here, if you feel like going to have a look.'

They thanked her profusely, shaking her hand as if she'd just awarded them a lottery prize. They left the museum feeling hugely encouraged by this small, perhaps meaningless clue and set off for Lower Beckton.

The villagers couldn't have been too delighted by the recent addition of two new housing estates, one at each end of the once tranquil settlement, but the increase in population had led to improvement in the roads leading to it, as well as better signage. It was easy to find, therefore, and surprisingly convenient to park close to the old village centre.

The parish church looked miserable in the rain. Its aged stones, coloured green on the northern side, kept watch over the leaning gravestones crowded into the small yard. Its ancient oak doors were locked. Even the porch was kept out of bounds by the heavy metal gates which denied visitors shelter from the elements. Looking at how much rubbish had blown under the gates and collected in the porch, Monica wondered how long it was since the church had last been opened. The place felt sad, badly in need of care from its villagers. It needed to be brought back to life with village fetes and jam and Jerusalem and money-raising enterprises to mend its no doubt leaking roof and the gaping holes in its stained glass.

Wading through the untended grass under umbrellas, Archie and Monica began the slow and fairly hopeless task of reading headstones. They had looked at so many in the last few days that they knew now what to expect; if the engravings were legible, the stones were too new to be of interest. If they were the right age, the engravings had worn away. And yet, still they searched, their jeans getting steadily wetter as they progressed through each area of graves with its waist high weeds and banks of nettles.

'This is getting us nowhere,' moaned Monica loudly, as her umbrella was caught up yet again by an overhanging yew branch.

'I agree,' replied Archie casually, 'so we'll just forget we saw this one and go and find some fish and chips, shall we?'

'Which one?'

'This one, belonging to an Edmund Elijah Ambrose and his beloved wife Louisa.'

Monica was there in an instant, high-stepping over brambles to reach the small grave against the low wall. The engraving had become almost illegible on the crumbling headstone. One corner had broken off so long ago that the break itself had become smoothed and softened by the weather, cutting in half a cherub in mid flight. Archie was squinting at what was left of the script, reading slowly and hesitantly aloud.

'In loving memory of Edmund Elijah Ambrose who departed this life on 21st May 1843. Also of his beloved wife Louisa who died 5th November 1841.'

Neither of them spoke for some time. Monica was vaguely aware of rain dripping on to her umbrella from one of the yew trees as she looked down at the wet stone in the neglected graveyard.

Edmund Elijah Ambrose's final resting place. Was this, then what Victoria had found?

'But is this *our* Edmund? And was he really Joshua's son? We still can't be sure,' she remarked quietly, as if afraid of offending the deceased. She took out her phone and took several photos of the stone and its inscription, trying to get as clear an image as possible of the faint lettering.

'Perhaps the church registers could tell us,' said Archie. 'Victoria must have found evidence to link these people together. So far all *we* have is a number of people sharing the same surname.'

Monica went in search of a notice board, finally concluding that the only notices were the ones attached to the inside of the porch. Because of the railings, it was impossible to get close enough to read the faded pieces of paper that hung limply from the small board. She gave up with a shrug. She was getting used to setbacks.

'I'll Google the church later,' she said, 'Presumably, we can find a contact number that way. Let's go and see whether the pub over there has a good fire, so we can dry off.'

The landlord of the Swan opposite the church had indeed lit a fire in the wide, stone grate. They hogged it. They pulled up their chairs to dry themselves, the legs of their jeans steaming pleasantly while the locals gathered by the chilly bar threw them filthy looks.

The pub didn't offer Archie's favourite lunch of fish and chips, but promised the best fisherman's pie in Dorset. When it arrived, and they were obliged to move to a table by the window to eat it, the pie didn't look like the best of anything. It was an unappetising grey colour inside, consisting of something which looked like fishermen's socks. Perhaps, they thought, this was the usual punishment for strangers who hogged the fire. But they were hungry, so they finished it, socks and all.

Monica looked through the window as she ate, watching as the rain dripped mournfully from the church roof opposite. In this weather it was difficult to recognise the village of Lower Beckton from Edmund's paintings, but Archie reckoned that a house on the corner, minus its modern extension, had been in one of the pictures. And coming to think of it, this pub had been featured too, though it had probably served better food in those days.

She could not escape the thought that tomorrow morning she had to leave this beautiful county. She had to depart from her perfect cottage before she'd had chance to spend much time in it. Even worse, she had very little in the way of results to show for her week. At least, though, she had found Edmund's grave, if he was the right Edmund. The dates fitted. Everything fitted. It just needed the proof to stick it all together, and then she'd know for sure that Victoria was right and that her museum was truly at risk.

'Let me cook you dinner tonight,' she said on impulse, 'partly to say thanks for all your help and for running me around in your car, and also because I'd like to spend my last evening in the cottage. Would you come over?'

He smiled.

'Only if there are fish and chips.'

THIRTY SEVEN

Diary of Joshua Ambrose, Saturday 21st September 1799

We walk
And nineteen thousand stars awake
To dance upon thy brow.

These past days have been a haze of happiness. Within the shelter of these hills, these vales, these small woods and copses, we have spent such contented hours. I try to hold an image of these days in my heart and to preserve them in poetry, for I know they cannot be ours for long.

Already the mornings are colder and damper. The wind is keener. Our summer is fading all around us.

My aunt continues to visit Mrs Blackstock whose problems greatly trouble her. Sometimes, in trying to maintain our flimsy pretence of correctness, I accompany my aunt on these visits. Susanna sits demurely at Mrs Blackstock's side. She fetches refreshments for us all and at times she raises her bright eyes to meet mine while the two ladies discuss domestic affairs.

Can my aunt truly be ignorant of whom I meet during my long days on the common? Does she not suspect, when I arrive home so late, how I have spent my time? Whatever she thinks, she remains silent on this subject. After all, she has warned me once and I am old enough to know what I am about.

And besides, there is more than the early dusk of a changing season to threaten us. My father has written to request my return. He hopes that the warmer air here has been of benefit to my health, but informs me that the town air of Wisbech is in need of me. Perhaps he is trying to be humorous.

Susanna knows too that the time draws near when she must return to Lower Beckton and her duties on the farm.

Yet still we hold on, prolonging these sweet, precious days, denying the change of season which is evident all around us. And my heart will be forever hers. Whatever happens, I know nothing will ever change that.

THIRTY EIGHT; Early April 2018. Day Seven of Holiday

Twist of Tinned Custard

Monica had thought about doing something fancy with smoked salmon, making it look pretty, a picture on a plate. But he wanted fish and chips. He was obviously a bit of a gourmet, this Archibald Newcombe-Walker.

So in the end, she bought frozen cod in batter and a packet of frozen chips from the village stores. She even added a dollop of frozen mushy peas to give it a touch of class. Determined to make at least a small effort, she made a rhubarb crumble for dessert. It was a bit of a gamble, she knew. He probably didn't like rhubarb.

He arrived exactly on time, clutching a bottle of prosecco and pausing to admire the home she had been renting for the week. He examined the great old fireplace and the heavy, darkened oak beams and seemed as charmed by the place as she was.

He hadn't been kidding about fish and chips and it was clear that she couldn't have produced anything better for him. He seemed to like the crumble, too, especially with the added twist of tinned custard. They chatted and laughed as they ate and toasted with prosecco their small success. Seated at the table by the front window, they watched as people and dogs returned from late strolls on the common, walking past in the gathering dusk.

'I am really going to miss this place,' she said.

He nodded and commiserated. They did not touch, not in the slightest way. They certainly never hugged, not even as newly found friends parting too soon. She was afraid to do that, afraid of what it might start.

They had never discussed anything personal. She knew that he had an ex-girlfriend or an ex-wife (he'd never made it clear which) in Leamington Spa, but that was all. And the last thing she needed to clutter her thinking with was a doomed romance. Besides, there was nothing to indicate that he was even attracted to her. He had been her fellow investigator for a few days, nothing more.

She told him that she'd looked up the Parish Church of St Mark in Lower Beckton on the internet. There'd been no phone number given for the vicar who looked after that and two other parishes, but there'd been an email address. She had written to the vicar immediately and, although time had run out now for looking at any available old records, she hoped she'd be able to speak to him once she was back home. And of course, she could always come back if necessary.

'And Ponders Mullen?' he asked, 'Any answer from there yet?'

'Nothing. The phone still rings out, unanswered. Vicar's perhaps on holiday.'

'But if you find proof of Joshua's marriage in Lower Beckton, you won't need to know whether the Williamses of Ponders Mullen were part of his family.'

'True. It'd be nice to know, though. It would be good for the museum to know where he stayed in his Dorset days. I'll go on trying when I get home.'

Archie left just after eleven, just after he'd discovered her unopened bottles of local beer in the kitchen.

'You like Silent Slasher?' he asked with a grin.

'I never got round to trying it,' admitted Monica. 'Take them as a souvenir of the Isle of Purbeck.'

'Thank you,' he muttered, looking hesitant as he stood in the doorway, but her rigid body language gave him no encouragement. He'd call and see her off in the morning, he promised. He would then check out of the Bankes Arms and travel on to Devon.

Monica's heart was heavy as she watched him leave, his coat pockets bulging with bottles of Silent Slasher. She wasn't sure whether the heaviness of her heart was because of her inadequate sleuthing, having to leave this perfect cottage and village, or the thought of never seeing Archie again.

Maybe it was all three.

THIRTY NINE

Diary of Joshua Ambrose, Sunday 29th September 1799

A Song for Summer Time

With clammy hands
Autumn comes to call,
Breathes misty fog
On all our hopes,
Blows once loved leaves
From bowing trees,
And licks with damp,
Chastising tongue.

And yet I sing
My song for summer time
And still we laugh and
Love and seek the sun.
Our sheltering hills
Must yet repel
Autumn's whining call.

They must stay deaf
To its lament, and we
Shall drown it with our voice.
So I shall sing
My song for summer time
And go on loving
Beneath the sun.

We always knew this moment would come, and come it has. Having said our last goodbyes, we wait in separate doorways of separate houses, preparing for separate departures.

My travelling trunk sits ready in the hallway of this house opposite the church in Ponders Mullen. My home for the last few happy weeks.

We held on for as long as we could, to our precious, short time together. I know I shall always keep this in a hidden corner of my heart, whatever life brings, and I believe the same will be true for Susanna.

She too will soon be travelling home, but at least on that subject there is good news. My excellent aunt has arranged, at her own expense, for Mrs Blackstock to receive nursing care and help in her home. My aunt's cook, Mrs Mollifer, has a sister who is in need of work and who seems a good and kindly soul. Mrs Blackstock is overflowing with gratitude for this generosity, for it allows Susanna to leave her aunt, knowing that she will be well cared for.

So, we are all content. We must be. Susanna is to see her family in Lower Beckton once more and her aunt can remain in her much loved home in Ponders Mullen.

But as the autumnal damp creeps in ever more, my cough worsens. It had almost gone, during those warm, carefree days, but with the first hint of damp it is back. Like the shadow cast by my father's letters, beckoning me home to my long-neglected duties, this sickness stalks me.

Early tomorrow morning, I must begin my journey northwards. I shall not hurry. I shall avail myself of as many overnight stops as the mood takes me and prepare my thoughts for home.

FORTY; Mid April 2018

Distinctly Troubled

Two large, round, yellow eyes blinked slowly at Monica from the office doorway. She watched as the grey Smutty sidled into the room before pausing to lift one paw gracefully to his mouth, grooming it with his long, pink tongue. He had just crunched his way through half a saucer of biscuits, scattering the rest over the floor to be walked into the carpet later.

Mrs Paynter from next door had gone away for a few days and had left the three Smutties in the care of the museum. In reality, things were not very different from normal. The cats continued to spend most of their time there, sleeping in their own baskets in the box room upstairs, or on Joshua's bed, if no one noticed. The only discernible change was the increased expenditure on Go-Cat and Felix.

The steady hum of voices from reception told Monica that business was good. Usually, so soon after Easter, even on a Saturday, visitor numbers were fairly low, but the opening of Joshua's room was continuing to make a real difference. A couple of nice features in local magazines hadn't done any harm, either.

Regarding her investigation, however, there had been very little progress since her return from Dorset. There was no reply yet to the email she'd sent to the vicar in charge of Lower Beckton, but at long last her phone calls to the incumbent of Ponders Mullen had been answered.

Her relief in finally connecting with the elusive vicar, however, had been short lived. He had gone away to search the old registers, but when he'd phoned back it was only to report disappointing news. There was no trace in the parish records of banns or any marriage involving Joshua and Susanna.

Monica remained in the dark, therefore, about whether the PD Williams of the old manor house in Ponders Mullen had been related to Joshua. It was disappointing, because she'd had such a positive feeling about that village and house. But if he'd ever stayed there at all, he must have moved to another parish before marrying.

She was trying to remain positive and still hoped for a reply from Lower Beckton. In the meantime, she decided to have another look at the scrapbook. She opened its wide leather cover carefully and examined the front end papers.

During one of her frequent sleepless nights, Monica had recalled Victoria's nagging to be allowed to handle the original scrapbook. She must have believed that something was hidden within its pages, but once she'd been to Dorset she had stopped asking. Presumably, this was because she'd found the evidence she needed down there instead.

In her frustration, Monica had begun to wonder whether Victoria had been right and whether it was worth another, more careful look inside the scrapbook. Had Joshua perhaps inserted a scrap of paper, even a pencilled word, between the leather cover and one of the end papers? It was the only place Monica had never looked.

She examined the end papers again, paying special attention to the edges where the blank paper had been pasted on to the cover. There was nothing at all that she could see. The glue and paper looked like they had never been disturbed and nothing had been written on the end papers themselves. For all its two hundred and forty-odd years of age, the book was in very good condition.

Still she continued to leaf through the book, no longer looking at what was written, but for any indication that something had been inserted between the pages. The corner of one page had been torn off, but that was hardly likely to....

'Monica!' Bernadette's call reached her from reception and she went through to help. The place was gratifyingly busy and she was soon immersed in selling tickets and giving out information.

'I'm nearly out of guide books,' Bernadette managed to utter before greeting two little boys and their mother who were approaching the counter. It was unusual for children to visit the Poet's House, unless it was the middle of school holidays and their families had run out of other options. Only on rare occasions did the kids seem genuinely interested in poetry. The thought occurred to Monica, as she hurried to fetch more books from the store room, that she should do more to make the museum attractive to children. She had to remember that they represented the future for places like this.

She was still thinking through various ideas as she returned to reception and filled the guide book display with fresh copies. The crowd had subsided a little now and when the door opened again it was to admit Mrs Sharpston. Monica grimaced before she could stop herself.

'Good morning, Victoria,' she managed with false cheerfulness, 'Come to have another look round?'

She didn't wait for a reply, busying herself with the gift shop displays. The bracelets and other items of jewellery were selling well, their stand looking sparse and neglected, and Monica kneeled down to pull a box out from the cupboard below. She selected a few blue and green beaded bracelets and earrings, amusing herself by arranging them on the display. Behind her, the latest arrivals moved from reception into the house and after a couple more minutes even Victoria had disappeared.

Bernadette and Monica exchanged looks.

'OK today?'

Bernadette knew what she meant.

'Yes, no comments this time. Just another look round, apparently.'

'Well, there're two room stewards up there, so it shouldn't be a problem. Coffee?'

Reception was still fairly quiet when she returned with the coffee and Bernadette was happy to chat for a minute or two. Victoria, she reported, had left after only five minutes. Her regular short visits and readiness to go on forking out entrance fees seemed pointless. She obviously didn't mind wasting money.

'She has lots,' explained Bernadette confidentially, 'Her family is loaded.'

Not exactly the best news Monica could have heard about someone who was paying for expensive legal advice against them. When more visitors arrived, she took her coffee back to her office and sat down, warming her hands on the mug, her thoughts a mixture of Victoria and the need to bring more children into the museum.

Which was probably why at first she didn't realise that the scrapbook was missing.

She had left it on her desk. She knew she had. Now there was nothing there but a few old biros and her closed laptop.

'How long ago did she leave?' she yelled to Bernadette as she ran into reception.

'Dunno....five minutes?'

Monica was out on the quayside within seconds, the cold wind snatching at her hair as she dodged the traffic to reach the riverside wall. Eyes scanning the view before her, she could just make out the woman's blonde head moving close to the bridge.

'Victoria!' she hollered, but her voice was carried away by the wind and drowned by traffic noise. She began to run, her knee joints which were used only to a swift walk these days, clicking and objecting painfully. She could see the head moving along the other side of the bridge and turning on to North Brink. Monica's knees gave her another warning twinge and she slowed to an undignified trot, but kept going. Past the Clarkson memorial and over the road to the bridge, she finally caught up with Victoria outside Lloyd's Bank.

'Look, this isn't funny,' she panted pathetically, 'Just give it back.'

But Victoria was only carrying a small handbag and wearing a short jacket; there was absolutely nowhere she could be hiding anything as large as the scrapbook.

'Give what back?' she asked in what looked like genuine puzzlement.

'Where did you hide it?' Monica insisted, 'It has to have been you.'

'I really don't know what you're talking about.' Victoria's confusion was fast turning into irritation.

'All right, but I....' Monica backed away and Victoria shook her head, as if pitying this strange woman.

It was a long, cold walk back over the bridge to the museum. The rest of the working day felt like it would never end.

That night, Monica dreamed again of the man walking on Corfe Common. He was the one she'd dreamed of before, the one who was definitely not Archie. Not with all that fair hair and those intense blue eyes. Last time, he had looked reassuring, but not anymore.

This time he looked distinctly troubled.

FORTY ONE

Diary of Joshua Ambrose, Tuesday 1st October 1799

What a miserable place this is! Charing Cross with all its noise and dirt is as vexatious to me as the persistent cough which has returned to blight my well being.

The journey so far, two long days of swaying and bumping along in the post-chaise, has been bleak enough to make even a stout man sick. Even before we left the narrow lanes of Dorsetshire, the driver and I were obliged to climb down and push the chaise out of the mire. The horses were tired by then and had to be changed, allowing us to rest a while at a rat infested inn in the middle of nowhere.

And so, wearily we came to London. I take no joy from its crowds, its yelling paper boys and vendors of everything under the sun, nor from its incessant traffic. The Golden Cross Inn is perhaps a little less blighted by vermin than other hostelries along the way, but it is still a draughty, unwholesome place. The ale has been too liberally watered down and the pastry I was served with on arrival contained a mysterious brown slop I have yet to identify.

There is a small, mean fire in my room and here I sit to write by the light of a cheap candle. It is dark outside now. My view from the small window, of the streets of Charing Cross, does nothing to cheer me. Even in the last of the daylight, this view was impaired by the thick layer of grime covering the glass, convincing me that London sits under a permanent shroud of soot and gloom.

But I am being unfair. Were I being entertained in a palace, my mood would be little better. Wherever I happened to be tonight, I would still be wretched. Leaving Susanna is the hardest thing I have ever had to do.

I know that once home I must act on my long-held understanding with Ada and set a date for our wedding. She is a good woman and will surely make me a passable wife. Perhaps in time this pain of parting from my beloved Susanna will fade, but her memory never will.

I read and re-read the lines that I composed during our sun-blessed days and they bring some comfort. Even the poetry written at the beginning, in longing and sadness, brings cheerful reminiscence now, because it ended in joy.

Nowhere can I mention her name, but my memories are hidden within safe words, in a language that only she and I will ever understand.

Tomorrow the chaise will take me from London, along the north road and eventually to Wisbech. I shall settle back into my old life and shall work conscientiously. I shall do my best for my father who despairs of me, and make Ada a good husband.

All these things are possible!

FORTY TWO; Mid April 2018

Mighty Tomes

They had looked everywhere.

They had all stayed late that afternoon, Monica, Bernadette, Angie and the volunteers on duty. They had searched every room in the house, in the gradually diminishing hope that the scrapbook would be unearthed, that it had merely been moved by someone, well meaning or not. But there had been no sign of it.

For Monica, it had meant a troubled evening followed by a sleepless night. By her own carelessness she had managed to lose the museum's most valuable asset. She knew that she should have called one of the trustees immediately. If she had, the police might even be involved by now. Yet, still she was reluctant to give up. While they continued to search and kept the problem to themselves, the book remained merely missing. As soon as she made the problem official, things would become a lot more complicated.

The next morning, she arrived at work very early. The Poet's House seemed quieter than usual, its silence almost heavy enough to mask the street sounds.

And then, although at first she thought her sleepless senses were deceiving her, the whispering began again. Growing ever louder, it seemed to fill the stair well before flowing out to the rest of the house.

She was not in the mood for this nonsense. Climbing the stairs, she began another hopeless search, knowing that really there was no point, that they'd done all of this yesterday. Just one more look around, she told herself, and then she'd have to phone Justin Loveridge, the trustee least likely to fire her on the spot.

The dining and drawing rooms on the first floor were definitely hiding nothing. She climbed the next flight of stairs and began to check the Reading Room again. The glass case which usually displayed the scrapbook taunted her with its emptiness, but she ran her eye once more over the bookshelves, over each and every title, just in case the missing book had been slipped in there by mistake or mischief. Nothing. And this room had been her main hope.

The whispering seemed to accompany her as she wandered into Joshua's room, switching on the concealed lighting. At first, the low energy bulb, always irritatingly slow to take effect, did nothing to relieve the room's deep shadows. Gradually though, the light grew in strength, filling the room with a soft glow.

And illuminating the scrapbook. The scrapbook which lay comfortably open on Joshua's pillow, as if it had just enjoyed a good night's sleep.

How on earth....

The whispering seemed for a moment to build, almost to a mocking chorus, but she ignored it. She picked up the big, old book, hugging it to herself in relief, and ran down the stairs to phone Bernadette, to tell her not to worry about coming in early.

Back in the office, she checked the book, making sure it was still all there, that it had not been tampered with. She still suspected that Victoria was involved, but they had searched after she'd left and found nothing. She would have had to break in during the night and avoid setting off the alarm, in order to move the book, and even someone as crafty as Victoria would have been hard pressed to manage that.

While the scrapbook was still on her desk, Monica resumed her inspection from the day before, looking to see whether anything had been hidden within its pages. After a few minutes' close scrutiny, she had to conclude that there was nothing to find. The scrapbook could tell them no more. She carried it back upstairs and locked it carefully in its glass cabinet, only then realising that the whispering had stopped.

It was still too early to be at work and, with the panic over, she wandered into the kitchen to make herself coffee. There was no point in going back home now, so she carried her mug into the office, to catch up with her emails.

There were a few Facebook and Twitter messages; comments on the museum's pages, all of them friendly or harmless enough. She hadn't been keen at first to expose the museum to the world of social media, but it seemed to be bringing in new visitors and that could not be bad.

Several emails could be deleted immediately, others quickly dealt with and removed. About half way down the list was one from an address she didn't recognise. She opened it cautiously, then smiled as she saw that the vicar of Lower Beckton had sent her a reply. It was just a single sentence, giving her a telephone number.

Seeing that it had just gone nine o'clock, she dialled the number. A hoarse voice answered after several rings and it seemed to take the owner of the voice a while to recall her name. Perhaps it was just too early in the morning.

'Ah, yes!' croaked the vicar, finally remembering, 'another lady from Wisbech! How is it up there on the Wash? Used to take the family up there to visit an aged uncle; nice little place. Now then, just give me an idea of what you need and I'll see what I can do. If it's similar to what the other lady wanted, I should be able to find the records quickly.'

Monica sighed inwardly, knowing that her request would be exactly the same as Victoria's. She gave him a brief outline of what she was searching for.

'Ah!' he laughed triumphantly, 'Knew you were going to say that! What was it, then? An early nineteenth century mass migration of Ambroses from Dorset to Cambridgeshire? As it happens, you and the other lady are very fortunate. Lower Beckton suffered a particularly nasty flood in the nineteen fifties, when the stream burst its banks and water came into the church. With all the other clearing up, no one noticed that the chest containing the church registers was sitting in water. As a result, many of the pages of the older records, which were at the bottom of the chest of course, were severely damaged and can no longer be read at all. Luckily, your man's marriage was right at the beginning of the 1800s. In a new book, you see. It was saved by the mighty tomes beneath it....'

The vicar's speech was broken off by a sudden gasp followed by a fit of painful coughing. He sounded as if he needed an urgent dose of anti-biotics. Monica waited patiently, feeling a bit concerned about the man's state of health. It was obvious that she hadn't called at the best time.

'Sorry about that....' he wheezed into the phone.

'Perhaps I should call back at another time?'

'No, no....look, I'm pretty sure where to find the records you need. Haven't long been put back since the other lady, you see. I'll find it all when I get back from the doctor's. I'll scan the pages if I can get the book to balance on my machine and then I'll email it to you. Other lady was here in person, you see. She could read it for herself, but I'll see what I can do. Quite getting the hang of this new technology.'

Monica smiled into the phone and thanked him warmly.

'And I hope the doctor helps you with your cough,' she added as he rang off.

It was just a matter of waiting now. It might take the ailing vicar a few days to fit her request in with the full schedule involved with caring for several parishes. He had been good about getting in touch, though, and it sounded like it wouldn't be long before she knew as much as Victoria.

FORTY THREE

Diary of Joshua Ambrose, Monday 21st October 1799

My state of health is much improved, or so I tell myself. The past few weeks of fever, pain and fearsome coughing have passed in a blur. My old friend, Dr Western, has poured so much evil, stinking medicine down my throat that there were times when I doubted he wanted me to survive at all, so foul was the taste of the stuff. Perhaps my devoted Tabitha, who spent much of the time dozing on my bed, thought so too, for she gave him the most disapproving of looks.

But he is a good fellow, George Western. We were recalling some of our grammar school days, our many merry hours of laughter and nonsense before he went off to study medicine and I was called to family duty. He needn't think I didn't see his pity, though. Being ill does not make me blind. I saw the way he looked at me, but if he thinks I'm ready to keel over, he is much mistaken.

Perhaps his sorrowful looks helped to spur on my recovery. I am not yet ready for anyone's pity. I knew it was time to return to the world and even the prospects of life as a Wisbech merchant and marriage to Miss Ada Imbridge felt attractive while I was confined to my room.

It was the darkness of my thoughts too, which hurried my return to work. Sometimes in the depth of night I would suddenly awaken, thoughts of Susanna raging through my head. Memories of wondrous times and the knowledge that she was lost to me, were tortures added to my sickness. In the end, I longed for pointless distraction, foolish conversation and work.

And so, today I returned to the quayside office and warehouse. A shipment of silk arrived from London on the Mermaid this morning and there is plenty of demand for it. Our order book was full even before the cargo had reached the port, and before the day was done the silk was packaged and delivered to our customers.

I know father watches me sometimes from his high desk by the front window. I feel his eyes on me as I work and I wonder whether the scratching of my pen on the pages of the ledger annoys him. Perhaps it simply concerns him that the future of the company he created rests in the hands of such a weakling.

Yesterday I paid a call to the Imbridges. In my determination to do what is right and necessary, I fear I called too soon. Barely free of the sick room, my looks were hardly those of a man recently returned from the fresh air of southern counties.

Ada looked pleased enough to see me. She even managed to dimple a little as she smiled and curtsied. Her conversation was as animated as ever as we spoke of Dorsetshire, especially when I described the ruined Corfe Castle. Yet I sensed something missing in her manner. Her eyes had lost some of their sparkle; her voice sounded somehow less lyrical. These had been the things which had most endeared her to me before I met my Susanna, and now these things are less than they were.

As for Mrs Imbridge, there was no mistaking her coldness. Her manners were frosty and her constant, unsmiling presence urged me to terminate my visit as soon as was polite. I wandered back along North Brink in puzzlement.

Had Mrs Imbridge sent her spies to watch my activities on Corfe Common? Or was it my distasteful coughing fits and incessant bad health that bothered her?

I wonder whether my mother has noticed a change in her behaviour. I must wait now to see whether my visit is returned, but I fear it will not. I have given up my Susanna and now there is a distance in Ada's manner which I could never have imagined before.

FORTY FOUR; Mid April 2018

The Other Lady

Marcia Hunter, of Phenland Phantom Phinders, was wearing her new T-shirt.

As she glided through reception in that other-worldly way of hers, her jacket flapped open to reveal a black Halloween ghost logo on a white background. Printed in spectral looking lettering above the ghost were the words "The Truth is In There". Continuing below the image was written "Come Phind it With Us."

Monica was certainly not in the mood for this.

'I see you have noticed our group's new T-shirt,' observed Marcia in her slow, dreamy voice, 'but I must not keep you. I know you are busy. I am calling to see if you would reconsider allowing our group to carry out an investigation of this atmospheric building....'

'No, I don't think so and anyway you'd be wasting your time. This place is not haunted.'

A snort from behind her was the sort of betrayal she didn't need. Bernadette, obviously with too much time on her hands, was listening openly.

'Aw, come on Monica, this place is so haunted that the ghosts are complaining about overcrowding!'

Marcia took a step forward, tucking her dark, bobbed hair behind her ear and adopting the ethereal expression she was so good at.

'Yes, I was aware of their presence as soon as I first walked through the door. We would not cause you any nuisance. We would need to spend a few hours here, not necessarily overnight, and would leave no mess. We have a very good reputation. You only have to look at our website to see the feedback we've had....'

'Look, I'd have to ask the trustees, OK? It really isn't my decision and....'

'Justin wouldn't mind,' interrupted Bernadette, 'I think the place gives him the creeps too. All that whispering and muttering....'

Marcia looked from Bernadette to Monica, sensing an imminent falling out.

'I am not here to cause trouble. Please take another of my cards and call me. We pay well and what we discover may help you to understand more about this house's past. Good day to you. Please get in touch.'

The two women watched her go.

'Thanks very much, Bernadette. That was way out of order.'

'I know and I'm sorry, but the peculiar goings-on here are getting a bit much. And Angie's still not happy. How you can spend so many hours here alone I just do not know. And how do you explain the scrapbook disappearing the other day then reappearing on Joshua's pillow? If that weird group can find anything out, surely it would be a good thing? And they pay, Monica. With everything that's happening, the more money we can make, the better.'

Monica nodded, still feeling tetchy. From her office came the imperious ringing of the telephone.

'I'll think about it,' she sighed as she went to answer the phone.

One of Mrs Paynter's cats was asleep on the desk, his elegant forepaws stretched across the trustees' quarterly report which Monica had been trying to make sense of earlier. She reached for the phone, trying not to disturb the cat, but managing to knock his back leg in the process. She gave his ear an apologetic rub as the voice on the line greeted her.

'Oh, hello Dad....no it was just a working holiday really, just a few days....oh, it was just a postcard....that would be lovely....yes, of course....not really, course I will....perhaps at the end of the summer when we're less....of course. Love to Mum and Adela....'

She expelled a long sigh as she replaced the phone on its unit. She should go to Stamford and see them all, she really should. It was nearby, her dad kept inviting her and they all meant well. Yet somehow, after the first few hours of everyone choosing their words carefully, things always dissolved into crossness. She invariably came away reminded that she'd never really been one of them, that she was the odd one out.

'What should I do with them, Smutty?' she asked the cat. He lazily opened one eye to peer at the disturber of his sleep. 'What should I do with the lot of them?'

Smutty made no comment but began to purr, which, considered Monica, made more sense than any of the words spoken so far that morning. She went into the small kitchen where Angie was busy making coffee and pulling trays of sausage rolls out of the oven.

'A bit quiet this morning?' Angie queried.

'Not too bad for a Wednesday and it's still early.'

Monica took three old saucers from the cupboard and began filling them with various mixtures of Webbox and Go-Cat, the dry biscuits making a ringing sound as they hit the porcelain. She filled three more saucers with water before carrying them all into the small store room next door. The clink of pottery as the saucers hit the tiles must have reverberated like dinner gongs to the feline ears around the house, for the three cats were there in seconds, tails up, heads rubbing against her legs.

Smokey, Smudge and Sooty, though the jury was still out as to which was which, put their heads down and began munching their biscuits. A symphony of clinking and crunching and cats' jaws hard at work filled the small room.

'Mrs Paynter will be back on Monday,' Monica explained to Angie back in the kitchen.

'Pity,' she replied as she placed a clear plastic cover over the sausage rolls, 'I love having them around.'

'Angie, they're always around. It won't make any difference.'

Wiping cat hairs from the trustees' quarterly report on her desk, Monica stacked the pages together and pushed them aside, pulling her lap top towards her. It had been several hours since she'd checked her emails and while the museum was quiet she took the opportunity to look again.

Hidden amongst the usual rubbish was an astonishingly early reply from the vicar of Lower Beckton. He obviously wasn't allowing poor health to get in the way of efficiency.

He had experienced no trouble at all, he wrote, in finding the very registers she needed. They still, he reminded her, hadn't been replaced in the trunk following the enquiry from the last lady. He hoped she was pleased with his detective work because not only had he found an entry showing the marriage of Joshua Ambrose to Susanna Harrington in 1801, but the baptism of their son in 1802. The other lady, he reported, had been quite delighted with the information.

I bet she was, breathed Monica, talking to the screen.

This was far more than she'd expected. She sat back in her chair, staring at the text, almost hearing the vicar's wheezing as he wrote. He had attached copies of both entries in the register and she clicked on the first attachment, her heart racing.

The writing wasn't at all easy to make out. The page the vicar had photocopied must already have been faded and damaged and the poor quality of the copy made it even worse. The book must have been large and unwieldy because the vicar had clearly had trouble in getting the page to lie flat on the machine. There were large, dark stripes across the page and places where the copperplate handwriting faded away to nothing. She could just about make out the names, though.

Joshua Elijah Ambrose, bachelor of the parish of Lower Beckton, had married Susanna Harrington, spinster of the same parish, on the twenty sixth of June 1801.

So Victoria was right. She had guessed what Monica Kerridge, curator of the country's only museum dedicated to the poet, had failed to grasp. Joshua had married a girl in Dorset and somehow no one in Wisbech had known about it. Was that really possible? Or had his family just refused to accept it?

Clicking on the second attachment only made things worse. The handwriting looked the same as the previous year's entry, the ink fading in just as poor a way.

Edmund Elijah Ambrose, son of Susanna and Joshua Ambrose of Lower Beckton, had been baptised on the third of June 1802.

Monica had forgotten to breathe, thoughts thumping around in her head as she stared, fixated on the ancient writing which was never going to bring different news. Joshua had died in September 1801. That much had always been certain. But what about his wife and their child, the child who had become fatherless long before his birth? Had anyone ever known about them?

Had anyone ever told them of Joshua's death? Or had Susanna simply believed that she'd been abandoned?

Poor Susanna! What sort of life could she and her child have had? Yet she had, despite everything, honoured the father-in-law she probably never knew, in giving her son the family name Elijah.

There was too much to think about and Monica occupied her mind for a few minutes in writing a reply to the vicar, thanking him for his trouble. He had told her everything she had gone to Dorset to find out and the news was as bad as it could have been.

Since the Poet's House would have been subject to the entailment provisions common at the time, it should legally have passed to the next male heir. That heir was Edmund, Joshua's son and Victoria's ancestor. However, it had passed instead to Joshua's nephew, his sister Rachel's son. It had all gone wrong, either because Edmund's existence was unknown or because it was ignored.

No wonder Victoria was so vehement about this! In her mind, the museum should have been passed down a very different line, to her. No wonder she was seeking legal advice. Who wouldn't, so long as they could afford it?

Monica sank her head into her hands at the desk. If she had been the kind of person who wept, she would have wept.

FORTY FIVE

Diary of Joshua Ambrose, Tuesday 29th October 1799

Now I know for sure that my understanding with Miss Imbridge is at an end.

She did not need words to tell me, however carefully she might have selected them. She told me with what was left unsaid, in her manner, in her look.

I was walking along the quayside to the office this morning. There had been a frost over night and the frozen mud in the ruts and cart tracks of the street were sparkling in the shade of the dark warehouses. There were fewer people about than usual and so I saw Ada approaching from a distance, long before she noticed me. She was hurrying, perhaps because of the cold, but there was about her some inner excitement which seemed to spur her on. Her steps were lighter than normal, her smile unmistakably radiant, before she realised that she was being observed.

When she saw me her demeanour changed completely. She slowed her steps and her smile faded. Her eyes remained bright, but by then they shone with concern, not pleasure in seeing me.

We exchanged all the usual polite enquiries, delaying what had to be said in an agonising way. At last I heard myself asking whether I might call on her again soon, but even as the words were spoken I understood the extent of my foolishness.

'I regret to say,' she voiced quietly, looking away and across the street, 'that we are unlikely to be at home....'

I suppose I nodded, accepted the blow, gave her one of my curtest bows and moved on to nurse my hurt pride.

I am bound to find out shortly in this small town of busy tongues, what is behind all this.

FORTY SIX; Mid May 2018

Haughty and Unpleasant

May arrived, accompanied at last by fine weather.

In the small herb garden at the front of the museum, sage bushes were sprouting new mauve leaves and the marjoram, thyme, oregano, chives, lemon balm and several varieties of mint were thriving. Even last year's parsley was making a new appearance. It wouldn't be long before Monica would be able to set out the seedlings which she'd been tending on the shelf of the downstairs storeroom, and fill the terracotta pots under the front windows with basil.

A pair of bay trees in large ceramic pots guarded the front door, and just to complete the picture, bees had arrived to buzz around the floral abundance of the tiny garden. Monica was quite proud of her gardening efforts, especially since she'd never been what you would call green fingered. It was surprising what you could achieve, she thought, when you really made the effort.

It was a pity therefore, that such a fine, sunny Wednesday in mid-May had to bring Victoria to the door.

With a cardboard shoe box tucked under her arm, she sauntered into reception and asked Bernadette if she could speak to Monica for a few minutes. Monica took her uninvited guest into her office, wanting to avoid being overheard, even though at that early hour there were few visitors about.

As usual, Victoria hadn't bothered to wash her hair. Perhaps she assumed that by pushing her greasy locks behind her ears no one would notice. Long, unkempt strands of it trailed across her shoulders, interrupting the busy pattern of her flowery cotton vintage dress. Judging by its enormous puffed sleeves, thought Monica as Victoria sat down and placed the box on the desk, the dress had last been allowed out in the nineties or even the eighties.

'I thought it only fair,' Victoria began, her head on one side as if choosing her words with care, 'to keep you up to date with the progress I'm making. My lawyers are carrying out their own research and of course there will be no quick results. You know how it is. You long to have an answer from them, one way or another, but then the one looking into things has three weeks' leave, then another goes off sick. However, despite the unusual nature of this case, I am given to understand that I can be hopeful. I am sorry, Monica. I know how much this museum means to you, but a huge mistake was made many years ago. Were it not for that mistake, I would now be the owner of this house. And I can't help feeling....'

She paused, waving her arms about theatrically before continuing, 'I can't help feeling that Joshua would have wanted his old house to remain as a home. I'm not at all sure that he'd have approved of his house becoming a museum. Just imagine! Hundreds of strangers wandering all over your home and poring through your books! Poor man would have hated it.'

So, Victoria thought she had inside knowledge of the poet's feelings, did she? Monica had to bite her lip, force herself to be polite. She really needed to get this woman out of the building before she said something really rude.

'Well, Victoria, thank you for the update, but I really must be....'

'Yes, I know you're busy, but while I'm here, just let me show you what I bought the other day.'

A new dress? Voucher for a hair cut? Monica's spiteful thoughts were at least some balm for her rising anger. She watched as her visitor lifted the lid of the shoe box to reveal a pile of yellowing paper and photographs.

'I advertised on the community website recently for any old photos or items which may have belonged to the Ambrose family. No, Monica, not from Joshua's time, but from the more recent Ambroses, my grandparents or great grandparents, for example. I wish I'd kept my maiden name when I married that loser, Mickey Sharpston. Haven't seen him for years, I'm happy to say. When I married him I hadn't studied the family tree and didn't value the name of Ambrose as I ought to have done. I didn't know that we Ambroses were directly descended from the poet....' She paused to take a breath and seemed to have lost her thread.

'So the box....' prompted Monica, wanting to get this over with.

'Oh yes. Well, I had an email yesterday from an old lady living on South Brink who had bought a whole load of stuff from a house clearance sale a while back. No one seems to know whose house it had come from. Apparently, the old lady nearly threw this box of bits away, but because some of the photos looked old, she decided to hold on to it and keep it in her attic. I offered her twenty quid and she seemed pleased enough.'

I bet she did, thought Monica, as she glanced at the pile of dog eared pictures and worthless junk Victoria was showing her. On the top was a studio photograph of an elegant couple dressed in their post First World War finery. They were standing by a pot plant in front of a screen showing some sort of Grecian temple. The gentleman looked haughty and unpleasant in his immaculate suit, his wife nervous in her calf length, droopy dress.

'I'm so happy to have this picture,' Victoria was explaining. 'On the back there are names and a date; 1925. These were my great grandparents, James and Mary Ambrose. Isn't that wonderful? It's the first time I've seen them. Then, there's this one.' She flashed another photo under Monica's nose. It was a less formal composition showing an adolescent boy on a bike, wearing a Fair Isle pullover and a flat cap. He looked like he was dying to clear off on his bike and escape whoever it was behind the camera.

'This is my granddad, Arthur Ambrose. The others,' she flicked through a pile of about twenty postcards and photos, 'are more recent, but interesting all the same. For some reason these things weren't passed down the family as far as me. Someone must have thrown them out, thinking they were valueless.'

'What's that?' asked Monica, intrigued, despite the situation. She picked up a silver thimble from the bottom of the box. It was so tarnished that it looked more like pewter. There was also an old piece of lace and what looked like decorations from a wedding cake. Victoria didn't seem to mind her looking, in fact she seemed to be enjoying sharing her new find. Perhaps she was short of friends, thought Monica, as she rifled through the box's contents. Pushed down the side was a folded piece of paper and she pulled it out, opening it.

'Oh look!' she said, 'Mark Appledore at Peckover House would like this. It's an auction ticket from a big sale they had at the house in 1948. Wonder what it's doing in the box?' She offered it to Victoria to look, who shrugged.

'No use to me. He can have it if he wants it.'

'I'll drop it round then, next time I'm passing.'

'Fine,' said Victoria dismissively, returning to the photo of her great grandparents and gazing at it again.

'Isn't it wonderful, though,' she was saying, 'To be able to see what your ancestors looked like?'

Monica stared at the woman across the desk. She walks in here, she thought, to tell me that the days of my cherished museum are numbered, and she expects me to think it's all wonderful!

FORTY SEVEN

Diary of Joshua Ambrose, Wednesday 30th October 1799

Ada is to marry my old school friend, Dr George Western. Old Imbridge must be rubbing his podgy hands together at the thought of securing such a catch for his daughter. George Western is heir to a considerable sum and property in Norfolk.

No wonder he looked at me with such pity while tending me during my illness! He must have known even then that I had lost more than simply my good health.

But he need not concern himself. The only wound I am suffering from is to my pride. He and Miss Imbridge have my blessing. She and I only did what our families expected of us and there never was an official engagement.

I wish only that I had known of this while with my Susanna. It is too late now to know that the only impediments to our marriage were our different levels in society and my father's loud disapproval.

I met a very gloomy Sam Mayberry in the Rose and Crown tonight. The bar was intolerably crowded. All the Saturday market traders, their booths and goods packed away for the night, were squeezed into the hostelries around the market place and on the quayside. Trade must have been good because the din of their laughter and raised voices was fairly bouncing off the old panelled walls of the inn.

Despite the jostling elbows, Sam and I managed to claim our usual seats in the corner by the fire. Sam's low spirits are due to his forthcoming marriage to Jane Neverson, an event which looms ever closer. She is the daughter of the senior clerk of the Wisbech and Lincolnshire Bank.

Poor Sam feels nothing but misery in his situation. Old Neverson's position in the bank is such that a match with his daughter promises to boost Sam's prospects considerably. Sam's family, of course, are the main architects of his fate and are delighted with the match.

I have not seen Miss Neverson, but Sam tells me she is very ugly. Twinned with his malodorous armpits, they should make a handsome couple.

Sam's problems have made me reconsider my own situation and to revel in my escape. I had grown used to the idea of marrying Miss Imbridge, but that would not have guaranteed our happiness.

Sam and I had just begun our third flagon of ale when Dr Western himself strolled in. He looked uncomfortable when he spied me and we exchanged cool nods, but there was no benefit in allowing him to imagine a grudge where there was none.

I went over, therefore, and shook him by the hand. I wished him the very best of luck for his forthcoming endeavours. He looked remarkably surprised and pleased. Before the night was out, we were all three sitting at the table in the corner, drowning life's uncertainties in a torrent of ale.

I remember staggering out of the Rose and Crown in the early hours and standing in the market place, Sam by my side. I faintly recall the whiff from the open sewer as we crossed over it, and not really caring.

Most of all, I remember feeling, despite my less than perfect circumstances, a sense of utter freedom.

FORTY EIGHT; Early June 2018

K2 is Blinking

'Hi everyone. Glad you could all make it here tonight. I know how much you're looking forward to investigating this marvellously atmospheric museum....'

Ron Rustleman paused to glance around the circle of seated people in the Poet's House reception hall. There were fifteen members of the Phenland Phantom Phinders present, including Marcia Hunter and himself, all sporting Phenland T-shirts, all eagerly attentive and bristling with anticipation. Joining them on this one occasion were the very reluctant Monica and the highly interested Bernadette.

'....and I'd like to thank Monica and Bernadette for allowing us to visit and explore this evening,' Ron continued. There was a flutter of applause and Monica nodded uncertainly.

The funny thing about Ron Rustleman, with his long iron-grey pony tail and large blue eyes in his middle aged face, was that Monica actually liked him. Unlike his second in command, Marcia, who managed to get up Monica's nose every time she spoke, Ron had an easy-going, natural manner. His voice was low and calming and he seemed kind and considerate. Despite her prejudices, Monica had taken to him as soon as he and Marcia had walked through the door that evening. The pair had arrived early, before the other group members, to begin setting up their equipment.

Monica had not wanted to go ahead with tonight's event, but in the end had given in to Bernadette's persuasion. Angie had refused to come, of course, being put off quite enough by the old house's peculiarities by day, without inviting a further dose of them at night. Monica had accepted at last that she could no longer ignore the odd things that were going on. She had finally agreed with Bernadette that if some explanation could be found for all the muttering, whispering and other unexplained occurrences, it could only benefit the museum.

And the Phenland Phantom Phinders were actually paying to be here. With so much uncertainty at the moment, it would have been stupid to turn down extra money.

'So, folks, you know how it goes. We have video cameras with night vision set up in the three rooms where it appears, from my chats with Monica earlier, that most of the activity occurs. I will also be keeping this mobile sound recorder switched on throughout the evening.' He pulled back the sleeve of his jacket to display the small, sleek gadget strapped to his wrist and was rewarded with a few appreciative cheers. 'My new toy! Marcia will, of course, be carrying the K2 monitor.

'Since we're a fairly small group, I think we can stay together and spend about half an hour in each room, seeing what we pick up. I make it just six o'clock, so if we aim to finish about midnight, that gives us ample time to take a break every couple of hours for coffee and to stretch our legs. At the end, when all the rooms have been investigated, we'll have a debriefing session and a quick look at any interesting camera footage or sound recordings. If there's still time after that, we can return to any rooms we need another look at.'

They began in reception, since they were already seated there. Monica had imagined these things always taking place in the dark and at six o'clock in an evening close to midsummer, with no curtains to dim the light, it seemed peculiar to be sitting in broad daylight with strangers, pretending to listen for ghosts.

'It's OK,' whispered Sukie, a girl in her late teens with long, bright pink hair and a couple of gold rings through one nostril, 'It'll be dark soon. You'll be, like, so into it, you won't notice.'

Monica smiled, still feeling self conscious. A hush fell on the group. There was a bit of fidgeting at first and most people were closing their eyes. Monica stared around the group, wondering how long this unproductive silence would go on for.

But then Marcia's dreamy voice interrupted the quietness, going on about what she could feel. Great sadness, she proclaimed. A lot of unhappiness. Someone else joined in, describing creativity marred by illness. Very interesting, but they'd have known all that from the guide book. And then:

'Something just touched my foot!' panicked a tall, blonde haired girl who was sitting with her back to the door.

'That's my bag, you idiot. I just moved it.'

A lot of tittering.

'OK, settle down everybody.' That was Ron.

'I sense frustration,' began another voice, so quiet that it was hardly audible above the sound of traffic that bumped rhythmically over a loose drain cover in the street, 'Frustration, yes. Being unable to speak freely....'

Silence.

'Anything showing on the K2, Marcia?'

'Slight reaction, just a flicker.'

There was very little else picked up in reception and after half an hour the group left their chairs and filed down the narrow, damp stairs that led to the cellars.

Monica only came down here when strictly necessary. The two main rooms, the old kitchen at the back and the wine store facing the street, were unwelcoming, mouldering places with a permanently stale atmosphere. The gloom, even on the brightest days, never completely lifted, relieved by only a few small windows and a low energy light bulb in each room. Even in Joshua's day, the kitchen must have been a pretty dark, unpleasant place to work in, but at least there'd have been warmth from the fire.

The group spread out at the bottom of the stairs, heading first for the wine cellar. Ignoring the pull cord for the electric light, Ron led them into the centre of the shadowy room with its cobwebbed, small windows set high in the wall. They trod gingerly between crates of dusty porcelain and dented pewter and avoided the pile of broken furniture in one corner, where various oddly shaped legs stuck out into the room.

'OK, step carefully, please folks,' Ron advised in his calm voice, 'Monica tells me this room is rarely used these days, except for storage....if you can manage to find a space between the boxes....that's great.'

Though the damp and the spiders with their trailing, dusty webs, made it uncomfortable in the cellar, nothing much else could be sensed. Even Marcia found nothing to say and the monitor in her hand refused to flicker. It was a similar situation in the old kitchen next door with its yawning, empty fireplace and up-ended broken table. After endless minutes of listening to traffic clanking over the drain cover outside, the group retreated up the stairs and returned to the bright, welcoming air of the small hall behind reception.

Monica closed the door to the cellars behind them and followed the others to the foot of the main stairs. This staircase, which looked rather too grand for its position at the back of the house, had once graced a much larger entrance hall which filled the greater part of the ground floor. The main reception rooms had all been on the floor above. When the house had been made into a museum, the ground floor had been re-divided to create the layout required for its new role. A pity, really. Monica wondered who'd be the first one to drone on about that, having read about it in the guide book.

The group settled quietly around the bottom of the stairs, some of them sitting on the broad lower steps. Silence gradually replaced the shuffling and fidgeting.

Monica closed her eyes and leaned against the curved wooden handrail. She was feeling tired now and wondered how they would manage to stretch this nonsense out until midnight.

'What's that?' squeaked a voice.

'What's the matter?'

'Did anyone else see it? It was a shadow; I swear it was a shadow moving up the stairs.'

'I felt something,' admitted another voice, 'Felt movement. There's something here.'

'It's OK, it'll just be one of the cats,' said Bernadette, 'Won't it, Monica?'

'Is that right, Monica?' asked Ron, 'Is there a cat here?'

'No, not tonight,' she replied, 'our neighbour promised to keep them all indoors.'

'Hairs are all sticking up, like, on the back of my neck,' observed Sukie, 'something's here all right.'

'Yes, K2 lights are flashing,' drawled Marcia, 'Oh yes, we certainly have company.'

Silence again.

'Someone's name beginning with J,' said another voice.

Oh please, thought Monica, tutting. Who didn't know that this was Joshua's house?

'This is ridiculous,' she muttered in exasperation. Bernadette nudged her hard and told her to pack it in.

'We must keep the atmosphere positive,' Ron reminded her calmly. In a louder voice, which resounded around the hall and half way up the stairs, he called, 'We are friends and wish only to speak to you. If you are still here, please give us a sign.'

Nothing. The mood in the hallway seemed to lift.

'Anyone fancy a break for coffee?' offered Monica.

The group split into small groups over coffee and biscuits, some wandering out on to Nene Quay. Bernadette and Monica served coffee and had little time to chat.

When ready to start again, the group headed up the stairs to the first floor, where the large, high ceilinged drawing and dining rooms were. Earlier, when Ron had asked Monica where she thought most of the activity was centred, she had mentioned the downstairs hallway, reception and Joshua's bedroom. She hadn't talked about this floor at all, but Ron still wanted to give these two rooms a full half hour each, just to see what might be picked up.

They walked into the drawing room. To Monica's unspoken discomfort, some of the group sat on the precious silk upholstered chairs, while others chose the floor. She and Bernadette stood by the door. It had gone eight o'clock by then, and although the June evening still provided plenty of light, it had a sleepy quality about it, the shadows long, like small patches of dusk.

'K2 is blinking,' remarked Marcia smoothly after only a couple of minutes, and a few heads bent over the machine with her. Monica crouched down to look over their shoulders. Rather than just the first tiny series of green lights on the panel being illuminated, as had been the case for most of the evening, an orange light next to it was blinking. The red bulbs at the far right of the display were still dark. Monica wondered briefly what would happen if they lit up.

'Picking up something. It's a man, I think,' Sukie was saying. Her head was silhouetted against the window, her pink hair more shadowed now.

'If you are here, please talk to us,' said Ron, 'We mean you no harm, only wish to speak to you. Do you need to get a message to anyone here?' He paused, listening to the absolute silence. No one moved. 'Do you perhaps need to talk to Monica? Have you been trying to speak to her? She is here now.'

Nothing; no movement, no sound.

'K2 still reading orange.'

'What does that thing do?' whispered Bernadette.

'Picks up, like, changes in the electro-magnetic field,' whispered Sukie.

'But....'

'Shush!'

Ron was pacing around the drawing room, concentrating and repeating his message periodically to unseen presences. The silence continued, everyone waiting, poised for something.

'You found....' The voice came from a dark haired, bearded man in a very creased Phenland T-shirt, who was seated by the window. He had said little all evening, but now all eyes were on him as he concentrated hard, his head tilted as if listening, blinking rapidly in the gloom.

'Mike? Have you got something?' prompted Ron after a while. The lights on Marcia's K2 monitor were flickering and for a fraction of a second the red zone flashed.

'Hard to make out,' Mike said quietly, 'but it sounds like....you found the....ring? The ring or something. Yes, you found the ring.'

Monica's heart gave a deep thud. Only she, Bernadette, Angie, Bertle Bodgit and the trustees knew about the carving of the ring on the skirting board upstairs in Joshua's room. Though the room stewards were aware of the patch over the skirting, hidden behind the chair, none of them had been shown the carving itself.

She felt Bernadette looking at her.

'Monica, does that have any significance to you or the museum?' Ron was asking. People were getting up and leaving the room and he came to stand by her.

'Yes,' she admitted, 'it's something to do with the research we're doing at the moment, but....'

Ron waited as she collected her thoughts.

'But I don't understand how your machine for measuring changes in the electro-magnetic field can tell you much. I mean, wouldn't your own electronic equipment just set it off?'

'Yes, radio frequencies from electrical equipment can be picked up by it, so we use an RF monitor in conjunction with it. You may have noticed Magnus, the bloke with all the hair, carrying another hand-held meter?' She hadn't, but let him continue, 'Well that's an RF monitor and it registers radio frequencies. If it reacts at the same time as the K2 monitor, we know there's nothing to get excited about; all we're picking up is our own gadgetry. However, just then, when the K2 was picking up so much activity in the drawing room, the RF monitor showed nothing.

'You have a presence here, Monica. The message Mike received was loud and clear. Someone wants to be heard.'

Monica was nonplussed. She had expected to snigger her way through the entire evening, to seethe with cynicism, but this felt so real, so serious.

They went next into the dining room on the same floor, but nothing happened to disturb the peace. She stood next to the wiry haired Magnus this time, watching how the RF monitor reacted sometimes, picking up radio frequencies. Across the room, Marcia's K2 monitor was quiet, its light steadily remaining on the green of no action.

After another coffee break, the group went wearily up both flights of stairs and began to work their way along the top floor. It was almost ten o'clock by that time and darkness had fallen. Lights had been switched on to help them up the stairs and between the rooms, but once inside each room, the lights were turned off again and they worked in the dark.

They squeezed first into the small box room, addressing the empty air for half an hour before moving into the Reading Room next door. Sukie said she felt movement in the room, thought she saw a shadow by the window, but no one else seemed to pick up anything. By the time they moved into Joshua's bedroom, they were all tired and showing it.

One of Ron's video cameras had been set up in the corner and he checked it as they all walked in. The Phenland

Phantom Phinders found corners to sit in, but to Monica's relief, no one attempted to sit on the bed. It was so fragile; it would probably have collapsed under their weight.

Cars continued to pass by in the street below; in the distance an ambulance wailed. Someone came out of the take-away up the road and hollered something. Yet in the room there was a heaviness which seemed to cushion them from most of the noise. They all felt it, even Monica. She sat on the floor and waited with the others, one eye on the K2 monitor.

'Someone's here,' reported Sukie, 'feels like the person from downstairs. This man had, like, a lot of sadness. Lived here a long time, but was, like, never really happy....'

Most of this, Monica silently told herself, could be picked up from the guidebook. The sadness bit could simply be guessed at.

'Would you like to tell us anything?' began Ron once more, addressing the air, 'We mean you no harm....'

'K2 is in the red zone,' announced Marcia with intensity.

Suddenly, from somewhere in the house, perhaps from the ground floor, came an abrupt, slapping sound.

'What was that?' panicked several people at once. Ron's calm voice broke through, still talking to the space around him.

'Was that sound from you, friend? Are you trying to let us know something? Monica would be grateful for any message you can give her.'

Would I? she queried silently. They had moved so far from what she knew as normal that she was no longer sure what she'd be grateful for.

'I'm aware of this man too,' remarked Magnus from somewhere in the darkness, 'His sadness comes from loss and disappointment. Too much has been lost. Too much....' his voice faded away to nothing.

Did the guide book say that? Monica was getting confused. Of course it didn't. When the book was written no one had known anything about Joshua's loss and disappointments. They hadn't known much at all, really.

'Keep on searching,' said Sukie, 'He's saying, like, keep on searching.'

Monica took a sharp intake of breath.

'Monica? You OK?' came Ron's voice. Everyone was moving out of the room and the light on the landing was switched on. Ron was lending her his arm, helping her up.

'You all right love? I take it that message meant something to you.'

'Yes,' she replied faintly, 'It did.'

'We'll get you a glass of water downstairs,' he said in a matter of fact way that belied all the silliness of the Phenland T-shirts.

They followed the others down the stairs. The whole group was subdued now, a little from tiredness but more from the effects of the evening. They believed beyond doubt that messages had been received that night from someone who had once lived in the house. Whether it was simply her exhaustion she couldn't be sure, but at that moment Monica believed it too.

Bernadette already had the kettle on by the time she reached the kitchen. She seemed perfectly calm.

'Sit down, Monica, I'll make the tea.'

Monica obeyed wordlessly, perching on the high stool next to the work top.

'I think we can safely accept, then,' Bernadette was saying, 'that this museum is haunted and that it's more than just our collective wild imagination.'

Someone pressed a glass of water into Monica's hands. She thanked whoever it was without looking up. People were taking mugs of tea from Bernadette, chatting in the hall and spilling back into reception, where Ron was about to do his summing up. There was a shriek, probably from Sukie, then rapid footsteps.

'I'm sorry love,' Ron was saying, 'but your display of guidebooks has fallen from the shelf. It must have been the sound we heard from upstairs. And they all appear to have fallen open at the same page.'

She took one of the books he was holding out to her, expecting to see it opened at the same page as before, showing the poem, "The Walk," but it had not. Instead, all the books had fallen open at the very first page. A sepia toned photograph of the Poet's House formed the background for a few lines of one of Joshua's earliest poems.

'Home.
Home to love, to hearth and fire

To that which ever does inspire
My heart to sing....'

These lines from Joshua's adolescent years had come from the scrapbook. They were part of a sweetly naive poem which showed how important his home was to him in his youth.

He needed her to keep it safe, she thought.

'Does it mean anything to you?' Ron was asking,'I mean in conjunction with the other messages tonight?'

'Yes,' admitted Monica, 'I believe it does.'

FORTY NINE

Diary of Joshua Ambrose, Thursday 19th December 1799

Winter has the town and the Fens securely in its grip. Its merciless fingers trail ice across ponds and freeze hard the rutted, puddle ridden roads. Out in the yard, the servants toil with the frozen pump, their fingers blue as they lug pails of icy water to the kitchen for their laundry and cooking. Even the Nene seems to flow more sluggishly, the ships creaking as they move against the quayside, as if their old bones ache from the persistent cold.

There was plenty of cash to be deposited at the bank this morning. Trade does not stop with the cold. We have done well with our latest purchases of woollen cloth from Yorkshire. Mr Watling, the draper in the market place, has purchased almost all of our stock, so long is his list of customers requiring fine wool to keep the bitter wind at bay.

I am growing accustomed to my lot. Compared with most wretched souls, I am fortunate. The clothes on my back are as good as anyone's and, although I would never have chosen the life of a merchant, it could hardly be said to be a poor one. I am grateful for my improved state of health and have pushed away my foolish dreams. It is best that way.

Pulling up the high collar of my new woollen coat, I hurried along North Brink, telling myself how fascinating the mud-brown river was. I stared into its sad depths for as long as it took to avoid looking at the Imbridge house and all its bustle.

At Christmas Ada is to marry my old friend George Western and the whole town is alive with talk of it. I hear old man Imbridge is buying in all sort of luxuries for the wedding feast, while his cooks labour to produce candied fruit and other fancies to grace the table. According to mother, there will be a mock turtle as the centre piece. It will look very grand to be sure, but why cannot folk simply admit it's just the head of some unfortunate calf which was in the wrong place at the wrong time? As well as that particular delicacy, there'll be pheasants, collared pig, a haunch of venison.... I can just imagine Ada, with her spiky little elbows, picking her uneasy way through that lot.

The Ambrose family will not be attending. Father has made sure of our absence at Christmas; we shall be visiting Rebecca in Outwell. For once, I approve of his decision. It will save much embarrassment.

By the time I reached the bank, the morning rush had died down and I was able to be served by dear old Sam. He was looking very serious, as he always does in his place of work, labouring under the austere glare of the senior clerk, his future father-in-law. Sam was wearing a small pair of spectacles which balanced awkwardly on his nose and appeared to require constant adjustment. He counted out the money I was depositing, the coins chinking into the wooden drawer in the desk. Then he took up his pen, dipping it with concentrated care in the large pewter ink well before entering the details of the transaction in the huge ledger on the desk.

Dear Sam, he has his future mapped out for him now. He needs only to nod and shake his head in all the right places, and the world will be his, so long as he never dares to have a will of his own.

Mr Peckover's new banking hall is an impressive, trust inspiring statement of efficiency. I also believe that, despite its stern air, its authority is a benign one. The bank's excellent reputation grows all the time and is a veritable shrine to good sense, commerce and investment.

As I was leaving the banking hall, something quite extraordinary occurred. Mr Peckover himself was entering his bank and, apparently without urgent business to attend to, he paused to ask after my family. To my great surprise, he went on to say he understood I had a love of books. This information must have come through Mrs Peckover's acquaintance with my mother; I cannot imagine father admitting to such weakness in his son.

If it truly is a weakness, it is one shared by Mr Jonathan Peckover, a man of sound business sense and one greatly admired by my father. Before I knew it, Mr Peckover was leading me into his fine house, through the elegant hallway, and we were turning into his library.

The north facing room struck me at first as rather dark. The library overlooks a very pleasant garden, but benefits too little from the daylight. A few tall shrubs grow rather too close to the windows and inhibit the already pale midwinter light. Yet, once noted, this small defect soon ceased to matter. A pleasant fire was burning in the grate, bringing cheer to the room, and when I saw the shelves of books, the magnificent collection put together by Mr Peckover with such consuming interest, the room gained a brightness all of its own.

It was hard to concentrate on what the gentleman was saying to me, so busy were my eyes as they flitted from one enticing title to the next on the overflowing shelves. I was aware of the honour of receiving attention from such a busy and important man, especially when he took the time to ask about the poetry I write, something which my own father never cares to do.

As Mr Peckover glanced at his pocket watch, I knew my brief visit was at an end. Yet, even that brought a pleasant development. When we have more time at our disposal, he said, perhaps I would like to browse through the library and look at one or two of the volumes? Naturally, I readily agreed!

As I write this, I am hopeful. I know at last that there is someone in this town who shares my love of books. Although I have my mother's and sisters' encouragement about my poetry, companionable discussions with Sam about the failings of the world, and the occasional inspiring coffee house lecture, with no one of my acquaintance can I discuss my love of books. With none of them can I share my interest in nature and the elements, the love of love itself, and the melding of it all into verse.

Perhaps soon I shall be able to speak of all these things.

FIFTY; Midsummer 2018

Seek the Smutties

Unusually, they were all in on Friday morning.

'OK, we need ideas,' Monica was saying to the small group of staff and volunteers, 'I have a few, but we need something good to draw in more families with children over the summer holidays.'

Though the museum was closed on Thursdays and Fridays and Monica normally had the place to herself, she'd decided to call a meeting to help with planning a way forward. It was already mid June and the school holidays would begin in under a month. Despite Victoria's threat, no one was ready to give up.

As well as Bernadette and Angie, ten of the volunteers had come in, everyone sitting in a circle in the reception hall. And then there was Bertle Bodgit, who was meant to be mending the leaking cistern in the staff loo at the back of the building, but who kept walking down the hall to have a good listen.

'How about some special snack boxes for children in the tea room?' suggested Angie, 'You can buy the boxes quite cheaply on the internet. They have pictures of fairies and things on them for girls, super-heroes or aeroplanes for boys. That sort of thing. I could fill them with whatever they wanted; sandwiches, little cakes, etcetera.'

'Nice idea,' agreed Monica, 'perhaps we could tie that in with a special event in the museum and find some boxes with appropriate designs?'

'Personally,' said Bernadette, 'I think we're missing a trick in not promoting this place as a haunted house.' She'd been saying this a lot lately, ever since the visit from the Phenland Phantom Phinders the other week. 'I bet we'd have double, even treble the amount of visitors, in no time at all.'

Monica sighed heavily.

'I know, Bernadette, but as I keep saying, this is a poet's house. It's a museum, not a freak show....'

'And I don't need reminding about it all the time,' said Angie with unusual crossness.

'But haven't you noticed,' ventured Emily, a volunteer room steward, 'how the activity has died down? I usually look after Joshua's room when I'm on duty and I was getting used to the odd noises, but I've not heard a thing for more than a fortnight now....'

'Oh great,' moaned Bernadette, 'we've killed off our best asset.'

'Good,' retorted Angie, 'Perhaps your pals at Phenland did a good job, then.'

'All right, everybody,' said Monica, 'Maybe we could consider something along those lines for Halloween.... just a discrete event, strictly for adults only, but I'm not at all sure it's the right thing to do. I'll have a word with Justin and the other trustees and see what they think.'

She did not add that the place might not even be open by then.

'Children's quizzes,' stated Enid, a room steward in her late sixties who had heard too many verbal battles, 'If we want to make the place more attractive to families we have to engage the children's interest. Make them think. Give them a quiz.'

'Absolutely,' replied Monica with enthusiasm, 'Thanks, Enid. So, how do we go about it? Question sheets? Clues on boards in the rooms about the poet and his work? How about....'

'Nah,' said a familiar voice from the doorway, 'Look, no disrespect intended, know whatta mean, but when you've seen one poem you've seen 'em all....'

'Err, thanks Bertle....'

'So you don't wanna bore the little buggers silly as soon as they get 'ere, sortta thing. My lad, right,' he waved his half eaten chicken drumstick in the air to emphasise his point, 'my lad would sooner be at a theme park or with his eyes stuck to his phone, so if you wanna get him moving during the holidays, and other kids like him, you'll have to make it interesting, know whatta mean?'

'Well, Bertle,' Monica smiled, 'what do you suggest?'

'Cats.'

'Cats?'

'Yupp. What's the first thing the kids look for when they come 'ere? While the parents are quoting *stanzas*,' he made a flouncy looking gesture with the drumstick, 'the kids are all squealing, know whatta mean, cos they've seen one of the cats. That's all they're interested in. If you make a cat trail, the kids'll wanna come and do it. Not real cats, mind. That'd drive the poor little buggers mad, but you could use toy cats or sommat. You could call it "Find the Smutties", or sommat. Know whatta mean?'

'Err, yes, I think I know what you mean....' trailed off Monica, bemused.

'Actually,' enthused Angie, 'I think Bertle's got a point. The cats are accepted as part of the house, so why not make a theme out of them? Any idea whether the Ambroses had a cat, anybody? If they did, we're home and dry.'

'That's settled then,' concluded Bertle, his mouth full of chicken, 'Bob's your uncle.' He left, presumably to finish mending the toilet.

'Did the Ambroses have a cat, Monica?' prompted Bernadette.

'I don't know,' she admitted, 'but I should think every house and warehouse this close to the river would have had a vermin problem. I think they would have needed a cat. Maybe Bertle's right. The kids love Mrs Paynter's three cats, so let's make a feature of them. We could hide little toy cats around the house and give the kids a quiz sheet with clues to locate each one. They could answer questions about Joshua and his poetry as part of the quiz and we could give them a prize at the end....'

'A cuddly cat key ring?' suggested Bernadette, 'They have loads in the shop catalogue. You can even have the ribbon on them printed with the museum's name.'

'Sounds perfect!' acknowledged Monica, 'Would you look into the cost of that please, Bernadette? Then we can work out how much to charge for the cat trail. Angie, why don't you look into that snack box idea of yours and then we can discuss it further. Do they make any boxes with cat designs? I'll get working on the quiz sheet. I'm determined to educate the little darlings, if it's the last thing I do.'

And, added Monica grimly to herself, with things looking so uncertain, this event may indeed be the last thing she did here.

FIFTY ONE

Diary of Joshua Ambrose, Thursday 23rd January 1800

At last, this afternoon brought an opportunity to accept Mr Peckover's invitation.

The penetrating damp and cold of this new year provides little inspiration and these days I write but rarely. Each morning seems bleaker than the one before, bringing nothing but duty and business.

Sam is relieved of his freedom now, his marriage to Jane Neverson reshaping his life. He still escapes for an ale or two with me in the Red Lion or the Vine, but he is no longer the Sam I knew. How can marriage so effectively rob a man of his humour and wit? Had I married Ada, would that fate also have befallen me?

Today's visit to Mr Peckover's library was therefore the very thing needed to lift my spirits. The comforting fire in the grate spread a warm, soporific glow through the room as I idled away happy hours immersed in poetry.

Many of Mr Peckover's books are works written by the Friends, serious essays based on Quaker philosophy and the way of life close to my new friend's heart. Many others are histories and there is a fine volume of the plays of William Shakespeare, another of the writings of Samuel Johnson. There is an ancient and fragile edition of "Don Quixote" by Miguel de Cervantes, but the books which inspire me most are by the great poets. There are collections of verse by Christopher Smart and Thomas Gray which interest me greatly.

When at last I could tear my attention from Thomas Gray's verses, my host invited me to a glass of port. I knew already how fine it was, because we sold it to him some time ago, but it seemed even better, shared as it was with a fellow of like mind, before a good fire in an excellent library. And so we whiled away a very pleasant half hour, weighing the merits of one writer against another. How glad I am that for all this excellent gentleman's devotion to his Quaker faith, he still enjoys a drink and keeps a good cellar.

Mrs Peckover, I believe was at home, for at times I heard the sounds of female laughter and the voices of children from the drawing room upstairs. The Peckover household seems a very happy one.

As I left the warmth of Bank House for the bleak darkness of late afternoon, Mr Peckover accompanied me to the door. He remarked that he would soon be calling on my father and added an invitation for me to call on him again, whenever I wished, to look at his library.

This is the one thought which has the power to brighten the gloom.

FIFTY TWO; Late June 2018

Rookery Something

It was a Tuesday in late June when Monica left Bernadette in charge of the museum and walked over the bridge to Peckover House.

The morning was cloudy but warm and everywhere roses were in full bloom, ready with perfect timing for the annual Rose Fair. As it had for years, the event would begin on Wednesday and continue until Saturday. Depending largely on the weather, the fair drew in thousands of visitors to the small Fenland town each year and gave trade a welcome boost. Even Monica's small museum was staying open on Thursday and Friday in the hope of attracting a few more visitors and, although the tiny herb garden at the front could hardly be said to follow the general theme, she had replaced the usual bay trees by the door with pots of white tea roses.

There was a coach parked outside Peckover; already the house was busy, though the fair was yet to begin. Monica waited on the pavement to allow thirty elderly folk to climb down from the bus and file into the front garden. A harassed looking member of staff was shouting out instructions about toilets and tea, desperately trying to hand out tickets to escaping pensioners. The sun was breaking through a milky mass of cloud and the group was more interested in pulling out sun hats from capacious bags than in paying him any attention.

Monica had clearly not chosen a good time to call on Mark Appledore. She hung around outside the house for a bit, wondering whether she ought to come back at a less busy time, but her dithering was interrupted by a distinguished voice drifting over the crowd.

'Monica Kerridge, have you brought more knackered old books for me to squint at?'

She turned round, but could see no one apart from the large group, which was making its uncertain way through the arch towards the tea room.

'Over here!'

Mark was standing just inside the open front door, his body almost absorbed in deep shadow. His pale face seemed to float, independent of his dark coloured clothing, in the dim light of the entrance hall. He looked like he was fighting another bad headache and losing.

He was just about coping with greeting visitors as they entered the house, his polished voice and hint of a painful smile doing their best to provide a welcome. He must have been standing in for room stewards who, one at a time, had gone for their tea breaks. Monica gave him a grin and walked up the steps to join him.

'It's not a book this time, but....'

'I'm back now, Mark, thanks,' a cheerful looking lady room steward took his place at the door, having finished her short tea break, and he shot her a grateful glance.

He beckoned Monica further into the hall and she pulled an envelope from her pocket, opening it to reveal the auction ticket she had retrieved from Victoria's box of family treasures.

Mark grimaced at it. He must have been hot in his grey scarf and sweatshirt, but he made no attempt to loosen the woolly folds from his neck. He backed into a shadowy recess next to the grandfather clock to keep out of everyone's way and Monica followed.

'How the devil does a thing like this survive?' he queried as he examined the small slip of paper in his hand, 'It's even in fairly good condition. We only have one or two scrappy versions, so this is a rare find. How did you come across it?'

She told him about the box of Ambrose family photos and how the ticket must have been lying, forgotten in the cardboard box for decades.

'I just thought you might like it for your archives,' she added. 'It ought to be here really.'

'Well, thank you, Monica Kerridge. Frightfully good of you to bring it over. I was thinking of putting together some sort of display next year, actually. Thought I'd concentrate on the three-day auction in September 1948, so this little chappy will be an excellent addition. Somebody's scrawled on it; could you read what it says?'

'No, I saw something was there, but the writing was so bad I couldn't make it out.'

Mark glanced around him for a moment, noting the steady flow of visitors through the house and the fact that the room stewards appeared to be coping well. The coach party was unlikely to return from the tea room and garden for a while yet.

'Let's go through to my office. We'll be able to see better in there.'

She followed him along the little back corridor, then along another passageway to his office. The room was well lit, benefitting from a large window overlooking the garden. Back in his sanctuary, Mark seemed to relax a little.

'Rotten headache today. Plagued by the damned things....'

He stood by the window and studied the ticket again. On the front was printed the lot number, 976, and underneath, in large, looped handwriting were added five words. On the reverse of the ticket two more words had been added in the same hand and all were equally impossible to interpret.

Mark looked intrigued, turning the ticket over in his hands and scrutinizing the badly formed words.

'The words beneath the number are, I think, "Twenty cat something...." oh and I think the last word is "misc"....ah of course, it'll be the Peckover sisters' cat baskets and all the other gear they must have stored up over the years for their cats. They adored them, you know. You'll have seen the cats' graveyard in the garden, of course.... yes, the writing on the front just clarifies what lot 976 was comprised of, "Twenty cat baskets and misc." As for what's written on the reverse....'

'Why would anyone want to hold on to twenty pieces of cat equipment?'

'Perhaps sentimental value, perhaps simply because one threw away less in those days.'

'True,' agreed Monica, 'perhaps more to the point, why would one of the Ambroses want to buy so much cat equipment?'

'Hard to say. Perhaps the poor chap was just giving his ear a good scratch when the auctioneer saw him. Now, as for the writing on the back of the ticket, I have no clue at all. It looks like nonsense. "Rood Shacks?" Meaningless. Ah no, that's a "y" at the end, so "Roodery Shacks?" What the devil's that? Rookery something? Could it be "Rookery Shacks"? An address?'

He passed the paper back to Monica and she peered at the two words on the reverse of the ticket.

'Yes, I see what you mean. If it's an address, it sounds in need of help.'

He smiled, then winced.

'I'll make a copy of both sides for you, just in case you ever need it for your own research. And thank you for bringing it; it really is a good addition to the collection.'

Mark disappeared for a moment and returned with a photocopied sheet, just as his radio stuttered into life and a crackled voice requested his help.

'Have to go,' he muttered, 'Will you see yourself out, Monica Kerridge?'

As she left through reception, the coach party was advancing like a slow but determined army towards the front door.

By the time she reached the Poet's House, it had become almost as busy as Peckover. Monica went to give Bernadette a hand, issuing tickets and selling items in the shop. She felt a bit guilty, knowing that she shouldn't have left the museum for such a trivial reason, but no one had predicted being so busy before the Rose Fair even started.

When reception quietened down, Monica moved into the tea room to help Angie. She brewed tea, refilled the coffee machine and made sandwiches to order. Time passed quickly and by five o'clock the three women were exhausted.

While Bernadette and Angie cashed up, Monica went upstairs to shut the windows, tidy up and close everything for the night. In Joshua's bedroom she paused for a moment, enjoying its peacefulness. From downstairs came the muted sound of tills whirring as they coughed out end of day records and from the street drifted the hum of traffic and the occasional raised voice. Apart from these normal, everyday sounds, there was nothing.

It really was true that since the Phenland Phantom Phinders had called, all the unexplained noises, the muttering and whispering, had ceased. There had been no more misplaced items and no more books had fallen from shelves.

If Monica had been less cynical, she might have wondered whether whoever had been causing so much disruption was satisfied that his messages had got through. "Keep on searching," the message had been. Whatever she believed about that night, and still she wasn't sure, she could not forget that simple, very relevant message.

Keep on searching. But was she? She seemed to have lost her way. Having discovered the worst about Victoria's ancestry and knowing that she meant to take the museum away from them, Monica hadn't a clue how to stop her.

Suddenly, despite the excellent business they'd done that day, she felt a wave of hopelessness and sank down on to the Windsor chair. The late afternoon shadows seemed to gather around her as she stared down at the floor, at her own sandaled feet.

'Monica!' called Angie up the stairs, 'Ready to go now!'

She pulled herself together and hurried down the stairs. With a smile she took the cash boxes from the two women and let them out through the front door. After locking up, she went into the office to collect her bag.

The front door bell rang, its shrill command piercing the silence, and she muttered crossly under her breath, wondering why so many visitors failed to read the big "closed" sign on the door.

She unlocked the door begrudgingly and opened it half way. A man in charcoal coloured walking clothes stood there. His dark hair looked untidy, his face tired, as if he'd driven a long way.

Archibald Newcombe-Walker had come to visit.

FIFTY THREE

Diary of Joshua Ambrose, Sunday 30th March 1800

This morning after church I rode out of town, along the course of the old Well Stream, leaving the straight lines of the modern canal behind. We enjoyed a leisurely pace, my faithful horse Adolphus and I, following the ancient course of a river long reduced to a defiant trickle.

Our morning was sunny, the spring sunshine golden bright, yet brittle too, as if it might be snuffed out at any moment. Behind us, stretched out across the sky, was an advancing bank of the deepest grey cloud, a curtain which tracked our progress, closing in at our heels. The birdsong, so confident a chorus as we set out, faltered as the curtain pressed ever nearer, fading to an occasional brave cheep from the hedgerows. Even Adolphus was anxious, his ears twitching nervously as he walked along the track. He knew as well as I that a storm was approaching and we quickened our pace.

Not far ahead was a line of animal byres, low wooden shacks at the edge of a field, and we made for them. Suddenly, the fragile sunlight was extinguished. Distant thunder rumbled its warning. The pall of cloud swept over us like a malevolent presence and the last daring trill of birdsong stuttered into silence.

We had not quite reached the shelter when the first fat drops began to fall, but we were safe before the deluge came. I dismounted and held Adolphus' reins, talking to him in the reassuring way I need to use for him. For all his great size, he has always been afraid of storms.

The roof of the dusty old byre leaked in several places and we had to move around to dodge the worst of the drips, avoiding the remains of broken ploughs and rusted scythes, left there and long forgotten.

We watched as the heavy rain fell in a shimmering cascade, sweeping across the dark soil of the Fen. There was another roll of thunder, closer now, and Adolphus began to move around in agitation, his ears pinned hard back, so that it was hard to keep hold of him.

Yet, for all its bullying threats, the thunder came to little in the end. It growled in retreat as the heavy drumming on the flimsy roof slowed to a less dramatic beat. Outside, the silver sheet of falling water thinned to a fine mist.

We ventured out into the sodden landscape, Adolphus easier now. We picked our way between the worst of the slippery mud and cloudy brown puddles. A cold wind was blowing across the fields, following in the footsteps of the storm, and the earth, with its feathery down of Fen grass, seemed to shake itself like a great dog, shrugging rain from its coat.

The great, purple-grey line of cloud was moving away, ahead of us now. Tentatively, the sun flickered back, briefly illuminating the rain drops suspended from hawthorns to crystalline perfection. From deep inside the hedgerows and stands of tall grasses the warbling and trilling of birds struck up again. Adolphus lifted his head and let out a long sigh, as if denying he had ever been afraid.

The retreating storm still hung like a leaden backdrop in the sky. The sunlight, bright and golden, flickered on and off, projecting a wonderful lightshow of clashing colour.

For a fleeting second, a tree on the horizon, fresh with young leaves, was lit up in a glowing, impossible green against the dark backdrop. Away to the left, a church spire was picked out, shining golden, lit like a torch. A flock of geese rose into the air to form a perfect V formation, their wings touched in a heartbeat of luminescence. In that glorious moment they seemed to hang there, a banner of lights across the sky. The sunlight skirted the line of the river, catching the tips of new, furry grasses, lighting them up in a honeyed display that flickered away to the horizon.

It did not last long, that wondrous light show. Gradually, the sunlight grew more constant and the thick cloud moved further away, losing its power.

We continued on our way for a while, enjoying the glories of spring after a hard winter. The sections of the old Well Stream which still hold water benefit from heavy rainfall and we could see the gleam of small pools between the bulrush and reeds.

Our ancestors abandoned this once efficient and fine river to its inevitable decay. In ancient times, the Well Stream brought trade to Wisbech. It was the life blood of the town, but in time its meandering course became blocked with silt and new channels were cut, scarring the landscape. And yet this old stream, though largely dwindled to nothing, still lives on as a series of long, unmolested pools. The life these small ponds carry, the teeming world untouched by man, is enviably unaware of his destructive actions.

We did finally manage to find a place to stop, Adolphus and I. There was a place by the stream where I could sit on a stump of willow and, covering the soaked wood with an old coat from the saddle bag, I rested there a while with my notebook and pencil. I tried to find fitting words to recapture the wonders I had just witnessed, while Adolphus grazed contentedly.

All was peace for an hour or so. What I wrote was of no great quality, but it was an opportunity for undisturbed thought, for I have much to think about.

I have decided to publish some of my poems. The idea first came to me while conversing with Mr Peckover. He mentioned a publishing friend of his in London and I noted down the gentleman's address. Mr Peckover has looked at some of my poems and encourages me in my new scheme.

Father cannot hide his pleasure in the elevated circles in which I move these days. With Mr Peckover's encouragement of my new enterprise, dear papa has even stopped referring to my writing as a waste of time.

Buoyed up by all this friendly optimism, I have gone so far as to write to Mr Peckover's publishing friend, Mr Wildernesse of London. Though I must pay for the satisfaction of seeing my work in print, Mr Wildernesse is very particular about the quality of work he publishes, his reputation being at stake. So now I must sit and wait while he considers my proposal.

For a while I must be patient and fill my free time with walks and rides in the countryside. And on a day such as this, nothing could be better.

FIFTY FOUR; Early July 2018

Lop-eared

Archibald Newcombe-Walker was standing awkwardly in front of Wisbech Castle.

'Smile!'

'No one says that anymore, Monica. Hurry up, we're in the way,' he objected, smiling anyway as he called out an apology to the group of people held up on the path while the photo was taken.

It was still early, but the sun, as if under orders for the annual Rose Fair, was already making its way through the cloud. It was going to be a perfect day. Archie's arrival on the eve of the town's four day event, through which Monica would have to be working, had not been the greatest of timing, but she wasn't complaining. She'd decided to make the best of the situation and show him around the town this morning before opening the museum.

He was staying at the Rose and Crown where they'd eaten last night. She still couldn't believe her own eyes that he really was there, that he really had driven to see her when his long touring holiday had come to an end.

Yesterday afternoon, when he had appeared without warning, she'd hardly been able to take it in. Things like that, unexpected, good things, had simply never happened to Monica. Her thirty three years' experience of life had convinced her that wonderful surprises only came to other people.

Since meeting him in April, she'd thought often of Archie. His was a soothing, happy memory, a balm to her usual jarring worries. Yet, despite these pleasant reminiscences, she'd never expected to see him again.

The pair of them had been "ships that passed in the night", as her mother would have said, people who meet once and never expect to meet again. And Monica would have agreed.

'I went home to Leamington after spending time in Cornwall and Wales,' he'd explained to her the night before, over his inevitable fish and chips (refined restaurant version), 'and I tried to settle into my new life. The business and all its pressures had gone, but I kept wondering how your investigation was going, whether you'd found out what you needed to know. So I looked up your museum on the internet and decided to come over, just in case you still needed a bit of help with your detective work.'

She'd stared at him over the top of her wine glass.

'Just like that?'

'Well, I gave it a couple of days.'

She didn't ask why he hadn't just phoned. It seemed unfair to put him on the spot and a pity to prick the bubble of his carefully prepared casual attitude. Because there was just something a little awkward about his manner, something which reminded her of her own behaviour when pretending something was unimportant.

They had met again early that morning. She'd wanted to show him the best parts of her small town before he had chance to see any less pretty bits. As yet, she'd not brought him up to date about the sad state of her investigation, insisting that it could wait until morning. Last night she'd just wanted to enjoy his company, the wine and the food, and to take a rare break from her worries.

They wandered into St Peter's Garden where rows of stalls had been set up for the fair. Though it was still early, the gardens were teeming with people who strolled in the sunshine and browsed the stalls, buying teddy bears, jam, cakes, crafts and plants. In the midst of it all, the old circular fish pond with its lazy fountain carried on as if nothing had changed. Just more hidden from view than usual, it continued to attract the same crowd of old boys, who rested on benches and discussed the matters of the day, as if there were no tombola going on next to them.

Monica bought a jar of rose petal jam and Archie unwittingly won a large, stuffed, lop-eared rabbit on the tombola when he was hoping for the set of screwdrivers. He duly presented the bunny to Monica, who was fleetingly aware that this wasn't like her at all, to be so girlishly dimpling, silly and blushing on being presented with a soft toy.

She carried the large creature into the church, so that she could show off the ancient building's architecture to Archie. The spacious church, with its two naves and two chancels, was as busy as the stalls outside, a myriad of visitors filling the aisles to look at the floral arrangements which decorated every surface and crevice.

Archie was drawn to the stone carving, dating from the 1250s, around the north door. Fantastical creatures, goggle eyed and slightly off-putting, reposed on the door surround. Among them was the Green Man, complete with flowing locks and beard.

'Did the stone masons not quite get the Christian theme?' queried Archie.

'More likely they were hedging their bets. The country people around here would still have been close to their pagan origins and natural magic. It probably wouldn't have seemed strange to them to mix old customs with Christianity.'

He nodded thoughtfully and they moved on, out of the north door and round to the sunlit side of the building. Monica still had an hour before she had to open the museum, so they ordered coffee and scones in the church hall next door. With the large rabbit, they occupied a table meant for four by the window, Monica knowing that this would be the nearest thing to lunch she'd have time for all day.

'So come on,' he chided as he smeared a large dollop of red jam on his scone, 'tell me what you've found out.

It was a pity to spoil such a bright and cheerful morning with news of her museum, but she'd put it off for long enough. She told him about the marriage and baptism records she'd received from the vicar of Lower Beckton, how there was no longer any doubt that Joshua Ambrose had married and had a legitimate son. She added that under the entailment laws which controlled the inheritance of the Ambrose property, the house should have passed to Edmund, Joshua's son.

'And instead it passed to the nephew.'

'Yes, to Joshua's sister's son, Richard Blunt. Presumably because the family was unaware of Edmund's existence.'

'How peculiar.'

'And like a red rag to a bull for Victoria Sharpston. She claims that the house, courtesy of her ancestor Edmund, should now be in her possession. She has her lawyers working on it and seems pretty confident that she can take the house from us. Even worse, she has this dreamed-up theory that Joshua wouldn't have approved of his home becoming a museum. In other words, Victoria plans to take the museum away from the trust, close it and use it as a private house. In yet more words, Archie, we are facing the loss of the museum within.... maybe a few months. And it isn't just a job, it's....'

She stopped, dropping the piece of scone she'd been trying to eat on to the plate. She was staring out of the window, blinking hard, troubled. He put his hand on hers. Just a brief, light touch, but it seemed to work. She turned her head to face him, her blinking slowing down, trying to smile.

'I know. It's more than a job,' he finished saying for her, 'It's a place you love.'

She nodded.

'I can't let her take it.'

'Then we'd better get to work. What else have you found out? Anything at all?'

'Nothing of any practical use. Well, there *was* the truly weird night with the Phenland Phantom Phinders ....'

'The what?'

She told him about that strange evening and her initial scepticism. She told him about the earliest messages which could, in theory, have been researched beforehand, then about the others, which in all reality could not.

'There were two main messages that night,' she explained, 'neither of which could have been made up without a lot of luck. The first was "You found the ring," or words to that effect. That was incredible. You see, as I think I told you before, in the spring we found a carving on the skirting board in Joshua's old room with the name "Susanna" and what appeared to be a ring symbol, like a wedding ring. Because of Victoria's regular poking about in the museum, we decided to keep the discovery a secret. After all, it was the first time we'd even heard of Susanna and it would just have encouraged Victoria. The only people who know about the carving, besides me, are the trustees, Bernadette, Angie and the handy man who discovered it. We've managed to preserve the area around the carving by covering it in such a way that it's practically impossible to read, unless you lie on the floor and stare at it. Even then, the light has to be just right.'

He was listening carefully. It was hard to tell from his face what he thought to the idea of supernatural communication.

'I see, and you said there was a second message?'

'Yes, the second one was simpler. It just said, "Keep on searching". By that time we were all exhausted. It had been quite a night. I never really believed before then that the noises in the house were anything other than pipes and floorboards. You know, the usual rational explanations, but now....'

'The sceptic has been converted?' he smiled.

'Well, I wouldn't go so far as to say that.... but maybe, oh I don't know!'

'Well, it seems to me the best thing you can do is to accept the advice you were given and stop worrying about where it might have come from. For now, do as it said and keep on searching. And if you will allow me to stay on for a little while, I believe I'm the right man for the job.'

'But you must need to get home....'

'Must I? As I told you once before, I have sold my half of the business. I'm starting to enjoy a few months of freedom after more than twenty years of hard work....'

'Well, yes, I remember you saying....'

'But you never asked me what the business was.'

'No, of course not! I hardly knew you. It would have been nosey.'

'You'd make a hopeless snoop, Monica. I was a private detective, private eye, call it what you like. And so, when it comes to outwitting Mrs Sharpston, I am the very man you need.'

FIFTY FIVE

Diary of Joshua Ambrose, Tuesday 13th May 1800

It is done. My manuscript has been despatched this morning. I handed the package to the Post Master myself and am assured that it will go with tomorrow morning's mail coach from the Rose and Crown. Mr Wildernesse, of the Wildernesse and Wilde Publishing Company, is expecting it, having agreed to take on the work.

Since receiving the publisher's favourable reply, most of my free time has been spent in editing and polishing my work. I finally chose twenty of my earlier poems, the best I have for now. My later ones are still unready for publication, too engrained with sadness and too much a part of me yet to be shared.

Some of the poems I have chosen seem naive now. They come from a time when I knew duty and the tedium of it, but nothing of heartbreak. Life was a simple matter of comfort and discomfort. No complications.

I remember scribbling this one after walking too far one December afternoon at around the age of nineteen.

A Fenland Night Walk

Darkness hovers near,
Its winter canvas close unfurling,
Its foggy kiss
And misty breath
Turning my face
To home.

Fog drifts and stalks
The inky hollowed wayside ditches,
Shadows me on limbs
Of smoking fur,
Turning my face
To home.

The moon is misted now,
Its lamplight shrouded, helping none,
Yet still the fog
Clings to my breath,
Turning my face
To home.

Tossing its grey smoke fur,
Briefly wild, briefly loyal,
It parts to make merry
With the saturated night,
Clearing my path
For home.

And so now I must wait again. Mr Wildernesse promises the first copy of my anthology in a few weeks and then I can revel in the vanity of seeing my own foolish words in print. I have called the work "First Thoughts" and hope that I never have cause to regret releasing these thoughts into the world.

While I wait, I am determined not to lack entertainment. Last night I took myself off to the Theatre in Deadman's Lane, a place of illusion and fantasy, its stage set with wonders. Sam being, as usual nowadays, engaged in some tedious duty, I was obliged to go alone and had one of the side boxes to myself. From there, I was able to look down into the pit and the gallery, both of which were teeming with boisterous townsfolk. I had an excellent view of the stage too.

In the main, the Lincoln Circuit Players didn't make a bad job of "A Midsummer Night's Dream", except for the fellow playing Puck. He was far too hefty for a fairy, his doublet constantly riding up to reveal his large, hairy belly. His pointed pixie ears seemed permanently askew, the wig they were attached to being too big and slipping over his eyes whenever he launched into a speech.

There was some wondrous scenery, meant to depict fairy land, or some such place, and some clever machinery that lifted Titania (played by a youth with a tad too many whiskers) on to the stage, as if by magic. Despite these clever tricks, the audience in the pit grew restless, especially during Oberon's rather laboured speeches, and I spotted a few stale buns being readied for hurling at the stage. When the first of their rude objections were hollered out, however, the offending persons were hastily removed from the building. It was a pity really. Oberon looked insufferably priggish and a well aimed missile at the back of his neck might have done him good.

What sport Sam and I would once have had with all this! We would have laughed until we dropped, finding humour in all the wrong places, perhaps thrown out ourselves for bad behaviour.

How I miss the old days with Sam!

FIFTY SIX; Early July 2018

Faintly Dismayed

On the Monday following Rose Fair, as soon as the museum opened, Mrs Paynter appeared in reception.

'I have to take the Smutties for their annual jabs today,' she announced to the first person she encountered. Unfortunately, it was Archie, who hadn't a clue what she was talking about.

He'd spent the weekend helping Angie in the tea room and now he'd been asked to tidy the shop displays, which looked like they'd been tossed about by a strong wind. Business had been good in the shop during the Rose Fair, but the place was showing the strain.

When Archie had offered to help, he hadn't meant like this, but if he was feeling used he wasn't showing it. He was clearly confused by Mrs Paynter, though.

He straightened up from tidying the Hi-Bounce Day-Glo bouncy ball display and looked quizzically at the small, rather stooped, elderly lady, who was holding a package towards him.

'Sorry?'

'Please tell your boss I've been knitting all weekend and I'm out of wool....'

'Good morning, Mrs Paynter,' sang Bernadette's voice from behind them, 'Archie, this is our neighbour, Mrs Paynter. She is the owner of the three cats you met yesterday and she's very kindly been knitting toy cats for our summer children's trail.'

'Ah, right. Hello there, Mrs Paynter....'

She merely nodded and pushed the paper package into Archie's hands.

'Must go, appointment's in ten minutes. Could do with some orange wool next. I'll make some marmalade cats. The grey's getting on my nerves.'

'All right, thank you, Mrs Paynter. We'll buy some and bring it round,' called Bernadette to the retreating back of the bustling old lady.

Bernadette turned to Archie and grinned.

'She's a dear lady, just a little eccentric. You've been a bit put on this weekend, I'm afraid, but it's your own fault. Fancy turning up just before Rose Fair! This place relies heavily on volunteers and will suck in every available pair of hands.'

'It's OK,' he shrugged, 'I quite enjoyed it. A change from what I'm used to.'

Monica appeared in the doorway and they both turned to look at her. She was smiling at Archie and the smile lit up her face, displaying her teeth in undisguised happiness. Bernadette watched the pair of them walk from reception with mixed feelings. In all the time she had known Monica, she'd never seen her look at anyone like that. All her usual reserve seemed to have been cast aside and she looked vulnerable as never before.

For some reason that she couldn't explain, Bernadette was suspicious of Archibald Newcombe-Walker. With so much uncertainty regarding the museum and her job, maybe it was natural to suspect anyone who appeared so conveniently out of the blue. Whatever the reason, her instinct told her there was something wrong about him.

As Archie and Monica reached the office, the phone started to ring and Monica picked it up reluctantly, signalling for him to wait, that she wouldn't be long.

She was doing most of the listening, and judging from her replies and her frown, it sounded like a call from one of the trustees. He knew from what she'd told him over the working weekend that such calls came frequently at the moment.

He was familiar by now with her small office with its desk in the centre of the room and the work table standing against one wall. From a long-held habit of observation, he'd made a mental note of the details. Unlike most offices, there were no family photographs, no holiday or Christmas snapshots. The only colour to break up the blandness of the walls was a dog-eared print of a Vermeer painting showing seventeenth century Dutch houses. Old sticky tape stains did nothing to relieve its scruffiness.

There was never much in Monica's in-tray. Either she received very little post of the paper variety or she was very efficient. Maybe both. There was one small peculiarity, though. Whatever arrived in or was removed from the tray, one piece of paper always remained untouched. It was a sheet of copier paper with a hand drawn cartoon of a pair of shorts with knobbly-kneed legs dangling out of them and a huge pair of boots on the feet. Quite what she meant to do with this item was anyone's guess.

While Monica continued her phone conversation, he went to look out of the small window. It was hardly an inspiring view; a small side yard containing nothing but three wheelie bins lined up against next door's fence. A small amount of litter had blown against the dingy looking green and blue bins and there were untidy tufts of grass growing by the brown one. Fortunately, visitors were spared this sight, which was in complete contrast to the neat herb garden at the front of the building.

He was still clutching the package from Mrs Paynter and, having had enough of looking at dustbins, he perched on the edge of the desk and opened the bag. Inside were two curious looking knitted items. They were both cats, neatly knitted in a hairy kind of grey wool, one of them in a sitting position, the other lying down. They both had small whiskers made of nylon thread and their eyes and mouth had been sewn on with black wool. One of the cats was distinctly boss-eyed, while the other looked faintly dismayed. Archie wondered whether it was deliberate. He was still staring at the toys when Monica's phone call ended.

'Am I interrupting something?' she grinned. He gave her a brief smile and placed the cats on the desk.

'Err, look Monica, this is all very nice, but I really should be getting on with what I came for.' He paused, surprised to see the carefree look fading from her face. 'Rose Fair is over and the museum did well from it, but if we're going to tackle Victoria and her plans we need to be doing some more digging.'

Her face had fallen completely and he wondered what the matter was. She was clearly pulling herself together, though, and beginning to nod soberly in agreement.

'Perhaps,' she ventured, 'we should check the Ambrose family tree. I mean, surely we shouldn't just accept what Victoria says at face value? I know her lawyers are encouraging her, so they must believe she's right, but....'

'I agree,' he replied briskly, 'it's somewhere to start. We need the right software, or.... don't suppose you subscribe to Predecessors.com or any of the other sites?'

'No, I....'

'Doesn't matter. If I could use your computer while you're working in reception today, I'll sort that out....'

She looked hesitant for a moment, definitely downcast. She nodded.

'Just one request,' he was smiling now, 'Can I get rid of this picture of the knobbly knees? It's a bit distracting....'

'Oh, that!' she laughed, snatching the piece of paper from her in-tray and turning it over, 'It's the information Mark Appledore from Peckover House gave me the other day. He must have used a piece of recycled paper to copy it on to for me. I took him an old ticket I'd come across, from the auction that took place at Peckover in 1948. The ticket came from Victoria's box of old pictures, by the way, the one I mentioned. There was something written on it, which he tried to interpret, and he gave me this copy, in case it was of any use to us here.'

'Why didn't you show me this earlier?' he snapped, taking the paper from her. He squinted at it, just as Mark and Monica had done, 'What does it say?'

'Well that bit under the auction lot number says "Twenty cat baskets and misc". The other bit was copied from the back of the ticket and is more of a mystery. Mark thought it might refer to an address. I think he made it out to be Rookery something. Shacks maybe.'

He stared at the writing for a few seconds, moving his head this way and that.

'At least it gives me something else to have a go at,' he said at last, 'Leave it with me, oh, and Mrs Paynter needs some orange wool.'

FIFTY SEVEN

Diary of Joshua Ambrose, Saturday 16th August 1800

Our house was already a cheerful one this evening when our servant Matthew brought the package I had long been awaiting.

We were all there, even Rachel and my young nephew Richard, who are staying with us for a few days. Young Master Blunt is now some fifteen months old and in his bold attempts to explore his world he stumbles around all over the place. He keeps us all busy whenever he is with us and at these times we are a happy family. Even father's stern features have been known to appear over the top of The Times and assemble themselves into something like a smile at the child's antics. Considering how easily the old man could disappear into the peace of his study, I find it surprising how rarely he does so. I can only conclude that he enjoys family noise more than he confesses. If only his stony old features would crack more often!

He still cannot forgive me for allowing Miss Imbridge and her fine connections to slip away. Were it not for my failings, the Ambroses would now be connected to the wealthiest family of merchants in the town, and an heir to the Ambrose property might even be hoped for.

But all that was pushed from my mind as Matthew handed me the package, newly delivered by the post boy. I went down to the hall, turning the parcel over in my hands before cutting the string and pulling away the many folds of paper. In an instant, both my sisters had joined me, exclaiming and merry, carrying the new book to show to our parents before I'd seen it properly myself.

I have young Richard to thank for giving the old man smiling practice, for I swear his crinkly features managed to summon up something positive. He even put down his newspaper to handle the book. My father smiling! Though not as well as my mother.

So now I have it, my first copy. Mr Wildernesse has done an excellent job, binding the work within a handsomely tooled leather cover and adding the title, "First Thoughts," like a proclamation in gold lettering along the spine and front cover. Even my name is added without apology.

Yet, what did I feel as that small volume lay in my hands, the product of so much work, of so much outpouring of thought and emotion? I had expected to feel proud and excited. Instead, I felt like an imposter, someone who had no right to shout about his work in so brash a way, placing it within a cover which proclaims itself worthy of opening.

How can this item ever be put on a shelf next to the works of William Cowper or even new and inspiring poets, such as Coleridge or Wordsworth?

I think the world would do perfectly well without hearing of Joshua Ambrose and his foolish scribblings.

FIFTY EIGHT; early July 2018

A Twanging of Springs

It was unusual, this level of heat in an English summer. Yet, it is often the way that during long periods of it, when day after day brings baking blue skies and temperatures in the high twenties, it begins to be accepted as normal. It becomes hard to imagine anything else.

The first week of July was like that. Children were still at school and the town seemed hushed, submerged in an unusual stillness, no one going out unless they had to. Only the rumble of lorries along Nene Quay indicated that the world was still at work.

On the Tuesday of that week, Archie stood by the half opened sash window of Joshua's bedroom, having agreed to stand in as a room steward. He would much rather have been getting on with his work on the Ambrose family tree, but Monica needed her computer.

In the last twenty four hours her mood seemed to have changed completely. All that girly carefree behaviour had disappeared, leaving her tetchy and miserable, and Archie couldn't understand it. Surely it couldn't have been anything he'd said?

Her low spirits didn't seem to affect her efficiency though. She was clearly a very practical person and he admired that. She had tried to combat the heat in the airless upper rooms by standing large electric fans on each floor. They were quite effective, but ugly, their white presence filling the still afternoon with their droning.

From the window, Archie had quite a good view of the town. If he craned his neck sufficiently, he could just about see the Clarkson memorial to the left, and to the right, across the river, the backs of the buildings in the Old Market. The two Georgian brinks followed the line of the river in their elegant way out of town, and although North Brink wasn't visible from this angle, he could see some of the houses on South Brink, their frontages a mixture of renovated, good looking buildings and run down, crying-out-for-help relics of a more refined age.

The Fenland town had not enjoyed a great level of prosperity for some years, but it had managed to hold on to much of its fine architecture. As these buildings were gradually spruced up, old Wisbech was beginning to emerge, peeping out from the indifference of past decades.

Archie yawned and turned away from the window. Being a room steward for the afternoon might have made a pleasant change from staring at the computer screen, but the scarcity of visitors on this hot Tuesday was making it a waste of time. He paced around a bit, sighed and looked at his watch. Almost half an hour had crawled by since the last visitors had left the upper floor and had gone downstairs for their tea.

He dawdled back along the upper landing once more, entering the Reading Room and catching a waft of cool air from the fan. The window in that room overlooked the side of the house and didn't provide much of a view, just the extended backs of neighbouring houses. He yawned again, wondering how soon he could have a tea break.

Suddenly there were footsteps clumping up the stairs. Loud, female voices were resounding across the landing. Archie made an effort to shake off his drowsiness and prepared himself to greet the newcomers.

Usually, on reaching the second floor, visitors walked straight into the Reading Room, since its door faced the top of the stairs, but these people were striding past, heading straight for Joshua's bedroom. Archie was about to join them, but instinct held him back.

The voices of the two women were expressing no curiosity whatsoever about their surroundings and clearly required no information from a steward. They were chatting noisily about nothing in particular. There was a lot of "and he said to me and I turned round and said" with no reference at all to the museum. For all the interest they were taking in the place, they might have been standing at the bus stop. Archie decided they had no need of his services and stayed out of the way.

After a couple of minutes the voices dropped to whispers. There were a few giggles, a few exclamations, and then;

'But come on, Vic, how can you be so sure?'

The name alerted Archie and his ears tuned in. He had spent hours recently in trudging through the website to construct Victoria Sharpston's family tree. The loud voice in Joshua's bedroom had to belong to the same woman.

'I'm pretty sure. It's complicated, but for heaven's sake, I'm paying them enough! They seem confident I've got a case and....'

'But, all that research they're doing, it's taking them an awfully long time. And let's face it, Vic, you practically did all that yourself before going to them.'

'Yes, but you see, this sort of case is very *rare*. They can't just leap into it without very careful preparation and I'd rather they *did* check all my research. It needs to be absolutely right, because this is going to cost tons more yet.'

'But is it worth it? I mean, this pile of old bricks must be worth zilch. Why do you want it? By the time you've paid for all that legal action, you could have bought a much better place outright....'

'That's not the point. Joshua was my ancestor. He was Edmund's father and this pile of old bricks, as you call it, should have been Edmund's. I owe it to him, as much as to myself. Entailment rules were unbendable and someone back in the early 1800s messed up big time. Edmund was cheated. All we have to prove is that a continuous line of legitimate male heirs existed from Edmund in the early 1800s to 1925, when the entailment provisions came to an end. After that date, it's just a matter of ensuring that family Wills would have passed the property down the remainder of the line to me. Under modern law, of course, as a woman I can inherit.'

'Flaming heck, Vic, rather you than me.'

'Good thing it's me, then, not you.'

There was a twanging of springs, then the sound of someone dropping their weight carelessly on to Joshua's bed. Monica had warned Archie about this. Very few visitors had the nerve to sit on the bed, even though there was no notice specifically prohibiting it. The bed was a fragile piece of furniture on very wobbly legs, and whenever a visitor took an uninvited rest on it, the stewards were asked to see off the offending bottom.

Archie had been eavesdropping on the visitors' conversation and had missed nothing. He was extremely reluctant to let them know of his presence, but now he had no choice. The women were taking too many liberties.

He had begun to stir himself from the Reading Room when a curious squeak from one of the women stopped him in his tracks.

'What's that down there?' shrieked the voice which was not Victoria's.

'What's what down where?' replied Victoria in a lazy tone.

There was another agonising protest from the ancient bed springs, followed by the scraping of something which sounded like a chair across floorboards.

'See what you mean. Looks like a little window....'

'No, it's just a patch of plastic covering some writing. Look, if you get down here you can read it. Looks like....err, Susanna 1801 and a blob....'

'What?'

There was a shuffling sound and another twanging of springs as Victoria, presumably, heaved herself from the bed on to the floor. There was a screech and a string of very loud expletives.

Monica had not had time, with all the activity during Rose Fair, to give Archie a proper tour of the house, but he could tell that the women had found the very thing which no one wanted them to find. He wasted no more time in holding back, striding rapidly along the short passage into Joshua's room.

'Good afternoon, ladies,' he greeted them with a polite, brittle smile, his eyes sweeping from the creased bedcover and displaced pillows to the two women crouching in the corner. Their noses were still close to the skirting boards, their generously sized backsides towards him. 'May I help you?'

They turned their heads and stared at him resentfully.

'I'll just tidy the bed cover,' he continued smoothly, 'This bed is not strong enough to take much weight, so we don't encourage visitors to sit on it....'

Victoria was recovering more quickly than her friend from the indignity of being caught out, hauling herself back onto her haunches and slowly, by holding on to the wall, back to her feet.

'What the hell is going on here?' she demanded, 'What do you think you're up to?'

Archie knew better than to be drawn into arguments with people like Victoria Sharpston. He took the small black radio from his pocket, and keeping his eye on the poisonously staring woman, spoke calmly into it.

'Monica, could you come up to Joshua's room immediately, please?'

There was a crackled response, followed by rapid footsteps on the stairs.

'To hell with that,' retorted Victoria, 'I'm going down to see her. I want to know just what's been going on around here.'

The two women met at the top of the stairs.

'What is it now, Victoria?' asked Monica in a resigned way, 'You're loud enough to be heard as far away as Peterborough.'

'I want to know,' growled the poet's descendant in very unpoetic tones, 'why I have been deceived.'

Monica shrugged.

'Come downstairs to the office, then. You're making the place look untidy.'

FIFTY NINE

Diary of Joshua Ambrose, Wednesday 10th September 1800

The summer has passed with painful slowness this year. Its sweetness, scents and softness did more to mock than to please me.

Whenever I looked at the fertile Fenland fields, warmed by summer sun, I remembered sunlight on the old stones of Corfe Castle and the warmth which spread to the hills and vales of our beloved common.

It is a year now since last I saw Susanna and I doubt there has been one hour in which I have not thought of her. How can I delight in a season as bountiful as this, when it brings such memories to taunt me?

I know not whether it is melancholy or the ever increasing dampness in the morning air which has caused my sickness to return. Whatever the cause, it seizes my throat and burns my lungs and I fear it will bring on the fever once more. Yet again, I have had to take to my bed.

As ever, our sweet Tabitha spends much of her time with me. Sometimes, when no ears are there to eavesdrop, I tell her of my troubles and she does not judge. She just blinks her big eyes at me and treads her circle dance on the bed cover. Usually, she curls up to sleep to keep me company, her purring a soothing presence while I too drift into sleep.

My old friend Dr George Western is once more paying regular visits to his hopeless patient. I must say that his newly married state suits him, but I do not envy him. If I must mourn the loss of Susanna for the rest of my days, I can at least do so freely. I reassured him only yesterday, when I caught him giving me that pitying look again, that he may spare himself the guilt.

In a lighter mood, he told me that he has purchased a copy of my book. He bought it from old Mr Partridge in the New Market, who by all accounts is doing a good trade with it. It appears my fellow townspeople are curious about a merchant who writes poetry.

The modest success of my work gives me some consolation as I am forced to idle here in my room. I have a foolish dream sometimes, in which the sales of the book spread, with the aid of some miracle, as far as the south coast and Susanna buys a copy and remembers me. Then I come to my senses and realise that by now she is likely to be wed. I picture her reading out a verse or two to her new husband, the pair of them with their heads together, and my mood goes spiralling down again.

My father's stern reminders that, as soon as I am well again, I must set my mind to marriage, do not help. He has a list in his fat head of suitable candidates. Some of them are minor gentry! Can he really not know how they laugh at him behind their smooth hands? We are tradespeople. We may be doing well from it, but like the Imbridges, we are only from trade.

We came from nothing. We have no pedigree to polish and display on the mantelpiece next to miniatures of our ancestors. The local gentry, even the poverty-stricken among them, look down on us. Some of them may have fallen on hard times, lost their land and most of their wealth, but no one can take away all that breeding. That is one of the few things which my father cannot order from

London. If he could purchase a shipment of breeding, he would certainly do so.

Further down his list are daughters of other wealthy tradespeople. If we cannot have class, we may as well increase our wealth; that's his thinking. With Miss Imbridge out of the running, he is bound to find some other unwary creature to burden with me.

He must have his heir and I am his only son. God help the poor old devil.

SIXTY; Early July 2018

Unwanted Toady

'It was all lies, wasn't it?' Victoria continued to shout, 'You knew all along about Susanna and pretended you'd never heard of her. It was one big cover up because you knew this place should be mine. I warn you, you won't know what's hit you when you hear from my lawyers! And right now, I'd like an explanation about that writing on the skirting board you're trying so pathetically to hide....'

She had hardly paused to draw breath since leaving the top floor and stomping down to Monica's office. Archie stood, grim faced with arms folded, behind Victoria and her now silent companion. Fortunately, there were no other visitors in the museum, no one to witness this tirade or in need of Archie's room stewarding skills. Even if there had been, he wouldn't have moved. Monica may not have admitted to being vulnerable, but he knew how worn out she was beneath her head teacher like facade and there was no way he would have left her alone in this situation. Behind him, in reception, the air was practically bristling with Bernadette's eavesdropping.

Monica was trying hard to keep a veneer of calm. She had hardly spoken a word since Victoria had begun her loud complaint, letting the woman's bitter speech run itself into stuttering silence.

The cats had been far less calm about the disturbance of their sleeping place by the open window. They had been languishing on a couple of old chairs, enjoying the rhythmic draft from the oscillating desk fan. Their drowsiness had been enhanced by the restful tones of Test Match Special on the radio, but when Victoria's noisy entrance had cut Geoffrey Boycott's views on English cricket stone dead, the cats had legged it.

Still Monica let the silence run on. Only the quiet commentary on the radio and the wheezing of the fan filled the stillness. Even from behind, Archie could see that Victoria's agitation and frustration were increasing with every second.

From the radio came the polite sound of anguish as another English wicket fell. It must, thought Archie briefly and irrelevantly, be a hot day at Lord's too. England seemed to be in trouble.

'Well?' demanded Victoria, her slate-hard eyes glinting, 'I think I deserve some sort of explanation!'

There was a hand on her arm; Philippa's. Victoria scowled at her. Stupid woman never knew when to stay out of it.

'Come on, Vic,' she cooed, 'nothing will be achieved like this.'

She shook her off, muttering something under her breath.

'No one is trying to deceive you,' replied Monica at last with infuriating calm, 'we have only just discovered the inscription upstairs. We're still researching it and are in no position to make any findings public. And you most certainly had no business poking around up there.'

'Of course I did. I have every right to protect what is mine. And,' she added, picking up an unusual looking knitted toy from Monica's desk, 'You can forget about your childish events in future. This museum needn't plan anything past Christmas.'

'Go away, Victoria, and get on with your legal meddling, or whatever it is.'

'I warn you,' the woman shouted, her anger spilling into the room, 'my lawyers have almost finished what they have to do and very soon the trustees of this museum, this crass insult to Joshua's memory, will be receiving a letter from them. A very significant letter.'

'Out, Victoria, or I'll call the police,' said Monica, 'Your noise is making my head ache.'

Archie stepped forward and picked up the phone from Monica's desk. He began to press keys.

'Oh, don't bother. I'm going, but you are going to regret this. Who the hell do you think you are?' She glared at Archie, 'Her guard dog?'

With that, she tossed the knitted cat back on to the desk, knocking over the tiny digital radio, and stormed out like Miss Piggy in a huff.

Monica and Archie watched her leave, shadowed by the other woman. Monica recognised her as the person she'd met in the Wisbech and Fenland Museum in the spring, the one who had feigned concern about the Poet's House. Philippa Renshaw; unwanted toady of Victoria Sharpston.

They heard Bernadette saying a few words, then there was silence. Or as much silence as there could be with another moan of despair coming from the fallen radio. A sixth English wicket had gone down.

'Sounds like we're really in trouble now,' said Archie philosophically, 'In more ways than one.'

SIXTY ONE

Diary of Joshua Ambrose, Sunday 5th October 1800

It was a mistake to attend the assembly at the Rose and Crown last night.

My sister had pleaded with me to accompany her. Rebecca loves to dance and at the age of twenty four it is natural that she should. Her head is full of dreams and she appears to want nothing more than to find an eligible partner, but she fears her advancing age will soon make her undesirable in the marriage market. It is a ridiculous notion and I have told her so.

Joining Sam's party for the evening, Rebecca and I arrived with the newly wed Mayberrys and Sam's parents-in-law, the Neversons. Mr Neverson, being both Sam's superior at the bank and his new father-in-law, is someone in whose presence my old friend can never relax. His professional future and any hope of meeting his wife's expectations depend heavily on his good conduct, both at work and at play.

I knew Sam would have preferred to be swallowing ale in a corner of the bar downstairs, or at the New Inn, but occasions such as this, with their irksome codes of conduct, have to be borne sometimes. Mr Neverson smiles only when strictly necessary and his wife does a fine imitation of someone chewing a wasp. I pity my old friend, I really do.

His new wife, Jane, is pleasant enough, but very serious. Who would not be, having been introduced to the world by clowns as jolly as her parents? Contrary to Sam's description of her, she is not ugly. However, the self righteous way in which she inclines her head, half closing her eyes as she preaches prudent house management and common sense, is most unattractive. She is too dour for Sam, whose allegiance to the banking world is due more to obligation than to genuine interest.

And yet, the straight faced Mrs Samuel Mayberry managed to surprise us all last night. Just when I was convinced that her features would never achieve anything resembling a smile, she declared that she was determined to dance! I saw my sister's astonishment and we exchanged amused looks.

We watched as Sam and his new bride danced, seeing how her sober face lit up. We observed too how fondly she smiled up at Sam. After that, she plagued him all evening to dance, seeming not to care that he has all the grace of a lumbering ox. He did his best to oblige, but I caught him several times with his eye on the wall clock of the assembly room, as if begging its hands to move more quickly.

When Sam declared he could bear to dance no longer, I gave in to his wife's pleading and partnered her for a short while. Meanwhile, Rebecca seemed to be enjoying herself, dancing two sets with the lawyer's son from the New Market. I forget his name; he looks intolerably wet to me, but no doubt we shall be hearing all about him at breakfast time.

Mrs Mayberry and I were just returning to our seats after a particularly lively Cotillion when she whispered;

'You know this will not do. You cannot spend your entire evening with me. There are many pleasing young ladies here who would make admirable dance partners.'

I only smiled and gave her a little bow. She was perfectly right and many of those "pleasing young ladies" were not so dreadful to look at. Some were even on dear father's list of "suitable girls". I therefore did my duty and made myself useful for the rest of the evening, joining the lines of country dance with a series of not too unpleasant young women.

Yet, what a waste of time it all was! I did as they wished. I even danced the Boulanger, joining the rest of the throng in the last dance of the night, yet there was not one woman in that whole public assembly who engaged my interest beyond the first few seconds. There was no one apparently capable of discussing anything more entertaining than the food on her plate. Among them all, there was no humour to speak of, no intellect and certainly no imagination.

Attending this sad event only made stronger the pain of Susanna's absence. I have not the faintest hope of ever meeting her equal.

I fear my father is destined to remain a disappointed old man and I a bachelor.

SIXTY TWO; Mid July 2018

Misguided Chivalry

At last Archie had Monica's office to himself. It was proving more difficult than he'd imagined to make any meaningful progress. He was hampered by the fact that he'd left his laptop at home and there were just not enough opportunities to use Monica's computer, when she didn't need it herself. But that afternoon she was showing a private group around the museum, allowing him the freedom to get on with things.

He could just hear her voice above the purring and droning of the desk fan as she led the group upstairs. He could tell she was having to rein in her irritation with one member of the party who kept interrupting her talk. He smiled to himself. Gradually, he thought, he was getting to know Monica. He was beginning to understand that her natural instinct to avoid people came into constant conflict with the needs of her job. Because of this, she seemed forever on the verge of snapping at the people who annoyed her, often having to work hard to control her temper.

He should not have come here. What had made him do it? It had been an ill judged decision, a spur of the minute thing, and after almost a fortnight in the Fens he was still asking himself why.

Had it merely been the silence of his home after being away for so long? Or were curiosity and a bit of misguided chivalry more to blame?

When, a couple of years earlier, his marriage had broken up, he hadn't been too troubled by the sudden emptiness of the small Leamington house they had once shared. He'd still had his work then.

Perhaps his real mistake had been in giving up the business so early. He'd just been so very tired, sick of the long hours and endless conflicts the job had involved. Taking a break from work and living for a while from his investments had seemed a good idea at the time. Once he'd had time to rest and recover, however, he'd started feeling directionless. His mid forties were far too young an age to give up work altogether.

To keep himself busy, he'd set out on that long touring holiday of the West Country, but it had only delayed the inevitable. Coming home, he'd once more been greeted by the intolerable silence of the house. So what had he done about it? He'd simply set off again, delaying once more the need to sort out a new life for himself. This trip to the Fens, then, was nothing but a delaying tactic. Or was it? He still couldn't be sure.

He'd given himself no time to think through his reasons. He'd hardly unpacked his bags from the holiday before he'd made the decision to look up Monica and her museum. The Poet's House had been easily found on the net, and his trusty sat nav had guided him there.

Monica, he thought as he stared at the search screen on the Predecessors website, was very difficult to read. It was hard to tell whether she merely wanted him there for his help and support or whether there were deeper reasons. After those first few days, when she'd been so obviously happy to see him, she had really withdrawn. What had caused such a sudden change? Had it been something in his manner? He'd been told before that his practical, matter of fact way often sounded colder than he intended.

Whatever was behind Monica's cooling off, it made a mockery of the fact that as he'd left Corfe Castle and travelled through Devon and Cornwall, he'd found himself thinking of her constantly. He'd kept wondering what she'd have thought of this village or that, or whether she'd have found a certain museum interesting.

So that was his answer. His reason for coming had been more than just an empty house and a lack of something to do. It had had more to do with Monica herself. It was anyone's guess whether she'd given him a single thought after they'd parted in Dorset and now any hope of romance was growing smaller by the day.

Still, it was probably a good thing. Right now they had a job to do and needed no complications.

He tried hard to concentrate. The incessant droning of the fan was making him drowsy, but he pulled himself together with an effort. This had never been a part of investigation he'd enjoyed, but this kind of background work was essential. So much of it these days relied on computers and even before they'd existed, there'd been long, tedious hours of searching through all kinds of paper records.

He'd made a certain amount of progress. He had traced Victoria Sharpston, née Ambrose, born in 1985, back through her father, Michael, who had been born in 1960 to Arthur and Jane Ambrose. Arthur had been born in 1926 to James and Mary. James had been born around 1899 and married Mary in 1923. Further back than that, however, the line became much harder to trace. Searching for the parents of James Ambrose was difficult without an exact birth date for him. None of the results which came up quite matched and Archie was getting a headache. He still had a yawningly wide gap to fill between Edmund's birth in 1802 and James' in 1899.

Victoria was boasting about having filled in all the gaps, so it had to be possible. He'd keep trying, but not today. He'd have another go when the museum was closed and he had a clearer head.

With a sigh of frustration he closed the family tree he'd started and returned to the computer's home screen. From upstairs came a burst of hilarity that sounded like canned laughter. Monica's talk was obviously going well.

He owed her better than this. From his pocket he pulled out a folded piece of paper with a drawing of knobbly knees on one side. He turned it over and attempted once more to read the few photo-copied words.

"Twenty cat baskets and misc," and then the almost illegible words from the back of the auction ticket. Roodery Shacks? Roolery Snacks? Rookery Shacks?

This little mystery intrigued Archie far more than the family tree and it was something he could get on with, headache or not. He opened the Google search screen and began to type.

SIXTY THREE

Diary of Joshua Ambrose, Saturday 22nd November 1800

A cheerful fire in an excellent library and a glass or two of Madeira can be dangerous things sometimes.

I spent a pleasant few hours this afternoon with my good friend, Mr Peckover. He gives me great encouragement with my writing, though I suspect kindness colours his appraisal of my work. It is true, however, that "First Thoughts" is doing uncommonly well, at least locally. People here share my understanding of the often harsh and bleak landscape which surrounds us.

Mr Partridge's shop in the New Market is constantly running out of stock. He sends his boy round for fresh supplies of books with pleasing regularity and this small success is balm for my melancholy and dark thoughts. I wonder sometimes whether I shall ever be free of their grip. The nights are the worst, when daytime cheerfulness has faded to black and dawn is too far away to take away the hopelessness.

But, together with the sales of my book, my conversations with Mr Peckover serve as excellent diversions.

He told me today that he has received a letter from Mr Clarkson, written from his farm in the Lake District. That admirable soul has suffered badly from exhaustion and overwork and has been quite ill, but he benefits greatly from his respite in the country with his new wife. It will be with mixed feelings, I suspect, that he moves with his family down to Bury St Edmunds, where his parents-in-law live. He plans to do so soon, and to renew his efforts against the despicable slave trade.

Mr Wilberforce, the Member of Parliament for Hull, who is such a great supporter of the anti-slavery campaign, suffered a heavy defeat of his bill in parliament several years ago, but he and his fellow abolitionists refuse to give up.

Once rested, Mr Clarkson vows to be back on the road, winning support for the cause. He is determined that the British Empire shall soon be rid of the trade that shames us all, and to free every poor mistreated soul from its evil.

Such determination in the face of so much opposition humbles me. My own inability to swim against the tide, to follow my heart's desire, is shameful. As I heard once more of Mr Clarkson's work, a puny rebellion rose within me, a sad little determination that I too should succeed.

Perhaps that is why, with the encouragement of the Madeira, I found myself speaking Susanna's name.

I have never before mentioned her in this town, not even to Sam. Yet, suddenly I was irrationally determined to keep her name secret no more. It felt good after so long to speak of her. At last, there is one person in Wisbech who understands my reluctance to marry and my indifference to every pretty face in the vicinity.

Mr Peckover, having read some of my later poems, had apparently suspected something of the sort. He believes this more recent work is worthy of publication. He adds that, even if I cannot marry where I wish, the emotion behind my words can still come to light. In his opinion, I should publish a second volume of poetry.

Still fuelled by wine and the determination to do more with my worthless life, I agreed to consider it.

In truth, the idea is not new to me. The poems I am thinking of publishing are mainly those penned in Dorsetshire. There are others too from a later time, when illness confined me to my room.

Now, free of the effects of Madeira, I must live with the fact that my secret is shared with another. I feel as sure as one could ever be, however, that my truth is safe with him.

SIXTY FOUR; Mid July 2018

All that Caper

'We need to turn right here, I believe. Parson Drove can't be far now.'

She nodded as Archie depressed the indicator switch, though there was no other car in sight, and made the ninety degree turn. It reminded her of driving with him along the lanes of Dorset, though these Fen roads couldn't have been more different.

Unlike the narrow, winding lanes of the Isle of Purbeck, where the high hedges on each side gave the impression of travelling through a tunnel, Fen roads were mostly straight. They followed the lines of the great, wide fields and were bordered by ditches, rather than hedges. And, unlike driving in the south, you could see across the fields for miles. Apart from an isolated line of trees or a distant farm building, the view was open, almost endless. You could see each junction coming up from far away. Whereas the south was hilly, leafy and hidden, this was flat, mainly treeless and open.

In a beauty competition between the two types of landscape, the Fens would have trouble coming second.

But at least you could see where you were going and Monica felt happy. Going sleuthing with Archibald Newcombe-Walker was something she never expected to experience again, yet here they were, seeking more answers to the same old mystery.

'I used the internet and looked up every variation I could think of for what was written on the back of the auction ticket,' Archie explained, bringing Monica up to date, 'and the nearest thing I could find was an advert for "Rookery Stacks," a guest house in Parson Drove. I thought it had to be worth a look.'

'Rookery *Stacks*. Of course, and being nearby, it makes some kind of sense. How finding this place could help the museum, though, I do not know.'

'Of course you don't. Neither do I, but it's worth following up every small lead. Most are dead ends, but any clue could turn out to be significant.'

Monica didn't reply, her thoughts a jumble of useless, disconnected threads. Archie appeared to be making some progress with the Ambrose family tree, but was hitting a few problems. Even if he managed to trace it all faultlessly back to Joshua, it would do nothing but prove that Victoria had a case. And presumably it had all been done before by Victoria, so they would still be no further forward. Somehow, though, Archie managed to sound optimistic. Perhaps it was easy to sound carefree, she thought crossly, when you had nothing to lose.

They were driving slowly through the long village of Parson Drove. They passed an ancient church on the right and a few old, noble looking houses on both sides of the road. This village had been the home of John Peck, Monica reminded herself, the locally celebrated diarist and farmer of the early nineteenth century. These had been his fields, his landscape, and he had tirelessly served the community here all his life.

'Do you have any idea of what the guest house looks like?' she asked, remembering that she ought to be paying more attention.

'From the advert I saw, it looked quite a narrow building,' he replied, 'the sort that stretches back from the road and is much bigger than you first think; perhaps Victorian or Edwardian.'

There were several buildings that fitted that description, but none of them had big, helpful guest house signs outside.

'Was there a house number?'

'Nope. Just Rookery Stacks Guest House.'

They had reached the end of the village without finding any sign of the place and Archie did a quick three point turn in the quiet road.

'OK, back again. This time, we'll slow right down and look a lot more carefully.'

'Don't you need a licence for this sort of thing?'

'Looking for a guest house? Hardly! I gave up my licence when I left the partnership, so I have to tread carefully, but at the moment all we're doing is exploring a bit of local history and researching public records. Nothing wrong with that.'

After several more three point turns and a lot of frustration, they finally found Rookery Stacks. The house faced away from the street, looking more as if it belonged to a narrow side road than to the main thoroughfare. Its sign was just about visible if you approached it from the right angle, but it was hardly likely to be attracting passing trade.

'Sorry, love,' said the cheerful woman behind the reception desk, 'we've no vacancies at the moment.'

She had a very short, gun metal grey haircut and was probably in her sixties. She was holding a duster and looked as if she'd been interrupted in the middle of her cleaning. The place smelled of budgies. It was an odour Archie remembered from an aunt's house he'd often visited as a boy, an aunt with a great love of small feathered pets.

'Ah, that's a pity,' he smiled, 'It looks like a nice, out of the way, quiet place to stay.'

'It is, love. I have my regulars, you see and they tend to fill the place up. People coming into the area on business, sales reps and the like. They know they can get some peace and quiet and a nice big breakfast here. I'm known for my breakfasts, in fact I....'

'Well, not to worry, I'll have to find somewhere in Wisbech then....' Archie glanced back at the woman as he began to leave. She was still standing there with her duster, still smiling and looking like she'd welcome a break and a chat. 'I love buildings of this age,' he continued, taking advantage of the situation, 'I noticed the terracotta roof finials as I got out of the car. They knew how to build in those days, didn't they? Has it always been a guest house?'

'Oh, for a long time, it has, certainly,' smiled the woman, dropping the duster on the desk and leaning with both plump elbows on the counter, 'Mother and father bought the place in the sixties and we've had it ever since. You should have seen the place then! My goodness, I was only in my teens, but I remember how run down and ramshackle it was. Lots of big, untidy animal enclosures in the back garden, tall weeds growing between them. Oh, it was such a mess! The old owners had died and the place had taken an age to sell. Reckon Dad got a bit of a bargain. Mind you, took him and Mum months to sort the place out and make it respectable again. Then we opened it as a guest house. I've been here ever since and took over the running from the parents a while back. Met the husband, he moved in. No need to move anywhere else, really....'

Archie had guessed correctly about her willingness to talk, but could see that finding out anything useful wasn't going to be his only problem. At this rate, it might prove challenging to stop her talking before nightfall.

'....and then of course it's the kids. Well, they're all settled here, moved down the road, so no way any of us will move now. My Ruby, she'll be a grandmother herself soon. Her middle daughter married a local boy and they've got a little one on the way....'

'That must be lovely....'

'Then my Peter, well he works for the farmer, same as Penny's dad did. Penny's his wife, you see. Don't suppose they'll move away neither, so I can count my blessings, not like the Catchpoles next door. Their Sonia went to New Zealand. Ooh, I'd hate that. All that caper with airports and travelling and....'

'Yes, it can be very frustrating. You mentioned animal cages at the back?'

She paused, looking affronted and disappointed that he could focus on such a minor detail, rather than the exploits, or lack of them, of her family.

'I mean,' he added hurriedly, 'I find it fascinating how a house develops and you obviously love your home. What do you think the house had been used for, why they needed all those cages?'

She smiled reluctantly.

'Well, I think it was some sort of animal place, you know....'

The telephone on her desk began to ring.

'What sort of animals?'

She picked up the phone.

'Rookery Stacks Guest House, hello....Margery! Oh, you're home now love, that's lovely....I was only saying to him last night I wondered when you'd be back, only 'cos....'

Archie gave her a quick wave and left her to it. He was losing his touch, he thought hopelessly.

Leaving the tiny reception hall, he followed the old brick path through the garden to where it turned down the side of the house and back to the road. Before leaving the garden he paused for a moment to look. His chatty informant had told him that there'd been animal cages here once, but it was hard to imagine now. The family had done a very good job in restoring peace and tranquillity to this small patch of ground. The perfume of deep red roses hung sweetly in the air, their thick, thorny stems climbing the warm bricks of the house and the drowsy buzzing of bees seemed to be everywhere. It felt like a world apart from the village road outside, even from the talkative woman inside.

In the centre of the garden stood a small statue on a plinth, surrounded by tall stemmed daisies. Archie moved closer for a better look. He smiled. The diminutive stone creature was lifting a paw to its mouth, its grooming frozen in time and captured forever.

'So,' he murmured to himself, 'this place was a cat's home.'

'That's right, dear,' erupted a voice close to his ear and almost causing him to bolt out of his skin, 'I thought I'd said. It was a cat sanctuary. A charity that took in abandoned cats. Everyone around here was sad when the owners died and the place had to shut, but my dad wasn't cut out for that sort of job, and besides....'

'Thank you, Mrs....'

'Mrs Jones. Hope to see you when you're next looking for a place.'

He shook her hand, smiling with practised charm.

'Yes, I hope so too.'

You're getting smoother by the day, he remonstrated with himself as he left the garden and found his way back to Monica in the car.

He told her about his small discovery and she nodded, showing little enthusiasm.

'But I still don't see how knowing that an ancestor of Victoria's gave some cat baskets to a cats' home is going to help us.'

'Neither do I, Monica, my dear pessimistic friend, but you just never know. Sometimes these seemingly unimportant scraps of information fall into place and add up to something worth knowing.'

'Great,' she muttered, 'so long as they get on with it.'

SIXTY FIVE

Diary of Joshua Ambrose, Monday 9th March 1801

Excellent business this morning.

This shipment of tea has proved to be a particularly good purchase and demand for it is high. Mr Anthony in the New Market has placed a good order for his coffee house and now the other establishments seem compelled to keep up with him. Mr Rudderham came in this morning to place a sizeable order and Mr Moules has asked to inspect the tea. He is always less forthcoming with his cash than the others.

Some considerable time has passed since I've written in this journal. Even now, all I have to report is dull, for these days I think of nothing but business.

I am reluctant even to work on my new collection of poems, though it is necessary that I do so. It is so very time consuming and encourages too much maudlin thought. I find it difficult to tell which compositions have true merit and which are merely sentimental foolishness. Each time I look at them, I am taken back to that other time, the time I dare no longer think about.

Since my silly outpouring to Mr Peckover last autumn, I have decided that the only way forward is self discipline and diligence.

Indulgence in memories of past happiness, however necessary it may be to prepare my work for publication, is a poor way to live. It robs a man of his good sense and pecks away at his resolution to lead a sensible life.

If I am to make the most of the situation I find myself in, if I am to marry and pass the family business on to a new generation, I must keep my head clear of old fancies. Memories of Susanna and reminders of what might have been do not help the serious task of finding a wife.

There is just one young lady I could tolerate. She is pretty enough. Miss Anderson is the daughter of a King's Lynn merchant and would bring connections of the type which make father rub his hands together in greedy anticipation.

Shall I be like him one day? Will I learn to put away old dreams and be content with a fine home and a warehouse groaning with exotic imports? Could I learn to love Miss Anderson?

But for now, whether the mood takes me or not, I must concentrate on completing my work for the new book. Mr Wildernesse, my faithful London publisher, claims to await the manuscript with eagerness. I imagine he is alluding to the large sum of money which must accompany the work. No wonder he loves my poetry! The vanity of seeing my own words in print comes at a considerable cost.

I shall call my new volume "Common Poems," in memory of a place where Susanna and I were once so happy.

SIXTY SIX; Late July 2018

Little Darlings

There were kids everywhere.

Bernadette had never imagined that they'd be so busy. When she, Monica, Angie and Archie had put up posters around town to advertise the "Seek the Smutties" children's trail, she had never expected this. She'd thought there might be a dozen or so extra visitors a week during the school holidays, but the response had been astonishing.

Perhaps it was because the timing was good; the trail had started right at the beginning of the school holidays. Or maybe, as Angie had suggested, it was because it was cheap.

Bernadette had ordered two hundred fluffy cat key rings to give out as prizes at the end of the trail. Each of them wore a red ribbon, printed with the name of the museum, around its neck, and these little prizes were surprisingly popular. She'd had to place another order already, and they were only in their second week.

As she called to Monica for more change, another family surged through the door. The three children rushed up to the desk and declared their intention to do the cat trail. Bernadette smiled at them indulgently as their mother searched through her pockets to find the right change. Even so, Bernadette's stock of pound coins was getting woefully low. She called out again and Monica eventually appeared, looking as down-beat as she had all day.

'What's up? Still shut out of your office?'

'Likely to be all day,' Monica nodded, 'You know what it's like when the trustees have one of their meetings.'

'Pity they had to choose a day when we're open. Pushing you out of your office isn't very practical, is it?'

'I suppose it was the only time they could manage,' she shrugged, 'A couple of them travelled up from London.'

'Important, then?'

Monica nodded. She looked close to tears, which was highly unusual.

'I couldn't get much out of Justin when he arrived,' she said, 'but apparently they've had a letter from Victoria's solicitors.'

'Oh hell.'

'Just what I said.'

'Are they likely to tell you what's going on?'

'Justin might later. I'll catch him before he leaves. Better get you that change.'

Monica disappeared as another group clattered through the door, the youngest children hugging teddy bears and eager to start seeking the Smutties. Once she'd handed out their tickets, Bernadette sat on her high stool behind the reception desk and leaned back against the wall. She could hear the children's excited voices as they ran upstairs in search of the first clue.

In the end, because Monica had been so busy with the trustees and the extra administration caused by their current problems, Bernadette had been the one to put the trail together. She had made the first few clues easy, to encourage the kids. Monica had insisted, however, that the children learned something about Joshua Ambrose's poetry and so the questions grew slightly harder as the trail went on. By providing ample information and clues, Bernadette hoped she'd done enough to engage the interest of a new generation.

But would future generations even be able to see inside Joshua's birthplace? Not if Victoria had anything to do with it.

The kids, whether or not they were learning anything, were certainly enjoying themselves. From all floors came the distant sounds of shrieks and giggling, of questions asked and answers given. Bernadette couldn't help smiling, despite the tension. This event was clearly a success and would bring in money. Surely that counted for something?

She knew that Monica was deeply worried, despite the help from dear old Archie. Bernadette was still unsure about him. He'd been around for a few weeks now, but seemed to have achieved precious little with his alleged detective skills. What he *was* good at, she thought with irritation, was worming his way into the everyday life of the museum. Even now, he was upstairs, supervising the kids. They should all be grateful, she thought meanly, that he hadn't ingratiated his way into the trustees' meeting and told them what to do.

By three o'clock the flow of visitors had reduced considerably and Bernadette was able to start tidying up, restacking children's books and restocking the tray of cat prizes. The house was far quieter now. Only the occasional voice reached her ears from upstairs.

It seemed a long time now since the museum's unexplained sounds had ceased. These days, when the place was empty of visitors, only the creaking of pipes and resettling of old timbers made any noise to fill the silence. Monica and Angie, of course, were relieved about the absence of whisperings and mutterings, but Bernadette sort of missed it.

Had it all stopped because Monica, courtesy of the Phenland Phantom Phinders, had finally received the message she was meant to hear? That made sense in a way, but there was little progress to show for it. Whoever it was who had stopped the whispering seemed to have uncanny trust in the abilities of the people running the place. In Bernadette's opinion, the stony faces of the trustees did nothing to inspire hope.

'Would you cover for me while I go and check upstairs?' Bernadette asked Monica when she next wandered in. Monica nodded and took her place behind the desk.

It was necessary to check the clues at the end of each afternoon, to make sure everything was still in place. Already, a few knitted cats had gone missing and Mrs Paynter was refusing to knit any more replacements. They would soon have to start using the spares bought from charity shops. Either that or tie the little critters down. Bernadette was forever finding toys stuffed into corners or lying on the floor, where the kids had chucked them.

Little darlings, thought Bernadette crossly as she retrieved a grey knitted item from behind a chair in the Reading Room. Why couldn't they just leave things where they found them?

'You've got a real cat too!' a little child chirped as she reached the top floor.

'Yes', Bernadette smiled, 'we have three, but they're all next door at the moment.' She glanced at the child's mother and continued, 'They get a bit nervous when there are a lot of visitors.'

'I can imagine,' replied the woman, 'especially when most of the visitors are five years old and tend to get over excited.' Her daughter chuckled.

'But you still have one,' the child insisted. 'She's asleep on the bed.'

'Naughty cat,' Bernadette tutted indulgently, following the child and mother into Joshua's room, 'He's not allowed on the....'

She was staring at Joshua's bed. It was mostly enveloped by shade from the long window curtains and the marmalade cat curled up on the bed seemed almost a part of the shadow. Its body, as it stirred to stretch its front paws, was becoming fainter with each passing second. By the time it had stood, yawned an almighty yawn and leapt from the bed, it had faded almost to nothing.

The woman and Bernadette exchanged looks over the child's head.

'She's gone now,' stated the little girl philosophically.

'Yes,' agreed Bernadette, 'It would seem she has.'

SIXTY SEVEN

Diary of Joshua Ambrose, Tuesday 5th May 1801

The post boy brought the parcel with the rest of the correspondence this morning. Father was away somewhere, counting his money, for all I knew, so I was able to unwrap my new book in peace.

I have to admit to pride in this volume. Mr Wildernesse has made a fine job of it. Its neatly tooled chestnut leather cover is a thing of such beauty that you could almost forgive anything found inside. Even the contents do not shame me. Perhaps I have become vain, but the reworking of these old poems seems to have been worthwhile.

Misery, melancholy, longing; they make excellent fuel for writing. The human soul at its most vulnerable has a way of creating beauty which is quite often absent in contentment. I may never offer anything of greatness to the literary world, but at least I have had the privilege of sharing my heartfelt words, my truth through poetry, when everything else is lies.

I leafed through the delicate pages and my eye fell on one.

The Walk

We walk
And nineteen thousand stars awake
To dance upon thy brow.

We tread
The darkening track of hill and vale
To reach our own quiet bower.

And time
She runs away and laughs at us,
Mocking every word.

And how
Shall we recall this ecstasy
When all is past and gone?

We'll long
For nineteen thousand shining stars
That danced and dance no more.

That danced and dance no more. The accuracy of that prediction hits me hard when I stare out of the murky office window at the dreary warehouse, while two clerks scribble away in the corner, one of them forever scratching his grubby neck.

What would I give now for shining stars? My resolve, to forget the past and to do as my family wishes, is weakening. In all honesty, it has been losing strength steadily with the passing days.

With my father's obvious approval, I have been spending a little time with Miss Anderson. It has been pleasant enough, but I have no feelings for her that are worthy of note. She is pretty, but has none of the intelligence or wit of Miss Imbridge (as was), nor the gentleness and inner beauty of my Susanna.

And so, I am determined that my ailing health will do me a service, that it will lead me back to Dorsetshire this summer. There is to be no more wavering. Miss Anderson, to be sure, has no high hopes of me. She would equally favour a dance partner of adequate fortune from her own town of King's Lynn. Besides, the assemblies are done now for the winter. She will not miss me.

My mind is quite made up. I shall seek out Susanna. If she is settled with some other lucky fellow, I shall return home and accept my lot. But if she is free and still values our time together, I shall claim her for my own.

My mother worries greatly about my health and is eager that I spend a few months in warmer climes. Father merely makes impatient noises and curses the feeble health of his disappointing son.

SIXTY EIGHT; Late July 2018

Tanned and Golden

'Just look at this!' Bernadette demanded, holding a knitted cat by one foot, 'The little buggers planted this one upside down in a vase in the sitting room with just his legs sticking out and look....'

'I notice you no longer call them little darlings,' muttered Monica, whose eyes did not budge from the computer screen on her desk.

'Monica, look at this!' Bernadette insisted, 'What the hell did they think they were doing? I'm going to have to take this home and mend it tonight.... Monica!'

Monica raised her head at last to look at Bernadette's exasperated expression and the damaged toy in her hands. The stitching which had attached the legs to the body had come undone and both back legs were hanging off. Its woollen stitched nose had also unravelled, a thick thread hanging down its face like a bad nose bleed.

'Oh, I'm sorry, Bernadette,' Monica frowned, still looking distracted, 'it's this email from Justin. More performance related questions. I just wish the trustees would tell us what's going on instead of asking more and more questions.'

'Perhaps they don't know themselves,' replied Bernadette, placing the damaged cat on the desk, 'The letter from Victoria's lawyers might just have been a warning shot. Anyway, I will finish cashing up and take this poor creature home and mend him. Good thing I have no life of my own....'

Monica gave her a tired smile.

'Not all the kids misbehave,' she reasoned to Bernadette's disappearing back, 'in fact they all seem to love it. It's a great success. You've done a fantastic job with it.'

But Monica's belated encouragement went unheard. Sounds of coins clinking in the till meant that Bernadette had shut the door and was cashing up. Monica returned to Justin's email and tried to concentrate, typing a few sentences and trying to remain positive.

The sound of determined, impatient knocking at the locked front door interrupted her again. Bernadette's voice reached her, heavily loaded with expletives. The sign outside showed pretty clearly that they were closed and the locked door emphasised the point. Surely whoever it was would give up and go away?

Apparently not. There was more knocking, more exasperated noises from Bernadette. Then there was a woman's voice, low and insistent, interacting with Bernadette's terse remarks and a child's high piping tones. A bit late for the trail; surely the kid could see that?

She went on typing.

'Monica,' Bernadette was back in the office doorway, her face a picture of long suffering, 'People to see you.'

People? Monica tutted loudly and finished typing a sentence before swinging out of her chair to walk despairingly into reception.

But she met them half way. They had almost reached her office, one of the children breaking into a run and making for the angle poise lamp on the desk. The mother called out something and the little boy stopped reluctantly, one hand still on the lamp's flexible neck.

Monica's eyes flicked from the child to the mother, looking at the woman's impossibly long, straight and perfectly groomed blond hair. Her peachy complexion was at its summertime best, tanned and golden. In fact, she always managed to look like that, whatever the season. Always tanned and always golden.

'Sorry to drop by unannounced,' said Monica's sister, 'but we were in the area and....'

'Adela,' she said, a little too flatly, 'what a lovely surprise.'

SIXTY NINE

Diary of Joshua Ambrose, Sunday 10th May 1801

Meet me, meet me, dearest love,
You know the place
Where willow reaches curtain long
And sweeps the sward where we belong
And covers every secret kiss,
Where love embraces
Sweetest bliss.

My small travelling trunk stands ready in the hall, for early tomorrow morning I shall begin my journey.

In a rare moment of indulgence, fresh from a successful meeting with a buyer of our silk, father granted me the use of the carriage. It will take me as far as Charing Cross, and from there I shall take the post chaise, the carriage being required for more important matters thereafter.

Last week I took a copy of my new book to Mr Peckover, as a parting gift. He alone knows my true purpose in travelling to Dorsetshire. He alone knows what is in my heart. He appears not to judge me, though he is fully aware of my father's wishes. He thanked me kindly for the book and wished me God speed and good fortune. I know my secret is safe with him.

I was never the less surprised when a package was brought to the house last night by one of the Peckover man servants. I opened it in some puzzlement. Inside was a small book with a cloth cover of bright blue; a volume of essays entitled "The Spirit Guiding Us" by Mr Jabez Crow. The thought occurred to me that Mr Peckover was sending me a gentle reprimand through this book of sober essays based on the Quaker philosophy he adheres to. Yet, as I opened the book, I realised he had written me a short note.

"To my dear friend Ambrose, as you travel south once more. May God go with you." Underneath he had signed it and penned in the date.

This gift means a great deal to me. It assures me of his good wishes and at the same time attempts to guide me with its philosophy. I shall keep it with me on my journey. It will provide a welcome diversion and may even help to still the turmoil in my heart.

SEVENTY; Late July 2018

A Little Miffed

So there they were, all of them in Monica's flat.

Edward, the little boy, was doing a lot of running around while Adela filled the place with her natural calm and radiance. They had ordered takeaways, Monica's fridge being unable to support any unexpected visitors. The kids had managed to smear something pink and oriental all over the kitchen worktop and on to the ear of a curiously large stuffed rabbit which dominated the sofa. Monica had taken a deep breath and tried not to complain as her sister's inadequate attempts with a damp cloth had only managed to spread the stain further into the rabbit's ear.

They were sitting down to chat now, or at least the two sisters were. Edward was still zooming up and down the long room and his baby sister was crawling around the carpet.

'So, who was the man we met in the doorway as we left?' Adela smiled craftily, 'He was less than delighted that you had surprise visitors, I could see. I think he was planning a little snuggling on the sofa with you tonight.'

They had met Archie as he'd come downstairs after a long afternoon of room stewarding. He'd found Monica on the point of leaving with her sister and family and Adela couldn't help but notice that he'd looked a little miffed.

'It's not like that at all,' Monica retorted, feeling a treacherous blush creeping over her face, 'He's a friend. He's helping me with some research, that's all.'

'Sure he is, and I'm the Fairy Queen,' Adela grinned, 'but, seriously, Mon, he seemed nice. Is he married?'

'No, divorced I think, but that's hardly relevant, I mean....'

'Just open your eyes, dear sister. He likes you.'

'No, he made it quite clear he's only here to help.'

Adela's response was a knowing look that was extremely annoying, but to her surprise, Monica found herself smiling. Her sister meant well and her way of spotting silver linings in every cloud could be infectious if you didn't watch yourself. In Adela's world, if you liked someone, they liked you in return. It was as straight forward as that and a perfect future was assured. Things just fell into place for her. They always had, and she couldn't understand that for other people, less beautiful, less perfect people, life didn't flow so easily.

To change the subject, Monica began to tell her sister about the problems facing the museum. She told her about Archie's work on the Ambrose family tree, how he'd managed now to trace it as far back as Edmund's grandson. When he'd finished, she said, he intended to look up some of the family's Wills in public records.

Described like this, things sounded pretty hopeless, yet Archie seemed to believe there'd be a breakthrough, something which could weaken Victoria's case. Adela listened attentively while Monica told her everything, nodding with a worried look while keeping one eye on her younger child. The baby was attempting to pull herself up from the carpet into a standing position, using the sofa.

'I will keep my fingers crossed for you,' Adela commented, 'I know how much the museum means to you. It's great that Archie's helping and I'm sure he'll stick around if you give him a bit of encouragement.'

'Like what?'

'Smile, Monica. Poor bloke is giving up his time for you and living expensively in a hotel meanwhile. Your dismissive manner and permanent frown can't be very encouraging. In fact....'

'How can you know?' Monica objected, 'How can you know how I look at him? You only saw him for thirty seconds.'

'Because I only needed thirty seconds to see how you are with him. As usual, you're covering up your feelings, afraid to show him how you really feel. I know you, Monica. You frighten people away with that mask of indifference. You can't expect Archie to read your mind and with so little encouragement, if you're not careful, he'll be off.'

Monica was bristling. It was the same old thing again, her elder sister telling her how to smile at the world, how if you smiled, the world granted you every wish. There was an awkward pause and Adela sighed, shifting her position on the sofa.

'I'm sorry, Mon, I didn't mean to nag. I just want you to be happy and so do Mum and Dad. They send their best, by the way.'

Monica grunted something and managed half a smile. The little girl at her feet had almost managed to pull herself up against the sofa. When the sisters had last met, during the previous November on holiday, this child had been little more than three months old. She hadn't done much more than sleep and cry, and the change in her was enormous. Monica reached down automatically to steady her and, feeling suddenly ashamed, she realised she couldn't even remember the little girl's name.

'Grace, darling, what a clever girl!' cooed Adela.

Grace, that was it. Grace. A beautiful name. Her small, pixie-like face was peering up at Monica, who had the strangest urge to pick her up. It was obvious, though, that her niece wanted to stand for herself. Her tiny hands were gripping the fabric of the sofa as her legs braced to pull herself straight. She was doing well, her back stretching and her arms reaching up as still she looked at Monica.

'I think she'd like you to pick her up,' came Adela's soft voice. Monica reached down and picked up the infant, placing her in her lap. Her little head was just below Monica's chin, her dark hair already a short mop of curls.

'She's quite small for her age,' Adela was commenting. 'The doctor said she's unlikely to be tall.'

Monica had hardly ever held a baby. She didn't really have a clue what she was doing and was sure she must be doing something wrong, yet Grace seemed thoroughly content, closing her big, brown eyes and settling down to doze on Monica's lap.

'Have you noticed?' Adela smiled, still speaking in that soft voice of hers, 'How much she looks like you? She has your eyes, your beautiful hair....'

Monica nodded, feeling foolishly tearful.

'I thought I was an oddball,' she found herself admitting, 'always the one left out. I never looked like the rest of you. I was even convinced at one point that I was adopted. Grace and I must have inherited a load of recessive genes from somewhere.'

Adela nodded and smiled.

'I *thought* you'd like to meet her.'

SEVENTY ONE

Diary of Joshua Ambrose, Monday 11th May 1801

A shabby hostelry this, but at least we are well on the way to London. We travel more swiftly in the family carriage and I am making the most of its comforts, for after Charing Cross it will be the post chaise. I am so eager to arrive, however, that I would gladly travel the rest of the way on horseback.

There is little to report about the journey so far. The late spring weather is sunny and agreeably dry, keeping the back roads free of mud, though their rutted surfaces are enough to shake a man to death as the carriage lurches and rattles along. It is not the state of travel I wish to write about, however, but the foolish thing I did before leaving home.

As a wayward child, I was often guilty of a very bad practise. On the eve of my leaving Wisbech, I found myself returning to the same childish habit. My old fruit knife was in my hand before I knew it and I was kneeling down, carving Susanna's name and the date into the skirting in the corner by my bed. It is less likely to be discovered there. I tried also to form a ring shape, but the knife slipped as I attempted to carve the rounded corners. It was a poor effort, but I meant it as a statement of my intentions.

Such foolishness! It will take more than that to make my dreams come true.

SEVENTY TWO; Early August 2018

White Missives

The place looked pretty grand, not bad at all for a care home.

Victoria brought her Jaguar to a halt by the kerb and switched off the engine, keeping the air conditioning on. She leant forward over the steering wheel to have a proper look at the place.

Lime Tree House must have been built around the beginning of the last century. With a small turret standing proud at each corner of the roof, the fancy brickwork and imposing front entrance, the house had clearly been built for a well-heeled Edwardian. Even now, it sat comfortably on its wide plot, its lawns still neatly trimmed and edged with flowering shrubs. Only the ramp, which covered half the width of the front entrance steps, provided a clue about its modern role.

The old girl must be doing all right, thought Victoria. She had to be, to have a room in a place like this. Aunt Edith must have inherited some of the family loot.

Victoria could easily have walked here from home on a summer's day as perfect as this, but she hated the heat and anyway, she didn't wish to be seen. Not yet. For now, she just wanted to look, to check the place out. There wasn't a soul on the quiet street, the only movement being the soft swaying of the topmost branches of the mature lime trees which gave the house its name.

So far, this had not been a good day. There'd been another letter, one of those slim, white missives on expensive stationery which at first she had found so exciting. They had felt like strong allies in the beginning, these updates from her lawyers, their embossed sheets so reliable and expensive in her hands. They had given her a buzz, their regular arrival convincing her that steady progress was being made. But lately, the letters had contained nothing more than invoices, and this morning's was another one of them. Just a paltry two lines long and a request for yet another payment!

It wasn't as if she'd ever been under the illusion of this being a cheap job. From the very beginning, her London lawyers had emphasised that this was no run-of-the-mill sort of case. Proving that she had a legitimate claim to the Poet's House, using archaic inheritance law, was far from straight forward. It required thorough investigation and research and only this firm, out of all those she had spoken to, had been willing to take it on. She'd felt grateful to them, had nodded in agreement when they'd mentioned the initial sum they'd need to begin their work. She'd told herself it would be worth it in the end. But since then she'd forwarded more thousands to them than she dared to think about, and judging by the tone of today's letter, this was far from the end.

She'd phoned them as soon as she'd opened the letter this morning, using her haughty telephone voice. Her lawyer was unavailable, apparently, most likely busy with a case involving sums even more eye watering than hers. His secretary had deigned to come to the phone, though, sounding even frostier than usual. Victoria had found herself wondering how long you had to practise, to perfect that cold, superior tone. The secretary's icy, staccato syllables had informed her that the situation had been made clear from the start, that this kind of work demanded a certain level of expenditure.

The secretary might as well have said that this case was always going to cost the earth. Victoria hadn't realised that the earth could be so expensive.

She had always enjoyed having money. Her father and grandfather had made huge amounts of it. They'd both been entrepreneurs, people who loved to take a risk with new projects. Sometimes, in fact many times, these gambles had failed and they'd lost serious amounts of money, but occasionally they had backed the right person, the right idea, and they had made their fortunes, one generation's added to the next.

Since inheriting her parents' money at the age of twenty, Victoria had not been obliged to work. Her wealth had doubtless been the main attraction for her waster of a husband, Mickey Sharpston. Once he'd gained free access to her money, Mickey had shown his true, unpleasant colours. She'd divorced him, of course, and her lawyers (different ones) had made sure his greedy fists hadn't held on to too much of her cash.

Victoria was used to feeling rich and, since Mickey had cleared off, independent. She'd never had to care much about how she spent her money and this confidence had fuelled her ambition to claim what she saw as her birthright, the museum. When her new lawyers had started talking about fees and expenses, she had waved it away as of no consequence.

She simply hadn't understood the enormity of this enterprise. What she'd always seen as her unshakable wealth suddenly looked a bit vulnerable. Already, she'd had to start encashing long term investments, money she had hoped not to touch, in order to pay the string of bills. At this rate she would have to get a job. Heaven forbid!

In the end, she'd slammed the phone down on the snooty cow of a secretary. Screaming profanities down the dead phone line had relieved a bit of tension, but hadn't helped much. She'd tried to calm down, to think logically.

There had to be something she could do herself, instead of relying totally on the lawyers, because for all their expensiveness they didn't seem to be getting very far.

Whenever she asked them for a progress report, their reply was invariably disappointing. They were apparently satisfied that an unbroken link existed between Joshua Ambrose and her, but that was hardly news, since she'd told them that to start with. There were other important factors, they reminded her, which had to be taken into account, and these were what they were working on.

She was not impressed. For the sort of money she was paying she expected instant results.

If only there were someone in the family she could talk to, someone who could give her advice or, even better, could supply some vital clue to help her case. But, she was an only child and had lost both parents. Her mother had had no siblings and her father had had just one brother who had gone to live somewhere in the West Country and hadn't been seen for years. Her family had gone from small to non-existent in a very short time. That was why she'd been so pleased to come across that box of family photos. It was only when looking through them that she'd remembered Great Aunt Edith, her dad's very old aunt.

But she hadn't even known whether the aunt was still alive. She couldn't recall anything about her dying, but no one had bothered to visit the old girl for years. Victoria's parents had been far too busy making and enjoying their money to give her a thought. Victoria did have one faint memory of her, however. She remembered an old, sharp voiced woman giving her biscuits, then scolding her for dropping crumbs. She recalled feeing nervous in the aunt's strange old house with its rows of creepy stuffed birds. She must have been very young; maybe five or six? So, how old would her aunt have been then? To Victoria as a child she'd seemed ancient, but she'd probably been no older than her late fifties or sixties at the time.

In her desperation to talk to a member of the family, it had seemed just possible that Aunt Edith was still alive. Victoria faintly remembered something about the aunt going into a care home and so she'd searched the local directories and on line. She'd reduced the initial long list to just the homes with familiar sounding names and then she'd begun phoning them.

Using her concerned and caring telephone voice, she'd asked each time to be put through to Miss Edith Ambrose. After a few failures and a few hasty apologies, she'd finally struck gold. Dialling the ninth number on her list, she'd received a cheerful assent and, before she'd known it, she was being connected with the old lady's room. She'd put the phone down in a hurry.

But now she knew that Aunt Edith was alive and where she was living; Lime Tree House, an exclusive home for the elderly and a veritable Edwardian pile.

But she wouldn't go in today. Today she was too angry with the world to pay a visit. She didn't want to put the old lady off right from the start.

She would return tomorrow.

SEVENTY THREE

Diary of Joshua Ambrose, Thursday 14th May 1801

This journey is determined to be a slow one. The weather turned to rain as soon as we were out of London and the roads rapidly deteriorated. Already, on more occasions than I care to count, the driver and I have been obliged to push the chaise out of the mire of these narrow lanes.

My driver is a melancholy soul who predicts that conditions will worsen, the nearer we get to the coast. But however slow our progress, however uncomfortable and dreary, with every turn of the wheel I am aware of our steady advancement towards Ponders Mullen.

One more stop now, one more night at another draughty inn with poor food, and we should be in Wareham by tomorrow. My good aunt promises me that her carriage will be there to meet me. From her, I shall soon learn how Susanna does. It is true that a letter could equally have obtained the same truth and saved the bother of this journey, but for some reason I cannot explain, I need to be there and find out for myself. If I find nothing but sorrow, then so be it.

Even if she is wed and there is no future for us, I would like to see my Susanna once more. Even for such sweet misery, my journey would not be wasted.

But, dear Lord, let her be unwed and thinking of me still.

SEVENTY FOUR; Early August 2018

Spikes Everywhere

Outside, though it was only three o'clock in the afternoon, the sky was rapidly darkening.

July had been hot and dry and the museum had done well from it, but now, on this first Tuesday of August, it was as if time had been called on good weather and the air was heavy with change. Outside in the yard, the birds seemed to sense it, reacting to the ponderous dark banks of cloud with nervous twittering and uneasy, darting flight.

Archie had Monica's office to himself, having been left to get on with his research while she tidied up in the cellars. In reception, Bernadette was dealing with a steady but reduced flow of visitors. Every few minutes Archie heard her voice ring out, merry and welcoming, as children went in search of knitted cats, their excited giggling filling the house.

In the distance he heard the first muffled sounds of thunder, and upstairs the children heard it too, answering each rumble with squeals. It was hard to know whether they were sounds of fear or excitement. The sky felt loaded with warning. It had to rain soon; tension was building to the point where a downpour would almost be a relief.

Archie pulled the sheet of paper out of the printer tray and glanced once more at the Ambrose family tree which had taken him so long to complete. After so much time and effort, all the thing did was to confirm what Victoria already knew. He'd found no weakness in it. With its direct links from Joshua's birth in 1770 to Victoria's in 1985, he might as well have added a few armorial shields and given it to Victoria as a birthday present.

He realised he was shaking his head as he looked at the family tree. He needed a breakthrough fast because soon he had to be gone. He couldn't stay in Wisbech much longer, not with a mounting hotel bill and an increasing sense of pointlessness.

He had almost given up with Monica. Being near her was like trying to get close to a hedgehog. He must have been nuts to believe he'd ever get anywhere with that prickly yet endearingly lovely woman. Every time he drew near, it felt as if she curled herself up in a ball, spikes everywhere. Sometimes, though, in a few quiet moments, he had sensed her looking at him. At such times he'd felt sure he hadn't misjudged the situation, that there was still hope. But then, if he went even so far as to ask her to dinner, she came out with a hasty brush-off. And the rest of the time she was just too busy or too wrapped up in her worries, even to notice he was there.

Yet, besides all that, his purpose in coming here had been a sincere wish to help. And after all the promises he'd made, he really needed to pull something good out of the bag. If things never worked out with Monica, at least he would have the satisfaction of having helped her.

He still had the family Wills and inheritances to look into, but apart from that he was stuck. His only option for now was to get on with the Wills and hope for a breakthrough. He put the family tree down and returned to the laptop. After a quick search, he found the government site he needed and began to work.

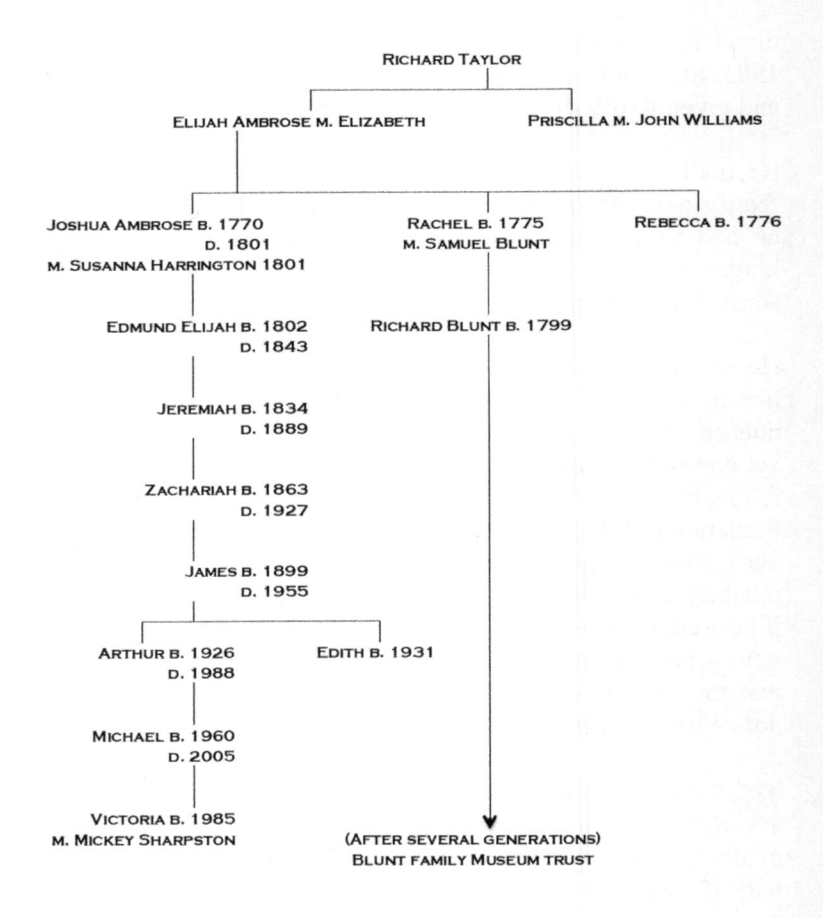

```
                          RICHARD TAYLOR
                ┌──────────────┴──────────────┐
    ELIJAH AMBROSE M. ELIZABETH        PRISCILLA M. JOHN WILLIAMS

    ┌─────────────────┬─────────────────────┐
JOSHUA AMBROSE B. 1770      RACHEL B. 1775        REBECCA B. 1776
      D. 1801               M. SAMUEL BLUNT
M. SUSANNA HARRINGTON 1801
      │                           │
EDMUND ELIJAH B. 1802       RICHARD BLUNT B. 1799
      D. 1843
      │
JEREMIAH B. 1834
      D. 1889
      │
ZACHARIAH B. 1863
      D. 1927
      │
JAMES B. 1899
      D. 1955
  ┌───┴────┐
ARTHUR B. 1926    EDITH B. 1931
  D. 1988
  │
MICHAEL B. 1960
  D. 2005
  │
VICTORIA B. 1985
M. MICKEY SHARPSTON         (AFTER SEVERAL GENERATIONS)
                            BLUNT FAMILY MUSEUM TRUST
```

He was familiar by now with the entailment provisions which had controlled the passing of the Poet's House only to legitimate male heirs. Because the family had apparently been unaware that Joshua had a son, the house had passed to his nephew, Richard Blunt. From there, it had eventually passed to the current owners, still called Blunt, who had created a trust and opened the house as a museum.

However, had the family known about Joshua's son Edmund, the entailment provisions would have dictated that the house passed to him. From Edmund it would have passed down the Ambrose line which Archie had so painstakingly researched, eventually to Victoria.

But in 1925 the Law of Property Act had been introduced and entailment laws had been abolished. From then on, inheritance of the property would have depended on each subsequent owner's Last Will and Testament.

Archie had to check, therefore, all the Wills on record since 1925.

Using the assumption that, had everything been done correctly, the house would have passed down the Ambrose line as far as 1925, Archie now needed to see what was written in the Wills after that date.

Presumably, Victoria's lawyers had done this already. It had to have been one of the first things they'd checked, but still it was worth looking at.

The owner of the family property at the time of the law change in 1925 had been James Ambrose, born in 1899. Using the details he'd researched, Archie began filling in the relevant boxes on the screen before clicking on the search icon. A number of records under the name of James Ambrose appeared in a matter of seconds and he went carefully through them, choosing the one which fitted best. He then went through the procedure of ordering a copy of the Last Will and Testament for James, before returning to the search screen to work on the next generation.

James had had a son, Arthur, Victoria's grandfather, in 1926. He had died in 1988. Again, using the information to hand, Archie completed the boxes on the screen for

Arthur. He ordered a copy of his Will before proceeding to his son, Michael, Victoria's father. He had been born in 1960 and had died in 2005, aged forty four. Again, Archie looked him up and ordered a copy of his Will.

With three documents ordered and paid for, Archie's initial satisfaction faded when he realised that he now had to wait ten working days before he received anything.

Another ten days, and not a single lead to work on in the meantime. He leaned back in the chair and sighed, listening to the rolling of thunder. The air was thick and muggy and even with all the windows open, the room was hot and stuffy.

Idly, he stretched out his hand and picked up a new silver photo frame from Monica's desk. He found himself smiling. Monica, who had never seemed to bother with family photographs, suddenly had one in her office. It was a very smiley picture; an attractive couple confidently posing with their two children. There was a fair haired boy of about five standing in front of his beaming father, and a dark haired baby girl, who seemed to be laughing at some tremendous joke, on her mother's knee.

What had caused such a change of heart in Monica? She'd said nothing about the visit from her sister that evening, but that was hardly surprising. She'd practically stopped confiding in him altogether. But something had made her put this photo in a hallmarked silver frame. Had her family at last found a way through those hedgehog prickles of hers?

If so, Archie considered as he rose from the chair to stretch his legs, it was a good thing. She might well need the support of her family soon. Already, her spirits had hit rock bottom because she was anticipating the loss of her museum, her job. Everything. However well the children's trail or any other event went, she knew the doors would soon be closing to visitors for good.

And Archie was no longer sure he could stop it happening. He had to go home; his time here was over.

SEVENTY FIVE

Diary of Joshua Ambrose, Saturday 16th May 1801

How good it is to be here again, back in the fresh green of the Purbeck Hills. How comforting too to be back in the village of Ponders Mullen, its old stone mellow in the May sunshine.

And most of all, how happy it is to see my dearest aunt once more and to hear all the local news.

The final part of my journey was comfortable enough, carried as I was in the luxury of my aunt's carriage from Wareham. I am grateful, however, that the travelling is done for now. The inns along the way were mostly damp and I fear were the cause of another bout of this wretched cough. I caught my aunt peering at me with some anxiety as we sat together this evening. Perhaps she caught me observing her too, for I see her health is not at all improved since I was last here. She seems always short of breath and every small exertion seems to tax her.

Whatever her own problems, she continued to look at me in concern. I wondered as we sat and sipped tea whether this was merely to do with my health or some news not yet imparted. For by then I had been back in my Aunt Williams' home for five or six hours without a single word being spoken on the subject dearest to my heart.

The maid Lizzie came in with more tea and still there was no mention of the Harrington family. I was assuming that my aunt continued to send help to Mrs Blackstock and must therefore have news of the lady's niece, but the minutes stretched by without the smallest reference to the family.

No matter how many savouries we ate or how much tea we drank, no matter how much I heard of Farmer Brownwig's prize flock of sheep or Mrs Peartree's bad teeth, we came no closer to any word of Susanna. I began to suspect that this was deliberate, but whether it was thanks to my aunt's teasing or a sterner reason to make me suffer, I could not be sure.

In the end, I had to be plain about it and ask after Mrs Blackstock. My aunt smiled and assured me that the lady's health was improved and that Mrs Mollifer's sister was well settled as her servant. This reminder of the Blackstocks seemed to unblock a torrent of information from my aunt, but my encouraging smile must have frozen on my lips as I came to appreciate her ability to describe the most trivial thing at length. I endured a full description of Mrs Blackstock's embroidery and her production of linen items, and by the time she had launched into exuberant praise of the lady's bramble jelly, I suspected my aunt of enjoying herself at my expense.

So, I had no choice but to ask outright about Miss Harrington. I was rewarded with an instant change in my aunt's countenance, complete with pursed lips and a wagging finger.

'Miss Susanna Harrington,' she pronounced with a degree of frost I'd scarcely thought possible in her, 'has had two proposals of marriage in the last twelve months. Both were from neighbouring farmers with good connections and both matches would have brought her family a degree of prosperity. Both young men were decent, pleasant looking, honest sorts and her family was hopeful that she would accept one of them. In either case she would have lived only a short distance away. The situation would have been ideal.'

My aunt paused, her hands folded neatly in her lap. I wondered whether she were preparing me for a painful conclusion, but the only emotion I could detect in her was one of suppressed anger.

'And what did she decide?' I shouldn't have asked, since her face gave me enough clues, but I needed to have it spelled out.

'She refused them both, nephew. Against the wishes of her family, she turned her back on both of them. The silly creature declared she would not marry without love! What, I ask, does love have to do with a situation like that? Of course, her real problem might have had something to do with the fact that two years ago a wealthy, careless fool arrived here and played with her affection, promising her I dread to think what, before remembering that he was committed elsewhere.'

A truly deserved reprimand. Anger filled the room and for a while neither of us spoke. My Aunt Williams is a good, gentle soul who rarely sparks to fury, but my conduct has caused her distress enough to do so. Whenever I imagined the effect of my actions on Susanna, I never allowed for the hurt and shame inflicted on my aunt.

I could only apologise in the most humble way. I must find Susanna now, not only to gladden my own selfish heart, but to right the great wrong I have committed.

I shall leave tomorrow, as soon as it is light.

SEVENTY SIX; Early August 2018

A Squeal of Hinges

The air was very still, dark clouds crowding the sky. Even to someone who didn't normally notice them very much, their heaviness was oppressive.

Victoria parked right outside Lime Tree House, a few feet away from the kerb. She'd never been very good at parking and today she could hardly be bothered with it at all. She aimed her key fob casually at the Jaguar as she left it, pressing the small black button and vaguely hoping the car was locked.

She strode up to the imposing front door and rang the bell, waiting in the heavy stillness of late afternoon. When, after a few seconds there was no response, she pressed the bell again, giving it a couple of good blasts to make sure someone heard. Still she waited, fidgeting impatiently on the doorstep before giving the bell another three sharp presses.

At last there came the sound of hurried footsteps from inside the building and the door was yanked open. A flustered face peered out at her.

'Yes?'

Victoria couldn't imagine why the woman sounded so rude and snappy.

'I have come to visit my great aunt,' she announced, 'Miss Edith Ambrose.'

'Better come in, then.' The woman shut the door behind the visitor and turned the key in the lock. She pointed at a large, open book on the hall table, 'Sign in, please.'

The aroma of cooking sprouts hung in the air and Victoria sniffed distastefully before scrawling her name on the page. She was rather disappointed. She'd expected the place to be as smart inside as it was outside, all fine carpets and gleaming ornaments, like the Hollywood mansions you saw in films.

'Miss Ambrose's room is upstairs, second on the right. Please do not stay with her long. She's very frail now and gets tired easily, though she's just had her afternoon nap and might be able to chat for a few minutes. Her dinner will be served, in any case, in half an hour.'

Victoria nodded and walked up the once elegant stairway, ignoring the wide, ugly lift which had been installed to the left. The stairs were carpeted in brown, horrible, hard wearing material and the paint on the banisters was chipped.

Outside the old lady's room she paused to collect her thoughts before giving the door a couple of sharp raps. The seconds ticked by without response, so, sighing heavily, she knocked again, more insistently this time. When still there was no reply, she opened the door cautiously and peered inside.

The gaunt face which glared at her from the high backed chair by the window wasn't familiar to her, but then it had been a long time. The woman looked extremely old and frail, as if the slightest breeze might blow her over.

'Come in, why don't you?' the old lady was grumbling, 'You people never wait to be asked, so just get on with it....' She screwed up her face suddenly, realising that her visitor was not one of the carers, 'Who are *you*?'

Victoria walked across to her, holding out her hand.

'I'm Victoria, Great Aunt Edith, you know, Michael's daughter.' She dropped her hand when it became obvious that her aunt wasn't going to take it.

Edith Ambrose seemed to be taking a long time to process this information.

'Michael's daughter, you say? You mean my brother Arthur's granddaughter?'

'That's right, auntie. I thought I'd come to see you.'

The old woman laughed suddenly, a squealing sound that was a bit alarming.

'Oh, you did, did you? And what prompted that, may I ask? Is it because I'm about to snuff it? I haven't seen hide nor hair of any of my beloved family since they put me in here five years ago. They sold my house to pay the fees for this place and Gawd knows how much longer that'll last. I suppose you've come to tell me the money's run out? I suppose you're dumping me on the scrap heap, or should I say an even worse scrap heap than the one I'm on already?'

'What? No!' Victoria tried hurriedly to work out who would have sold the old lady's house and paid the fees here. It could only, she thought, have been her dad's brother, the uncle who went to live in Cornwall or somewhere. She couldn't even remember what he looked like. 'No, auntie,' she continued more calmly, 'No one is trying to make you move out of here....'

'Well, that's a pity. Food's ruddy awful. Perhaps the council place would have been better after all.'

Victoria ignored this contradiction and sat down in a high backed chair while her aunt fumbled with the switch on the small table lamp by her side. The room had been growing progressively darker as the storm outside rumbled ever closer and the sudden lamplight brought the bony face into sharp relief. It seemed to Victoria like an eerie presence floating in a bubble of light.

'So, then, great niece, what do you want? Let me see. I last saw you when your father brought you to visit when I was living in Elm. I quite liked your father, though he hardly ever came to see me. Better than his brother by far and I was sorry when he kicked the bucket. You were a small thing then, all pigtails and freckles, but a bit full of yourself, even then. So why, I repeat, have you come to see me for only the second time in our lives?'

Victoria swallowed hard. She hadn't expected an easy chat, but the old woman was making this harder than it needed to be.

'Well,' she began hesitantly, starting to relate the version of events she'd thought up earlier, 'I've been researching the Ambrose family tree and have hit a few snags. I just wondered what you remembered of family Wills, things like that....'

'Wills! Ah, now we're getting to the point, aren't we?' She squealed with laughter, hurting Victoria's ears, 'Wasn't your inherited fortune enough for you? After a bit more are you? Well, I can tell you that everything was handed down correctly, according to all final Wills and

Testaments. And I don't blame my father at all for what he did, if that's what you're getting at.'

'Your father?'

'Bit of a parrot, are you?'

Victoria ignored her tone and ploughed right on. It was even darker outside now, the growl of thunder louder. The pool of light illuminating the old lady's head was spreading further across the room, showing up the nylon threads in the cheap carpet.

'I wasn't aware that your father, my great grandfather....James? I wasn't aware that he'd done anything....'

'Oh, aren't you? Well, you're the only one then. For years that's all anyone spoke about. They thought he was an old devil for cutting off his son and heir, but he had good reasons, I can tell you. Put the light on, will you? I can hardly see; it's so damned dark in here.'

'It's already on. Cutting him out? You mean his son Arthur, my Granddad?'

'Who else? My dear brother, Arthur. While I was forced to stay at home and look after our father, Arthur was away all over the place, doing his deals, as he called them. But all he appeared to be doing was gambling his money away, backing unlikely projects and losing a fortune every time. Arthur didn't even come home to see father when he was really ill, even though on one occasion the thoughtless idiot was only living in Leicester. Meanwhile, I could feel my youth slipping away as I went on nursing father. I didn't really *resent* the time I spent with him. He was a lovely man, never lost his appreciation for what anyone did for him. It was just for so very long. All my girlhood friends were getting married and leading exciting lives while I was simply growing old.... I grew old looking after father while Arthur mucked about and threw his money after bad causes.'

'But Granddad *made* money! Some of his projects must have been good bets!' Victoria protested wildly, the real implication of what she was hearing not yet sinking in.

'Perhaps later, yes. But all father and I saw was that he would go on all his life wasting any money he got his hands on. Father thought that if Arthur inherited the family money as well, it would just be gambled away.'

'Granddad was not a gambler! You talk as if he spent his life in casinos and betting shops! He worked hard and so did my dad after him!'

'Maybe so,' acknowledged the old lady, 'I'm just telling you the reasons for father's decision to cut Arthur out of his Will.'

The truth finally hit Victoria like a body blow. For a moment she couldn't speak. She felt the colour drain from her face and saw the old woman watching her with obvious enjoyment.

'So....you took the lot, did you?' Victoria managed at last to squeak, 'I bet you were pleased with yourself, dripping all that poison about your brother into your father's ear while you were playing Florence Nightingale. No wonder you're living so well here!'

'Watch your tongue, girl. You know nothing about my circumstances. My money was hard earned. When father died in 1955, I went to work as a secretary and continued to do so until I was sixty. Yes, I did inherit from father, not that it's any of your business, but it was just a modest amount to compensate me for the years I'd given up to look after him. The money which funds this place is my own life savings and the money from my house. And my pensions, of course.'

'So where....who inherited?'

'You mean you really do not know? Did neither your grandfather nor your father tell you?'

'No....' Victoria's voice had become very quiet.

'Well, it was the Rookery Stacks Cat Sanctuary. That's where the Ambrose money went.'

'The *what?*'

Miss Ambrose smiled the broadest smile she had managed in years.

'Father loved animals and there was this place over in Parson Drove which took in neglected creatures. It was mainly cats at first, hence the name, but gradually they began helping all sorts of animals abused and neglected by people. Dad saw all this money being wasted by his son, while those good people were doing what they could to help so many poor creatures. They were running the place on a shoe string and father wanted to help them, so, apart from a few small legacies, he left his money to the cat sanctuary.'

'The Ambrose fortune went to a cats' home....' Victoria's voice was barely audible.

'It certainly did. The place isn't there anymore, of course. The people who ran it died in their eighties and other sanctuaries took over the work. Humanity was gradually becoming a little more aware of its responsibilities towards its fellow creatures by then.'

'I don't believe it,' whispered Victoria. The old lady, whose hearing didn't seem to have diminished much with age, caught the comment and laughed.

'No and I don't expect Arthur could either! You should have seen his face when they told him about the Will! I couldn't help but notice he managed to turn up *that* time! It was priceless! He even tried to get me to halve the small legacy I'd been given. I'm surprised you never heard about it. Maybe it was pride....'

'And maybe,' snarled Victoria, 'He just made his own money and thought damn the lot of you!'

'Yes, could be you're right,' Miss Ambrose acknowledged philosophically, 'Oh, but don't just take my word for it. Pass me that tin from over there, will you? Damned carers keep moving it, putting it away while I'm asleep. Bloody interfering lot.'

Victoria fetched the biscuit tin the old woman was pointing at, from a table near the fireplace, and passed it to her. She watched as Aunt Edith opened the tin lid with a rusty squeal of hinges and leafed through papers, carefully easing out one folded sheet. She gave it a quick glance before handing it to Victoria.

'Here. Keep it for your research. I won't be needing it anymore.'

Victoria didn't really want to take it, but felt her fingers close around the stiff old paper. It had been typed out in official language; a professionally produced Last Will and Testament, and the name Rookery Stacks Cat Sanctuary stood out clearly from the page. She rose to her feet a little unsteadily and looked one last time at her great aunt.

'I don't suppose we'll meet again,' the old lady was saying, 'I'm sorry for your disappointment. None of this was your fault.'

'No,' replied Victoria, 'But I suspect you had a great deal to do with it. Good bye, Aunt Edith.'

She hardly remembered reaching the street outside or driving the car home. She was hardly aware of the low banks of leaden cloud or the flashes of lightning that forked the sky. It was finished. All her hopes, her dreams for regaining the museum, were dead.

The passing down the line of the Ambrose fortune from the early 1800s, despite everything she had believed, had been interrupted long ago. Having survived intact for over a hundred years, it had been thrown away by an old man who resented his son's entrepreneurial spirit. Yet no one had breathed a word of it to her.

Despite what she'd said, she suspected Aunt Edith was right, that her grandfather Arthur's pride had made him shrug off his disinheritance and had spurred him on to make plenty of money for himself. No wonder he had disposed of the old family photographs! Perhaps he'd never even told his own son, Michael, about his loss and disappointment.

The money which Michael had inherited had not been the original Ambrose money at all, but a new fortune made by

Arthur. Michael had added to it through his own endeavours, and passed it on his death to Victoria.

So, why on earth had her expensive lawyers not found out about this long ago and stopped wasting her money? Were they perhaps trying to find a way around it? But there was no way. It was over. In order for her to prove a legal right to the Poet's House, she had to show a continuous line of inheritance through the family, and that line had ended in 1955 with her great grandfather's actions.

If anyone had the right to the museum, it was the now defunct cat sanctuary.

So her lawyers could go begging for their cheque. She was so furious and disappointed that she hardly knew what to do with herself. She paced around the house, putting the kettle on and then forgetting it, throwing herself at last on the bed and giving in to angry tears.

In the morning she would write to her lawyers, putting an end to their research and action. Then she would make an official complaint against them. They wouldn't know what had hit them. Through her sobs, she was already composing in her head the most deadly and damaging sentences for her letter.

Outside, hard and heavy, the rain at last began to fall.

SEVENTY SEVEN

Diary of Joshua Ambrose, Sunday 17th May 1801

The journey to Lower Beckton was a comfortable one, thanks to a last minute intervention by my aunt. In the early hours, just as I was about to order the chaise, Aunt Williams offered me the use of her carriage. I had expected no such favours, but her good nature overcame her dissatisfaction with my conduct and made my travelling easier. I left her a copy of my new book to read while I am away and she seemed pleased to receive it.

By midday I was standing before The Swan Inn at Lower Beckton. I left my aunt's driver to stable the horses and to please himself for an hour or so, while I went the rest of the way on foot.

I was hoping that, like all good folk around here, the Harringtons had completed their church-going for the day and that I might find them at home. Other than that, I had no plan.

Following the landlord's directions, it was only a short walk along the lane to the Harringtons' farm. By the time the house with its thatched, low eaves came into view, my shoes were wet and heavily caked with mud. The lane was too narrow in places for avoidance of the wide puddles and seas of mud to be possible, but that was nothing compared to the churning state of my heart and mind.

And then, turning the last corner, there it was, Susanna's home. The yard which surrounded the house was a neat, well-ordered looking place with a number of animal byres and a family of contented looking hens clucking over scattered grain. The house itself was not elegant, but like the out-buildings, looked solidly built of local stone, its upper windows set into the thatch in a very pleasing manner.

I stood in the yard for a minute or two, my indecision in as bad a state as my shoes. Like the coward I am, I was delaying the moment when my hopes could well be dashed once and for all. Finally, cursing my foolishness, I kicked off the worst of the mud and strode forward to knock at the door.

Before I reached it, however, a movement from the side of the house caught my eye. Around the corner bustled a figure carrying a basketful of vegetables for the kitchen. Her hair was escaping its loose knot and one side of her gown was hitched up and gathered in her belt. She stopped abruptly as she saw me and then the contents of the basket were spilling on the ground as her hands flew up to cover her mouth.

I hurried to her, gathering up turnips and potatoes and dropping them into her fallen basket. And then I turned my attention to her, to the beloved face behind the soil blackened hands, and then she was in my arms.

She was weeping, my Susanna. She was weeping because this fool of a merchant, who had been too cowardly to do his heart's bidding, had returned at last.

As we walked and talked throughout that long, wondrous afternoon, she told me that in her heart she'd always known I would return. Far wiser than I, then!

A man cannot delay for so long and then reappear without making his intentions clear, and so I waited no longer. Mrs Harrington, a strict, hard working yet kindly woman, released her daughter from her duties for the afternoon. We were free to wander, to plan the future and to talk of all that had passed. All our troubles, fears and obstacles seemed to melt away in the May sunshine.

I had to wait until Susanna's father was finished in the fields before I could speak to him. Sunday or not, a farmer's care of his animals cannot be neglected.

He must have looked at this puny body with its pale, soft hands and wondered what sort of husband I would make for his daughter. Perhaps, however, my good prospects and his wish to see his daughter finally and happily settled played their part. I found Mr Harrington to be a man of good sense, and from what I heard at the inn, he is well thought of and respected in this rural community.

Susanna and I are to be married in a month's time. I must return to Ponders Mullen tomorrow in my aunt's carriage and then I shall come back and take a cottage here, in Lower Beckton.

There is much to do and it will be best done from here, rather than from Aunt Williams' home. It grieves me to acknowledge it, but I cannot share my good fortune yet with her. Such tidings are best left until we are wed, when the spread of news can no longer prevent our marrying.

My happiness is so great that it eclipses every past misery and though I know there will be problems to be faced, I have no care for them today.

My face hardly knows how to stop its smiling.

SEVENTY EIGHT; Mid August 2018

Multi-Coloured Mayhem

Monica was standing by the office door and for once she was smiling at him. That, he thought, was as far as things ever went. And even the smiles weren't as dazzling as they had been at the start.

If anything, in the last couple of weeks she'd become even more prickly, shrugging off any attempt of his to take her out or put a casual arm around her. It was all pretty hopeless and time to call it a day.

Sometimes, though, he still saw a glimmer of hope. Occasionally, she apologised for her unfriendliness, explaining that with everything going on, she couldn't really be herself. Whatever that meant.

'There's an email for you,' she was saying as she watched him open the laptop and enter her password, 'I haven't opened it and wondered if it's the information you've been waiting for.'

'I hope so. It's been a couple of weeks now.'

Angie called something from the kitchen and Monica disappeared, leaving him to scroll down the list in the mail box until he found the item he was looking for.

There it was at last, the reply from the government records service with the documents he had requested. Archie clicked on the attachment and after a couple of seconds the Last Wills and Testaments of James, Arthur and Michael Ambrose began to fill the screen.

He reached with one arm to switch on the desk lamp without taking his eyes off the screen. Outside, the sky was an unpromising flat white, packed with clouds and too indifferent either to rain or to cheer up. The lamplight lifted the gloom a little, redistributing the shadows into new corners.

He looked at the oldest Will first, that of James Ambrose, who had died in 1955. His eye followed the long paragraphs of legal wording, trying to get to the point. As James' wishes slowly unfolded, Archie stared more and more incredulously at the screen. He went on reading, gathering information with increasing disbelief. There was a lot of it; it seemed the old man had loved the sound of his own wishes, and when Archie finally reached the end of the document he sat back in the chair and took a deep breath.

Monica had to know this. He needed to find her.

Bernadette looked up without smiling as he entered reception.

'Is Monica about?' he asked.

'I think she went to the shop. Angie needed something for the kitchen. She'll be back in a minute or two....ah, hello again,' she interrupted herself, smiling as a woman and child entered the room from upstairs, 'Did you manage to find all the Smutties today?'

'Yes, even the one hidden in the flower pot,' replied the little girl. Bernadette raised her eyes to the ceiling. The group of noisy kids who'd been in earlier had obviously been mucking about with the clues and toys again. She smiled indulgently as the child selected another fluffy cat key ring prize for her collection.

'Thank you,' smiled the five year old with practised politeness, 'she wasn't there today though.'

'She?' prompted Bernadette.

'The orange cat on the bed. She's my favourite. I looked for her, but she wasn't there today. The grey ones were....' the little girl opened her arms to express herself, '*everywhere*, but no orange one. Not today.'

'Ah,' acknowledged Bernadette, realising what she meant, 'No, she isn't always there. She, err, moves around a lot.'

The mother and Bernadette exchanged smiles and then the visitors were leaving with a cheery wave and promises to return soon.

'What was all that about?' asked Archie when the door had closed behind them.

'Oh,' Bernadette shook her head dismissively, 'You wouldn't want to know.'

'Wouldn't I? What makes you think that?'

Bernadette's constant refusal to have anything to do with him, even after weeks of working together in a small team, was really getting on his nerves now.

'Look, it's nothing. Those visitors came a few weeks ago and the little girl told me about a cat lying on Joshua's bed. I was clearing up after the trail as usual and went into the bedroom, ready to shoo one of the Smutties off the bed. Only it was none of our cats lying there.'

'Go on....' Archie was frowning, clearly listening, and she was encouraged enough to continue.

'A cat was there all right, but a sort of marmalade colour and very indistinct. And I swear to you, as crazy as this sounds, it disappeared. It just faded away to nothing before our eyes.'

Archie's frown had deepened. He'd heard some things in his time, but....

'Oh, I knew you wouldn't believe it,' Bernadette blurted angrily, 'You're as sceptical about it all as Monica. That's why I never told her about the cat. She was relieved when all the muttering and whatever stopped after that visit from the Phenland Phantom Phinders, even though we received messages that night which could only have come from Joshua himself. That evening, I tell you, even Monica couldn't find any "logical" explanation for what was said, and now this marmalade cat....'

'Why assume I'm a sceptic? Actually, I like to keep an open mind and I'm not about to dismiss out of hand what you're saying.'

She nodded uncertainly, clearly regretting telling him.

'OK, well I saw what I saw, and so did the little girl. We couldn't both have imagined it.'

'I didn't say you did,' smiled Archie, 'As I said, I keep an open mind.'

'Well maybe,' Bernadette allowed herself the smallest of smiles, 'you aren't quite as bad as I thought you were.'

'Bet he's over the moon to hear that,' remarked Monica, as she entered through the front door, wiping her feet on the mat.

'Monica,' said Archie, the smile leaving his face completely, 'Have you got a minute?'

She looked at him and nodded silently, sensing bad news. She took off her jacket, folding it with exaggerated care over her arm.

They were all startled as the door burst open, shoved with such force that it thudded against one of the toy displays and missed Monica's arm by millimetres. The impact disturbed a box full of bouncy balls, sending them pinging and pounding all over the place in multi-coloured mayhem.

'Oh Victoria, not now!' groaned Monica.

Bernadette ignored the visitor and went chasing after the acid green and bright pink balls, thinking that this might have been funny had it not been so ominous.

Victoria looked like she hadn't slept in a week. Her hair, always favouring the greasy look, was even more firmly plastered to her forehead than usual and her summer dress was a creased mess of faded poppies and little red bows.

Monica and Archie were staring at her in unified and fearful expectation. Bernadette gave up with the balls and she too stopped to await some kind of announcement. They were joined by Angie, who ran in from the kitchen.

Victoria took a deep breath and prepared herself for her speech.

'This morning,' she enunciated, 'I have been in communication with my lawyers.' She paused for effect, looking at each of her audience in turn before continuing, 'and as of today they will no longer be acting on my behalf. I have terminated my contract with them. I am no longer pursuing a claim to this property.'

No one reacted for the long seconds it took for her words to sink in.

'You mean,' responded Monica at last, 'that you're giving up? Just like that?'

'I mean you can *keep* your museum.' She managed to make this simple statement sound mildly insulting.

'But what about your inheritance?' Monica just couldn't understand and couldn't help asking. Victoria looked impatient now, angry.

'My inheritance? If anyone had the right to inherit this, it would have been a load of cats which kicked the bucket years ago. My great aunt kindly informed me shortly before her death that, even had the entailment of this house been correctly dealt with, it would simply have ended up in the possession of a cats' home. And even that cats' home has gone. So, as I said, Monica, you can keep your museum. And I am suing my lawyers for every penny they've got!'

At last her audience was reacting; laughing, incredulous, the three girls all hugging each other. Only Archie stood still, staring at Victoria. She met his look and shrugged.

'So, what now, Mr Newcombe-Walker? Time to move on? What's next on your agenda?'

He only stared back at her. No one else seemed to have heard, being too busy congratulating each other on their sudden change of fortune.

And then, quite incredibly, Monica hugged him. In fact, she was practically throwing herself into his arms. She'd hugged everyone else in her relief and joy, her normal reserve temporarily cast aside, and she obviously wasn't too shy to include him in her celebration. He made the most of it, holding her close for a moment before she sprang free again.

When he looked back towards the door, Victoria was on the verge of leaving.

'Err....sorry about your aunt,' Angie said, thinking she ought to. Victoria made a scoffing sound in reply before flouncing out, leaving the door wide open.

From somewhere in the house came the sound of whispering, intense, excited whispering, but everyone ignored it.

SEVENTY NINE

Diary of Joshua Ambrose, Wednesday 3rd June 1801

The cottage I have taken is a pleasant enough place on the main road, close to the Swan. It is tolerably pretty and as good a place as any for a couple to begin their married life in. I have hired two servants; a housemaid and a man to tend the small garden. We have no need of more, Susanna and I.

For we cannot remain here long. Once married, we shall only have the summer; after that I must look to my responsibilities in the Fens.

Much has passed since I last wrote in this journal.

I know now I was right to keep my news from my aunt, recent events having reinforced that certainty.

My decision to move out of my aunt's house was made for two reasons. The principal one was my determination not to involve her in the family strife my marriage will inevitably cause. Much as I long to share my happiness with her, I know my news would bring her as much anguish as joy. This way too, she cannot be accused of keeping a secret from my parents.

The other reason I have chosen not to remain as a guest in my aunt's home is a far more grievous one. From Mrs Blackstock we have learned of a sudden and alarming deterioration in Aunt Williams' health. Her heart, long understood to be weak, is failing, and she has taken to her bed. Her physician is in regular attendance but regrets he can only soothe with his medicine; he cannot hope for her recovery.

I shall visit her again tomorrow but must remain silent about my plans. The very last thing she needs is further vexation. She must remain ignorant of my marriage until after the event.

I am relieved to hear from the vicar here that banns for my marriage need not be read in my aunt's parish of Ponders Mullen. No one in the village, therefore, will hear the news in church and carry it to my aunt. Since I have taken up residence in Lower Beckton in sufficient time, banns need only to be read in my new parish.

Sadly, our deception extends to keeping Mrs Blackstock in the dark, as the dear lady would be bound to talk. Susanna, though it saddens her to keep the news from her beloved aunt, understands the necessity of saying nothing until we are wed.

What a web of deceit I am weaving through my shameful conduct!

But I shall make things right. Once the ceremony is over, I shall inform them all, first of all Aunt Williams, then everyone in Wisbech.

EIGHTY; Early September 2018

Strangers in Distress

'Don't mind if I do!' Angie giggled as Archie refilled her glass.

'What about you, Bertle?' continued Archie, bottle in hand, 'More prosecco?'

'Nah, mate. No offence, but this stuff ent really my cuppa tea. Don't wanna be funny, but it tastes like rats' pee to me. Got any beer?'

'Err....'

'Beer's on the worktop, Bertle. Just help yourself,' said Monica as she breezed out of reception. Bertle had been his usual devious self about staying on for their celebration. He'd been fixing the ball cock in the visitors' loo just after they'd closed and had been making a lengthy job of it. When Justin had arrived, complete with a case of prosecco and other goodies, Bertle simply hadn't left.

It had taken a week or two before Justin had been free to attend the party for staff and volunteers. In the end, they'd decided to hold it after the doors closed to visitors on a Wednesday evening. That way, they'd have the following morning, when the museum was closed, to clear up. Archie had supplied a tiny Bluetooth speaker and his small selection of nineties music was playing in reception from his phone. They were all in the mood for a celebration, as modest as this was. Justin, having made an earnest and enthusiastic speech about the new way forward for the museum, was now in tedious sounding discussion with

Bernadette by the bouncy ball display. He looked very well oiled already.

Angie had put together a counter top full of party food and they were all helping themselves. There was a lot of laughter and a good atmosphere as around twenty volunteers and staff celebrated the removal of the threat to the museum. Archie, a glass in one hand, was filling his paper plate with tiny prawn sandwiches when Monica managed to trip over Bertle's foot and lunge into her fellow investigator. He shot out the arm holding the glass in a misjudged attempt to stop her falling, spilling fizz down his arm and her front. For once, she didn't push him away, snuggling against him instead. Funny the things drink could do to a person, Archie thought, abandoning his plate of sandwiches and ignoring his sticky, wet arm. She was smiling up at him, happy and relaxed at long last.

But for Archie it was too little, too late, too drunken. It was September already and time for him to go. He wouldn't say so tonight, though. Tonight was a time for celebration and he wouldn't spoil it.

'So, come on, tell me what 'appened,' Bertle was demanding loudly to no one in particular. 'I mean, one minute it's all doom and gloom, sortta thing, and your poet's 'ad this son what no one knew about, and now 'ere we all are, getting the beer out. What 'appened to him and the son, then?'

'It's complicated, Bertle,' Bernadette began, interrupting Justin's talk of budgets and planning. She looked like she needed rescuing. Monica and Archie went to join her and Justin's monologue resumed, largely to thin air, with scarcely a pause.

Bertle was still waiting for an answer, a bottle of Elgood's bitter in one hand, a pork pie in the other, but Justin went on talking, oblivious of everything. In the corner, Angie was prodding at Archie's phone, trying to put together a more suitable play list for a party.

'We're not altogether sure what happened to our poet and his son, Bertle,' Monica broke in over the top of Justin's projections for the next financial year, 'though thanks to Victoria, we know a lot more about them than we did....' A burst of cheering drowned out her last few words, 'The biggest mystery we have yet to understand is why the family never knew about Joshua and Susanna's son, Edmund.'

'Or why they deliberately ignored him....' put in Bernadette.

'Yeah, they sound real iggerant,' put in Bertle.

'Oh, I don't think they would have ignored him,' said Justin, finally managing to switch his attention to a new subject, 'It would have been important to the Ambrose family that the estate was passed correctly down the male line, in accordance with entailment provisions. So, we have to assume that they never knew about the child. It is equally possible that they were unaware of the marriage, because there is absolutely no mention of it in any of the letters or contemporary writing that we have.'

'Maybe,' suggested Monica, 'he simply died before he could tell them about his marriage. We know he was ill and it's come to light now that he returned to Dorset, to Lower Beckton in fact, in 1801, the year of his death. It's possible that he never managed to tell anyone in Wisbech.'

She leaned back towards Archie as she spoke, as if reclaiming him, and he put his arms around her. Bernadette raised her eyebrows and said nothing.

'But his wife!' objected Angie, 'Poor girl would have been abandoned, and with a baby too! Surely she would have contacted his family! Surely she would have wanted them to know about her son!'

'Yes,' acknowledged Justin in a voice that was growing more unsteady by the minute, 'that's the real mystery. Their marriage must have been carried out in secret. Perhaps after his death she was too proud to seek his family's help. Maybe she had no need of them. Perhaps she went back to live with her own family.'

'It's a horrible thought,' added Angie in a sorrowful voice,' but he could have died on the journey home and never had the chance to tell them.'

'Flamin' 'eck!' grunted Bertle as he swigged from his beer bottle, 'Sounds like the soaps the missis watches on TV.'

'Does a bit,' agreed Bernadette, 'or one of those Italian operas; all death and misery.'

'Quite,' said Justin, 'More prosecco anyone?' A few glasses were held out to him and he smilingly refilled them like an inebriated Santa Claus.

Archie said nothing, leaning to kiss the top of Monica's head. He'd put his glass down somewhere and couldn't find it, but was reluctant to move from his comfortable position to find another.

He was no longer very interested in Joshua Ambrose and his secret marriage. For a rather indifferent poet, he had caused more than enough trouble for one lifetime, yet the repercussions of his actions were still creating havoc two centuries later.

Archie was more interested in his own plans. He'd been all set to leave in the morning, had intended just to tell Monica and go. The museum was saved, apparently. There'd been nothing left to keep him here.

But Monica, having waited two months to thaw towards him, had had to go and choose this moment, which was almost too late, to show him some affection. If he hadn't been so delighted about it, he'd have been furious with her.

'Speech, Monica,' Bernadette was insisting, 'I think you should give us a speech!' A few encouraging cheers rang out from the group gathered around the buffet table.

Bernadette was probably thinking that anything would be better than more of Justin's rambling shop talk.

'You've already had one,' Monica protested with a smile.

'No, Bernadette's right,' agreed Justin as he took a big bite out of a crab sandwich, 'We need to hear from the curator. Come on, say a few words, Monica!'

Archie felt her wriggle out of his arms and he grinned indulgently as she took up a position of authority in the centre of the room, collecting her thoughts. Justin refilled her glass and, noticing that Archie was without one, picked up Bernadette's coffee cup from behind the counter. Giving it a cursory check, he deemed it clean enough and filled it with fizz for Archie.

'OK, then,' Monica began, big eyes sparkling, 'I want to say thank you to all of you for being such a loyal and enthusiastic team, especially in the last weeks of so much uncertainty. At last, we can look to the future. The kids' trail, which ends this week when the little loves return to school, has been a great success.

'There is so much else we can do to bring families in and, thanks to all the new information that has come to light recently about our poet, during the winter we shall be making new displays for the Reading Room. But enough forward thinking, let's concentrate on tonight! Thank you again; dig in, there's plenty more booze and food! A toast then, to every one of you, and....' raising her glass to the ceiling, 'to you, Joshua. I hope you're happy with the way things turned out.'

'And to the marmalade cat!' added Bernadette as they all drank.

'Who?' Monica's smile took on a puzzled look.

'Yes,' agreed Archie, 'To the marmalade cat!' Everyone cheered, though only he and Bernadette had a clue what they were talking about.

The front door opened very slowly. No dramatics this time. Victoria just stood there, watching them all. The music, as if with rehearsed timing, came to the end of its play list and stopped, leaving an awkward silence. Bernadette groaned.

'Who forgot to lock the door?'

'You did,' giggled Monica. There was, after all, nothing the woman could do to threaten them anymore.

'I too, would like to propose a toast,' said Victoria quietly, 'to Archibald Newcombe-Walker.'

The sniggering continued; only Archie had stopped smiling, straightening up to face the uninvited guest across the room. Monica shifted her position and clung to him even more tightly, resenting the intrusion and wishing the woman would just go away.

Since no one was offering her a glass, Victoria scanned the room and eventually spotted an abandoned and sticky looking one on the guide book stand. She didn't seem bothered by the state it was in and Justin, looking a little confused, stepped forward to fill the glass for her.

'So,' Victoria continued at last, raising her glass, 'I would like to propose a toast to Archie, to thank him for his unerring helpfulness and charm and for coming to the aid of strangers in distress. It must be said that, had it not been for dearest Archie, I could never have begun my action against you all. After all, it was he who helped me in my time of need, when I was lost and alone in Corfe Castle, searching in vain for my ancestors. I shall be eternally grateful for his leading me in the right direction, to Edmund's grave in Lower Beckton....'

She certainly had their attention now and no one was laughing any more.

'Don't be ridiculous,' objected Monica, but Archie noted that she was no longer clinging to him so tightly.

'It is not ridiculous to give thanks where they are due, Monica,' continued Victoria smoothly, 'and surely you have your own gratitude to add to mine? Shall we both drink to the health of Mr Newcombe-Walker? After all, he was such a busy so-and-so down in Dorset, wasn't he?

There he was, touring around, helping me, moving on, then I do believe he returned to Corfe and happened to bump into another stranger who was researching the same family. Of all the coincidences! Yet, his knightly virtues knew no bounds and he sprang to her aid too, didn't he, Monica? No doubt, it was easier for him the second time around. He knew just where to guide you to, didn't he? Clever chap, our Archie! Come on, then, everyone, don't be stingy. A toast to Archibald Newcombe-Walker, everyone's friend and saviour!'

There was silence in the room as Victoria drained her glass, placing it with a smack on the counter. Monica hardly realised that she'd eased herself away from Archie. She hadn't a clue how to react.

Archie was staring at Victoria, his eyes narrowed. One of the cats wandered in, casually sniffing at Victoria's feet before sitting in the centre of the room and lifting one back leg to commence a rigorous grooming of his nether regions.

'You can always rely on a cat to wash 'is bum at the worst time, know whatta mean? Really iggerant sometimes,' chortled Bertle, 'I'm off for another beer....'

Bernadette released a nervous giggle and they all watched Bertle as he plodded towards the kitchen.

'What's all this about, Archie?' asked Monica wearily. He glanced at her wretchedly before turning his attention back to Victoria.

'Victoria is right; I did help you both. I spent quite a lot of time down in Dorset this spring, sometimes doing round trips and returning to places I wanted to see again, and,' he looked at Monica, 'I was in Corfe Castle when I met

Victoria. I had nothing much to do for a few days and she was desperate to discover her family's past. She was searching the church records in Corfe and nearby parishes because of the supposed connection between the common and the poems, but I could tell she was wasting her time. All her passed-down family memories were from the Dorchester area. I suggested she transferred her search to the villages around there and I offered to help. We eventually found Edmund's grave in Lower Beckton.'

'You mean that all the time I was trying to find out about Edmund, you *knew* where his grave was?' uttered Monica, 'How could you keep up a deception like that? How could you string me along, pretending you knew nothing about Joshua Ambrose, making out you were discovering everything for the first time?'

'Yes, come on, Archie,' smirked Victoria, 'Explain yourself.'

'I always knew there was something wrong about you,' Bernadette muttered. She bent down and picked up the cat, as if to protect him from the toxic atmosphere. Having finished washing his bottom, he rewarded her with a lick on the nose.

'Look, I'm sorry, Monica,' responded Archie, ignoring the interruptions, 'I always knew I'd have to tell you eventually....of course you're angry. I'd only just left the business and was still used to treating my clients with confidentiality. So, it seemed natural not to mention, when I later met you in the same village, looking for the same family, that I'd come across all this before with someone else. I know that neither of you were my clients, but the habit sticks. By the time I was getting to know you better, Monica, it felt too late to tell you. And quite honestly, I didn't expect to see you again. Not that that's any excuse, of course.'

'Oh just leave it, Archie. Just go, please,' she said, her face stiff with suppressed emotion, 'just go.'

'Well,' announced Victoria, as Archie remained where he was, 'I'll just leave you all to get on with it, shall I?'

Everyone ignored her. The door closed behind her with a thud, leaving heavy silence in the room. Archie was the one to break it.

'Why let her do this to us?' he asked in a low voice, 'I know it all sounds bad, but....'

'Sounds bad? Archie, *she* was the one threatening the museum, the reason why I was down there looking. Of course you couldn't have known that at first, but you should have told me later, when you understood the connection. The museum visits, the searches around graveyards, all the difficulties....all the time you knew how it would end, because you'd already gone through it all with her!'

'Not all of it. We never looked in any of the museums. You and I found a completely new lead in the Dorset County Museum. It was valuable information about Edmund which Victoria never picked up. She and I just searched the parishes around Dorchester....'

'What difference does *that* make?' she snapped, 'I thought I could trust you, Archie. Please just leave. Let's stop this before....just go.'

He nodded quietly, put his coffee mug down on the counter and left. No one knew what to say, but they knew the party was over.

'Flamin' 'eck, that was quick,' said Bertle as he re-entered the room from the kitchen, 'I've only just started me beer.'

EIGHTY ONE

Diary of Joshua Ambrose, Sunday 28th June 1801

On Friday afternoon, Susanna and I were married in the parish church in Lower Beckton. Susanna's family all turned out for the event and afterwards we had a fine party. There was dancing in the barn, the whole village arriving to share our happiness. Everything was as merry as could be, truly a time of joy, laughter, music and dance. And plenty of cider; my good father-in-law made sure of that.

If only town assemblies and balls were half so entertaining as this country merriment! I miss none of their stiff formality. My only sadness was that my aunt, mother and sisters were not there to share our joy.

And now the new Mrs Ambrose and I are settled into our small but charming cottage in Main Street. My life, I have to confess, is as close to perfect as it could be.

I am to lend a hand to Susanna's father for a few weeks. I have offered to help him with the sale of his wool, as I believe I can get him a better price at market than he is currently achieving. It will be a pleasant change from my work in Wisbech and, however idyllic my summer here promises to be, I shall not be idle.

I know this cannot go on forever. Before long, I shall have to return to my responsibilities in Wisbech and find us a townhouse there. I tell Susanna about the life she will enjoy as a merchant's wife. She will have fine gowns and every pretty thing, enjoy the polite society that her new position will afford her. She smiles, but not brightly, at the prospect. Despite the promise of such a future, it will not be easy for her to leave her family and this close-knit community behind.

But such thoughts belong to the end of the summer, not to the present. Now is the time to be happy, to reap the harvest of so much longing and hoping. Any difficulties will be faced when the time comes.

EIGHTY TWO; Early September 2018

Delicious Ammunition

So what was the problem? He'd known for a while it was time to move on.

Archie was packing his clothes into the suitcase without much care, stripping the hotel room of any sign that he'd ever stayed there. By the time his bulging case was standing by the door, the room was just an untidy version of the one he'd moved into two months earlier.

As if he'd never been there at all, never left Leamington in a hurry and come to Wisbech.

And in truth, he might as well not have done. All his research and poking about had come to nothing in the end. The museum was saved, but not through any brilliant detective work on his part. And Monica, who had finally begun to thaw towards him, was finished with him. He had deceived her and she was unlikely to forgive him for that.

Yes, it was time to leave; time to go home and consider his future. But it felt uncomfortable. This was not the right way to leave.

He knew he should have told Monica ages ago about meeting and helping Victoria. Having failed to tell her while they were in Dorset and hardly knew each other, it should have been the first thing he'd told her on arrival in Wisbech. And yet, it had all seemed too good to spoil. The way she'd greeted him, walking with him around the Rose Fair, the sunshine, the happiness of it all, had been too good to ruin with a silly confession, and so he'd put it off again. Later, when the future of the museum had looked so bleak, she'd withdrawn into herself and the idea of adding this small revelation to her other troubles had seemed out of the question.

And all the time he had been expecting Victoria to say something. The way she'd looked at him on that hot afternoon in Joshua's room, when she'd first recognised him! But she was clever. She'd been saving this delicious piece of ammunition for when it could be used for maximum impact.

He shrugged on his jacket, room keys in his hand. He pulled up the handle of his case and wheeled it out of the room, closing the door behind him with a decisive click. There would be no returning to it.

He would leave that morning and drive back to Leamington Spa, but first he had an apology to make.

EIGHTY THREE

Diary of Joshua Ambrose, Sunday 18th August 1801

Why is it that times of great happiness inspire so little will to write, yet grief and sadness bring an immediate need for pen and paper?

These past weeks have flown by in a haze of happiness. In my thoughts, it is as if the sun has permanently shone, yet there has been rain enough to freshen the pasture and keep it good for grazing. My beautiful Susanna has made our small cottage into a comfortable home and a haven of peace, a refuge I return to with a happy heart after each day's labour.

I enjoy my work here and trust my father-in-law is satisfied with the new customers I have found for his wool and cider. What I have learned in the merchant's trade is indeed put to good use here.

My happiness during these last two months has been as close as anyone can get to perfection. Must it be true, however, that for every man, if fortunate enough to find such contentment, it can never last?

For we have had the most terrible news.

The message came on Tuesday and we left straight away for Ponders Mullen. There was nothing to be done; my dearest Aunt Williams had passed away in the night. Her maid Lizzie found her lying peacefully in her bed when she went to wake her that morning at seven o'clock.

My sorrow in losing her is great, and terrible thoughts haunt me, depriving me of sleep and peace. My aunt enjoyed a contented life and has no doubt gone to a better place, yet still I grieve. I ask myself how severely my selfish actions may have troubled her already weakened heart. I shall never know, but I shall always wonder.

She is to be buried tomorrow in the little parish church of Ponders Mullen, a place she must have looked upon almost every day of her adult life. The whole village will be there with Susanna, Aunt Blackstock and me, but my parents will be absent. Naturally, I wrote immediately to my mother, for I know how deep her sorrow will be in losing her sister. The time my letter will take to reach her, added to her journey time, however, will make her attendance impossible.

All this serves as a sober warning that I can keep my new status from my family no longer.

I plan to leave in a month. I shall travel to Wisbech and tell my family everything. I shall go alone to break the news and to find a new home for Susanna and me. Afterwards, I shall take my wife to be introduced and to charm them all.

I do not relish the thought, any more than does Susanna, of leaving our cottage and the farm, but I have always known this is how things must be. Susanna understands, smiles sadly and accepts.

She is a country girl, my Susanna. I know that adapting to town life may not come easily to her and that my beloved Fenland, with its endless skies and flat tranquillity, will be a stark contrast to the rolling hills she has known all her life.

I must get about my business now. Susanna and I have much to do. After the funeral, we shall close up my aunt's house and leave her affairs in the safe hands of her Dorchester lawyer.

It is truly a sad business.

EIGHTY FOUR; Early September 2018

All Smoothed Down

He could see them both through the window, clearing up in reception. Bernadette was clutching a black bin liner and gathering up used paper plates and other debris from the night before. Her face was a picture of disgust as she bent to recover something shrivelled and unrecognisable from the floor. Further away, Monica was pushing a vacuum cleaner over the tiles, the racket it was making drowning out his ringing of the door bell.

He rang again and knocked hard on the door. He even tried waving at the women through the window, but neither of them glanced his way. Increasingly frustrated, he gave up with the door and stood peering through the glass until eventually Bernadette's cleaning brought her to face the window. He waved frantically and at last she looked up and saw him.

She had known he was there all along; he suspected that from her unmoving, stony expression as she finally let him in. She had been ignoring him, making him suffer. Her expressionless mask in place, she stood back without any greeting as he entered the house. Monica was still vacuuming, apparently unaware of his presence. Her head was down, intent on the floor tiles, yet when he touched her arm she didn't flinch. She simply glanced at him, switching off the vacuum cleaner with her foot.

'Monica, I....' he began. He wished Bernadette would go away. Monica was waiting, her face as stiff and cold as her colleague's. 'Monica,' he started again, feeling Bernadette's ears tune in behind them, 'I didn't want to leave without giving you a proper apology. I know I should have told you at the beginning about meeting and helping Victoria before I met you, but the time never felt right. That's no excuse, I know. I'm just sorry for letting you down.'

She glanced at him again and it seemed an age before she spoke. Bernadette had stopped picking up rubbish and was openly listening.

'It doesn't matter now,' Monica said at last with a weary sigh, ignoring Bernadette, who was tutting loudly behind them. 'I was so angry with you last night. Why the hell couldn't you have found the right moment during two whole months to tell me? Keeping me in the dark gave Victoria even more ammunition to hurt us with....' Monica put down the hose of the vacuum she'd been holding and sat on the tall counter stool. He followed her, leaning against the reception desk, his back to Bernadette. Monica sighed again, looking like her head was hurting. 'Then, this morning I was thinking that tiny bits of power and petty revenge are like food and drink to Victoria. It would be a victory for her if she destroyed our friendship over this, so let's not give her that. She has lost her battle and I don't think we'll see much more of her now. I'm glad you came back, Archie.'

'Oh, for....' muttered Bernadette.

'Well, actually,' he said, 'I've only come to say goodbye. I really do have to leave. I must go home and sort things out.'

For an unguarded moment, Monica looked even more upset than she had by Victoria's spiteful revelation. Bernadette made a scoffing sound.

'Archie', she needled, 'you really do have a way with words and timing. Where did you learn to be so sensitive and tactful?'

They both ignored her as she walked out, presumably to throw her black sack into the dustbin.

'Do you *have* to go?' Monica asked quietly after a pause, 'You've seen nothing here but trouble and you did so much to help me through it. Couldn't you stay a bit longer and see some better times?'

She put her hand on his arm, a pleading gesture he'd never expected to see. It didn't seem at all like her.

'But, it's never going to work, is it?' he reasoned, 'All these weeks, you've been pushing me further and further away. And besides all that, I cannot live forever in a hotel. I still have a house to run and my investments can't go on stretching to such fine living.'

At least Archie was smiling now. Monica wasn't. She looked like she was on the verge of tears.

'When you first came here, I thought you were telling me you weren't interested, that it was business only. My sister tried to warn me. Said I should be careful not to push you away. She was right. As usual.'

He wasn't at all sure how it happened, but suddenly he was holding her. Her head was resting against his shoulder and he was stroking her hair. She was like a wounded creature. Her hedgehog prickles, if they'd ever been there at all, were all smoothed down.

'I really do have to go home,' he said into her hair, 'but perhaps I should just sort things out in Leamington and think about a change of address....'

She moved her head so that she could peer up into his face.

'You mean you'd move here permanently?'

'Would you want me to?'

'Yes.'

'Then, I'll do as I've thought of doing many times; put the house on the market and move here. Perhaps dear old Rookery Stacks might have a vacancy for when I come back next time!'

'Perhaps they might,' her face was right against his now, 'or there's always my sofa-bed. It's a very useful thing, for putting up friends when they need somewhere to stay. It has a pull-out bit and everything, but you'd have to share it with a giant stuffed rabbit....'

He smiled broadly and found he was kissing her, that she was responding in a way that he'd almost stopped hoping was possible.

EIGHTY FIVE

Diary of Joshua Ambrose, Thursday 17th September 1801

There is really no point in writing this. These words, like all my earlier ramblings, will soon be ashes, turned to powder in the fire.

This worthless habit of writing down thoughts is something I should have abandoned long ago. Everything must change now. No more hidden thoughts; the time for openness is long overdue.

So, tonight when I reach the inn at Charing Cross with its grimy view over London, I shall burn my diaries. Each and every one of them.

This journey is more arduous than most; the old sickness with all its horrors is back. Each bout of painful coughing leaves me as weak as a kitten and I am so damnably tired. Despite the constant swaying and jolting of this conveyance, I know I have slept for much of the last two days on the road. On several occasions I have come to suddenly, seeing how the countryside we are passing through has altered. Then the coughing begins again, its bloody evidence something I have learned to dread.

Perhaps the sickness is worsened this time by the knowledge of what must be told on my arrival. I do not relish the disappointment I shall cause my father, nor my mother's pain. Nor is my well being improved by leaving Susanna behind.

Our time together has been too short for such an early parting, but it seemed wiser to deliver the news alone. Better for my wife to arrive later, when all the anger has died down.

Was it a lack of faith in this coming interview that made me purchase, at the last moment, the lease on our Lower Beckton cottage? My dear aunt did not forget me, though she left, as was necessary, her home to her husband's family. Her small but gratefully received legacy made the purchase of the lease a matter of simplicity. Should things not go to plan in Wisbech, I can at least be sure of my Susanna's future security.

Having done all I can for now, I long to sleep, even in a bed as mean as those at Charing Cross. I must be well for when I reach home. I must recover my strength to face father.

All I need is rest, then surely all will be well.

EIGHTY SIX; Early September 2018

Merely Mislaid

Archie's smile was fading.

He'd agreed to stay an hour or so before leaving and help to finish clearing up. He was mopping the kitchen floor with a squeegee, removing the sticky residue spread around by Bertle last night when he'd spilled prosecco over some of the worktops and the floor tiles. The tacky mess had stuck to everyone's feet, resulting in a trail of black, gluey footprints that led in all directions from the kitchen. Bertle, Archie surmised, must have had this little accident before comparing the stuff to rats' pee.

When Archie had said he'd stay to help with the cleaning, he'd imagined working alone with Monica, that they'd have the remainder of the morning together. But in typical Monica fashion, she'd failed to get the point and was already back behind her computer screen in her office. To make things worse, it was Bernadette who was keeping him company. She was working far too close to him, lips pursed as tightly as a mouse trap, and taking far longer than was necessary to clean the worktops. As if she didn't trust him enough to let him out of her sight.

And Monica was making him nervous, the way she was staring at the computer screen. Every time he passed the door and glanced in, she was staring in the same fixed way; not typing, just looking puzzled.

It was all right, he reminded himself. He had deleted everything. Without considerable effort, she wouldn't be able to look through his research.

And surely, now that the threat was gone, she wouldn't bother. Would she?

He couldn't help feeling uncomfortable. All was apparently resolved, yet still it felt as if something hovered over them, ready to swoop. As he went on mopping the floor and ignoring Bernadette's hostile glances, he felt increasingly tense.

He'd had enough. He dropped the mop with a crash and strode into Monica's office. Bernadette's eyes followed him and he could hear her tutting. Monica looked up from the computer and smiled, her dark eyes lighting up and radiating reassurance.

It was all right. She hadn't found anything.

'I really must set out soon,' he said, 'but how about an early lunch first? We could go to the White Lion for a change.'

'That would be lovely,' she replied happily, 'I just have to finish this, though. Sorry, Archie, but it's important and I must get it done this morning.'

He gave her a cheerful nod and left her to work in peace. He picked the mop up from the floor and put it away in the store room before going into reception and checking that all the debris from the party had been cleared away. There was a black bin liner by the door and, glancing inside, he saw that it was full of bottles and paper plates.

'That's for recycling,' Bernadette informed him unnecessarily, 'Needs taking to the blue bin. Oh, and then the bin needs standing out on the pavement for tomorrow's collection.'

'Fine,' he replied as he picked up the bag, trying to infuse a little friendliness into the single word. They were going to have to try to get on if he was coming back.

Outside, the wind was picking up, stirring the tree tops in Mrs Paynter's back garden and blowing an old crisp bag across the yard. Archie bent down to retrieve it, adding it to the rubbish he tipped into the blue bin. He wheeled the bin down the side passage and across the front garden to the roadside.

A car was slowing down outside the museum, parking over the double yellow lines. He ignored it as he manoeuvred the bin into its normal position near the front gates.

He heard the car door open and he looked up, expecting to be asked for directions. A stooped, tired looking middle aged man was making his way over to him, an apologetic smile on his face.

'Excuse me, but this *is* the Poet's House Museum, isn't it?' Archie confirmed that it was, 'Well I hope you don't mind me delivering this by hand, but I've been clearing out my aunt's things from her room at the care home and there's so much to get rid of. I'm her executor, d'you see, and I found this envelope in a tin of letters and documents. Do you work here? I mean, can I leave it with you? Quite honestly, there's so much to do and I'd like to get back to Cornwall today....'

Archie took the white envelope the man was passing to him. On the front, in shaky handwriting, was written, "For the Poet's House, Wisbech".

'Of course,' Archie nodded, 'I'll see that it gets to the curator immediately. Thank you for dropping it in.'

The man thanked him and was off again, driving swiftly away. Archie walked back down the side of the house towards the yard, clutching the envelope.

Perhaps someone had left the museum a donation. It happened sometimes; people died and left the place small sums. He paused in the side passage and already his fingers were working their way beneath the seal of the envelope. Before he'd even thought about what he was doing, the envelope was open.

He leaned against the house wall, his curiosity getting the better of him and hoping Monica would forgive him for opening the museum's post.

What his fingers pulled out of the envelope, though, was not a donation. There was no cheque, no bank notes, just two pieces of paper folded together; a letter and some sort of official looking typed document.

He straightened out the pieces of paper and, holding them out of the wind, began to read the letter. It was written in the same shaky hand as on the envelope and was undated. It was simply headed "Lime Tree House, Wisbech".

'To whomever it may concern,' it began,

'In sorting out my few remaining papers in preparation for the inevitable, I find that I am still in possession of the enclosed document. It relates to the Last Will and Testament of my father, James Ambrose. Knowing of your museum's dedication to the memory of my ancestor Joshua, our town's most beloved poet, I entrust this document to you.

Sometimes the truth lies hidden for years. Sometimes it is merely mislaid.

I trust you will know how best to deal with it.

Yours faithfully,

Edith Ambrose (Miss)'

Miss Edith Ambrose. This had to be Victoria's great aunt, the elderly lady who had given her the bad news about the cat sanctuary. And before her death she had been putting her affairs in order, which for some reason included sending information to the museum.

Archie's heart was thumping heavily as he turned to the enclosed document. He recognised it immediately.

It was the codicil to James Ambrose's Will, something he'd received full details of through his application to the government records site. On the morning of Victoria's arrival, when she'd come to tell them she was giving up and withdrawing her claim, he had been looking at this very document on the screen. He had been reading it slowly and carefully, its implication gradually sinking in.

It was because of what he'd read in this codicil that he'd found Victoria's sudden decision so bizarre.

The codicil had been added several years after the Will had been written and it looked like a death bed stirring of conscience. The main Will had, apart from a few small legacies, left everything to the Rookery Stacks Cat Sanctuary, blatantly denying James' son, Arthur any inheritance.

Yet, as James had lay dying, it seemed he'd felt some remorse and a slight change of heart. He had had this codicil added. Archie didn't have to read the paper copy he now held in his hands, as he'd read the digital version before, over and over again. He had gone through it many times in his mind since.

Briefly, James had conceded that, although the main aspects of his Last Will and Testament should remain in place, he now wished that his principal residence should pass to his son, Arthur.

His principal residence, whichever that was. As far as Archie could tell, in James' time the Ambroses had owned several properties, most of which were rented out around the town. The house they lived in themselves, their principal residence, had been a large Victorian farm house close to Murrow, a village near Wisbech.

Presumably, that house was correctly inherited, according to the Will and its codicil, by Arthur. There was nothing to suggest that any errors had been made in carrying out all of James' wishes.

However, as Victoria had frequently pointed out, there had been a gross error right at the start of things, when the old entailment rules were incorrectly applied, when no one knew about Joshua's son, Edmund.

Had those rules been correctly applied, and the Poet's House passed down the line to James, surely *that* house would then have been the one classed by the family as their principal residence?

Archie had no idea about how a lawyer might look at this, but it occurred to him that they could have a field day over it. Even to his non-legally trained mind, it seemed highly likely that, if everything had been done properly from the beginning, the Poet's House would have been excluded, courtesy of the codicil, from the Rookery Stacks inheritance.

The Poet's House would have gone to Arthur.

And Arthur would have passed it to his son Michael, who would have passed it to his daughter Victoria.

She had been right all along. So why had she given up so suddenly?

Archie held the document up towards the light. He could see tiny holes and rusty pin marks where the codicil had once been attached to the main Will. Had Miss Ambrose, Victoria's great aunt, been the one who had separated the two parts of the document? When she had given Victoria the main Will, had she deliberately kept back the codicil?

If so, it would explain Victoria's reaction and her conclusion that the whole estate had been left to the cat sanctuary. But Archie had found a digital copy of the entire document, including the codicil, quite easily through the internet. So, why hadn't Victoria's expensive lawyers?

Perhaps, he thought, with a glimmer of logic, she'd simply not given them enough time. She had terminated their contract. As soon as she'd read James' Will she'd given up. She had withdrawn her claim and stopped paying her legal bills. She'd had no idea that the codicil existed, and it seemed likely that her great aunt never intended that she should.

Miss Edith Ambrose, rather than sending the codicil to Victoria, had chosen to send it to the museum. She trusted them to do the right thing with it.

The right thing. So what *was* the right thing? Handing the codicil over to the family, to Victoria, would be the honest thing to do, but it could also mean the end of the museum, and Miss Ambrose would have known that.

If giving the document to the family wasn't the right thing, what was?

Archie looked once more at the old piece of paper with its stilted sentences and crookedly typed lines and knew that it spelled out a further bout of bad news for Monica.

Once his decision was made, he wasted no more time. Carrying the envelope and its contents, he walked from the side passage, through the front garden and, dodging the Thursday morning traffic, across the road to the river. He stood for a few moments, looking over the wall into the choppy brown water of the Nene. The tide was going out, carrying chip packets and what looked like an old boot, with it. The wind was blowing strongly, bringing the first tang of autumn as it buffeted his face.

Tucking the letter and envelope under his arm, he held the codicil between his fingers and began to tear. The old paper put up no resistance, its dry texture yielding readily to destruction. By the time he'd finished, the document was no more than a pile of confetti in his cupped hands. He opened his fingers and let the wind take the fragments, a brief shower of dust that danced and billowed away. He thought he saw some of it landing on the water, crumbs reduced to nothing as they travelled out to sea.

He shredded the letter next, followed by the envelope, all of their remains reduced to dust and carried away on the tide.

Sometimes the truth, he thought with satisfaction, lies hidden for years. Sometimes it is merely mislaid.

And sometimes it's just blown away.

He had the strongest of feelings that this was exactly what the old lady had intended. The truth had merely been mislaid. Well, sort of.

Back inside the house, the atmosphere seemed to have lifted, but of course that was just his imagination.

'Come on, what kept you?' chided Monica, as she greeted him with a dazzling smile, 'We really should go.'

'Yes,' he agreed, taking her hand, 'let's go to "luncheon".'

AFTERWORD

1801

Mr Jonathan Peckover, Quaker and greatly respected partner of the Wisbech and Lincolnshire Bank, stands on the stone bridge over the river to watch the procession. He follows it with his eyes as it makes its solemn, silent way from the quayside house towards the Butter Cross.

He leans forward slightly, resting his gloved hands on the smooth stone of the bridge wall. It will soon be October and already a bitter wind is blowing, adding its own bleakness to the occasion. It whips the browned leaves from the trees and catches the black silk veils of the lady mourners. There are just three ladies in the group, Jonathan notes, not four as he might have expected; Mrs Elijah Ambrose and her two daughters. There is no weeping widow accompanying them, no fair hair escaping from a veil, no sign at all that his friend brought home a wife.

Once the small, sad group has disappeared from sight, Jonathan starts to walk again, hurrying unseen along the southern side of the fine, newly built Crescent. He manages to reach St Peter's ahead of the mourners, who make their sedate and dignified progress behind the coffin, along the far side of the Crescent.

He slips into the back of the church, this church which is not his own but which he respects. He follows the service and leaves with the large congregation to stand by the open, ready grave.

Mr Elijah Ambrose, white faced, stiff and mute, stands motionless while the women mop with handkerchiefs eyes hidden by veils. Even as they stoop to throw flowers on to the lowered coffin, whispering a few anguished words, he does not move. It is as if he cannot. His is such a small, desolate family group, shrunken by early death, reduced by grief.

And to Jonathan's eyes, it is certain that there is no widow beside them, sharing this tragedy.

He had to come today and see, just to be sure. And now, he has to conclude that his friend failed in his purpose in going south. He must never have found his Susanna, his fair haired girl. Those two small details are all Jonathan ever knew about her, her Christian name and the colour of her hair.

To him, the wretchedness of the scene is intensified by her absence. Only the dark veils of Joshua's mother and sisters, tossed about in the wind like the crisp, prematurely dead leaves from the trees, are there to mark Joshua's passing. To mark his passing alone in the chaise, before ever he reached home.

Jonathan Peckover takes one final glance and walks sorrowfully away.

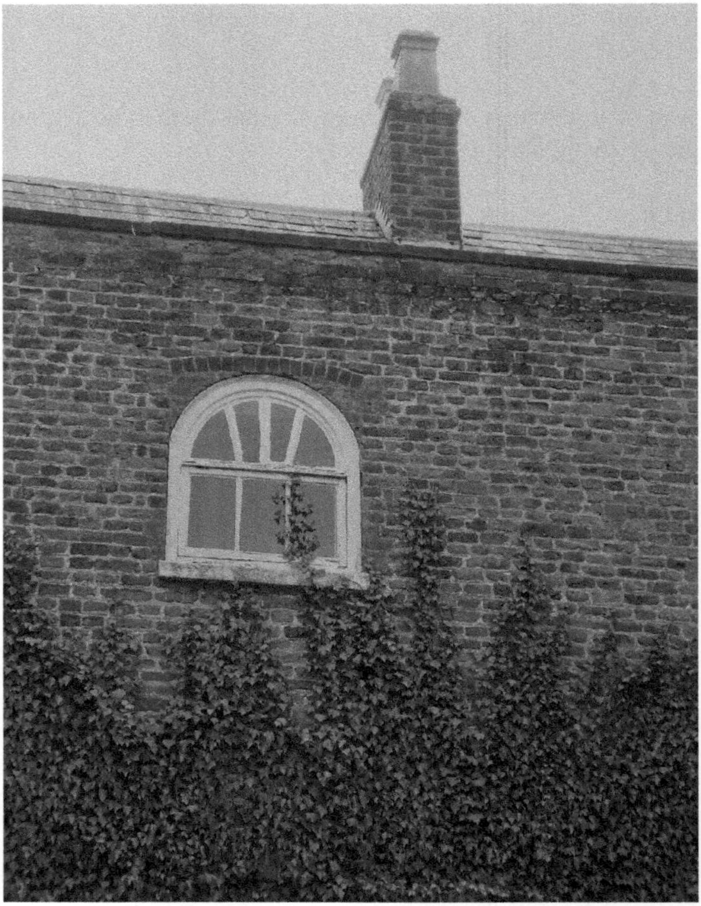

AUTHOR'S NOTE

Thank you...and a little explanation.

The poet, Joshua Ambrose never existed. He is merely a figment of my imagination.

I have to say though, that during the last few months of writing about him, he has become almost real to me. At times, I've caught myself looking for his headstone in St Peter's churchyard or wondering why he isn't mentioned in local history books.

Many of the people he mentions in his diary, however, are real historical characters. I have tried to portray Thomas Clarkson, Jonathan Peckover, Joseph Medworth, Oglethorpe Wainman and the Reverend Dr Caesar Morgan as accurately as possible, based on the often sparse information available.

Wisbech in its prosperous Georgian heyday, being home to so many notable characters, must have been an interesting place. For citizens with the leisure to make the most of all this Fenland town had to offer, life here was bound to have been good.

In weaving these characters and their times into Joshua's story, I am, as ever, truly fortunate to have been helped by many kind people.

My heartfelt thanks go to:

John Clarke LLB AKC, retired solicitor, for his advice on inheritance matters. (Any errors are mine alone!)

The staff of the National Trust's Peckover House, especially to Ben Rickett for lending me his alter-ego and Carole French for instructing me on book cleaning.

Geoff Hill, for his help in researching parish records.

Wisbech and Fenland Museum, a treasure house of local history. One of its displays is dedicated to Thomas Clarkson. His "slave chest" is still there to be seen, together with many of its original contents.

The Dorset County Museum, Dorchester.

And, as ever, I am extremely grateful to my very patient husband Tony for his long hours of proof reading and for his unfailing encouragement. And for one of the poems!

And to everyone who reads this book....a big thank you.

Bibliography:

'Cemeteries, Graveyards and Memorials in Wisbech' by Bridget Holmes

'Wisbech's Secret Princess' by Christopher Donald

'History, Gazetteer and Directory of Cambridgeshire' by Robert Gardner